Praise for Stephanie Grace Whitson

"As usual, Stephanie Grace Whitson skillfully weaves unforgettable characters with an unforgettable time in history. Step aboard the *Laura Rose*. You will definitely enjoy the ride!"
—Nancy Moser, bestselling author of *The Journey of Josephine* and *Mozart's Sister* on·*A Captain for Laura Rose*

"Stephanie Whitson is a master storyteller who has once again woven a tale of adventure, romance, and inspiration that will touch your heart. *A Captain for Laura Rose* is a novel rich with exciting details of riverboat life during the nineteenth century, and the well-drawn characters will steal your heart. Don't miss this exceptional read."
—Judith Miller, award-winning author of the Home to Amana series on *A Captain for Laura Rose*

"Whitson captures the reader's attention from the first sentence. You will not want to put the book down. The characters in the first Quilt Chronicles book are well thought out and well defined and wonderful to read about as we learn their stories."   —*RT Book Reviews* on *The Key on the Quilt*

"No one immerses me in a story world like Whitson."
—Colleen Coble, author of the Lonestar series and the Rock Harbor series

"Whitson writes amazing stories."
—*RT Book Reviews* on *The Shadow on the Quilt*

"Whitson delivers a charming, realistic coming of age story with plenty of conflict, humor, romance, and a good message...."
—Vickie McDonough, award-winning author of the Heartstrong series on *Unbridled Dreams*

A
CAPTAIN FOR
Laura Rose

A
CAPTAIN FOR

Laura Rose

A NOVEL

STEPHANIE GRACE WHITSON

New York • Boston • Nashville

Copyright © 2014 by Whitson, Inc.
Discussion questions copyright © 2014 by Hachette Book Group, Inc.

All Scripture quotations are taken from the King James Version of the Bible.

The Author is represented by Books & Such Literary Agency, Inc., 5926 Sunhawk Drive, Santa Rosa, CA 95409 www.booksandsuch.biz

FaithWords
Hachette Book Group
237 Park Avenue
New York, NY 10017

faithwords.com

Printed in the United States of America

RRD-C

First edition: March 2014
10 9 8 7 6 5 4 3 2 1

FaithWords is a division of Hachette Book Group, Inc.
The FaithWords name and logo are trademarks of Hachette Book Group, Inc.

The Hachette Speakers Bureau provides a wide range of authors for speaking events. To find out more, go to www.hachettespeakersbureau.com or call (866) 376-6591.

The publisher is not responsible for websites (or their content) that are not owned by the publisher.

Library of Congress Cataloging-in-Publication Data
Whitson, Stephanie Grace.
   A captain for Laura Rose / Stephanie Grace Whitson. — First edition.
      pages cm
   ISBN 978-1-4555-2905-6 (pbk.) — ISBN 978-1-4555-2906-3 (ebook) 1. Women ship captains—Fiction. 2. River boats—Missouri River—Fiction. 3. Pilots and pilotage—Missouri River—Fiction. 4. Missouri River—Fiction. I. Title.
   PS3573.H555C37 2014
   813'.54—dc23
                                                                              2013032578

Dedicated to the memory of God's extraordinary women
in every place
in every time.

Part One

It takes a real man to be a Missouri River pilot, and that's why a good one draws down as high as a thousand dollars a month. If a Mississippi boat makes a good trip to New Orleans and back, its milk-fed crew think they've turned a trick. Bah! That's creek navigatin'. But from St. Louis to Fort Benton and back—close on to five thousand miles, son, with cottonwood snags waitin' to rip a hole in your bottom and the fastest current there ever was on any river darin' your engines at every bend and with Injuns hidin' in the bushes at the woodyard landings—that's a hair-on-your-chest, he-man trip for you!

—Captain Louis Rosche, 1866

Chapter 1

St. Louis, Missouri
March 1867

With a little frown, Laura Rose White turned away from the hotel window. If wishing to see her brother on his way back to the family's temporary home could make it happen, Joe would have appeared in that pool of light created by the glowing street lamp on the corner long ago. But the streets had remained quiet the entire time Laura watched and worried—save for the night crew charged with keeping the city from drowning in manure and whatever debris the citizens of St. Louis flung or poured or spat onto the paved streets.

The familiar screech of a steamboat whistle sounded, and Laura closed her eyes. How she longed to return to the only place that would ever feel like home. She imagined herself standing next to Papa as he piloted their steamboat upriver, past forested banks and small towns, through the ever-changing river channel and, finally, to the far reaches of civilization in Montana. But Papa was gone now, and what was left of the White family was in danger of losing everything.

Rubbing her arms to keep from shivering, Laura glanced toward the polished walnut door that opened into Joe's room.

Each of the bedrooms on either side of the suite's sitting room also had private entrances from the hall, but Joe hadn't come in that way, either. She would have heard him. After all, she'd spent the better part of the last six nights curled up on the sofa here in the sitting room, ruminating over the problems plaguing the family business, wondering why repairs on their steamboat were taking so long, and wishing Joe were more like Papa. More forceful. More capable. More respected. More...everything. He might have passed the pilot's examination with what Papa proudly called "flying colors," but it took more than a license to manage everything involved in moving freight up the river many rivermen had labeled a "steamboat graveyard." In light of the past few days, Laura was beginning to fear that Joe didn't have "more."

Tonight's insomnia, however, was less about the family business woes and more about Joe's increasing fascination with eighteen-year-old Miss Adele MacKnight. As if the family didn't have enough problems, Joe was spending time with a young lady. And not just any young lady. A *MacKnight*, for goodness' sake.

As faint, predawn light began to filter in through the tall windows, Laura looked from the doorway of the room she and Mama shared to Joe's door and the empty room beyond and, finally, back out the window, past the street lamp on the corner, and toward the St. Louis levee.

Mama said that worry was a sin. "Be anxious for nothing," she said. Laura might not know the chapter and verse, but she'd seen Mama live it. She was living it right now, because instead of worrying about Joe and Adele MacKnight or business or anything else, Mama was snoring in the next room. How had Papa slept through it? Maybe he snored worse.

Mama had always been the keeper of the family faith. The closest Laura could come to praying was talking to Papa. *Please, Papa. Would you talk to God and ask Him to help us?*

I'm sick of carpeted floors and heavy draperies and luncheon in that musty hotel dining room. I miss Bird's cooking and...and I just want to go home.

Captain Jacob and Mrs. Margaret White and their two children had lived aboard steamboats for as long as Laura could remember. They'd journeyed through the deep waters of the Mighty Mississippi on floating palaces that took them all the way down to New Orleans and faced the challenges of the Big Muddy, when Papa took charge of humble, stern-wheeled mountain boats half the size of their more impressive side-wheel sisters.

Papa always said there was nothing on earth quite as satisfying as besting the Big Muddy, and he was right—as far as Laura was concerned. She and Joe and Mama needed to get back on that water, and soon. Every single day they spent in this infernal hotel, every meal they had to buy in the dining room, drained their already suffering bank account. And what was Joe doing about it? Laura snorted softly. He was calling on Finn MacKnight's younger sister. *Glory be.*

What on earth Joe saw in rude, bombastic, rabble-rousing Finn MacKnight, Laura could not imagine. And yet Joe had called the man "friend" for years. He'd refused to blame that friendship for his own past problems with strong drink, in spite of the fact that MacKnight had very nearly gotten Joe thrown in jail for public drunkenness more than once.

Images flashed in her mind of Papa hauling his drunken son up the gangplank and on board the *Morning Star*, the packet they'd lived on before the *Laura Rose*. She remembered the tears Mama had shed and finally, kind, gentle Papa's voice raised in anger as he fired Finn MacKnight and banished him from ever working on a steamer piloted by Jacob White again. The attempt to end MacKnight's influence in Joe's life had worked—for a while. But now the Whites were stuck in St. Louis waiting for one of the steamboat's boilers to be replaced, and who had Joe taken up with again but Finn MacKnight—and his sister.

Laura began to pace. Past Joe's bedroom door, over to Mama's room, and then to the windows and back again, in a triangular path that would eventually wear down the fine hotel carpet if Laura had to spend many more nights like this one. She had to *do* something. The question was...what? She had no more say over the family business than Logjam, the fearsome-looking dog they'd rescued off a pile of floating debris a few years ago. And she had even less to say about Joe's friendship with the MacKnights. He'd made that very clear a few days ago.

Laura and Mama had come back to the hotel after meeting with Bird and Hercules Perrin, the cooks who reigned over the galley aboard Captain White's steamboats. Mama wanted to linger in a shop, and Laura decided to talk to Joe—again—about the need to replace the engineer who'd somehow over-looked the fault in the boiler welds. As she was passing the hotel dining room, there was Joe, seated at a table for four. Socializing instead of pounding the pavement in search of a contract and a crew. Laura bustled upstairs, and when Joe finally returned to the suite, she was waiting. But she'd barely said a word when Joe raised his hand to silence her.

"The boiler is taking longer than we expected. There's nothing we can do about that but wait. I told you I'd hire the crew—including a new engineer—and I will. As to contracts for freight, I've made contacts, but there's no point in pursu-ing them until we have a packet to load. And if I want to have a nice lunch with friends in the meantime, I'm going to do it."

Laura bit her lower lip to keep from starting an argument. The last thing she wanted to do was turn into one of those women who made a vocation of nagging the men in their lives. If she felt trapped, that wasn't Joe's fault. He hadn't cre-ated the world in which a woman with a head for business or a talent for piloting a steamboat was little more than an annoying oddity.

But if women couldn't be licensed to pilot steamboats, why had God given Laura the talent for it? And she did have talent. "No one reads the water like you, Laura," Joe had said. "I'd give anything for that gift."

Joe's expression softened. He patted the gloved hand she'd put on his arm and gentled his voice. "I understand your being worried. We've had a run of bad luck, and this is hard on all of us. I also understand that you might have certain reservations when it comes to the MacKnights. But, Laura, Fiona is—"

"A lovely Christian woman," Laura interrupted. "I know that. Mama said as much."

He arched one eyebrow as he peered down at her. "You've been checking up on the MacKnights, have you?"

"Not in the way you mean. I merely asked Mama if she'd called on the elder Miss MacKnight since we've been back in St. Louis. It would be perfectly natural, given their past acquaintance."

" 'Past acquaintance' being a euphemism, I suppose, for family commiserating with one another in regards to their wandering sons and brothers?"

Laura ignored the jab. "As I said, Mama speaks well of Miss *Fiona* MacKnight. Says she's a lovely woman, even if she is a bit—frozen in time." When Joe grinned, she sniffed, "You know what I mean."

"I do. But Finn's older sister hasn't really had much chance to be anything else. She was only in her twenties when Adele arrived on her doorstep. Not that that was easy on Adele, either. Can you imagine being raised by people who don't want you?" He shuddered. "If it's any comfort to you, I'm not aware of Adele's displaying a single tendency toward rabble-rousing. She's charming and, from what I've seen, every inch a lady. And no matter what you think, my past difficulties were not Finn's fault."

They were not going to agree on the matter of Finn MacKnight, and there was no point in having a fight about it. "I know I shouldn't judge," Laura said. "I'm just—protective of you."

"In case you haven't noticed, sister, I'm all grown up."

"Of course I've noticed," Laura said. "And so has every other young lady who's seen you since we've been stuck in this hotel." She smiled. "You turn heads, Joseph. You're a handsome steamboat pilot who's inherited controlling interest in a nearly new packet. People assume you have money now. Don't you see how romantic that is?"

Joe frowned. "So Adele is interested in me only because she thinks I'm rich?"

Adele was interested. *Oh, dear.* Laura took a deep breath. "I didn't mean it that way."

"Good. And for your information, I do not turn heads. That's Finn's calling, not mine."

"He's dark and dangerous-looking," Laura said. "You're the blond-haired boy every mother hopes her daughter will bring home one day." She hesitated before adding, "All I'm saying is that there could be more to Miss MacKnight's interest in you than you've realized."

"That's enough," Joe said, as he strode toward his room. "You've done your sisterly duty, and now I really must insist that you mind your own business."

Joe had been out late every one of the three nights since that conversation, and as far as Laura knew he'd made no headway solving any of the business problems. *Business.* Laura stopped pacing. That was the real worry, after all. The White family packet had had more than her share of trouble since Papa died: broken spars (both of them on the same stretch of river), groundings, storms, flaming arrows from Indians, a leak in the hull that ruined cargo, and a small kitchen fire. Last year's shipping season had been fraught with near disasters, to the point that Joe had begun to doubt himself as a pilot. And now they had to replace one of the boilers. Had that problem gone undiscovered, it could have caused a disastrous explosion.

Some of the old-timers on the river had begun to hint that "old" Captain White's new packet had fallen prey to a curse. One absurd rumor reported that, on the night of a full moon, a roustabout had looked up at the wheelhouse and seen the ghost of Captain Jacob White standing at the ship's wheel—in the very spot where he'd dropped dead two years ago. No one seemed to question the roustabout's sobriety at the moment of his chilling vision. Nor did anyone wonder how a man could look up from the levee and recognize the man at the wheel. Or, for that matter, know that Papa's supposed ghost was standing "in the very spot where he dropped dead only two years ago." Of course logic didn't matter when it came to superstition. Things like that slithered in and out of the saloons on the levee with amazing speed.

Was that the reason Joe was having trouble hiring a crew? Were people afraid to work aboard the *Laura Rose*? The *Laura Rose*. Laura would never forget the day a little over two years ago when Papa had led her, blindfolded, down to the levee. When he removed the blindfold, he directed her gaze upward. "Look carefully, now. There's a new piano just waiting for Mama in the dining saloon, and Joe's to be first pilot. But there's a surprise for you, too."

When Laura saw her own name spelled out in tall, black letters just below the wheelhouse windows, Papa laughed out loud. She could still hear his booming voice. "Now, that's a banner headline for the *Daily Democrat* if ever there was one: 'Jacob White's Daughter Speechless.'"

Swiping at bitter tears, Laura returned to the sitting room

sofa and lay down in a vain attempt to sleep. Moments became an hour and one hour became two. As Laura fidgeted, the silence in the empty hotel room where Joe should have been sleeping seemed to seep through the closed door and form a cloud of worry that enveloped the sitting room in unrelenting gloom.

A thump in the hall just outside the sitting room door made her jump. It was odd how every little sound caught her attention here at the hotel. Folks who'd never traveled by steamer sometimes complained of the noise, wandering the decks, deprived of sleep and longing for silence. Laura loved every whistle, every groan, every holler, every creak. But here at the hotel, whispers in the hall could wake the girl who'd never had trouble sleeping on board a clattering, creaking pile of wood powered by a growling, grunting steam engine.

She sat up with a frown, listening intently. Muffled laughter. Definitely coming from Joe's room. A thud. Laura looked at the door. Another thud. And...laughter? *What on earth...* and then...a crash. And a moan. A *moan*?

Rushing across the room, Laura grasped the brass door-knob and flung open the door. "Joe? Joe...what's wrong? What's—" The words died in her throat as she caught sight of her bleary-eyed brother sitting on the edge of the bed, his coat off, his waistcoat and shirt unbuttoned, his tie dangling.

"Hey...Lllrrruuuh," he drawled, "iss okay..."

But it wasn't any kind of "okay." After nearly two years of hard-won sobriety, Joe reeked of strong drink. And the person to blame was kneeling on the floor, helping Joe take off his shoes.

"Finn brought me home." Joe pawed his friend's shoulder. "Heeesss a good fren'."

Friend? Laura stared at MacKnight. When had Finn MacKnight ever been a good friend—at least in the true sense of that word? If it weren't for his "friend," Joe would never have had to learn how to stay sober in the first place. Rage clogged Laura's throat. The words she wanted to cast at the man couldn't get out. Instead, she stood motionless, trembling.

MacKnight moved first. Standing, he grasped Joe by the shoulders and pushed him back. Joe murmured something as his legs were lifted onto the bed, and MacKnight literally launched himself across the room to grab the pitcher off the nightstand. He barely managed to get it in place before everything in Joe's stomach came rushing up and out.

Laura took a step back, nauseated by the smell of alcohol and vomit.

"Go," MacKnight said. "I'll see to him."

The very sound of the man's voice made Laura want to scream. Instead, she backpedaled to retrieve the pitcher of clean water from the washstand in the room she and Mama shared. At least Mama was still asleep. That was something. Donning her wrapper, Laura returned to Joe's room where MacKnight was busy undressing him. He stopped when Laura came in.

She unlatched the window and threw up the sash, then took a deep breath of the cool, fresh air. The indigo sky was fading to pale gray-blue. MacKnight had kept Joe out all night. How could he seem so unaffected? Maybe he'd left off drinking a while ago. Maybe he wasn't as vulnerable to the effects as a man who hadn't imbibed for nearly two years.

Taking a deep breath, Laura said, "There is no need to make a pretense at protecting my female naiveté. As you no doubt recall, I've spent many a night tending my brother when he was this way." It was all she could do to swallow the rest of the venom she wanted to spew. She spoke over her shoulder. "You should be the one to go."

"I will," he said. "In a moment."

Laura heard the rattle of a belt buckle, the sound of cloth

sliding across cloth as MacKnight slipped off Joe's pants. "I've covered him up. Can you get his shirt while I hold him?"

She didn't have the energy to argue with him. It was taking all of her meager stores of self-control not to scream like a madwoman. And so she swallowed and did as MacKnight suggested. He lifted Joe to a sitting position and then perched on the edge of the bed and cradled Joe against him while Laura pulled the shirt off. It had not fared well through the night. With a grimace, Laura balled it up and stuffed it into the laundry bag hanging on a hook by the door. MacKnight lowered Joe back to the bed.

"Is there anything else I can do for you before I leave? I've—I'd stay, but—there's someone waiting."

Of course. There would be "someone" waiting, wouldn't there? Laura resisted the urge to ask her name. At least Joe hadn't brought *that* vice to his hotel room. And what, she wondered, would the Misses MacKnight think if they knew about that?

MacKnight went to the door, then hesitated, his hand on the brass knob. "The hotel staff is discreet, Miss White. You won't need to worry about gossip. For your mother's sake, I mean."

Ah. So the fact that there was some trollop waiting in the lobby wouldn't be noised about. How thoughtful of him to reassure her.

MacKnight retreated to the nightstand and reached for the pitcher. "I'll...um...empty this."

"You've done quite enough." Laura nodded toward the door. "Please. Just go."

MacKnight dropped his hand. With a last look at Joe, he nodded. "As you wish."

Laura followed him out of the room, leaving Joe's door cracked open behind her. When MacKnight turned left and headed for the stairs, Laura turned right and made her way to the water closet shared by the entire floor. She emptied and rinsed the pitcher, then refilled it with fresh water before hurrying back to Joe's room. He was asleep, his breathing deep and even.

It took Laura a moment to move the washstand near enough to his bed so that if he was sick again, he'd be able to reach the bowl. By the time she was finished, anger and resentment had transformed, plunging her to the brink of despair. Back out in the small parlor, she returned to the window, looking out on the city. A whistle sounded from the direction of the river. On the street below, a horse-drawn streetcar appeared from around the corner, pulled by a team of bays that seemed already weary of the work. Laura leaned forward until her forehead was touching the cool windowpane. Closing her eyes, she wept.

Chapter 2

As Adele sat in the hotel lobby waiting for Finn, fear clutched at her midsection. A fear even worse than what she'd felt when Papa died. She'd felt both afraid and forlorn back then. But the alarm inspired by Finn's barely disguised rage tonight when she disobeyed him had nearly taken her breath away.

She should have done what he said and stayed behind at home while he saw to Joe. But Adele had always had better luck getting men to see things her way. Now, as the moments ticked by and she sat alone in the hotel lobby, she began to doubt that she'd made the right choice.

She looked toward the hotel doors. Maybe she should go now. It would give Finn time to cool off before she had to face him. Fiona would be in bed by now. She almost rose to leave, but then Finn's words rang in her ears.

"You wait here," he'd said between clenched teeth. "And so help me God, if I come back down here and you're gone—I'll march you to the nearest convent and give the nuns whatever it takes to convince them to throw away the key to your room." And with that, he'd slung Joseph over his shoulder and carried him up the stairs and out of sight.

Adele had always known that Finn was a powerful man, but the way he carried six-foot Joseph White—why, it was as if Joseph was nothing more than a rag doll. Just thinking of the look in Finn's eyes and the power in his stride as he hurried away almost made her feel ill with fear. *Breathe. Breathe. Think. Think.* Finn had never harmed her, but she had never seen him this angry, either.

"Are you all right, miss?" The hotel desk clerk stepped out from behind his polished desk and crossed the lobby to check on her.

"Oh, yes," Adele lied. "I'm fine, thank you. I'm just waiting for my brother. He—um—he was seeing a friend of ours to his room."

The clerk cocked one eyebrow. "And who would that friend be?"

"Mr. Joseph White," Adele said and lifted her chin. "*Captain* Joseph White of the *Laura Rose.* I'm certain you've heard of him."

The clerk nodded. "Yes, ma'am." He clucked his tongue in mock sympathy. "Sad, the run of bad luck they've had since the old captain passed on."

"Yes." Adele nodded. "Those of us who are their friends are doing what we can to help." And they were. Joseph had seemed so discouraged when first he came looking for Finn a few days ago. Finn had gone with Joseph to speak to someone about repairing a boiler. He'd helped write the newspaper advertisement intended to attract crew. And that had been the beginning of...everything, at least as far as Adele was concerned.

Fiona had invited Joseph to eat supper with them that first evening. Adele had noticed Joseph noticing her, and she'd made it a point to make him smile. He'd said something about how she'd grown into a lovely young woman. After that, Joseph found a reason to stop by every single day. Finn and Joseph and Fiona and Adele even dined together at the hotel where Joseph and his family were staying. When Adele wondered aloud about why Joseph's mother and sister didn't join them, Fiona leaned close and shushed her. Which of course meant that Adele had, once again, said something of which Fiona did not approve.

Joseph, on the other hand, seemed to delight in every word Adele said. He began to look less glum. He even kissed her once—a very chaste kiss, but a kiss, nevertheless. Everything had been going along wonderfully. Until tonight.

Looking toward the stairs, Adele wondered what horrible thing had happened to land Joseph in the gutter. Or almost in the gutter, anyway. She wondered what was happening upstairs, and she had almost decided to ascend and walk down the hall in hopes of hearing—or seeing—something that would tell her, when Finn finally came bounding back down the stairs. Adele rose to meet him, but instead of offering his arm and leading the way outside and toward home, Finn said they needed to talk and he didn't want to chance Fiona's overhearing their conversation.

"We'll talk here," he said. "Follow me." Then he shoved his hands in his pockets and led the way down the deserted hallway off the lobby, past the shops that catered to the hotel clientele, and to the far end of the hall where the hotel had set up a rather dreary attempt at a café, just outside the ballroom entrance.

It was an eerie experience, following Finn's hulking form through the shadows, hearing her own footsteps echo across the empty space. When Finn pulled out a bentwood chair and ordered Adele to sit down, she complied, clutching her hands in her lap.

He sat opposite her, leaning forward as he spat out the words, "What in the name of all that is holy are you up to, you little minx? And don't you dare lie to me."

Adele swallowed. It would not do to let her fear show. Taking a deep breath, she said quietly, "I don't know why you'd think I'd lie." She forced herself to meet Finn's flashing dark eyes. "Everything happened just the way I said it did. Milton

Lawrence was walking me home from the ice cream social, and we saw a man stumble and fall. Milton rushed to his aid, and that's when I realized it was Joseph—Captain White—in an . . . umm . . . compromising condition." She feigned wide-eyed innocence. "Surely you wouldn't have wanted me to leave him there? What if he'd been discovered by the police? Or robbers?"

Finn leaned back. "You say Lawrence was walking you home."

Adele nodded.

"From the ice cream social Fiona helped organize."

Again, Adele nodded.

Finn folded his arms across his chest. "The last time I attended with Fiona, the Presbyterian church wasn't anywhere near the saloons on the levee."

Adele swallowed. She ducked her head in what she hoped was a convincing display of feminine modesty. "Milton wanted me to walk down to the levee. I think he's jealous, although I can't imagine why. Joseph is *your* friend. I'm just in the way when the two of you get to talking about steamboating. But I mentioned Joseph's coming to dinner at our house and then our dining at the hotel with him, and before I knew what had happened, Milton was boasting about his uncle's side-wheeler and coaxing me to walk with him to see it."

"In the dark?"

Adele shrugged. "I know it was a bit scandalous. We should have had a chaperone, but Fiona was busy and— She approves of Milton. You can ask her. Besides that, Milton's a perfect gentleman. And it wasn't all that dark, anyway. Most of the steamboats' dining saloons were lighted up from within. Many of the cabins, too." She sighed. "It was really quite beautiful, and we didn't plan on being gone long. I doubt anyone would have even noticed our absence—if Milton hadn't behaved like a boor."

She didn't really care what people thought, but it wouldn't do to be quite so honest. She dared a glance in Finn's direction. "It was just a walk. I gave Milton what he wanted—which was admiration of his uncle's steamboat—and then we headed home. As I said, he was a complete gentleman. Until we encountered poor Joseph." She paused. "And then Milton— Well, I got very angry when he said something rude about Joseph. You know how I can be. You and I both have our papa's temper." When Finn said nothing, Adele continued, "I'm afraid I slapped him, and then I ran home to get you." She let a tear trickle down her cheek. "I don't see why you're angry with me. It was all very upsetting, and I was just trying to be a good friend to Joseph."

"What is this 'Joseph' nonsense, anyway? You've been raised to know better than to assume such familiarity with a man you aren't related to."

What did Finn know about how she'd been raised? He hadn't been around for most of it. On the other hand, when a man was angry, a girl might just as well agree with him than stir him up even more. "You're right," she said quickly. "I just— I feel so badly about all his troubles." She sighed. "And I admit it. I think about him a lot. I enjoy his company. Maybe I do have...hopes." She allowed a prim little smile. "You've seen Milton Lawrence. Can you blame me?"

Finn gulped. For a fleeting moment, Adele thought he might laugh. But he recovered quickly, and once again she was looking at the stern-faced half brother she'd been dumped on years ago—the half brother who'd spent most of those years away from home, either on the river or in the war. The half brother who had the gall to sit there and pontificate about how well she'd been "raised." The fact was, she barely knew Finn. The brunt of raising her had fallen to Fiona, who'd done her duty with a determination that would have been admirable if it hadn't been so...dutiful.

Two years ago, not long after Adele turned sixteen, Fiona had begun to hint about this young man or that in the church congregation. When Milton Lawrence's name kept getting repeated, Adele realized that Fiona was bent on marrying her off. After all, Papa's estate wouldn't be divided until Adele was twenty-one—unless she married. And weren't they all weary of waiting?

Now Adele was eighteen, and three more years of waiting had begun to look like a lifetime. She supposed Finn might be tired of waiting, too. Maybe they were already rich, and they just didn't know it. Maybe Finn didn't have to worry about getting a new job, now that he'd stopped being so wild. He might even be able to afford to buy his own steamboat, if only they didn't have to wait three more years. In which case, Adele thought, Finn should be happy about her interest in Joseph White. Unless, of course, Finn thought Adele wasn't worthy of his friend.

Maybe that was why he was so angry right now. Maybe Joseph liked her more than he'd let on, Finn knew that, and he didn't approve. As if Finn had a right to look down his nose at anyone. Adele could not understand why Fiona fawned over their brother the way she did. Oh, Finn was charming and handsome, but to see him through Fiona's eyes, you'd think Finn Graham MacKnight was going to be the next president of the recently re-United States.

Fiona had worried herself sick the entire time that Finn was off marching into God-knew-what during the rebellion. She'd rolled bandages and made little sewing kits for the soldiers until one would have thought that winning the war was entirely up to her.

As for Finn, he'd come home as if he'd been on an extended hiatus with his best friends. People talked about the "horrors of war," but as far as Adele could tell, Finn hadn't been horrified. He'd returned to his old ways, drinking and womanizing and giving pious Fiona even more reason to pray.

Well, no matter what Fiona and Finn did or said, Adele was not going to marry boring, beak-nosed Milton Lawrence who, at the ripe old age of twenty-two, was already the victim of a receding hairline. Not with someone like rich, handsome Captain Joseph White smiling that way every time he saw her.

Joseph had to be at least a little rich...didn't he? Even with the problems he'd talked about with Finn. After all, he owned the *Laura Rose*. And even if he wasn't all that rich, that kiss had made her feel...well, she wasn't quite certain what to call the emotion that had stirred deep inside her when Joseph's lips touched hers. But whether she could name it or not, she wanted to feel it again. Often. What's more, Joseph was part of a devoted, close-knit family. What would it be like to be part of a family like that? To be the girl who made two nice women's son and brother happy—instead of the disliked half sister they couldn't wait to get rid of? She meant to find out.

Adele swallowed. She had to be very careful with Finn just now. She must seem inclined to please. It would not do to pick a fight. Not tonight. And so she gave Finn her most innocent smile as she said, "When we were sitting on the front porch the other night after supper—when you'd gone inside to get those foul-smelling cigars you love—Joseph said I made him laugh. He said it was nice to laugh in such lovely company." When Finn remained silent, she continued, "He even told me about the apple orchard. And how you took the blame he deserved and never let anyone know that he was the one who threw a rotten apple at that parson." She gave him her wide-eyed, admiring look. "I'm so thankful you were home tonight, Finn. I was just plain terrified that something awful would happen to Joseph before we got back."

"Which brings me to my next question." Again, Finn leaned forward. "I told you to stay at home. I told you I'd handle it. But you followed me. Why didn't you do as you were told?"

Because I wasn't about to stay home and chance another one of Fiona's tongue-lashings. Of course she couldn't say that, either. Finn would never allow Adele the Upstart to criticize Saint Fiona. "I should have obeyed. I'm sorry. I just—I just couldn't sit there alone, worrying." Finally, the tears came. Goodness, but it had taken her long enough to muster them. Her voice wavered as she repeated, "I'm sorry."

Finn studied her for a moment. She swiped at a tear. Looked down at her gloved hands. Finally, he rose to his feet. His voice was a bit softer as he reached for her arm. "We'd better get you home. Fiona's going to be fit to be tied. She had to be expecting you to be there when she returned from the social."

Adele bit her lip, then confessed that, before running after Finn, she'd arranged her pillows and bedding so that if Fiona checked Adele's room, it would appear that she was fast asleep. "I didn't want her to worry needlessly," she said. When Finn stopped in his tracks and looked down at her, Adele didn't need the glow of light from a street lamp to know that he was frowning with disapproval. She gave a little shrug and a sigh. "I suppose you never did such a dastardly thing when you were only eighteen."

He barely managed to mask a chuckle this time. In fact, he had to clear his throat more than once before he managed to speak. "First of all, we both know that society is not nearly as forgiving when it comes to a young *lady's* reputation. Things that people might overlook in a boy can ruin a young lady's life. You know very well what my own mistakes have cost me." He paused. Cleared his throat. Finally, he said, "Adele, being like me is hardly the thing to recommend you to St. Louis society or, for that matter, to Joe's mother and sister. If you truly are bent on pursuing..."

His voice just sort of faded away. And just like that, with what she took to be Finn's understanding, if not his outright approval, of her intentions, all of Adele's disconnected longings, each one of Joseph's recent smiles, and a single, somewhat chaste kiss, distilled into one earnest desire. She was indeed bent on pursuing Joseph. On escaping Fiona's self-righteous do's and demanding don'ts. On becoming a steamboat captain's wife. The very idea of standing up on the texas deck of the *Laura Rose* and waving good-bye to St. Louis sent a thrill down to her very toes. The idea of sharing the captain's cabin with Joseph set her heart racing.

They were nearly back to the house when Finn rumbled, "Let's agree that if Fiona is still up, you'll hurry on to bed and let me handle things."

"With pleasure," Adele said. They'd taken a few more steps before she braved a question. "Does that mean you believe me about—everything? That you approve of me and Joseph?"

"It means," he said, "that I want things said in a way that spares Fiona as much worry as possible. You and I have both given her enough of that for a lifetime."

Fiona. Of course. He always thought of Fiona first.

***

As dawn tinted the eastern sky pink, Laura dressed and left the hotel. She was more exhausted than ever, but she had to do something to keep Mama from suspecting the truth about Joe. Making her way down the stairs and across the hotel lobby, she paused outside just long enough to take a deep breath of fresh air and to cast a longing glance toward the levee. Finally, turning her back on the river, she made her way up to a small café across the street from a pharmacy. She ordered coffee, and the moment there was a sign of life inside, she crossed over—narrowly missing landing one booted foot in a steaming pile of manure—and pounded on the door. "I am so sorry to bother you at this early hour," she said when the pharmacist finally answered, "but I wonder if you have any dyspeptic tea already mixed? My brother is quite ill."

The flustered proprietor motioned for her to come in. As he moved about behind the battered counter taking up this tin or that apothecary jar, he grumbled about the hour, the weather, the condition of the streets, and sundry other issues. With a pinch of this and a palmful of that, the balding old man mixed a quarter pound of various aromatic herbs that he assured Laura would create the best dyspeptic tea known to man. One bag ready, he reached for another jar. "Alternate with mint tea for best results," he said and, without waiting for Laura to agree to the additional purchase, prepared a small sack of that. "You'll also want some ginger for—"

"Thank you," Laura said quickly, "but I must go. Perhaps I'll return later for the ginger."

Weary and out of breath, she fumbled the key in the hotel room door lock, startled when the door opened from the inside, and there stood Mama in her dressing gown. "When I woke and you were gone, I was worried. You should have left a note."

"I'm sorry," Laura said. "You were snoring when I—"

"Snoring? Don't be ridiculous. I do not snore." Mama pulled Laura into the room and closed the door, eyeing the packages. "I smell mint?"

"Joe was feeling poorly"—Laura held up one sack—"dyspeptic tea." She held up the other. "Which the pharmacist suggested I alternate with mint. He wanted me to buy some ginger as well, but I suspect he was just exacting financial revenge for my insisting that he open up so early."

"Insisting?"

"I pounded on the door until he answered."

Mama gazed toward Joe's bedroom door. "Joseph called

out in his sleep. He was having a bad dream." She reached for the bags still clutched in Laura's gloved hand. "Let us make very strong tea. Gallons of it."

Laura's heart lurched. *Joseph.* Mama called Joe that only when she was upset with him. "I was in such a hurry, I forgot to ask the desk clerk to have a pot of hot water brought up so that I can make it." She turned toward the door, intending to leave again. "I . . . um . . . I'm sorry Joe's being ill woke you. I'll tend him, Mama. And don't worry. I'm certain he'll be fine. I don't think it's anything serious."

"Raising the window was a good idea," Mama said. "You might take the shirt he's nearly ruined down with you to have it laundered." She opened one of the bags of herbs and inhaled the aroma. "Tea may settle his stomach, but I don't suppose it'll do much for the headache he's bound to have." Her voice wavered. "He needs to get back on that river. He just doesn't do well in the city." She cleared her throat. "Strong tea every hour, I think. Until he realizes the dangers of risking such 'illness.'"

"I'm certain it isn't dangerous, Mama."

"That would depend on your definition of the term." Mama headed for Joe's room, pausing in the doorway just long enough to say, "Would you mind opening the rest of the windows, dear? We need fresh air. You're kind to want to protect me and Joseph, but the stench of drunkenness is nearly impossible to hide. Especially from an angry mother."

Chapter 3

"Mama?"

Laura stood in the doorway watching as her bleary-eyed brother lifted his head from his pillow and squinted at the little woman jerking the drapes open to allow sunlight to pour into his room.

"Yes, Joseph," Mama said. "You called out in your sleep earlier."

"I woke you? I'm sorry, Mama."

Mama motioned for Laura to come near. "Laura's made you some tea. Sit up, now, and have a sip."

Joe groaned. "Can it wait until I..."

Mama's voice was firm as she said, "It cannot. There is cargo to load and a steamboat to pilot. And before any of that can happen, we must deal with whatever is going on with you." She motioned for Laura to hand him the steaming cup of tea. "Drink it, now. A strong cup every hour. That's what the doctor ordered."

"D-doctor?" Joe laid his head back on his pillow. "I don't need a doctor." He grimaced at Laura. "Did you call a doctor?"

Laura shook her head.

"*You* did," Mama said, "when you called out in your sleep. I heard you and here I am, and I am quite certain I am all the doctor you'll be needing today." She paused. "Unless, of course, you decide to repeat this foolishness. In which case you will most definitely need a physician, because I will sew you between the sheets while you sleep and knock some sense into you. Now sit up and drink this tea."

Joe sat up and drank the tea.

"Good. Now sleep. I'll be back with more in an hour." Mama headed for the door. "And try to groan less, Joseph. It's unbecoming. There is no need to sound like a bull elephant in search of a mate."

Laura slapped her hand over her mouth as she retreated into the parlor. When Mama closed the door to Joe's room, she began to laugh. "Land sakes, Mama. A bull elephant?"

Mama grinned. "Your papa took me to the circus when we were courting. It was quite...memorable." She put her hand to her waist. "My stomach just growled." She looked toward Joe's room. "I don't think we dare leave him alone right now, but I'd love some eggs. And toast. And potatoes. And sausage, if they have it. On second thought, never mind the sausage. I don't imagine Joe would appreciate that aroma until we've settled his stomach."

"I could have a tray brought up," Laura said. "Would you like orange juice as well?"

"That would be lovely."

And it was.

Mama made good on her promise to treat Joe's "dyspepsia" with a vengeance. After only a few hours, he was begging Mama to let him get dressed—and to leave off making him drink tea. "I'm going to float away."

"Indeed you are," Mama said. "On a steamboat, with not one drop of strong drink to distract you from the important job of being a proper Missouri River pilot."

With a sigh, Joe confessed, "Problems just keep piling up." He sounded miserable. He looked over at Laura, who was standing in the doorway, his freshly laundered shirt over her arm. "I talked things over with Finn and...I thought I could handle it, but then I couldn't, and I thought, *Just one little drink.*"

Mama put her hands on her hips. "And of course everyone knows that strong drink is the perfect solution to problems. Why, solutions just magically show themselves when a man launches himself onto waves of bourbon and gin." She motioned with both hands, like a dancer mimicking a pounding surf.

Joe shook his head. "I'm sorry for putting you both through this." He glanced at Laura. "Thank God for Finn."

Laura sputtered. "Don't you *dare* thank the Almighty for the man who dragged you back down into the muck!"

Joe frowned. "What are you talking about? The only thing he did was pick me up off the street and haul me back here. Last night was completely my doing." He rubbed the stubble on his chin with the back of one hand as he muttered, "And now that I think of it...I wonder how..." He groaned. "I have to apologize to Adele. She must have been terrified."

Mama looked over at Laura. When Laura shook her head—*I don't know what he's talking about*—Mama asked, "What does Finn's younger sister have to do with any of this?"

Joe frowned. "I don't remember...exactly. But I think she...No, she was with someone." He thought for a moment. Finally, an odd smile replaced the frown. He motioned for the shirt. "I need to get dressed. I have to find both her and Finn and apologize."

Mama intercepted the shirt as Laura moved to hand it over. "If Miss MacKnight witnessed last evening's debacle, I have no doubt you owe her an apology. But that will have to wait until the effects are fully eradicated."

"I'm fine, Mama."

"You are not fine. You are 'hung over,' as they say." Mama shook her head. Her voice wavered as she said, "I cannot believe we are back in this place, Joseph."

"We aren't," Joe said quickly. "I mean it. I just— I lost hope for a moment." When Mama opened her mouth to speak, Joe hurried to say, "I know. I know. 'Only a weak man seeks solace in a saloon in place of solutions.'"

Mama smiled. Nodded. "Indeed. And it's even more critical that you believe that if you are thinking of courting that young lady."

"I'm not."

"Ah, but you are," Mama said gently.

After a moment, Joe nodded. "Yes...I suppose I am. Do you mind?"

Mama seemed to ponder before answering. "I don't think it's a particularly fortuitous time," she said. "But once you've completed the first trip upriver, our situation should be markedly improved—right?"

Joe nodded. "A good trip would do wonders."

"Then perhaps you'll want to ask permission to correspond with the young lady while we are gone."

Joe nodded, then looked Laura's way. "Please don't make assumptions about the MacKnights." He glanced over at Mama and then back at Laura. "Finn has reformed, and Adele is—Well, I think she's enchanting."

Laura took Joe's empty cup and retreated into the other room, relieved to escape all the talk of Finn and Adele MacKnight. She didn't really know Adele, but it would take more than a testimonial from Joseph to convince her that Finn MacKnight had changed. Not long after Papa fired Finn for being a bad influence on Joe, the close-knit world of pilots had resonated with news about MacKnight's continued bad behavior. Something about his being drunk at the wheel of another steamboat. As for the other night, even if MacKnight wasn't inebriated, he'd had "someone" waiting downstairs. Ladies were expected to feign ignorance about such matters, which made the fact that MacKnight had admitted it to Laura even more appalling. *Reformed, indeed.*

Why on earth had Joe gone to Finn for business advice? As for Adele, if she was anything like her half brother, things were happening too fast. Laura could not shake the mental image of her brother as the moth fluttering about a flame, unable to resist the attraction to things that would do him harm.

They had to get back on the river, and soon. That was all there was to it.

✶

Adele spent most of Saturday helping Fiona garden. Helping Fiona with her *infernal* garden was how Adele really thought about it, but it wouldn't do to let that show. Finn had smoothed things over about the late night, but men accepted that a matter was over once it had been discussed. It didn't work that way for women.

Even if Fiona never knew the details regarding Joseph's role in last night's escapade, there would be consequences for Adele's having left the ice cream social without permission— even with Milton Lawrence. She was determined to manage those consequences in a way that promoted her plan in regards to Joseph White. That meant earning Fiona's favor. And so, here she was, getting filthy in the oversized garden Saint Fiona tended so that she could share the abundance with "the poor."

"Not so deep," Fiona called from the opposite end of the row. "Lettuce seeds barely need to be covered."

Adele nodded. She filled the furrow in partway. "Is that better?"

"Much." Fiona straightened up, arching her back and grimacing. "I appreciate your help," she said. "As will the needy we'll share with this summer."

Why couldn't the "needy" grow their own food? Adele wondered. *Goodness.* Most of them had spent a big part of their lives growing cotton. Surely they knew how to grow food. But of course she couldn't say that. She reached for a packet of seeds. "Peas next?"

From Adele's point of view, it was the longest day in recent memory. Finally, late in the afternoon, Fiona said they'd done enough and they could get cleaned up and have a glass of tea out on the porch. They were doing just that when a tall, slim figure approaching from the direction of downtown caught Adele's attention. Her heart thumped. As he came near and she saw the bouquet clutched in one hand, a thrill of triumph coursed through her.

"It would appear," Fiona said from where she sat knitting in the wicker rocker nearby, "that you have a visitor."

"He's probably coming to see Finn," Adele said, even though the truth was obvious.

Fiona snorted. "And I suppose he's bringing the flowers to me."

Adele looked over at her. "Is it all right?"

"Does what I think matter?"

"Of course it does."

Fiona said nothing, but when Joseph got close enough that they could see the bouquet more clearly, she looked over at Adele. "Purple hyacinths? Does he owe you an apology?"

Adele shrugged. "I doubt he knows anything about such things." And yet she hoped he did, for purple hyacinths meant *I am sorry. Please forgive me.* She would welcome the opportunity to show Joseph just how forgiven he was—as soon as she found a way for them to be alone.

❀

Mama chuckled as she closed the door behind Joe. "He charged out of here like a wild animal being sprung from a cage."

Laura knew how he felt. Mama had always had a gift for

nursing, but below the gentle surface today there had been just enough flint to send a secondary message: *Don't you dare put us through this again*. From the way Joe responded, Laura was certain he'd gotten that message. When he'd mentioned calling on Adele MacKnight, Laura realized that more than avoiding Mama's wrath would help him keep his promise in regards to temperance.

"You don't have to worry about me," he'd said when he finally emerged from his room after a sponge bath and a shave. "Lesson learned." He'd spent the next few minutes discussing ways to overcome the superstitious rumors about the *Laura Rose*, among their other problems. Laura suggested they offer a bonus if the boiler repairs could be finished within forty-eight hours.

"That might work," he'd said, "but we can't afford it."

"We can't afford not to do it," Laura insisted. She gestured at the room around them. "We can't keep paying for hotel rooms. You said that we need more than one trip this year to catch up, and if we don't get under way soon—"

"All right," Joe said. "We'll do it." He stood up. "Monday morning. We'll go by the bank and check the account—"

"We should send word to Tom Meeks to meet us there," Laura said, referring to the clerk. "He'll have an idea of where we stand in regards to expenses." When Joe nodded, Laura promised to track down Meeks at the boardinghouse where the remaining crew was staying while they waited for the return of the *Laura Rose*.

Joe nodded. "Good idea. We'll consult with Tom, and then we'll head for the repair yard."

"With cash," Laura said. "There's nothing more compelling than a pile of cash."

Joe looked over at Mama, who had been a silent witness to the conversation. "See what I have to deal with? A woman with a head for business."

"Your father always said it was a wise man who knew when to listen to a woman," Mama said. "In fact, I seem to remember God Himself telling a man named Abraham to do the same."

Joe threw up his hands in mock surrender. "All right, then. So be it." He grinned at Laura. "May I go now, *Sarah*?"

After Joe left, Laura walked into the bedroom she and Mama shared. Opening her trunk, she pulled a ledger book out of the top tray.

Mama spoke from the open door. "What on earth?"

"I thought it made sense to keep the business books with us." Moving a potted fern out of the way, Laura set the ledger book on the low table in front of the sofa, then perched on the edge of an upholstered cushion and leaned over, squinting at the rows of numbers.

Presently, Mama replaced the fern with a lighted gas table lamp. She settled next to Laura. "Tell me what you see in those numbers."

Pending disaster. But she didn't want to worry Mama, and so Laura took a deep breath and muttered, "I'm not completely sure. But if there's a way to economize, we need to find it, because if offering a bonus to get the boiler fixed works, then perhaps we could overcome superstition the same way."

"It's come to that? We have to offer a bonus to get people to work for us?"

Laura shrugged. "I hope not. But if Joe hasn't filled the open spots on the crew by Wednesday, we'll have to do something." She took a deep breath. "We *must* be under way by Friday, come heck or high water."

Mama reached for Laura's hand. "Let's pray."

Laura bowed her head. She doubted that the Almighty cared much about the details of steamboating. On the other hand, she was quite certain He cared about Mama. Having her pray for the *Laura Rose* couldn't hurt.

❄

Late Saturday, a discouraged Finn MacKnight stood with his
back to the river, staring toward the familiar doorways spilling
light and music and raucous laughter into the dark night. It
had been months since he'd gone through one of those doors.
How long would it be before the allure finally, once and for all,
lost its hold over him? Would he ever be free of temptation?

He moistened his lips, imagining the first jolt. And then
the next as the second and then, maybe, a third shot burned
its way into his gut, seared his thoughts, and eventually
numbed everything, making life easier.

Except that it didn't. Not really. Whiskey might make the
demons that called him a worthless failure recede for a time,
but they always came back. Eventually, it took more than a
shot—more than three—more than half a night of steady
drinking to silence them. And then, dreams launched him
back to hospital duty during the war, and that gave different demons free rein to resurrect the images of severed limbs
piled near the hearth of an upstairs bedroom in a plantation
house they'd used for a hospital after the Battle of Franklin.

Even tonight, standing here on the St. Louis levee, that
memory made him shudder. He'd nearly killed himself trying to drink it—and others—away. Guilt was mixed in there
somewhere, too. The guilt of returning whole, when most of
his friends either died or lost something. He hadn't lost anything but himself.

He'd finally realized that drinking didn't really help all
that much. He always woke up, and then he had to face Fiona,
who just kept loving him no matter what he did. Finn had
finally decided that hurting his sister was worse than facing
memories and guilt. So he quit drinking. He made the rounds,
looking for work. But no one would hire him. And on nights
like this one, when the past and the present melded together

and everything about life looked hopeless, it was almost as if the light spilling out of those saloon doors had claws that could latch on to his lapels and drag him in.

His head down, his heart pounding, Finn marched away from temptation, his throat burning with a phantom thirst just as powerful as the pains the amputees in the military hospital felt in limbs that were no longer there. As he walked, he swore at himself—for being weak, for being a failure, for squandering the chance he'd had to learn from Captain Jacob White, for ruining his chances to have the only life he wanted.

He marched south, along the levee, painfully aware of the number of steamboats tied up just off to the left. He didn't look at them. He'd spent the day going on board one after the other, only to be told there was nothing for him there. Not that they weren't hiring, mind you. There was nothing for *him* there.

Now as he trudged toward home, something else came to mind that helped Finn quicken the steps leading him away from temptation. Something from just last night. He'd seen anew the fear in Adele's eyes when she told him about Joe's being drunk. He remembered the sneer in the hotel clerk's eyes when he walked past with Joe slung over his shoulder. And last, he saw the despair in Laura White's eyes. There'd been rage, too. It was easy to deflect rage, but despair on the part of a beautiful woman? That was another thing entirely.

He must have seen all those expressions before. As many times as he'd been hauled home drunk, he'd been in a position to see them over and over again. But liquor dulled the senses. That was, after all, the point. So the sneers and the fear and even the despair—and surely Fiona had felt despair as well—hadn't had much effect on the man who cared only that his demons be silenced.

Last night had changed that. Last night, he'd actually witnessed what a man's drinking did to the women who loved him. That shamed him in a way he'd not felt before. Shamed him so that the very idea that he'd just been contemplating having a drink made him blink back unbidden tears. *I'm sorry, Fiona. I'm so sorry.*

Fiona's steadfast loyalty was almost embarrassing at times. Not to mention her ironclad insistence that God concerned Himself with the affairs of all men. Finn had never doubted that God was interested in the affairs of some men. But he was fairly certain that it took a host of Fiona-prayers to keep the Almighty from launching lightning bolts every time He took notice of Finn MacKnight.

He looked up at the starlit sky, then back toward the long row of steamboats, nearly a mile of them, lined up along the levee. There had to be a job for him on this river. He could not give in. Not to defeat and most certainly not to whiskey. If it came to it, he would beg.

At the far end of the levee, he headed off down the road that curved into the countryside, skirting along the well-groomed gardens of the Demenil mansion, where he paused to look out over the river. Was it his imagination, or was it an especially clear night? The air smelled... *like the river, and that's not particularly sweet.* On the other hand, something was different. Something inside. Something he owed to those eyes he'd taken notice of the other night, Laura White's among them. He smiled. She'd hate that. Hate thinking that Finn MacKnight had read the hurt behind her rage.

Finn decided that tomorrow he'd check in on Joe, and maybe give him a talking-to. After all, if Joe was setting his cap for Adele, it was Finn's duty—even if he was only a half brother who'd been completely derelict when it came to things like "duty" in the past.

After seeing Joe, he'd return to the levee and look for work. Again. He'd considered begging Joe for a job, but after seeing the look in Laura White's eyes last night, he knew he couldn't do that. It would be asking Joe to consider not only going against his own father's judgment but also standing against his sister. It wouldn't be right to come between them. He would have to find another way.

Tomorrow was the Sabbath. Maybe he'd go to church with Fiona and Adele in the morning. It would be good to see Fiona's gray eyes light up with something besides disappointment. As he headed back into town, Finn began to whistle softly.

Chapter 4

It took God less than twenty-four hours to answer Mama's prayers about the family business problems, and Laura a split second to question part of that answer—if indeed God was the reason things changed so quickly. She and Joe didn't have to offer a bonus to the shipyard repairing the boiler after all. In fact, the *Laura Rose* came churning her way upriver late Sunday afternoon.

Elijah North, the boat's carpenter, brought the news, and the family wasted no time packing trunks and hurrying down to the levee just in time to see the *Laura Rose* slip into an open spot between the *Nashville* and the *Bluebelle*. The moment the gangplank was lowered, their dog Logjam shot on board and was trotting about the perimeter of the main deck like a guard making the rounds.

"Where'd he come from?" Joe laughed. "I thought he was supposed to be staying with the Perrins."

"That he was," a familiar voice boomed. "Launched hisself right out my wagon the minute he saw that *Laura Rose*."

With a little exclamation of joy, Mama hurried to the wagon to greet the beloved couple who'd worked for Captain White since Laura was a child. The moment Hercules— a physical monument to his unusual name—helped his wife down, Mama took Bird's hands in her own and leaned in to kiss her on both cheeks. Hercules wasted no time beginning to unload provisions.

Laura followed Mama and Bird up the gangplank, listening as they chattered away about this soup and that dessert. Making her way up the steps from the main deck to the hurricane deck, and then on to the texas deck, she paused to revel in the thing she liked most about St. Louis—the view of it from the deck of a steamboat. And that's when the thing happened that made her question what Mama had called "answered prayer," although it began innocently enough.

"We won't need to offer that bonus now," Joe said. "I was thinking we might use it to fill the open spots on the crew."

"Good idea," Laura said. There was no point in telling him she'd already thought they should do that.

He nodded. "All right. I'll have a few of the men put the word out, first thing tomorrow."

"Maybe ask Tom to help you arrive at a figure? I'll take him the ledger book as soon as our trunks arrive from the hotel."

Again, Joe nodded. "And I'll follow up on the military contract. Supplies and troops up to Fort Rice."

"Can we get that job?"

"I think so, as long as I can assure them we'll head upriver by Friday."

That was good news. But there was something else. Something that was making Joe uncomfortable. She could sense it.

Joe cleared his throat. He took a deep breath. "Miss MacKnight invited me to dine with them this evening." He paused. "I'm going to offer Finn a job."

It wasn't really a great surprise. They needed crew members, and MacKnight needed work. Laura had had time to think about it, and as long as Mama didn't object and MacKnight minded his own business down on the freight deck, he wouldn't be able to do them much damage. But then Joe delivered the blow that Laura didn't expect.

"We need a licensed second pilot. Someone the inspectors will recognize."

She clutched at the railing. Finally, she croaked, "You're making him second pilot?"

"I know what you're thinking."

"I seriously doubt that," she snapped.

"Well, for one thing, you're thinking that our own father fired him." He paused. "I talked to Mama, Laura. She agreed that everyone deserves a second chance. Even Finn."

He'd already talked to Mama? Before telling her? Tears threatened.

"I know you want to be a licensed pilot more than anything, and believe me, if I could make it happen, I would. Then it could just be the two of us taking the *Laura Rose* upriver. But I don't have the power to change the inspector's mind, and if we don't have a full crew, including a second licensed pilot, no one, much less the United States government, is going to trust cargo to us. Think of it, Laura. There's two thousand men stationed at a dozen posts upriver, and most of them are supplied completely by steamboat. We can't risk losing that kind of revenue."

She said nothing.

"I hate it that you can't be licensed, but it's just the way it is. You're a great pilot. I know it, and Finn will realize it, too. He'll likely be handing you the wheel by the second time we stop for wood." He paused. "It doesn't have to change anything. You'll still be up in the wheelhouse as much as ever. Please, Laura. Just give him a chance. He's been looking for work, willing to do anything, but no one will hire him. Adele is really worried about him."

Adele. So that was the real reason Joe could ignore the past. Reality hit. Being a cub pilot taking orders was the best she would ever do. It hadn't been so bad when the licensed pilot was Joe. But taking orders from Finn MacKnight? What had he ever done to prove himself? As far as anyone knew, his life was little more than a mediocre litany of failure. He went off to war and came back—unremarkably, as far as Laura knew. He got in trouble, dragged Joe down with him, and acted so badly that Papa, one of the kindest men in the world, fired him. And then, instead of learning his lesson, he continued to drink—and womanize, which was worse. And this was the person she was supposed to work with? Work for? Take orders from?

She turned away.

"Laura, please—"

When Joe reached for her, she warded him off. Somehow she managed to make it to her cabin before the dam burst. Once inside, she buried her face in her pillow to muffle the sound, crying out her disappointment and anger.

❈

Standing next to Joseph on the levee, Adele pointed to the freshly painted railing bordering the hurricane deck of the *Laura Rose* and sighed. "It's as if she's trimmed in lace." She looked up at him. "She's beautiful, Joseph. Just…beautiful."

He put his hand over hers. "I'm so glad you think so. See those crates and boxes? Those are full of weapons, ammunition, and supplies for several of the forts between here and Fort Rice. Those two wagons? Those are military ambulances. Now you see why I haven't been able to spend much time with you these last few days."

Adele squeezed his arm. "It's not as if I haven't heard Finn going on about how much hard work it's been to get everything arranged." She paused. "I understand. Just don't think I haven't missed you terribly."

As Joe escorted her on board, he explained again just how completely the business of running the *Laura Rose* had taken over his every waking moment. He seemed eager to make up for having had to decline two invitations to dine at the MacKnights', and Adele was eager to let him display his knowledge and his prowess, too. What was this, she asked, why was that, and goodness, how did he know so much about every little detail of the steamboat? When he led her up the gangplank and a massive brindle dog approached, she feigned a moment of terror, leaning close.

"That's just Logjam," Joe said. "He's been part of the family since he was just a pup."

"Well, he certainly did grow up," Adele said, with a little shiver. "It looks as though he's contemplating having me for tea."

Joseph squatted down and held out his hand. "Come here, boy. It's all right. This is Adele."

The dog tilted its fine head and peered at her. He wagged his stump of a tail, but he stayed put.

Adele forced a little laugh. "All right, then. It's a truce." She tugged on Joseph's arm and he escorted her up the stairs to the hurricane deck, where he showed her the cabins, which were much smaller than Adele had imagined, and the dining saloon, which wasn't nearly as sumptuous as she'd expected.

"You should see it by lamplight," Joseph said, pointing to the brass oil lamps hanging overhead. "And wait until you taste Bird and Hercules's cooking. The *Laura Rose* serves the best meals on the river."

He spoke as if she would be part of his life as a captain. "That sounds wonderful," she murmured. They were alone, and for the briefest moment, Adele thought he was going to kiss her again. But then the cook and Joseph's mother and sister came breezing in. Adele greeted the White ladies.

After being introduced to Bird—*what an odd name*— Adele said, "I never imagined one of the smaller steamboats could be so inviting." She pointed at the piano along one wall. "I asked for a piano once, but Fiona just said MacKnights aren't musical." The wistfulness in her voice must have been just right, for as Mrs. White excused herself and Joseph's sister—something about a problem with one of the grocers delivering food—she told Adele she was more than welcome to play the piano anytime she was on board.

Anytime. Again, a hopeful sign that maybe, just maybe, she would soon be drawn into the family fold. In the wake of the ladies' departure, Joseph led her outside again. Together they stood at the front of the hurricane deck, looking out over the levee and watching as roustabouts hauled still more freight onto the main deck.

Adele pointed to Finn, who'd just shouldered a crate of something and was hauling it on board. "I thought you were making him second pilot."

"I am, but we're still a little short on crew, and he volunteered to help." Joe paused. "Truth be told, I should be down there, too."

Adele sighed. "I'm sorry. I don't want to be in the way. Finn can escort me home—or maybe you should just put me on the streetcar. There's a stop just on the corner from the house."

It was exactly the right thing to say, because once she began to talk about going, Joseph said he wouldn't think of putting her on a streetcar and why didn't she take Mother up on the invitation to play the piano? He could get some work done, and then she and Finn could dine with the family that evening. He was about to send word inviting Fiona to join them as well when Adele mentioned Fiona's Ladies' Aid meeting, wording it carefully so she didn't tell an outright lie—because while there was indeed a meeting, it always concluded by late afternoon.

"Then we'll send word that you're dining on board the *Laura Rose*—just so she doesn't worry."

"You're so thoughtful," Adele said, gazing above them at

the wheelhouse. "You must feel like a king reigning over his kingdom from up there."

"I feel like a king right now," Joseph said, and when he looked down at her, her heartbeat quickened.

Adele fluttered her eyelashes, murmuring, "I don't suppose it would be proper for us to be seen up there. But I'd love to see what it's like—just so I can picture you at work while you're away."

Taking her hand, Joseph led the way, helping her up the narrow, ladderlike stairs to the texas. Adele hesitated at the foot of the ladder they would have to ascend to reach the wheelhouse, exclaiming over the view. "Oh, it's beautiful! So beautiful!" She held back for a moment before murmuring, "I wish I could go with you tomorrow."

With a glance toward the levee, Joseph pulled her after him, around the corner, alongside the family's private cabins, and just out of view of the levee. "Will you write to me, Adele?"

She nodded. "Of course."

He lifted her chin to encourage her to meet his gaze. "And will you wait for me?"

She caught his hand. "Yes. Oh . . . yes."

When Joseph put his lips to hers, she leaned in. His hands found her waist and then slid upward, exploring. She caught her breath and pretended to step away, ever mindful that the door to his cabin was just behind them. He followed, his blue eyes flashing with desire. Adele clasped her hands about his neck and took another tiny step toward the cabin door. "I love you, Joseph. So much."

He fumbled to open the door to his cabin, then drew her inside.

Laura stared down at the bill of sale in her hand, then glared over at the stubborn, little, bespectacled man standing beside the wagonload of groceries. "I don't know what you think you're doing," she said, "but I've seen Tom Meeks's ledger and I know for a fact that you agreed to a price well below this." She scanned the columns. "In fact, overall I'd say you've marked up every one of these items at least 30 percent since Tom gave you the order."

The little man shrugged. "What can I do? Costs rise, Miss White." He looked past her toward the *Laura Rose*. "I'm sure Mr. Meeks would understand, if only—"

"But you aren't talking to Mr. Meeks, are you? You're talking to a part-owner. And I can assure you that Mr. Meeks will agree with me."

"Well, now, is that a fact?" The grocer slipped a thumb beneath each suspender and rose onto the balls of his feet. "How about we get Mr. Meeks down here? Or better yet, Captain White? He'll settle the matter."

Mama put a hand on her arm just as Laura opened her mouth to let her temper do the talking. "I'll go get your brother, dear," she said. "In the meantime, perhaps you'd want to check a few things over." She leaned close, whispering, "The last time we took delivery from this outfit, the flour was full of weevils." Then, with a bright smile at the grocer she said, "I'm sure you won't object to my daughter's doing that, now, will you? It will facilitate things once Joseph settles the matter of the bill."

Laura set her jaw and looked away just as a familiar voice rumbled, "What's this? Hello, Reynolds. Is there some trouble?"

"Nothing we can't handle," Laura said as Finn MacKnight walked up, swiping his brow with a well-used kerchief.

"Didn't mean it that way," MacKnight said. "Just— Reynolds and I are old friends, aren't we?" He put a massive hand on the grocer's shoulder and gave it a friendly shake. "Don't tell me you're up to your old ways now. You'll find you can't pull the wool over Miss White's eyes."

The grocer's face reddened. "And who said anything about pulling wool over anyone's eyes? Costs go up."

MacKnight nodded. "True, but not after two gentlemen have shaken hands on a deal. And I was there when you and Joe did just that. Miss White says you added 30 percent?" MacKnight clucked his tongue. "Joe's not going to appreciate that, Edgar." He gazed toward the *Laura Rose*. "You wouldn't want it noised about that you tried to cheat your way out of an agreement by taking advantage of a lady, now, would you?"

The little man turned to Laura and asked her to hand the order back. He made a show of cleaning his spectacles and sputtered nonsense about a misunderstanding and a mistake and finally, pulling a pencil out of his shirt pocket, he lined out the total and adjusted it. Downward by 30 percent. He handed the bill to MacKnight. And Mama *thanked* him for saving her the trouble of finding Joe or Mr. Meeks.

With a smile at Laura, Mama said, "I'll fetch Hercules so he can begin unloading."

"I'll get Hercules, ma'am," MacKnight said, holding up the bill. "Need to deliver this to Meeks anyway." Touching the brim of his cap in a little salute, he strode off toward the packet, leaving Laura and Mama to inspect the order.

"Well, ladies," the grocer said with a forced smile, "you just take your time. If Edgar Reynolds knows anything, it's that the ladies are the ones who really make the world of commerce go round." He made a show of winking merrily. "We men just pretend to be in charge."

Clamping her mouth shut to keep from saying something she'd regret, Laura joined Mama at the back of the grocer's wagon.

Mama gazed toward the *Laura Rose*. "On second thought," she said, "why don't you leave this to me? I'm certain you'd rather be on board...polishing the wheel up in the wheelhouse or...something."

Polishing the wheel? What on earth— Laura glanced up at the wheelhouse just in time to see Miss MacKnight's head bob into view. Stifling a sigh, she headed for the *Laura Rose.* To babysit Joe and Finn MacKnight's little sister. Which was ridiculous, because Joe wouldn't listen to her any better than the grocers or the crew or...anyone else. Of course every single one of them heeded Finn MacKnight when *he* gave an order.

"Laura Rose."

Laura glanced back at Mama.

"Nothing makes a person more miserable than discontent. The Lord knew what He was doing when He made you a beautiful woman with unusual talent."

Laura nodded. It was the best she could do. If only she could be as certain of that as Mama. If only Papa hadn't died. If only Joe believed in her enough to stand up for her. Enough to champion her. If only.

Chapter 5

Laura woke before dawn Friday morning. Finally they would be leaving St. Louis behind. Laura loved her little cabin on the texas deck, outfitted with a narrow bed, a washstand, and a small trunk. Other people might like Persian carpet, but Laura just wanted to plant her feet on the blue and gray rag rug beside her bed on board the steamboat. The rug woven by the cook's sister. The rug here at *home*. Lighting the lamp on her bedside table, she hurried through her morning toilette, raking a brush through her hair and stuffing it into a snood before stepping into her unmentionables.

"Miss Rogers says that snoods are on the way out," Mama had said.

Sweet Mama. Ever hopeful. But Laura had no patience with the torrent of Titian red curls that sprang to life no matter what Mama tried in the way of irons and smoothing compounds, pomades and rinses. As far as Laura was concerned, if God had intended for women to mess with such things, He wouldn't have created snoods in the first place.

After donning a blue plaid waist and skirt, Laura pulled on the worn leather boots Mama called "those hideous things." Laura loved them. She'd soaked them and let them dry on her feet—just as she'd heard someone say the soldiers did—and they fit beautifully. What's more, the thick soles gave her feet purchase on the wheelhouse ladder. "Which would you rather, Mama, that I control my skirts or wear dressy boots? I can't do both."

Stepping outside her cabin, she took in a breath of fresh air and smiled up at the sky. And then...she remembered. Disappointment and a feeling of helplessness washed over her at the fresh realization that leaving St. Louis meant kowtowing to the new second pilot. Mama's words came back: *Nothing makes a person more miserable than discontent.* Mama was right, of course. When the morning breeze wafted the aroma of cinnamon and baking bread her way, Laura headed for the dining saloon. She would not let Finn MacKnight ruin her enjoyment of Bird Perrin's famous cinnamon rolls, or anything else. So help her.

Laura had finished not one, but two rolls and as many cups of coffee before Joe ducked his head into the dining saloon. "You haven't seen Finn, have you?"

"Why are you asking me? He'll hardly check in with the cub."

"He said he'd be here just before daybreak."

"Can't help you." Laura rose to take her dishes to the galley just as Mama came in.

"I thought we'd be under way by now," she said. "I hope there's nothing wrong."

"Finn's not here yet," Joe explained. "I've told Elijah to hold off bringing up the gangplank." He glanced at Laura. "We can spare a few minutes."

"Half the Missouri riverboats left days ago," Laura said. "And we have to take two trips this spring. One won't be enough."

"Don't you think I know that?" Joe retorted. "I won't leave without at least trying to find him."

"And what will you say to—"

"Lieutenant Swift?" Joe finished, referencing the officer in charge of the troops on board. "I think we can trust Bird's cooking to keep the lieutenant and his men happily occupied long enough for Elijah and me to make a quick search. I'll head for the house, and Elijah can make the rounds—elsewhere."

Elijah and me? Of course. Now he had an excuse to sneak one last kiss from Adele MacKnight, who had seemed strangely self-conscious when Laura entered the wheelhouse late yesterday.

As Elijah and Joe headed over the gangplank, Laura stepped to the edge of the hurricane deck and leaned down to call out, "Start at the Broken Spar. As I recall, that's a favorite haunt." Joe glowered up at her. She marched away, pacing the perimeter of the hurricane deck even as she watched Elijah and Joe head across the levee. As expected, Joe hurried off in the direction of the MacKnights, while Elijah did exactly as Laura had suggested and disappeared inside the Broken Spar.

It wasn't long before Mama found her, rounding the hurricane deck for the third time. "I told him this would happen," Laura said.

Mama smiled gently. "We must hope for the best."

Half an hour later, the two ladies were waiting on the freight deck, at the foot of the steps leading down from the hurricane deck, when Joe and Elijah trotted back up the gangplank.

Neither man had found MacKnight, but now Joe had a new worry. "There was no one at home," he said, shaking his head. "Something's wrong."

"Undoubtedly," Laura agreed. Sympathy for MacKnight's sisters flickered. They'd probably hoped he really had reformed. Now they would bear the brunt of whatever had happened. Again.

"Could you for one minute think something besides the worst about my best friend?"

"We've been waiting for *thirty* minutes, and you know as well as I do that that represents time we cannot spare."

More arguing ensued, with Mama finally intervening.

"Laura's right about one thing, Joseph. We cannot let one man's personal problems dictate today's events." When Joe seemed about to protest, Mama held up her hand. "You wanted to give the man another chance and you have. Whatever the reason for his failure to appear, I have no doubt we will learn it in due time. If Mr. MacKnight really wants to catch up to us, he will find a way. In the meantime, if someone objects to Laura's serving as second pilot at the last minute, we'll just have to find a way to deal with it."

And so it was. Laura and Mama stood side by side in the wheelhouse just behind Joe, watching as he deftly maneuvered the packet into the channel of the mighty Mississippi River. When Joe gave the order for the engineers to reverse gears so the paddle wheel could propel them upriver, Laura gazed back at the row of saloons on the levee and wondered where Finn MacKnight was sleeping it off today. Again, she felt a twinge of regret—on behalf of his poor sisters, out searching for him, even as the *Laura Rose* made her way upriver. Searching... and then facing what she had faced only last week in that infernal hotel. Ah, well. Fiona MacKnight undoubtedly knew all about dyspeptic tea. As for Adele, Laura had no doubt that Joseph would hear from her often as the steamboat wended its way toward Fort Rice. As her namesake churned away from St. Louis, Laura set her face toward the future—and she could not pretend to regret that Finn MacKnight would not be a part of it.

Joe had little to say for most of the first day out, but he did agree that if the weather stayed calm and clear, they should run all night. Other than stopping at two of the woodlots that dotted the banks of the river to take on more fuel, that's what they did. Laura took her turn at the wheel, and by the time Joe had had his lunch and was ready to relieve her, they were over a hundred miles from St. Louis.

"If the rest of the trip goes this well," Laura said as she left to rest, "we just might set a new record."

Joe shrugged and said nothing.

Determined to tease him out of his bad mood, Laura said, "Don't tell me you wouldn't love heading back home with a giant number 20 hung between the smokestacks."

"If we make it to Fort Rice in twenty days," Joe said, "I will personally rally the crew and march to Inspector Davies's office and demand that he give you the pilot's examination."

Laura glanced over at him. He wasn't smiling yet, but he didn't look quite as glum as he had when they left St. Louis. "I'm going to hold you to that."

❄

Four days into the trip upriver Laura felt, rather than heard, something different about the way the *Laura Rose* was moving through the water. They'd made good time thus far, in spite of the fact that recent gray skies and an almost constant drizzle had cast a pall over the crew and passengers. Today, though, when Laura stepped outside to check the sky, a gust of wind snatched the hat off the head of a passenger standing on the deck near the railing. As dark clouds gathered on the horizon, Laura told the passengers they might want to seek shelter, then headed for the wheelhouse—by way of her cabin, where she retrieved a woolen cape as protection from the increasingly chill wind.

She was partway up the ladder to the wheelhouse when a sharp crack sounded, and lightning struck a tree at the top of a nearby bluff. Laura yelped when the tree exploded, showering the deck of the *Laura Rose* with sparks and burning debris. Crew members hurried to stomp out the glowing embers. When another gust of wind grabbed the steamboat and nearly spun her about, Joe bellowed for more power, narrowly averting disaster just as a dark tail dropped out of the underbelly of a shelf of clouds in the distance. Seconds seemed like eons as Joe inched the *Laura Rose* ever closer to the bluffs. The cyclone came on, ripping trees from the earth as it churned its way closer, ever closer.

Standing beside Joe, Laura grasped one of the spokes of the ship's wheel with both hands and hung on as they watched the terrifying, dizzy dance. At last, the cyclone lifted and disappeared back into the sky. A downpour arrived in its wake, sending sheets of rain spilling off the decks until it was as if everyone on board the *Laura Rose* was trapped behind a waterfall.

The cold, heavy rain lasted for days, and by the time the sodden *Laura Rose* pulled up to the levee at St. Joseph, Missouri—mile 479 out of St. Louis—both crew and passengers were weary and out of sorts. Joe had gotten increasingly depressed as the trip went on and, day after day, the clerk had no mail for him.

"Mail gets delayed," Laura said. "It'll all catch up. Eventually. It may even be here at St. Joe."

She'd intended it to be a play on Joe's name, but he didn't get the joke. And still there were no letters from Adele. In the interest of making up for lost time, Joe and Hercules joined the rest of the roustabouts, discharging freight in a steady drizzle. Later, Laura and Mama ordered both men into the dining saloon, where they huddled over cups of hot tea while Laura piloted the steamboat north along the banks of the brand-new state of Nebraska.

Joe's mood continued to darken as time went on and still, no news came of the MacKnights. Laura tried to cheer him up, to no avail. "She really was quite smitten, Joe. Anyone could see that." She nudged his shoulder. "And when all the letters catch up to us, I'll take an extra shift. You can take an entire day alone in your cabin to moon over Miss MacKnight." All that got was a weak smile and a shrug.

Laura began to worry. Was Joe lovesick or...sick? He wasn't eating much. Even Mama seemed concerned. And then an unseen enemy launched an attack. Chills and aches, fever and coughing began to hopscotch their way from cabin to cabin, until half the passengers on board were feeling poorly. When Bird fell ill, Mama helped with the cooking. At Sioux City, she sent Elijah North into town to summon a physician to see Joe, who'd taken to his cabin and was fighting an incessant cough and a fever.

At first all the Sioux City physician did was sit at Joe's bedside, watching him breathe and listening to him cough. Finally, he reached out to palpate the area beneath Joe's jawline.

When Joe jumped, the doctor had Mama pull the drapes back from the windows and hold a lamp high while he peered into Joe's mouth. He laid his palm on Joe's forehead. Finally, he looked over his glasses, first at Laura and then at Mama. As he stood and reached for his bag he said, "I'll tend him at the clinic for a few days. You can pick him up on your way back downriver."

"But," Laura protested, "he's the pilot."

The doctor shrugged. "Wasn't the pilot today, was he? Won't be for some days to come." When Laura began to protest again, the man folded his hands across his ample stomach and said, "That's a full-blown quinsy about to erupt in that young man's throat. I'll try a diaphoretic first, but if that doesn't bring him around—" He looked over at Mama. "I don't think you want to deal with the results of a purgative while you're chugging upriver, do you?"

Joe stirred. He winced with the effort of talking. "Go on to Fort Rice. Pick me up on the way back."

"But—no. I can't, Joe."

"You can."

"It's not a matter of *can*. It's the crew. They won't hear of it."

"Get Tom Meeks in here," Joe croaked. "Elijah North. And Lieutenant Swift." When the three men stepped into his cabin, Joe ordered Mama and Laura and the doctor to leave. Whatever he said in their absence, it was enough.

"Don't you worry about a thing, Miss," Elijah said to Laura as he headed off to speak with the crew. "The old captain taught you, same as he taught your brother. Anyone has any doubt, he'll answer to me. We've all got a reason to see the *Laura Rose* on her way. We'll do it." He winked. "And if any of 'em tries to sneak off, I'll set Logjam after 'em."

Laura winced internally when Lieutenant Swift "graciously" said something about the United States Army trusting that Captain Jacob White's daughter could do the job until a "proper pilot" could be located. Bless Mama, she spoke up to defend her.

"My daughter is all the 'proper pilot' the *Laura Rose* will ever need, Lieutenant Swift." Whatever the lieutenant muttered, Mama disapproved. "Now you listen to me, young man," she scolded, like a teacher reprimanding a student. "I know what my husband taught his children, and Laura learned it as well as her brother. In fact, she has a talent for certain aspects of piloting that Joe has never mastered. Do not doubt, sir, that your men and your cargo are in very capable hands."

With a more convincing statement of confidence, the red-faced lieutenant took his leave.

As soon as he was out of earshot, Mama put her hand on Laura's arm. "I meant what I just said, dear. What I do *not* have a great deal of confidence in is this Dr. Grym." She paused. "I'm going to stay here in Sioux City with Joseph."

"But Mama—"

"We must both be brave now." She squeezed Laura's hand. "It'll be all right, dear. Joe's right. You can do this." She smiled. "There's bound to be a woman pilot one day. Who better than the daughter of Captain Jacob White? Why, I wouldn't be surprised if the crew is so impressed with you they demand Inspector Davies give you the examination the minute you get back to St. Louis. Now come and reassure your brother. Tell him all he needs to worry about is getting well."

And so that's what Laura did. Moments later, when two crew members arrived to help Joe make his way to the doctor's clinic, she helped Mama pack a bag, then walked her to the gangplank. Before heading ashore, Mama set her bag down and reached for Laura's hands, holding them as she prayed.

"Lord God in heaven, protect my girl. Give her knowledge that You are near. Help her to remember every single thing she's been taught, and please reveal the rest as she needs to know it. Take her hands in Yours and pilot the *Laura Rose* through all that is to come. Please bring her back to Joe and me both swiftly and safely. And please, Lord…if there be idiots aboard, keep their mouths shut." With a little laugh, Mama ended her prayer "in Jesus' name." She reached for her bag, then hesitated and said, "Depend on what you know, Laura Rose, and when that's not enough, call on God. He made the very water you're navigating. He can see the snags and the sandbars. He knows the way. Trust Him to take you through."

All Laura could muster was a nod and a whispered "I love you, Mama" as they hugged. Logjam came and sat next to Laura as Mama headed ashore. Whining softly, he thrust his nose into her palm. She stood watching, until Mama was little more than a black dot at the far end of the muddy trail leading away from the river and toward the row of false-fronted buildings along Sioux City's main street.

Turning back around, Laura felt rather than saw all the pairs of eyes watching her. "All right, then!" she hollered, hoping authority sounded in her voice. "The weather's good and the water's high, gentlemen! I intend to make Dillon's woodlot by nightfall, and there'll be a double portion of dessert if we make it."

Bird had often said that one sure way to a man's heart was to fill his stomach with good food. Laura hoped it was true. She lifted her chin and headed for the wheelhouse. Once there, she blinked away tears of regret. She'd wanted to pilot her own steamboat...but not like this. Never like this. For a fleeting moment, she almost wished that Finn MacKnight had shown up.

Chapter 6

With a quick intake of breath, Finn woke. The house was quiet. He opened his eyes. Turned his head just enough to see that the chair beside his bed was unoccupied, a blue and white quilt folded neatly over the chair back. Fiona's Bible lay open on the needlepoint footstool pushed to one side of the chair. *I guess I'm going to live.* Fiona hadn't left his side for— How long had it been? He didn't know. It took everything in him just to lift his head enough to see out the window. *Daylight.* But what day? He'd been hurt on a Friday. Hurrying to pick up a last-minute wagonload for the *Laura Rose*—one Joe didn't know anything about but would be glad to have, since the shipper was willing to pay a premium to get his product north in a hurry. *His product.* Nails. Seventy-pound kegs of nails.

The whole thing happened because of a yellow dog chasing a stray cat. The dog nearly bowled Finn over. For half a second he thought it would be all right. Thought the other guy who'd been helping him load the kegs might save it. But neither of them saved a thing. Finn lost his balance and fell, and a keg broke over his right leg. He didn't remember much after that beyond hearing someone bellowing in pain and then realizing through an odd fog that he was the one making that ungodly sound. He remembered someone shouting for a doctor. And

Fiona, her face grim, pulling his head into her lap and trying to soothe his brow with...a kerchief? Yes. A damp kerchief. Dipped in a bucket of water. Someone had brought water.

He frowned, remembering how everything had seemed to slow down. How he seemed to be captured behind a transparent curtain: present, but unable to communicate. *Communicate.* Had anyone sent word to Joe? Of course. Adele would tell him. She'd probably written a letter every day.

How many days had it been? Time had passed in a blinding flash of pain that seared memory. Somehow he'd shuddered his way through it. Closing his eyes, he concentrated on his toes. He could move his toes. Thank God for toes. *I won't let them take your leg. You have my word.* Thank God for Fiona, too, always a woman of her word.

Grimacing, Finn pushed himself upright in bed. Planting his hands on either side of his torso, he lifted himself and moved back. Only inches, but pain swept through him and a wave of nausea hit. He waited until it passed before trying again. Sweat dripped into his eyes. Maybe he shouldn't have tried to sit up. But he just didn't have it in him to slide that leg toward the foot of the bed so he could lay flat again. Pulling had to be better than pushing, didn't it?

He bent his good leg and placed that foot flat on the mattress. Now that he thought about it, the pain was different today. If he stayed still, he realized that the agony had been replaced by a deep, penetrating ache that was bad enough on its own and yet—bearable. Leaning his head back, Finn closed his eyes and slept.

❄

"I assure you, Miss White, that every possible precaution was taken, every medical advancement utilized. There was, quite simply, nothing I could do."

Laura had refused to sit down when she reached the clinic in St. Joseph. She'd made good time to Fort Rice and back, but she'd had her fill of being the only pilot on board. As far as she was concerned, the sooner Joe was back on duty, the better. She might even apologize to him for her attitude about MacKnight. She smiled to herself. Once Joe was back, they could run at night again. And who knew but that they could set a record to Fort Benton on the June rise? Together.

She was anxious to see him and Mama. She'd missed them and was looking forward to the return trip to St. Louis. Once there, Joe would do what he'd only joked about before: He'd go with her to speak with the licensing inspector and somehow they'd convince the man to give the pilot's examination to a woman. But not to just any woman. To Laura Rose White, the daughter of Captain Jacob White, the sister of Captain Joseph White, and part-owner of a nearly new packet that she had singlehandedly taken upriver from Sioux City to Fort Rice and back—without a single grounding. And wasn't that something?

But then the doctor started speaking, and as his words sank in, so did she—into the chair he'd offered when his assistant first ushered her into his spartan consultation room.

"Say it again," she croaked.

"Say what again?"

"Everything." She brushed a curl out of her face with a trembling hand. "I—I need to hear it again."

The doctor took his place behind his desk. "Captain White grew very ill indeed. You were quite right to allow me to bring him to my clinic."

Clinic. Half a dozen military cots lined up along one wall with sheets nailed to bare rafters and drawn back by bits of twine hooked about bent nails hardly qualified as a clinic, did it? The idea of Joe dying there—she forced herself to listen to the doctor.

"As I had suspected, the captain developed quinsy. The poor lad lingered very near death for two long nights. But then, on the third day, he rallied. Your mother and I were quite relieved. His fever broke around supper time, and by nightfall he was sitting up in a chair. He was even able to take a little tea and toast. He began to talk about plans for the future. He mentioned a young lady, as I recall. A Miss MacKnight." The doctor cleared his throat. "It is a pity the young lady's letters didn't arrive before he ... um ..."

"Letters?"

The doctor nodded. "You'll find them in your mother's bag."

Laura glanced at the worn leather bag sitting on the corner of the doctor's desk.

Clearing his throat, the doctor continued. "Your brother also mentioned a second trip upriver—all the way to Fort Benton—yet this season. Taking advantage of the June rise, he said."

"I don't understand how someone could be doing so well and then— How could things change so suddenly?"

With a sigh, the doctor explained, "The fever returned that night, and everything settled in his lungs." He put one palm to his chest, as if to illustrate his words. "There was nothing to be done at that point, other than to keep him as comfortable as possible. And we did our best." He paused. "Your dear mother was very brave through it all, Miss White. And an excellent nurse. Not once did she complain or indicate that she wasn't feeling well herself. The first suspicion I had that anything might be out of the ordinary was a complaint of unnatural fatigue. She asked me to recommend a boardinghouse where she might rest until the *Laura Rose* returned. I was escorting her there myself when it became clear that she was suffering from something much more serious than fatigue. Of course I brought her back to the clinic immediately. And I stayed with her." He cleared his throat. "She was quite feverish and then—" He broke off. Shook his head. "She did not suffer long, Miss White. She passed away in her sleep."

As tears spilled down her cheeks, Laura reached for the thin, gold wedding band resting next to Papa's pocket watch along with Mama's Bible and a union case.

"I am very careful about protecting my patients' valuables," the doctor said matter-of-factly. "I wanted you to see that everything is here." He paused. "Please feel free to inspect the contents of the case as well. You'll see that all is in order."

Laura just stared at the leather bag. All was in order? He meant well, of course, but...nothing was in order. Laura couldn't imagine that anything would be "in order" in her life ever again. Taking a deep breath, she slipped the wedding band on the small ring finger of her left hand. She opened the union case and looked down at the photograph of Papa in his Federal uniform and, opposite him, a seven-year-old Joseph White holding Laura, dressed in her christening gown.

There was a stir in the doctor's waiting room. A bark. Laura turned about and looked behind her just as the doctor's young assistant opened the door, an apology on his lips. "I am sorry, Dr. Grym, but this man—"

"It's all right, Cardiff." The doctor motioned for Elijah North to come in. Logjam padded along beside him.

"I told him to stay," Elijah said, pointing at the dog. "He wouldn't." Logjam snuffled along the edge of the desk and then, with deep sigh, sat beside Laura. "Thought you might need... When you didn't come back right off..." Elijah's voice trailed away.

Laura slid to the edge of the chair. Twisting Mama's ring about her own finger as she spoke she said, "We've several bales of furs to deliver to St. Louis."

"Ma'am?" With a frown, the doctor looked past her to Elijah North.

Laura rose from the chair. When the doctor leaped to his feet, she said, "We'll pay what we owe you when we collect on the freight bill in St. Louis." She looked down, concentrating on putting Mama's Bible and the union case back into her satchel as she said, "You and the un—undertaker." Swiping at the tears spilling down her cheeks, she looked over at Elijah. He looked grim but seemed to understand without her having to say the words. She didn't know if she could have just yet. "Please ask Tom Meeks to write out cards for them, noting what we owe. Those cards we leave for the wood hawks when we stop at wood yards should be sufficient." She glanced back at the doctor. "Will that be all right?"

He nodded. "Of course."

Laura slipped the watch into the pocket of her skirt. She closed Mama's bag. Taking a deep breath, she said, "I will want to bring my mother and brother h-home. If you would tell the undertaker that I'll be in touch about making those arrangements later in the year."

"Of course, Miss White. Whatever you want." Again, the doctor looked over at Elijah. "I'll have the contact information ready for your clerk."

As Laura took the bag in hand and turned to go, Logjam pressed against her, almost as if offering mute sympathy. Tempted to kneel down and fling her arms around the dog's neck and sob, Laura reached into her pocket and curled her fingers about Papa's watch, concentrating on the cool sensation of the golden disk against her moist palm.

Elijah put his hat back on his gray head and offered his arm, but Laura didn't take it. If she took hold of him now, she wouldn't want to let go, and it would not do for the crew of the *Laura Rose* to see her clinging to grizzled Elijah North's arm like some weakling. She had to appear strong, whether she felt that way or not. Clutching the small bag to her breast, she walked alongside him, her head bowed, her mind whirling. They were in sight of the steamboat when Laura looked over at Elijah and said quietly, "Will they leave?"

"Ma'am?"

"The crew. They expected things to be different once we got back to Sioux City. They tolerated me at the wheel—but it wasn't supposed to go on. Do you think they'll leave? We—I—I have to get those furs to St. Louis." She had to do a lot more than that, but it would all be moot if the crew abandoned the *Laura Rose* now.

Elijah took a moment to answer. "There might be one or two coldhearted enough to consider it, but even they aren't going to want abandoning a lady on their conscience—especially when doing that would mean forfeiting the bonus they were promised when they signed on in St. Louis. If they mean to collect, they don't have much choice but to stay." His voice gentled. "Besides that, miss, you've proven your mettle. You're a fine pilot, and every man on board the *Laura Rose* knows it, whether they'll admit it or not."

Whether they'll admit it or not. That was just the thing, wasn't it? They probably wouldn't admit it, and without the support of some seasoned rivermen, she was going to be hard-pressed to keep her livelihood.

As she and Elijah approached the levee, Laura stopped and looked down at the *Laura Rose*. Grief and weariness washed over her. Returning to Sioux City was supposed to mean the end of her solo struggle to best the river. The end of being alone up in the wheelhouse.

Chapter 7

The crew had obviously heard the news by the time they saw Laura walking back beside Elijah North. Like a musician responding to a conductor's raised baton, each man paused for a fleet second. Then, with a glance around, they set down whatever was in their hands and removed their hats, standing with heads bowed as Laura walked by.

At the top of the gangplank, Laura turned to Elijah. "I just need—a moment. Ask them to assemble up by the capstan engine in an hour, would you?"

Elijah nodded, and Laura quietly made her way up the stairs to the texas deck and her cabin. Logjam followed her, but then he paused at the door. "Good dog," Laura said. He knew the rules. No animals in the cabins. Then again, he was waiting, every fiber of him obviously hoping to be invited in. Laura hesitated, staring in, remembering her and Joe's delight when they first saw their brand-new cabins, large enough to accommodate washstands and dressers. Neither of them would ever have to share the public washrooms down on the hurricane deck. As if that mattered. Stifling a sob, Laura spoke to the dog. "I'm changing the rule," she said, gesturing for him to step across the threshold.

Logjam curled up on the blue and gray rag rug, his snout

resting atop his front paws. He watched as Laura set Mama's bag atop the little trunk beneath the cabin window and, opening it, took out Mama's Bible and the union case and set them alongside the bag. Next, she reached for the small stack of envelopes, each one addressed to *Captain Joseph White, Laura Rose, St. Louis packet bound for Fort Rice, Dakota Territory*. Poor Joe. Thinking Adele hadn't written.

When she set down the stack of mail, she noticed something jutting out from Mama's Bible. Another letter...this one opened. She turned it over, envisioning Mama reading it to Joe to cheer him up. *But there'd been time for only one. After that—*

Taking a deep breath, Laura untucked the flap. When she removed the single sheet of paper, something dropped into her lap. A pressed rosebud. Adele had written a line from a poem over and over again, around the edges of the notepaper. The words "Oh, my love is like a red, red rose" framed the text.

> Dearest Joseph,
> The sun is shining today, but my world is gray because you are not part of it.
> Finn is on the mend, although Fiona and I fear that the effects of his accident will linger. But he is brave and strong, and we will not give up.

Finn was "on the mend"? What did that mean? What accident? Joe's words sounded in her memory. *Something's wrong.* Joe had been so certain of MacKnight. So eager to have him aboard. With a frown, Laura continued reading.

> I have made ginger cakes for Fiona's Ladies' Aid and taken them to the church for her, for she cannot—or will not—leave Finn's side.

Closing her eyes, Laura pressed her fingers against the place just below her left brow that had begun to throb. In a wavering voice, she muttered aloud, "You were right, Joe. I—I'm sorry. You were right about him that morning."

Taking a deep breath, she returned to Adele's letter.

> I plucked this tiny rosebud from the bush in the churchyard. You undoubtedly remember what happened near that rosebush. I actually took two buds. One is inside the locket you gave me. And here is the other.
>
> If the river is kind, it will bring you back to me within the next 21 days. I pray the river—and God—are kind, dear one. I have kissed the place where I sign my name. I long to kiss your lips (and more) again.

Laura's cheeks were flaming by the time she finished the note. What must Mama have thought—if she had indeed read this aloud to Joe? Was this the way lovers spoke to one another? What could Adele have been thinking, to put such thoughts to paper and then chance the letter being waylaid and read by other eyes?

Laura sighed. She would have to call on the MacKnights when she got back to St. Louis. Adele should have the letters back. But oh, how she dreaded that meeting. A new burden descended. She skimmed the love letter again. Finn MacKnight was "on the mend," but there was some cause for worry. Adele wasn't the only person she would have to face.

Setting the letter on the tiny bedside table, Laura lay down, staring up at the rough board ceiling overhead. She would have time to think about all of that later. Right now, she had to decide what to say to the crew.

It hurt too much to think about Joe and Mama. She would focus on practical matters—at least for now. Because if she thought about Joe and Mama any more right now, she would want to sink beneath the covers and never get out of bed again—and that would not do. Mama hadn't done that when Papa died. Mama would want her to carry on.

Laura began to tally the accounts receivable in her mind. The government owed the owner of the *Laura Rose* for hauling two hundred tons of freight to Fort Rice—not to mention passage for the men. Two hundred tons at nine cents a pound. Around $36,000. Add to that the money from other freight along with passenger fares—less the grocery bill and the money owed various woodlots—it was next to impossible to know exactly where she stood.

For a moment, panic threatened. Papa had taken out a loan to have the *Laura Rose* built. He'd paid off half of it, but that left at least ten thousand dollars still owed. They hadn't paid the foundry for the new boiler yet, and other bills would no doubt surface, along with those from the physician and the undertaker in Sioux City. Thousands and thousands of dollars passed through the hands of dozens of people on any given river run— dozens of *men*, not one of them with any expectation of doing business with a woman. Not one of them open to the idea of ever doing business with a woman—apart, that is, from the occasional shopgirl in towns along the way. Or, perhaps, the wife of the owner of a general mercantile. Laura pressed a palm to her forehead, trying to ease the pounding headache. She was saved from dissolving in tears only by the sound of a pathetic whine. Logjam had risen and now sat next to the door, his dark eyes pleading.

Rising and crossing the cabin to let him out, Laura took a look at herself in the mirror above her washstand. She looked more like a disheveled harpy than someone a roustabout and an engineer might actually take seriously—even if given financial incentive to do so.

Quickly, she took her hair down, brushed through it, and pulled it up into a tight bun fastened at the top of her head.

She couldn't do much about the blotchy complexion. The sun wreaked havoc on her fair skin, and her emotions always showed in half blushes, pink cheeks, a red nose, or a combination of all. It was hideous, but there was little she could do about it. The same could be said about her hair. After a few hours at the wheel, she always looked bedraggled.

"I can't even control my own hair," she muttered. "What makes me think I have any business in the steamboat business?"

Reaching for the union case, she opened it, staring down at a young Captain Jacob White in his Union Army uniform. Papa had kept steamboating all through the war, even though it had been much more dangerous to shuttle supplies through waters that ran along the shores of Confederate states. It was the one time he'd insisted that Mama and Laura remain behind, and the one time Mama had accepted being separated from her husband. They'd rented a little house in Omaha, Nebraska, because Papa said it was far enough from the action that he wouldn't worry about his girls.

She and Mama had worried so about him and Joe. Mama had tried to keep Laura occupied with schoolwork, but they'd both lost sleep. Finally, though, they'd gotten their men home, safe and miraculously unharmed. Laura put her fingertips to the glass.

A poem that Mama had made her memorize for school came to mind.

I have no wit, no words, no tears;
My heart within me like a stone
Is numb'd too much for hopes or fears;
Look right, look left, I dwell alone;
I lift mine eyes, but dimm'd with grief
No everlasting hills I see;

My life is in the falling leaf:
O Jesus, quicken me.

Taking a deep breath, Laura looked in the mirror one last time before heading off to speak to the crew.

※

Finn winced as he lifted his right knee to try and place his foot flat on the bed. It didn't seem like it should be a difficult thing to do, but he might as well be trying to lift a log for all the progress he made. He looked over at the calendar hanging beside the bedroom door and counted the days. Twenty-nine of them. Twenty-nine days in this bed. No wonder he was as weak as a kitten. At this rate, he'd miss any chance to find work down on the levee. He looked around him. The idea of being cooped up in this house for weeks on end.

He squinted at the words printed across the bottom of the calendar. "Rejoice and be glad," it read. He grunted. He'd rejoice and be glad, all right. Just as soon as he had the strength to quit this bed and find work.

He looked across the room at the crutches standing in the corner. Out of reach unless he wanted to drag himself over there. He was only supposed to use them when there was someone to stand behind him—something about his balance being affected by all the time he'd been in bed. But Fiona's chair was within reach. He could use that for balance.

Leaning as far as he could, Finn managed to get a grip on the edge of the chair and pull it closer by a couple of inches. It took three tries and a chorus of grunts, but he finally managed to get the chair close enough. If he could stand up, he could begin to encourage his right foot to assume its proper place in line with the upper leg, instead of its turning in like that.

He had no intention of hobbling around as if he'd been born with a clubfoot for the rest of his life. Just the thought sparked a burning sensation in his gut that felt dangerously close to panic. Or fear. What if he didn't regain the use of that leg? What if he never worked on the river again? Trembling, he spun about and lowered his legs so that both feet were flat on the floor. Well, almost flat. As close to flat as he could manage for now. His leg throbbed; his heart raced.

Moving the chair so he could grasp the back with both hands, Finn took a deep breath, leaned forward, tensed his thighs, and powered himself upright. He looked down at his bad leg. Managed to lift it just enough to maneuver the foot and replant it. Try as he would, he couldn't get the foot flat on the floor. He'd practice. It would get better. It had to.

With his weight balanced on his left leg, Finn lifted the chair and walked it forward on its front legs. Just a few inches, but far enough that he could take a small step. Just a baby step, while he held on to the chair for extra support.

Fiona appeared at the door. "Where on earth do you think you're going?"

"Just practicing," he said and did his best to give her one of the cockeyed smiles that usually distracted her long enough for him to steal the cookie or the piece of candy or—to take another step. This time, though, Finn was the one who was distracted. The foot didn't cooperate, the leg above it wobbled, and he was too weak to save it. He ended up on the floor.

Fiona's reaction made him almost wish he'd hit his head and blacked out. "Finn Graham MacKnight! I declare! What do you think you're doing? Behaving like some naughty child, that's what. You heard what the doctor said. I turn my back for one minute, and here you are—"

"Stop squawking," Finn groused. "I'm fine."

She wouldn't listen. She kept at him, wondering how to get him off the floor, wondering if he'd reinjured something, wondering what the doctor would say, clucking like a mother hen.

"Hush, Fiona. Just—hush and leave me be. I'm fine. The last thing I need is you running around like a chicken with her head cut off. I fell. I'll probably fall a lot in coming days. Now get out of here and leave me be."

His frustration mounting, Finn grabbed the leg of the blankety-blank chair. At full strength, he likely would have launched the thing through a window. All he could manage now was to tip it over. When it hit the floor, Fiona jumped back. Finn looked over at her. She was standing with her back to the open door, her face white, her chin trembling, her eyes blinking in a vain effort to keep from crying.

"Don't cry," he muttered as he hoisted himself back to a sitting position, his back against the side of his bed. Fiona let out a strangled sob. He swore at her to stop, and then he couldn't seem to hush himself. Fiona took another step back and had just turned to flee when Adele appeared in the doorway, her green eyes blazing.

"Just listen to yourself. Swearing at the woman who's been by your side for weeks. How dare you speak to Fiona that way!"

"It's all right, Adele," Fiona murmured. "He doesn't mean it."

"It is *not* all right," Adele snapped. She glared at Finn. "If you want to yell at someone, yell at me. Lord knows I've been little or no use as a nurse this past month. But *Fiona*—Finn. She's worn out that sad little rug by her bed. On her knees. For *you.* She's given over all her Ladies' Aid activities. For *you.* She's skipped meals and missed sleep. For *you.*" Adele took a breath. "Don't you *dare* tell her to leave you alone. If she'd left you alone, you'd probably be drunk in some ditch somewhere. If she'd left you alone, you wouldn't still have that leg!"

The air in the room crackled with emotion. A fly buzzed in, made a wide, looping circuit, and flew out again. Finn took a deep breath. "Adele's right," he groused. He took a deep breath. "I've no call to speak to you that way, Fiona."

Fiona's voice wavered. "Y-you've had a difficult time. Don't be hard on yourself."

Adele looked at Fiona, frowning. "And you haven't had a difficult time? Lord have mercy, Fiona." She shook her head. "Sometimes I do not think you are real."

✸

Thanks to the promised bonus, the crew stayed on. Tom Meeks pored over the books and reassured Laura as to the situation with the accounts. All would be well, he said, barring "unforeseen challenges" and assuming, of course, a second trip upriver before summer. As the *Laura Rose* descended the river, her lone, unlicensed pilot clung to routines and duties. Thankfully, the river was kind.

When it came to giving orders, Laura played that carefully, relaying instructions through Tom and Elijah. She eschewed the usual duties of presiding over meals—she was, after all, in mourning—and in that way was able to keep the *Laura Rose* moving every day until the last sliver of daylight had surrendered to the night.

For two weeks, Laura stayed in the wheelhouse until she was so tired she could barely stand. Once the packet was tied up for the night, she returned to her cabin and lay down on her side, staring at the photo of Papa until she fell asleep. The poem she'd memorized years ago kept coming to mind, and on nights when she couldn't sleep, she found herself whispering it into the dark. She hadn't thought much about its meaning back then. Now she wondered what had happened to the poetess to inspire such devastating words.

> *My life is like a faded leaf,*
> *My harvest dwindled to a husk:*
> *Truly my life is void and brief*
> *And tedious in the barren dusk;*
> *My life is like a frozen thing,*
> *No bud nor greenness can I see . . .*
>
> *My life is like a broken bowl,*
> *A broken bowl that cannot hold*
> *One drop of water for my soul*
> *Or cordial in the searching cold.*

Mama would not be pleased to know that Laura skipped over the three or four lines that appealed to Jesus for help. She didn't know why, but those words made her feel guilty. After all, why would Jesus have any interest in answering someone who so seldom thought of Him?

In the end, she told herself that she had no time to contemplate religion. She needed every ounce of energy just to survive each day, wondering whether or not those ripples on the surface of the water meant a snag waiting to destroy the *Laura Rose*, if those clouds would bring a storm with high winds, if she could trust this channel to take her past that sandbar. All she had energy for was keeping the *Laura Rose* safe. It was, after all, the only thing she had left. The only thing.

On the day the *Laura Rose* finally reached the mouth of the Missouri River and churned its way into the deeper waters of the Mississippi just north of St. Louis, Elijah told Laura that between the good cooking and the good pay, he believed word of mouth on the levee would bring her all the crew she needed to keep the *Laura Rose* busy on the river.

"She's a fine packet, Miss White," he said. "Many's the captain who will be proud to take her out. As for pilots, I think you'll have your pick."

Of course Elijah meant well, but the underlying assumption was clear. Laura would be looking to hire a captain and two pilots. What Elijah felt her role would be, who could say? Without the excuse of an avoidable emergency, it would be scandalous for a lone woman to travel aboard a steamboat in the company of hired men, and while such scandal might not particularly bother Laura, it might eventually affect potential passengers. She could not let gossip and rumor ruin the *Laura Rose*'s reputation. That would besmirch Papa's legacy, and Laura would have no part in that.

Still, during the lonely nights as she lay alone in her bed, she allowed herself to resurrect the fairy tale in which she was not only the admired captain but also the first pilot of the *Laura Rose*. As Mama had said, there would be a female pilot one day. "Who better than the daughter of Captain Jacob White?"

Who better, indeed? Dare she think it possible? What would it take to convince the inspector to give her the examination?

Finally, on the morning of April 23, two weeks after heading downriver from Sioux City, Laura peered through Papa's spyglass and caught sight of the steeple of the old cathedral near the St. Louis riverfront and the forest of steamboat smokestacks ringing the curve of the levee. Strengthening her grip on the wheel, she called out orders, keeping her eyes on the river and her mind on the task at hand. Not until the *Laura Rose* had slipped into a gap between two other packets did the familiar sights of St. Louis penetrate the armor of duty that had kept her going.

As the gangplank lowered and the crew began to unload freight, Laura thought ahead. She would collect on the freight bills owing. Pay the crew. Dole out the bonuses. And then...what? The future yawned before her like the mouth of an unexplored cave. Again, she wondered about facing the inspector in regards to the pilot's examination.

Elijah North appeared at the top of the wheelhouse ladder. "Sweetest landing anybody could have expected," he said. "You've done the White name proud, miss."

Elijah's kindness did what nothing else had in recent days: It broke through her defenses. Backing away from the wheel, Laura plopped onto the simple, unpadded bench below the back wall of windows. When Logjam came to her and rested his chin on her knee, then looked up at her with mournful eyes, that burst the dam. Sliding to the floor beside the dog, Laura threw her arms about his neck and sobbed.

Elijah came near and bent to pat her shoulder. Then he handed her a clean kerchief, sat down on the bench, and waited while she cried. Finally, when her tears were spent, he directed her to look up through the windows and into the sky. "Way I figure it, that break in the clouds right there— that little patch of blue? That's the window the Almighty's opened so your folks can see the *Laura Rose*—see what you've done. How proud they are, miss. How very proud."

He stood to go, pausing at the top of the ladder just long enough to say, "The boys'll handle the cargo and the details for now. You get yourself a good, long sleep. I'll tell 'em to check back tomorrow late in the day. Give you time to get the accounts squared away. Sound all right?"

Laura nodded. *Sleep.* It would be good to sleep without that sixth sense holding her accountable to any odd movement, any rise in the wind, any little thing that might endanger her steamboat. *My steamboat.* For all the dreams she'd dreamed, she'd never wanted it to happen this way. To take over because someone got hurt—or died. To own the *Laura Rose* because she was the only one left. *The only one.*

Bitter tears flowed as Laura hurried down the ladder and to her cabin. Once there, she didn't even bother to undress but sank down on the bed and into the oblivion of exhaustion.

Chapter 8

"*No.*" Finn shook his head in denial, even as he failed to make his foot obey. A little thing like flexing his foot and making his toes point to the ceiling had left him soaked in sweat—and a failure. Again. Silence reigned in the room for more than a moment. Neither the doctor who'd just removed the splint designed to keep Finn's lower leg and foot at right angles nor Fiona said a word.

Finally, the doctor cleared his throat. "I—um—I believe the bone is healed. I'll leave the splint off, if you'll promise you won't do anything foolish."

"Define 'foolish,'" Finn grumbled.

"Well...abandoning the crutches, for example."

"I *am* going to walk again," Finn said.

"Well, of course you are," the doctor said. He reached down to flex the foot. "You can walk now, Mr. MacKnight. You just need a little help."

Finn grunted. "You said the bone was mended. You said it was miraculous that I didn't lose much muscle." Again, he tried to flex his foot and lift his toes. Again, he failed.

"Mended bone will eventually hold you up, but you need ligaments and tendons attached to those bones to have much flexibility. You can see from the shape of things—literally—that some of the tissue has healed in a less-than-ideal fashion." The doctor paused. "On the other hand, it has healed, and that is a very good word. Which takes me back to my initial warning. The ankle remains a concern. It's a complex structure, comprised of no fewer than seven bones. To be quite frank, I honestly don't know how much range of motion you will regain."

Finn frowned. "Are you telling me I'm to be a cripple for the rest of my life?"

"I am telling you that I don't know how much range of motion you will regain. And that if you stress either the injured limb or that joint prematurely, the results could be catastrophic."

Catastrophic. How ironic. To have survived the war and come home whole, only to lose the use of a leg now. Just now when he was regaining...everything. Everything important. Just when he'd determined to be a better man. Clenching his jaw, Finn looked away.

The doctor took up the splints. As he leaned them against the wall beside the crutches, he said, "You demanded that I save your leg. With the help of your devoted sisters, I have done so. I am no prophet. One year hence, should you and I encounter one another here in St. Louis or on board one of those floating barges you call a mountain boat, you may be ambulating on your own. You may have a cane at your side. You may still be on crutches. But you will have two legs." The doctor held up two fingers. "Given the nature of the injury, that is its own miracle."

Finn looked down at his crooked leg. *Some miracle.* Who in his right mind would hire a man with only one good leg to work on a mountain boat? Perhaps when Joe got back—no. He wasn't going to be taken on as some charity case.

The doctor gathered his things and left. Fiona followed him out, leaving Finn to stare down at his crooked leg. Again, he grunted. Reaching for the crutches, he made his way into the kitchen and then toward the back door. He made his escape while Fiona spoke with the doctor in hushed tones.

Market basket slung over her arm, Adele took notice of the daffodils and snowdrops blooming in the yards along either side of the street. Adele hadn't paid much attention to such things until lately. Being in love had made her more sensitive, she supposed. How sad that poor Fiona had only her garden and her ungrateful brother to love; that she'd never known romance.

How wonderful to be in love with a handsome steamboat captain who would, any day now, take her away. As she made her way up the block toward the little corner market, Adele began to hum. She hadn't heard from Joseph yet, but she would. He loved her. She knew he did. That last kiss and... the rest... were proof.

Joseph would do the right thing by her. Everything was going to be just fine. In fact, it was going to be better than "fine." He'd asked her to write and to wait. He'd also shown her how busy his life could be. She would neither scold nor worry. As she walked along, she reached up to touch the locket that held a single tiny rosebud. And she smiled.

She could not wait to stand on the deck of that brand-new steamboat and wave good-bye to Finn and Fiona. To have everyone know when they looked up and saw her on the texas deck that she was the wife of Captain Joseph White and, therefore, the mistress of the *Laura Rose*, the one who sat at the head of the table in the dining saloon, the woman the passengers toasted.

Yes, indeed. It was going to be a wonderful life.

Rounding a corner, Adele passed Miss Rogers's Emporium, lingering at the sight of a particularly exquisite length of white lace. How long, Adele wondered, would it take a dressmaker to make a wedding gown? She hadn't dared ask a soul, lest a rumor get started.

Thoughts of a wedding gown led her to thoughts of money. How long would it take the lawyer who meted out the MacKnights' monthly allowance to write the check representing Adele's third of her father's money? More important, how much would it be? Adele had no idea just how much Papa had been worth. That wasn't exactly the kind of question a girl could ask outright.

The house Fiona had selected for them to live in after Papa died was modest to the point of being dismal—at least to Adele's way of thinking. It wasn't even brick, for goodness' sake, let alone two stories. Fiona said it was "perfectly adequate." Now that Adele thought about it, that phrase was the essence of the difference between them. It was the reason Fiona gave nearly every time Adele wanted something. "Perfectly adequate" might be all that Fiona expected out of life, but Adele wanted more.

Finn wanted more out of life, too. At least he had before the accident. Even Fiona had said so. "You wait and see," she'd said not long after Joseph talked Finn into taking the job aboard the *Laura Rose*, "this is only the beginning for Finn." She'd looked at Adele with a broad smile. "It won't be long and he'll be Captain MacKnight again."

One thing about Fiona, when it came to Finn, she was persistence personified. Even the melancholy plaguing him in recent days hadn't made her give up hope. If Adele had been of a mind to be the jealous type, Fiona's obvious preference for her brother would have given her reason. Happily, she wasn't. She was, in fact, fond of Finn in her own way. He didn't make her sit through Bible readings and prayer times, he never preached at her, and he never pointed out potential suitors the way Fiona did—as if Adele were a commodity to be moved to its next destination—as Mrs. Martin Lawrence, for goodness' sake.

Finn understood about Martin—and about her loving

Joseph, too. Lately, he'd been almost brotherly. Fiona, on the other hand, seemed to feel it her duty to keep watch over Adele and Joseph. As if Joseph couldn't be trusted. Why must Fiona always be suspicious of every little thing?

Adele paused in front of another shop window. Oh, Miss Hart had an entirely new display of bonnets, and wasn't that emerald green one just divine? She looked about her. How refreshing it was to be alone for a change. Fiona would have nagged if they'd been together and Adele so much as took note of something lovely in a shop window. *It's simply not acceptable to buy things on credit against your next month's allowance, Adele. Papa provided more than enough for your needs—and your wants, if only you'd be more reasonable about the latter.*

Reasonable. It seemed that lately, Fiona had a new speech for every occasion, each one justified by the fact that in "only" three years, if she didn't marry, Adele would be in charge of her own affairs. It was Fiona's duty to prepare her. *Duty.* How Adele despised that word. And all the words on Fiona's list titled "What a young woman should be." Things Adele was not and never would be. Things Joseph didn't care about one whit.

She studied the hat in Miss Hart's window. Those iridescent green feathers would bring out her eyes. She could just imagine the effect it would have on Joseph if she wore that hat—and a matching ensemble—to welcome him home. No matter what Fiona thought, a girl didn't go to hell for overspending now and then. And what was one more transgression, anyway? It would be worth a flap with Fiona to see the look in Joseph's eyes. *It's my money and I'll do what I please with it.* With a glance toward home, she stepped into the shop.

Setting her new hatbox on a countertop just inside the mercantile door, Adele handed Fiona's list to the storekeeper and waited while he filled the order. She'd just asked to see a pair of white lace gloves—perfect for a spring wedding—when Fiona's friend, Jessamine Powell, came into the store. Adele laid down the gloves. The last thing she needed was to have Mrs. Powell mention her admiring white lace gloves to Fiona. The green bonnet battle would be enough for one day.

Mrs. Powell's more-than-adequate black eyebrows drew together the moment she saw Adele. "Oh, my dear," she gushed, "isn't it just the worst news? I couldn't believe it. That poor family. Struck down that way. How is your brother holding up?"

"Finn? He's... The doctor says that only time will tell. For now, he's using crutches. He'll mend. He has plenty of energy for being difficult, I can tell you that." Adele sighed. "Of course Fiona says that's a good sign. She doesn't seem to mind his foul moods. You know how it is. Finn can do no wrong in Fiona's eyes."

"Oh—you thought I was asking about your brother's injury." Mrs. Powell gave Adele's arm a friendly squeeze. "Of course your handsome brother has been in our prayers, but—no, dear. I was wondering how—oh—it's just terrible. I suppose your brother will be glad he wasn't on board that packet after all. Although I don't know that it was contagious. That poor girl, though, left all alone in the world." Mrs. Powell shook her head. "Lila Lawrence heard that she intends to have the bodies brought back and reinterred alongside Captain White. I suppose there will be a proper service then." She paused. "The Ladies' Aid must offer a funeral luncheon." The eyebrows wiggled and waggled as Mrs. Powell droned on. Finally, she seemed to notice that Adele hadn't spoken.

"Oh, no." She put a gloved hand on Adele's arm. "You haven't heard. I can see that now." She lowered her voice. "Captain White and his mother were both taken ill between here and Sioux City. Miss White went on with the cargo while her mother helped the doctor tend the young captain at his infirmary. Her brother insisted, they said. But—they've *died*, Miss MacKnight. The both of them. Within a few days of one another. And that poor girl left all alone.

"Did you know that she could pilot a steamboat? It's the talk of the levee the way she brought the *Laura Rose* back, all by herself— But goodness, what's to happen now? She can't exactly live alone on board, now, can she? Even if she could hire help—without a chaperone? What a scandal that would be..."

The voice kept yammering, but Adele didn't hear the words. Pulling away from Mrs. Powell, she staggered over to the counter and reached out with one hand to try to support herself. The hatbox went flying. A flash of green netting and feathers, and the world went black.

✹

Laura had just fallen asleep when someone knocked on her cabin door. She felt groggy and disoriented for a moment, but then she remembered. She was supposed to talk to the crew. No, wait. That was tomorrow. Elijah had told them to be back tomorrow around four in the afternoon. She reached for Papa's pocket watch. She'd been asleep for less than an hour. With a groan, she called out, "Yes? What is it?"

"Miss? It's Elijah. Need to talk to you."

Laura rolled out of bed and crossed the room, opening the door just enough to see the troubled look on Elijah North's face.

"I made him wait down on the freight deck, ma'am, but there's a Mr. Danvers here. Says he needs to talk to you right away." He lowered his voice. "I did my best to get him to come back Monday morning, but he says it can't wait."

Laura closed her eyes for a moment. "Do Bird and Hercules happen to still be on board?"

"Yes'm. You know Bird. She never wants to leave that galley until it looks like there was never a meal cooked in there."

Dear Bird. She said it made her feel good to come back to a galley that looked brand-new. "Tell her I'm sorry to interrupt the cleaning, but ask her if she'd mind brewing a pot of strong coffee and serving Mr.—What did you say his name was?"

"Danvers, ma'am. Wilson Danvers, Esquire. And he put the emphasis on the *Esquire.*"

An attorney. Laura opened the door a little more. "Would you take Mr. Danvers into the saloon? Tell him I'll be there shortly. And, Elijah—"

"Yes, Miss White?"

"Where's Logjam?"

Elijah smiled. "Keeping an eye on 'Esquire,' I expect."

Thanking Elijah, Laura poured tepid water into the bowl on her washstand and rinsed her face, then smoothed back her hair. Perhaps she should change, but she just didn't have it in her to face that trunk with its crinolines and silk dresses. *Mourning. I should be dressed in mourning.* She didn't think she could feel any worse, but the prospect of black veils and black gloves and black petticoats and black waists and black...everything...settled a new weight of grief about her shoulders. Smoothing the rumpled dress she'd just slept in, she headed off to meet Mr. Danvers—Esquire.

Logjam lay across the doorway opening into the saloon. When he saw her, he rose and followed her to where an elegant-looking man dressed in a fawn-colored frock coat and dark brown slacks was sitting, his legs crossed, his top hat on the table before him.

The moment Laura entered the saloon, he got to his feet, introducing himself with a little bow. "Allow me to express my heartfelt condolences for your grievous loss."

Laura nodded, then turned to Bird who'd just brought in a coffee tray. "If you'll trust me to clean this up, you and Hercules are free to go. You heard that I wanted to speak with the crew tomorrow?"

"Yes'm," Bird said. "Four o'clock. We'll be back."

Danvers looked after Bird, then turned back to Laura. "You have loyal people."

"I beg your pardon?"

He glanced over at Logjam. "And a downright intimidating dog."

Laura took a sip of coffee. "You'll excuse me if I don't take time for casual conversation. I don't mean to be rude, but—"

"Business. Yes. That's why I'm here." Danvers took a deep breath. "I represent a group—the details aren't really all that important—suffice it to say that these men thought very highly of your father, and they wish to see you relieved of any undue burden caused by a most untimely tragedy. I've been empowered to offer you eighteen thousand dollars for the *Laura Rose*. Payment to be made in cash upon transfer of the title. We realize, of course, that there will be a delay—estate matters and all of that. You will wish to seek counsel." He sat back. Smiling. "We are prepared to be patient."

Laura frowned. "I don't know what you've heard, Mr. Danvers, but the *Laura Rose* is not for sale."

"You can't have sold to someone else. We hold first rights."

"First rights to what? I can assure you, and anyone else interested, that our accounts payable will be current within the next few days."

Surprise sounded in the man's voice as he leaned back. "You don't know."

"Don't know what?"

"Well, ma'am, that you don't actually own the *Laura Rose*."

"Of course I know," Laura said. "There's still a note due for about half the construction cost. And according to my preliminary calculations, it will be paid—probably by the end of business on Monday."

Danvers looked away for a moment, thinking. Then he reached for his hat. "I do apologize. I—we—thought you

would have a more current understanding of your situation."
He reached into his coat pocket and withdrew an envelope.
"The offer remains on the table. Once you've spoken with
Captain White's attorney in regards to his estate—and then,
of course, with the bank, I'll call again. Or"—he pointed to
the address on the envelope—"you are welcome to call on me
at any time. I am at your service. And now, if you'll excuse
me—I do apologize for bothering you prematurely. We really
did not know that you wouldn't be aware of the situation."

Situation. He'd used the term twice. Her headache was
back. "Please. Mr. Danvers. Of what 'situation' are you
speaking?"

Danvers shrugged. "It isn't my place to say. I'm sure your
counsel—it's Mr. Hughes, isn't it?—I'm sure Mr. Hughes
will explain everything." He looked about him. "I thought he
would have hurried aboard as soon as word came of the *Laura
Rose*'s return."

Why would Mr. Hughes hurry? What was going on? She
took a deep breath. "Whatever you may have heard, Mr. Danvers, I have no intention of selling my father's pride and joy."
She paused. "And even if I were, I'm fully aware of the value
of a nearly new packet. The *Laura Rose* is worth significantly
more than eighteen thousand dollars, and to be quite frank,
I don't appreciate your apparent assumption that I wouldn't
know that."

"Under the circumstances," Danvers said, "we believe it's a
generous offer."

"And I repeat, what circumstances? And who is 'we'?"

He flicked an imaginary bit of lint off the brim of his hat.
"Now that I realize Mr. Hughes hasn't spoken with you, it
would be indelicate of me to speak of it." He donned the hat.
"Forgive me for my unfortunate timing. I'll tell the others
that you were unaware of the state of things and that you
need time to speak with Mr. Hughes."

Well. If the man was going to speak in circles, he might as well go. Laura rose and held out the envelope.

"You'll want to keep that," Danvers said. "I do understand your being upset with the way the matter came to light," he said. "But trust me, Miss White. You won't get another offer as good."

If he thought he'd brought something to light, he was a fool. All he'd done was confuse her. "Since I'm not entertaining offers, I don't imagine that will keep me awake tonight." Laura motioned for him to precede her out of the saloon and showed him to the stairs.

Elijah North was sitting on the bottom step, whittling. When Danvers descended, Elijah tipped his hat, then stood. Closing up his whittling knife, he tucked it in his pocket, watching until Danvers was off the packet.

Laura went down to speak with him. "Do you know anything about some mountain of debt against the *Laura Rose?*"

Elijah looked at her, clearly surprised. "The old captain kept his personal finances very private. As did the young captain."

Laura looked toward the city. "That man—and whoever he represents—wants to buy the *Laura Rose*. He seemed to think I should be relieved to have an offer."

"There's bound to be gossip, miss. Folks wondering what will happen now."

Laura looked behind her, up the sweeping steps and to the texas deck beyond. Something about Wilson Danvers, *Esquire*, and the way he combined mock politesse and insistent kindness sent a chill through her. Why would he assume she was selling? What "situation"?

She needed to find Mr. Hughes.

After Danvers left the packet, Laura climbed the stairs to the hurricane deck where she stood watching him make his way across the levee and into the city. When he stopped to speak with someone, she lingered, filled with new dread when whoever it was shook Danvers's hand, then proceeded in the direction of the *Laura Rose*. She'd descended the stairs and was waiting at the gangplank when the unknown man hurried up and handed her an envelope.

"From Mr. Hughes, ma'am. With sincere condolences." Hat in hand, the messenger said, "I was to wait for your reply."

Ambrose Hughes. Papa's attorney. Laura opened the envelope and read.

> Dear Miss White,
> The occasion for this note saddens me deeply. While I do not wish to cause undue alarm on your part, I must emphasize that it is imperative that you and I speak at your earliest convenience concerning matters regarding your father's estate and business dealings—things that Joseph put in motion before your departure for Fort Rice. There are issues about which you must be informed—and quickly. I shall explain everything to your satisfaction, only do not delay in coming to my offices or in sending word as to when and where I might call on you. I shall be dining at seven o'clock this evening on the second floor of the Planter's Hotel, and would not consider it rudeness on your part should you decide to join me. If this is simply not possible, then perhaps you would meet with me tomorrow—the Sabbath notwithstanding. I have instructed my man to await your reply.
>
> Most sincerely at your service,
> Ambrose Hughes

Hughes's flourishing signature brought to mind the image of a kindly gentleman with a froth of white hair, clear blue eyes peering through spectacles, and the habit of dressing in outdated fashion that, Papa had always said, was a considered choice intended to disarm "the enemy" in the courtroom.

"People tend to underestimate Ambrose because he looks like such a fuddy-duddy," Papa said. "And he likes it that way. He says it has given him an advantage on more than one occasion."

The troubled tone of the note did not match Laura's memory of Ambrose Hughes, whose office smelled of expensive cigars and old books. She didn't hesitate. "Please tell Mr. Hughes that I will join him for supper this evening."

"Thank you, ma'am."

She was on her way back to her cabin to change when she reversed direction and tracked down Tom Meeks. She waited while Tom read Mr. Hughes's missive before recounting the conversation with Danvers. "Do you have any idea what either man might be talking about?"

Meeks shook his head. "The captain kept his personal finances very private." He smiled. "I do know he trusted Mr. Hughes. I'd say that you can, too." He paused. "Don't know much about Danvers. What I do know is just...rumor."

"I take it those rumors aren't particularly positive in nature."

Tom hesitated. "I wish I could say different, but...ma'am. I don't know anything good about him."

"Thank you for being so frank, Tom. I have a late meeting with Mr. Hughes. Hopefully, he'll be able to clarify things for me." She paused. "I'm sorry to have to ask, tomorrow being the Sabbath and all, but would it be possible for you to have the initial accounting finished in time for me to give the crew promissory notes when I meet with them? I know they'll be in a hurry to cash in on the bonus the minute the banks open Monday morning."

Tom smiled. "Happy to do it, ma'am. I never have been much of a Sabbath-keeper."

Laura turned to go. She was just about to ascend to the

texas when Elijah called after her. "Ma'am? Seven o'clock...
It'll be dark before that supper's over."

Laura smiled. "And if the streetcars aren't still running, I
promise to ask Mr. Hughes to see me home. And thank you.
It's very kind of you to care."

The old man smiled. "Can't help it, ma'am. Been watchin'
over you since you was this high." He held his hand out to
indicate the height of a small child. "Old habits die hard."

Surprised when tears welled up in her eyes, Laura swallowed before saying, "That's not a habit that needs to die. I
appreciate having someone watching out for me."

Elijah nodded, then diverted the attention to the dog at
his side. "She's got both of us watchin', doesn't she?"

Logjam chuffed and wagged his tail.

※

Later that evening, Laura sat across from Ambrose Hughes,
her mind racing as she tried to take in what he'd just told her.
There had to be a way out. *Oh, Joe. How could you?*

"I am so sorry, my dear." Mr. Hughes reached across the
table and squeezed Laura's hand, then pointed to her cup of
tea. "Perhaps you'd like something stronger?"

Laura shook her head. If ever she'd needed a clear head,
it was now. Taking a deep breath, she said, "I hope you'll be
patient with me, but I need to say this back to you in my own
words. To be certain I truly comprehend."

"It requires no patience on my part to see you through
this, Miss White." Hughes sat back. "Your father was more
than a client. I considered him a dear friend. In fact, I was
involved in his decision to have the *Laura Rose* built. He'd
waited a long time to realize that dream."

Laura nodded. Again, she remembered Papa's joy as he led
his family aboard.

"Building the *Laura Rose* was a bit of a gamble, but not a

foolish one. His stellar reputation secured immediate financing. The only thing that makes your current position so tenuous is the added…ahem…situation."

The situation. Laura nodded. "As I understand it, then, I was correct about still owing half the construction costs. That's $12,500, and the loan is held by Boatmen's Bank." Mr. Hughes nodded. Laura continued, "That would not be an undue amount of debt—especially in light of our making yet another run this spring—except for the fact that before we left St. Louis, Joe took out a second loan of $7,500 from the men represented by Mr. Danvers." She swallowed. "To buy a house. A rather grand house."

Hughes nodded.

"The interest rate is high, and Mr. Danvers and his clients have a reputation for taking advantage of situations like mine." Suddenly, everything the man had said took on ominous tones. He hadn't really been smiling. He'd been leering. Practically rubbing his hands together with glee at the prospect of taking the *Laura Rose* away.

Mr. Hughes's voice was gentle as he said, "I am so sorry, my dear. I did everything in my power to convince your brother to wait. He said that Miss MacKnight had admired the house once when they were out driving together. He was afraid it would sell before he had time to go through the usual channels." He shook his head. "I thought I'd talked him into waiting. I truly did not know that he had gone ahead with this other arrangement until Danvers knocked on my door early this morning.

"As for Mr. Danvers, he told me he'd wait until you and I had a chance to talk. Clearly he had no intention of doing so." He sighed. "He has had some success in the past with such tactics. Frightened women often make rash decisions." He smiled at Laura. "You are to be commended for keeping your wits about you and sending him packing."

"He said they would be patient," Laura said. "I assumed that meant he'd wait until the *Laura Rose* made another trip."

"Let us hope that's true."

"But you don't think it is."

Mr. Hughes grimaced. "Danvers isn't the only problem. The bank made their loan to your father. They were willing to extend it to your brother as a licensed captain, but they have no obligation to do you the same courtesy."

"If they don't, then I must pay the $12,500 balance on the loan now?"

"Yes. And since your brother used his share of the equity in the *Laura Rose* as collateral for the Danvers loan, even if you do repay the bank, you'll fail to repay the second loan, which means Danvers and his partners become part-owners of the *Laura Rose*."

"So I have enough to pay either debt, but not both," Laura said. "Unless I sell the *Laura Rose*." Mr. Hughes nodded.

"What if I sell the house?"

"We can most certainly try, but real estate transactions take time, and Boatman's has already been more than patient."

He was right, of course. The bank loan should have been paid off by the end of last season. Easily. "How long do I have to repay Mr. Danvers?"

"I think," Hughes said, "that you should proceed as if the note will be called immediately—which, I regret to say, is a legal option as defined in the very fine print of the contract Joseph so hastily signed. Sadly, my experience with Danvers and his cohorts leads me to suspect that, if you refuse to see things their way, they will do just that."

"What I don't understand," Laura said, "is why they didn't just call in the note. Why bother with the pretense of offering to buy the *Laura Rose*? Isn't the result the same for them? I mean, if they call the note in—" She broke off.

"When he made the offer, he made no mention of its including the repayment of the loan, did he?"

Laura thought over their conversation. "No, he didn't. He made no mention of a loan at all."

"If that was the case, then they would expect to be repaid from the proceeds. You would have to pay them back a good portion of what they pay you for the *Laura Rose* to satisfy the loan. So they not only would own the *Laura Rose* completely, but they would also have the loan repaid in full. A very good deal financially for them."

"Do they really think me so foolish as to agree to that?"

"It's hard to say, but even if you refuse, they benefit. You see, for people like those Danvers represents, the world of banking and finance involves a certain dance," Mr. Hughes said. "Extending an offer creates an illusion. They can appear to be generous men attempting to help a poor, defenseless lady. They can use your refusal to claim that they tried to work with you. They can make the point that it is, after all, a business, not a charity, and they have investors they must answer to." He shrugged. "That may not be the entire line of thinking, but you get the idea. They maintain a veneer of respectability. Just beneath that veneer, they take advantage of every jot and tittle of a nefariously worded contract to force the desired result."

"That's despicable."

Hughes nodded. "It is. But it's also entirely legal."

Laura took a deep breath. "Can you convince Boatmen's to extend the loan for the construction costs? If they'd consider that, I could meet this other obligation right away. You could sell the property while I'm gone."

"Gone?"

"Well...yes. It's even more important than ever that the *Laura Rose* make that second trip upriver." Laura paused. "I'll have to hire pilots—I was hoping to convince the inspector—

but there isn't time for that now." Her mind whirled with things to do. Lure contracts for freight, meet with the crew, dole out bonuses, take on supplies—she looked over at Mr. Hughes. "If everything goes smoothly, we might be able to pull out midweek. How soon do you think you can get a decision from Boatmen's?"

"I'll do everything in my power to work something out and report to you by the end of business day Monday."

Chapter 9

The pounding. The roaring. The seasickness.

Finn pulled the covers down just far enough to be able to see out of one eye. Just far enough that it felt as if the shaft of sunlight shining in his bedroom window had slit his eyeball. With a grunt, he burrowed under his pillow, cursing the pounding...the roaring...the seasickness. The pounding. The shouting. *His name.* Somewhere in the distance, someone was shouting his name. Keeping his eyes scrunched shut, Finn pushed his pillow away from his right ear. And groaned. *Fiona. Not now. Give a man a chance to sleep.*

"Finn MacKnight."

His feet were cold. Suddenly cold. *What the—?* He groaned. "Not now, Fiona."

"Yes, brother. Now."

With a yelp, he snatched his feet beneath his covers and half sat up, peering at the daft woman standing at the foot of his bed with a...poker in hand? She'd tickled his bare feet with a poker?

"What is it? What's wrong?" He blinked, wincing against the bright light.

Fiona retreated to the door. Hands on her hips, she said, "For one thing, a fine specimen of manhood like yourself wasting his life away." She paused. "You have exactly ten minutes to get into the kitchen or I'll be forced to come back in here and help you wake up. And you won't like how I do it. Now get your backsliding self cleaned up. We've something to discuss."

Fiona left, but not without closing the door with a loud— well, not a slam exactly. Thank goodness for that. He didn't need any more noises pounding against his temples this morning.

With a sigh, Finn fell back against the pillow.

Fiona called through the doorway. "And don't you dare come to my breakfast table reeking of that saloon."

He sat up, dangling his legs over the side of the bed. That's when the church bells began to ring. *Oh, no.* Fiona had stayed home from church on the Sabbath. She would read hellfire and damnation over him from the Good Book while he ate breakfast. And Adele would sit there looking saintly while she enjoyed every minute of the show.

Hobbling to the washstand, he scrubbed his face then studied his reflection in the mirror. *You could have done a thousand things besides what you did yesterday. Could have gone a thousand different directions.* Well, he'd tried. While Fiona talked to the doctor, he'd headed through the back gate and up the alley, past the very church Fiona attended so faithfully and toward the levee, which still drew him like a magnet.

All he'd intended to do was get some fresh air. And exercise his bum leg. But then he saw the *Laura Rose* nosed up to the levee, her freight deck empty, the doors to the passenger cabins wide open, the only sign of life on board a lone figure sitting near the paddle wheel, his legs dangling over the side, a large brindle dog next to him.

Where was Joe? Why hadn't he come to see Adele as soon as— Finn had just started to make his way onto the packet when Jack McCoy came alongside. Pointing at the *Laura Rose*, he said, "Be glad you got away with only a smashed leg."

Finn looked over at him. "What're you talking about?"

McCoy told him about Joe and Mrs. White, finishing with the news that talk on the levee had resurrected the idea of a curse stalking the *Laura Rose*. "Not that I'm one who believes in such nonsense." He shrugged. "Guess it doesn't really matter whether I believe it or not, though. Way I heard it, the minute the crew collects on their bonus, they'll be done with her." He paused. "Best thing the little lady could do would be to sell her to the highest bidder."

Stunned, Finn made his way into the Broken Spar alongside McCoy, where everything the man had said was brought home over and over again. The misfortunes of the *Laura Rose* were the talk of the levee, and the rumor mill included an early offer to buy out Miss White. Finn's good fortune at "only" hurting his leg was celebrated again and again as old friends welcomed him back into the fold. They all wanted to buy him a drink. His thoughts a muddle over Joe and Mrs. White, his heart pained for Adele, he stayed put, trying to make sense of it all. He said no to the whiskey, but after a while, the ale began to take its toll. Eventually, it just didn't seem to matter.

His head pounding, Finn peered again at the unwashed, unshaven, hungover face in the mirror. "You're an unredeemed son-of-a-sandbar, Finn MacKnight." Taking up his straight razor, he went to work. Moments later, he thumped his way out into the kitchen, dropped into a chair at the table, and leaned down to slide his crutches out of sight beneath it.

At first, he avoided giving out the news. "I've come to take my punishment," he said, "but before you get started, let me save you the trouble. I'm an ungrateful wretch. The good Lord saved my leg and I should be praising Him instead of feeling sorry for myself. It's past time I proved myself to be the man you know me to be."

"Am I so predictable as that?" Fiona poured him coffee.

He took a sip. "You've sent Adele off on an errand. You always do that when I've done something like—yesterday." He raked through his shaggy hair, surprised by the fresh wave of remorse that washed over him. "I am sorry," he said, and he really meant it. "The pain— I went for a walk after the doctor gave me his verdict—although you can hardly call it walking. And the crutches just seemed to take me in the old direction." He shook his head. "I ran into Jack McCoy down at the levee." He paused, bracing himself before broaching the topic of the tragic news about the White family.

"Does that mean you've heard about your friend?" Fiona sat down with a sigh. Her hand trembled as she took a drink of coffee. "Of course. That explains..." Her voice trailed off.

Reaching out, Finn clasped her hand. "It won't happen again. I mean it this time."

Fiona pulled her hand away. "Adele is resting in her room, poor thing."

Her face was a mask of sorry. Finn sat forward. "She knows? How?"

"You'll remember I sent her to do some marketing yesterday morning."

Finn nodded. Fiona had made a habit of sending Adele on errands when the doctor visited.

"She ran into Jessamine Powell at the mercantile. Jessamine's brother works down on the levee." She paused. "As the saying goes, 'News travels fast. Bad news travels fastest of all.'"

Finn just sat. Fiona added, "Poor Adele was so staggered by the news she fainted dead away. Jessamine helped to revive her, then brought her home. She's fine physically, but Finn, she was so pale and trembling. I think she truly cared for Joseph White." And then, after a brief pause, Fiona clucked, "The poor girl."

Which "poor girl" was she thinking of now—Adele or Laura White?

"We must go to her today and offer our condolences. And then—we have to help her."

Ah, Miss White. Finn nodded. "All right." He glanced toward Adele's room. "When do you think Adele will be ready?"

"I see no reason to delay," Fiona said. "A woman alone attracts wolves in sheep's clothing as surely as vultures flock to a carcass." She peered at him over her coffee cup as she took another sip. "Miss White will be needing at least one other pilot. A good man who will look out for her interests. Someone she knows she can trust."

Finn sat back. "And you're thinking that's me?" He stifled a laugh.

"Why not you?"

"Well, for one thing, the first time she saw me since her father fired me, I'd just hauled her inebriated brother home." When Fiona opened her mouth to say something, he held up his hand. "For another, even though Joe talked me into helping him out—and even though Miss White had to know it was necessary—you can be sure she despised the idea of my going on that trip as second pilot. And last, let us not forget that as far as she knows, I was off in some saloon the morning I was supposed to report for duty a few weeks ago."

"But you weren't. You weren't in a drunken state when you helped Joseph home, and the only reason you didn't report for duty that day was because you were lying beneath seventy pounds of nails." Fiona paused. "Goodness, Finn, she'll have to understand that."

"Doesn't mean she'll have any confidence in me as a pilot." He paused. "The old captain worked with Ambrose Hughes. He's a good man, and he'll give good counsel. In fact, he'll probably advise her to sell the packet and be done with the headache—and the heartache. I wouldn't be surprised if prospective buyers are already lining up to take advantage of the situation—a poor choice of words. Hughes won't allow them to 'take advantage.' He'll see that things are done fairly."

Fiona challenged him. "And is that how you see it, then? She's to just give up on the only life she's known? Sign away her home, without another thought?"

"I didn't mean it would be easy. It's terrible, what's happened."

"Don't I remember hearing something about her running away from school when she was a girl?"

Finn couldn't help but smile. "You remember that, do you? That was a while ago. When Joe and I were just starting to feel our oats."

"And not long after Adele came to live with us," Fiona said. "I took comfort in knowing I wasn't the only woman on the earth with the equivalent of a wild colt on my hands."

"I believe the term you want is 'filly.'"

"So much the worse, society being what it is in regards to young ladies who don't toe the proverbial line." She paused. "My point is, Miss White fought to have a life on that river. Why would she want to sell the *Laura Rose*?"

Well, now that she put it that way— Finn took another drink of coffee. "There's nothing I can do, Fiona. Unless she asks for help."

"You could offer your services again. You're a very good pilot, Finn. I remember the old captain saying that."

Blast the woman's memory. Had she forgotten that the praise was couched in the old captain's apologies for firing him? *He's got more promise than any cub I've worked with, Miss MacKnight. But I just can't countenance any further shenanigans. Until he wants it more than he wants a drink, I won't allow him to set foot aboard a steamboat I'm responsible for.*

"No one is going to trust a packet loaded with cargo to me, Fiona. Especially not Laura White."

"But her brother had already hired you. Surely she'd give you a chance—for Joseph's sake."

She had to be the most stubborn woman on the face of God's green earth. "A man with crutches makes hardly half a pilot—no matter what he knows about the river."

Fiona pressed her lips together. Taking a deep breath, she said quietly, "Did I tell you I saw Harry Congers the other day? He and his wife just had their second child. Harry works in the office at Lemp Brewery. Losing both legs hasn't stopped him." Before Finn could say a word, she said, "George Holland. Remember him? He was right-handed, but he's learned to write with his left—and that hook he has for a right hand? He's back working as a bank teller. Hasn't let it stop him. Ben Hissem—"

"All right," Finn said. He held up his hand. "I get your point. I'll go back to looking for work—with my pride swallowed. Will that make you happy?"

"It will do for now." Fiona rose and headed for the back door. Taking the egg basket down from its nail, she said, "Would you knock on Adele's door, please, and tell her I'm making a light breakfast? She'll say she isn't hungry. Tell her she will need her strength, because we're going to pay our respects to Miss White later today." She unlatched the screen and answered Finn's unspoken question as to why he was being assigned to Adele. "You know I have little patience with her emotional outbursts. If she needs a shoulder, yours is broader." With that, Fiona opened the door and headed out to gather eggs.

※

Early Sunday afternoon, Laura faced the assembled crew and delivered the speech she'd written with Elijah North's help—the speech designed to state honestly her predicament with just the right balance of feminine appeal and professional strength. She needed their help, but she wanted them to have confidence in her—to believe that she was far from being either helpless or hopeless. She'd stood before the mirror in her cabin, her hands clasped before her, for the better part of the morning rehearsing. Now she stood on the third step of the hurricane deck stairs so they could all see her.

"And so," she concluded, as she looked out over the assembled crew, "that is the situation. Your bonuses are not in jeopardy, but the future of my steamboat is—at least insofar as her being mine is considered." Her voice wavered. She lifted her chin. "The *Laura Rose* is my home. I don't want to lose her. I need your help to find two licensed pilots—or, if the Good Lord has a miracle in the offing, one licensed pilot willing to take on a female 'cub.'" Stifled laughter rippled through the two dozen men below her. She forced a smile, even though the laughter rankled. They knew she could do the job. Why did they laugh?

When Logjam barked, the men looked toward the levee. The dog was standing at the head of the gangplank, looking toward a buggy that had just pulled up next to a freight wagon. Laura's spirits dipped. *The MacKnights.* Certainly Adele deserved sympathy, and her sister was nice enough. As for the man holding the reins—she wasn't sure how to feel about him. The old resentment simmered the moment Laura caught a glimpse of Finn.

The older Miss MacKnight climbed down without her brother's assistance. Which was odd. But then she pulled a pair of crutches out from beneath the buggy seat and waited while MacKnight maneuvered awkwardly to lower himself to the ground. Once he'd tucked the crutches beneath his arms, he hobbled to hitch the buggy while Adele climbed down unaided. *What on earth...*

Laura dismissed the crew and turned to face her visitors with a sense of dread. As the women ascended the gangplank—with their brother bringing up the rear on his crutches, the sight of Adele's pale, grief-stricken face made Laura think of the notes she'd put back in Mama's bag. Asking Elijah to show the MacKnights into the dining saloon, Laura hurried up to the texas to retrieve Adele's letters.

Taking a deep breath, she headed into Joe's cabin and made a quick search for anything he might have written before taking ill. She found one half-finished note tucked into the drawer of his bedside table. She stood for a moment, staring down at the beautiful script. Joe had always had better penmanship than she did. Tears threatened. Closing her eyes, Laura inhaled the familiar aroma of Joe's favorite cigars and his cologne. The very air in the cabin belied reality. It was as if he'd just stepped out. Surely he wasn't really gone.

A soft whine and the sound of Logjam scratching at the door saved her from a flood of tears. Letters in hand, Logjam at her side, she headed down to the dining saloon.

❦

Adele sat weeping quietly as she looked down at the small bundle of envelopes Laura White had just handed her. Opening the lone unfinished note Joseph had penned before taking ill, she remembered his arms about her, his hand at her waist, his lips on hers. The passion that had at once frightened and thrilled her.

"Joe was very fond of you," Miss White said.

"I loved him so," Adele croaked, her voice breaking. "Thank you for keeping them. For returning them to me." She took a deep breath. "If it isn't too painful...I was hoping...could you tell me what happened?"

"Adele," Fiona chided, "it's too soon for this. Miss White shouldn't be expected to—"

"No," Miss White interrupted. "It's all right." She reached

out and squeezed Adele's hand. "You loved him, too. It's nice not to be alone in that."

Adele hadn't thought of that. Miss White had no one to share her grief with. The notion of just how completely alone she was made Adele's eyes fill with fresh tears. "Fiona's right. I shouldn't have asked."

"We would have been sisters," Miss White said, and her voice was gentle. "It's all right that you asked." She told the story in simple terms, in a clear voice that didn't waiver until she got to the part about arriving at the doctor's office in Sioux City and hearing the awful news.

Adele was amazed by Miss White's inner strength as she spoke.

"I'll bring him back," she said. "I've been too distracted by other matters to make the arrangements, but there will be a memorial service once I get Joe and Mama back here beside my father—where they belong." She looked down and took a long, deep breath. "Sadly, other business has arisen that requires my attention before I can see to it." She paused then and looked over at Finn. "Obviously the crutches explain your absence the morning we departed." She paused. "I'm afraid I have judged you rather harshly. I apologize."

Finn shrugged. "From what you know about me, I'd be surprised if you'd drawn any other conclusion." There was an awkward pause, and then Finn reached for his crutches. "If you'll excuse us now, I'm certain you have more than your share of things to do." He looked at Fiona. "We shouldn't linger."

Fiona stayed put. "You'll forgive my intrusion, I hope," she said to Miss White. "But there's more to this visit than condolences."

Finn practically barked the words, "Now is not the time, Fiona."

"Now is precisely the time," Fiona insisted. She didn't move.

Finn glared at her. "No. We should go."

Fiona remained seated. Muttering a curse under his breath, Finn offered an awkward bow in Miss White's direction. "And now it is I who must apologize." He glared at Fiona. "If I could drag you out of here, I would. Since I can't—" Again, he looked at Miss White. "My sister is overzealous and out of order. I am sorry." He thumped his way out of the saloon, calling for Adele to come with him.

Adele hesitated.

"Go," Fiona said. "I'll be along directly."

He had a mind to leave and let Fiona ride the streetcar home. But then a gentleman wouldn't do such a thing, and he was trying to become a gentleman. And so Finn went and sat in the buggy fuming, waiting for Fiona.

"She means well," Adele said, as she climbed up beside him.

He snorted. It was high time that Fiona MacKnight retired from the business of rescuing him. Even a man doomed to limping through life had his pride, didn't he? And Fiona had about as much subtlety as a charging bull. Now that he thought about it, that's what made him the angriest: Fiona's ignoring him just now when he stood up and ordered her to desist. She'd acted as if he wasn't even there. Treated him like some imbecile who needed his big sister's help. His leg might be crippled, but his mind—and his pride—were still very much intact.

When Fiona finally inched her way down the gangplank, he remembered. She was deathly afraid of water. She probably hated being on that gangplank alone. Well, it served her right. Besides, by the time he managed to climb back down and get to her, she'd be ready to climb up into the buggy, and she was certainly capable of doing that on her own. And so he waited, and the moment Fiona had settled behind him, Finn cracked the buggy whip and headed off.

Fiona made one attempt to say something. Only one.

"Not now, Fiona," Adele said quickly.

By some miracle, Fiona listened to her. Which was good, because if Finn had dared to say one word, profanity would have burst out of him like floodwaters obliterating a dike. As it was, Adele's occasional sniff annoyed him. He glanced over at her just as she swiped a tear from her cheek. Reaching into his coat, he handed her a clean handkerchief. Then he glanced behind him at Fiona who sat, her lips pressed together firmly, her cheeks pink, her chin lifted. He knew that expression well. Fiona MacKnight was a proud woman. So certain she knew what was best for them all. So strong-willed. So *wrong*, with her nonsense about his magically becoming respectable. How had she said it? Oh, yes, he was supposed to become "the man the Lord Christ died for him to be." What did that even mean?

He was too far gone to become a saint, and he would not be bullied into doing things Fiona's way. The woman needed to find something besides reforming her brother to occupy her time. He was still angry when the house came into view. Instead of pulling into the drive and heading back to the small barn at the back of the property, Finn stopped the buggy in front of the house.

"I'm going for a drive," he said, without looking back. His voice dripped with sarcasm as he said, "You'll forgive me if I don't help you down."

Chapter 10

Laura waited until she was certain Fiona MacKnight was off the hurricane deck before going to the dining saloon door. From there, she watched the woman cross the levee and climb aboard the waiting buggy. It didn't take any special powers of deduction to see that her brother was still angry—very angry, from the way he cracked that buggy whip and headed off.

A man and his pride. Ah well. At least he was man enough to know she'd never trust him with the *Laura Rose*. It was a shame he'd been injured, but sympathy wasn't nearly enough to make Laura rethink her opinion of Finn MacKnight. Shaking her head, Laura crossed the open deck to stand at the railing and look out on the city. She was still there when the street lamps came on, dotting the darkening city with globes of light. Still wondering what to do. Hoping the crew was, even now, doing what they could to recruit a pilot—or two. As the sun dropped toward the western horizon, things quieted on the levee and music spilled from the doorways of the saloons in the distance.

Laura was about to retreat to her cabin when Logjam, who'd been snoozing on the leeward deck around the corner from the dining saloon, began to bark. Just as she turned to see what he was barking at, Captain Jack McCoy came into view. Logjam positioned himself between Laura and the visitor.

McCoy threw his hands up. "Hey, fella. No harm intended. I'm just here to offer Miss White my condolences. And my help, if she'll have it."

Logjam's hackles smoothed down, but he didn't offer to move from the space between Laura and the captain until she said, "It's all right, boy. I know Captain McCoy. He and Joe were cub pilots together." When Elijah called for the dog from down below and he backed away, Laura apologized.

The captain smiled at her. "Not a bad idea to have someone looking out for you." He crossed the open deck, pausing a few feet away and leaning against the railing. "That's actually why I'm here."

Something about his smile made Laura uncomfortable.

"You and your *Laura Rose* are the talk of the levee. Surely you know that."

"So I've heard."

"Sadly," McCoy said, "the talk isn't all that good. Rivermen are a superstitious lot."

"Don't tell me that nonsense about a curse is making the rounds again."

"Nonsense or not, it could make things difficult for you. And I hate to see that happen." He took a step forward.

Laura glanced toward the stairs, wishing Logjam had stayed nearby.

"I noticed the MacKnights leaving earlier. Too bad about what happened to Finn." He paused. "The fact that he was loading freight intended for the *Laura Rose* hasn't helped quiet the rumors."

She was not going to stand here and discuss superstitious nonsense with the man. "You said something about offering help. Does that mean you're applying to be one of my pilots?"

"Are you really offering seven hundred a month?"

"Is that your price?" It was an outrageous figure.

McCoy seemed to be considering, but then he shook his head. "I'm contracted to the *Colonel Kidd* for the rest of the season. You'd have to buy that out."

"And I can't. Now, if you'll excuse me—" If the direction of the wind didn't change soon, she was going to need smelling salts. How did crew members endure sharing the wheelhouse with a man who never washed?

"Rumor has it you were the only pilot for most of this last run. That true?"

"It is."

"Heard something about you wanting to be cub to a licensed pilot. Taking another run. All the way to Fort Benton this time." He paused. "You should have heard the laughter."

"My crew wasn't laughing when I came close to beating the record for reaching Fort Rice," Laura said. "We made it in twenty-five days."

McCoy's gaze dropped to the hem of her dress, then lingered in a couple of places. He took his time about looking her in the face. "Twenty-five days," he said. "Impressive. I almost wish I wasn't duty-bound to stick it out aboard the *Kidd*. I can't deny it's more than a little enticing to think of sharing space with someone as fine-looking as you."

Laura took a step back. "Perhaps you'll let me know if you hear of anyone interested in the pilot's position." Where was Logjam? What had happened to Elijah North?

McCoy moved closer. He touched her shoulder. "Luke Trask. Do you know the name?"

Laura shook her head.

"He's been in a bit of trouble, but nothing too terrible. I could talk to him for you. He owes me a favor." He winked at her. "Of course, if I talk him into helping you, then you'll owe *me* a favor. But we can work that out between the two of us."

Laura took a step back. "I don't—think so."

"Come now, Miss White. This doesn't have to be difficult. It might even prove mutually satisfying." He snaked one arm about her waist and pulled her close.

Her heart in her throat, Laura slapped the man's filthy face as hard as she could. Breaking free, she charged toward the stairs. With a snarl Logjam raced past her, latched on to the seat of McCoy's pants, and dragged him farther away. Elijah North came next. Grabbing McCoy by the scruff of his neck, he wrestled him to the edge of the deck and slung him over the railing. A mighty splash sounded, and North turned to face her. "You all right, miss?"

Apparently McCoy could swim. Laura could hear him swearing and splashing about. She nodded. "I—yes—no—" She pressed her palm to her midsection. She could hardly breathe.

"There, now miss, it's all right. He didn't—hurt you—did he? I only moseyed over to the Sandbar for a bit to sound out the situation. Thought I might rustle up a few more crew members, maybe even get a bead on a pilot. Didn't think it would do any harm to try to help. Took Logjam with me—should have left him here."

Laura swiped at her tears. "I'm fine," she sniffed.

"There now, child," Elijah took her hand. "It'll be all right."

Laura nodded agreement. But deep inside, doubt whispered.

"What you need is a good rest," Elijah said. "I'll make you a toddy and Logjam here will stand guard while you sleep. Things will look better tomorrow morning. They always do. You head on up. I'll bring that toddy directly."

When she'd donned her wrapper, Laura propped her cabin door open with Mama's satchel, then climbed up on her bed and pulled Mama's afghan about her shoulders. Logjam came to the edge of the bed and rested his chin there, looking up at her mournfully. When she leaned down to pat his head, he licked the back of her hand. Just once, but it was enough to startle her and to make her laugh.

"You did good, you know." She scratched behind one of the dog's ears. He strained against her hand, then put one white paw on the edge of her bed. "Are you trying to beg your way up here now?" With a soft whine, the dog removed the paw and rested his chin back on the comforter. He moved only his eyes. Back and forth, from comforter to her face and back again. "I'm going to regret this," Laura said as she patted the space beside her. Who would have thought a big dog could move that fast?

Elijah arrived, cup and saucer in hand. He spoke to the dog first. "Well, look at you."

"A reward for his part in the recent rescue," Laura said.

"You do realize you've a permanent fixture unless you lock him out?"

"I imagine so," Laura tucked her feet beneath Logjam's warm body. "I don't mind."

"You'll mind when you wake up in the morning and his head is on your pillow." Elijah chuckled as he reached down to pat the dog. "You stay on the job, now, y'hear?" As he started to leave, he hesitated. "Been thinking on the matter of a pilot. Didn't rustle up much interest over at the Sandbar."

"The curse of the *Laura Rose*?"

He shook his head. "Darned fools."

"I'll find someone," Laura said. "I have to."

Elijah nodded. He scratched at the whiskers along his jaw. "Funny thing about that dog," he said. "He doesn't take to the people you'd expect him to like. Folks fawn all over him and get the cold shoulder. Then he seems to watch over others that people don't like much. It's almost like he sees past their skin to what's inside."

"Well, he's certainly right about Jack McCoy," Laura said with a shiver. "His hackles went up the minute the man stepped on deck." She looked down at Logjam. "And I tried to tell you he was Joe's friend. I'm sorry."

Logjam wagged his tail.

Elijah continued, "On the subject of young Cap'n White's friends—couldn't believe my own eyes this afternoon when I saw him sprawled out right next to Finn MacKnight's chair." He nodded at the way the dog had stretched out next to Laura. "Just like that. Making himself right to home. You remember that?"

Now that he mentioned it—she did. Laura cocked an eyebrow. "Is this your way of telling me I should consider a one-legged pilot?"

Elijah grinned. "No ma'am. I'm just the ship's carpenter. It's not my place to tell the owner what to do. I was just commentating on Logjam and how he's generally a pretty good judge of character."

After Elijah was gone, Laura settled back and closed her eyes. When Logjam burrowed closer, she reached over and began to rub behind his ears. The dog sighed with pleasure.

"You wouldn't like him if you knew his past," Laura muttered.

❉

Laura spent Monday morning doing everything she knew to do to prepare for another trip upriver. First, she ordered handbills to post about the city that announced the departure of the *Laura Rose* on Friday, May 3, "Taking freight and passengers for..." and she listed virtually every one of the sixty stops between St. Louis and Fort Benton, Montana—to take up more space, since she couldn't follow the usual pattern and include the names of the pilots alongside that of the clerk.

"No pilots' names?" The printer's voice sounded doubtful as he stared down at what Laura had written to order the handbills.

Laura shrugged. "Put down that we're leaving at five o'clock p.m. on Friday. And across the bottom it should say, 'For freight or passage, apply on board to Tom Meeks, Clerk.' Now, how soon can you have those printed up?"

"No later than tomorrow noon, I expect," the man said.

"Make it noon today," Laura said, "and I will personally bring some of my cook's cinnamon rolls to the print room before we pull away from the levee on Friday."

The man smiled. "I'll see what I can do."

After leaving the printer, Laura intended to visit the first dress shop she passed. It was time to face the issue of proper mourning. But instead of stepping inside a shop, she wandered to first one and the next, gazing in the windows, unable to force herself to go in. Instead of buying mourning clothes, she fled back to the *Laura Rose* and the comfort of familiar surroundings. Drawn to Mama's cabin, she crept inside, surprised to find Mama's best black skirt and waist still hanging on the back of her door.

I should try them on. I bet they'd fit. But for some reason, after she'd taken the clothes off the hook, she couldn't quite make herself put them on. Laying them aside, she opened the small box atop Mama's trunk and stared down at the mourning brooch Mama had worn every Sabbath since Papa died. The finely wrought gilt edge framed equally fine hair work. Bird found her there, the brooch in the palm of her hand, tears dripping off her chin.

"Oh, child," Bird said and opened her arms. Laura stepped into them, clutching the mourning brooch in her palm as she wept. Finally, she pointed at the waist and the skirt on Mama's bed. "I went shopping, but I just couldn't. We were about the same size. I thought—"

"You remember what your mama said about all that?"

Laura nodded.

"She didn't want you putting all that mess on when your

papa died—and she wouldn't want it now. All those veils and petticoats and such. I was on the *Isabelle* when we passed that other steamboat. That bunch of widows standing at the top of the steps on the hurricane deck. Widows been down to Vicksburg to claim their own. You know what your papa said 'bout that? He was still talkin' 'bout it when I took him and your mama supper that evenin'. 'Margaret,' he said, 'I can't get it out of my mind. It looked like a dark cloud of misery haunting that packet.' And then he looked at your mama and said, 'You think it helps those poor women to dress like that? Or does it just prolong their grief?'" Bird nodded. "And then I heard it with my own ears. He told Miz White that if he was to die first, he didn't want her going around like some big ink blotch. And ain't that what made her tell you and your brother not to do such?" Bird put Mama's waist and skirt back on the hook. "She wouldn't want you doin' this, child."

"People will think I'm being disrespectful."

"Anybody thinks that doesn't know you and doesn't understand what a woman has to put up with to pilot a Missouri River steamboat." Bird paused. "You want a black armband, I'll make it." She pointed to the brooch Laura was holding. "You want to wear your mama's mourning brooch, that's all right, too. But she wouldn't want you going around the *Laura Rose* like some old woman with nothing left to live for—all the color gone out of her life."

Laura took a wavering breath. "There's so much I don't know...so much I have to decide...so much to do."

"I know, child, I know." Bird gave her shoulder a pat. "Hercules and me, Elijah North and Tom Meeks, and that dog: We're here. We'll do what we can to help." She smiled. "Got a little idea about how to get you the crew you need. Hercules said I best come right back aboard this morning and say it."

Laura returned the mourning brooch to its place in Mama's jewelry box. For now that was where it belonged. Bird spoke up as soon as Laura had closed Mama's cabin door and joined her at the railing.

"What I think is, we give the crew another reason to sign back on," Bird said. "One they can eat. A big banquet right out here on the hurricane deck where the whole levee sees it. And we do it up big. Roast beef sandwiches piled high. A cold slaw. Deviled eggs. Hercules's oyster stew, if we can get good oysters. And two kinds of cake. Maybe even ice cream." She hurried ahead, as if warding off an expected objection. "Now, I know maybe you think it ain't fittin' to be doing such, what with your brother and mama just passing. I understand if you feel that way, but to my mind, they's no better way to honor your family than to keep the business going. Carry on. Don't give up. So Hercules said I should tell you the idea." Bird paused. "You just let me know what you think—once you decide."

Laura was doubtful—but not for the reason Bird had raised. "That's a lot of work for just the two of you."

Bird nodded. "Yes'm. I thought of that. Maybe you'd let me have my sister to help. You remember Ruby. She's the pretty one."

Laura chuckled. Ruby Stokes was, indeed, the prettiest of Bird's sisters. The kind of pretty that turned men's heads when Ruby walked down a street, her hair wrapped in a bright kerchief, her ebony skin gleaming. She sometimes caused herself trouble with her regal bearing and a penchant for defending every aspect of her freedom. "Who could forget Ruby?" Laura said. "I just didn't realize she was working as a cook."

"She ain't. Not yet, anyway. She's been hoping to make a change from chambermaid on the *Colonel Kidd*."

The *Colonel Kidd*. Jack McCoy's packet. *Oh...my. Poor Ruby.*

"Ruby taught me nearly everything I know about baking, Miz White."

"Say no more. Let's get Ruby hired and make a plan." She paused. "How soon do you think we can serve this feast?"

"We start cooking by the end of the day," Bird said, "you could be the talk of the levee by this time tomorrow. In a good way. Take those rumors right out of their mouths and stuff some cornbread in instead."

"I assume you'll want to do the bulk of it in your kitchen at home," Laura said.

Bird shook her head. "No, ma'am. Folks need to see it all came from the galley right here on the *Laura Rose*. That way they'll know they get the same good food whether they come to work for you or book passage." Bird smiled.

Laura nodded. "All right. You come up with a list of what you need and I'll—"

Bird held up a piece of paper. "Got it all right here." She smiled. "Hercules said we ought to be ready for when you said yes." She pointed toward the levee. "He drove me down in the wagon. Ready to take me and this list to the grocery. Long as Mr. Meeks signs to make the order official."

Laura laughed. Maybe things were going to be all right after all.

Chapter 11

Laura had looked at Papa's watch for what must have been the hundredth time when finally, late Monday afternoon, Mr. Hughes stepped into the dining saloon where she'd been sitting at Mama's piano, trying to pick out the melody of an old hymn. The old man's expression said it all.

"As bad as that, is it?"

"I am so sorry, my dear. I pursued every avenue I could think of, but I could not get Boatman's to extend. They just— The risk is too great." He sighed. "If I could have told them you'd already secured a respected pilot and contracted freight—but then there is the matter of that second mortgage. I am sorry to say that the terms must stand."

"That means they expect payment by the end of business on Friday," Laura said.

"I'm afraid so." He sank onto the chair beside her. "I even contemplated using my own funds, but the truth is I'm in no position—"

"No," Laura said quickly. "I wouldn't want you to do that."

"I'm afraid there is still more bad news." He reached into his coat pocket, withdrew an envelope, and handed it over. "Danvers and his cohorts have filed a legal claim. They're calling in the second mortgage."

"But—he said they'd be patient."

"In this case, my dear, 'patience' will be extended for only the next forty-eight hours."

The words fell like blows. Laura pulled the document out of the envelope and skimmed the first page. Gibberish, as far as she was concerned—although the intent was clear, the words FORTY-EIGHT HOURS printed in capital letters and underlined. Her heart pounding, she folded the paper back up. "I've sent Elijah and Tom Meeks out to put up handbills announcing a Friday departure for Fort Benton. After that, Tom's going to call on some of our past shipping clients. If that yields contracts, would you be willing to go back to the bank for me?"

Hughes hesitated.

"I'll ask only if I have something concrete for you to present to them. Something new," Laura emphasized. "And I'll want to go with you. If they're going to turn me out, the least they can do is tell me to my face."

Hughes's expression changed. He actually smiled. Nodded. "I believe I see a glimmer of the old captain in his daughter."

Tears threatened. Clearing her throat, she asked, "As to the Danvers matter, when, exactly, does my forty-eight hours begin?"

"Now, I'm afraid."

Laura nodded. She pulled Papa's watch back out of her pocket. "Shall we say that was at 3:50 p.m.?" She held the watch up so that Mr. Hughes could see the time. He nodded. She looked toward the deck just beyond the dining saloon doors. "We're serving quite a buffet out on the hurricane deck for lunch tomorrow. Perhaps you'd want to join us." She told Hughes about the plan to entice the crew back. "Bird seems to think that two kinds of cake and Hercules's oyster stew will dispel superstition." She hurried to add, "Of course a crew is useless without a licensed pilot at the wheel. I do know that."

"If I had any influence in that regard, you know I'd help," Mr. Hughes said.

Laura nodded. "And I thank you." She rose. "I think I do have an idea, though. It's worth trying, at least."

Half an hour before the offices were supposed to close, a breathless Laura Rose White stood in the lobby of a square brick building just a block over from the St. Louis levee, staring with trepidation at the black lettering that read:

STEAMBOAT INSPECTION SERVICE
UNITED STATES DEPARTMENT OF COMMERCE AND LABOR
PHINEAS DAVIES, INSPECTOR

Taking a deep breath, Laura turned the brass doorknob with a gloved hand and stepped inside. The bent, bespectacled clerk standing behind the long oak counter a few feet from the door called out, "This is the Steamboat Inspection Service, ma'am." Assuming she must have made a mistake.

Laura nodded. "Yes, I know. I wish to see Inspector Davies, please."

"You have an appointment?"

"I'm afraid not," Laura said, summoning her most charming smile. "But if you'll only tell him Miss Laura Rose White is asking to see him, I'm hoping he'll have mercy on me."

"Miss White," the man said. He squinted and adjusted his spectacles. When he swallowed, his Adam's apple bobbed up and down, just above a none-too-clean collar.

"Yes," Laura said. "The late Captain Jacob White's daughter. The late Captain Joseph White's sister."

Recognition flashed in the man's watery gray eyes. He glanced over his shoulder at a green painted door to the right of a row of filing cabinets, then back at her. The Adam's apple bobbed again. "If you'll please just wait—there." He gestured at a row of chairs to the right of the main door.

"I don't mind standing. Hopefully the inspector won't keep me waiting long." Laura gazed past the clerk and at the green door. "He is in, isn't he?"

"He is." The clerk adjusted his collar. "I'll just— I'll be right back."

"Thank you." Laura clasped her hands before her, trying to looked relaxed in spite of her racing heart. Mama would have said to pray before setting out on this errand. *Please. Papa. Mama. Do you see me? I need help down here. Please ask God—help.*

"Miss White? Miss Laura White?"

Laura started when the booming voice called her name. With a casual wave in her direction, Davies turned and went back into his office. The clerk stood by the door like a sentinel standing at attention as she passed by. When she thanked him, he bobbed his head, then closed the door behind her without a word.

Mr. Davies stood behind his desk, mopping his brow. Apparently, walking to the door of his office was a great exertion. Which was no wonder, given the man's bulk. The cheeks that puffed out above the exaggerated sideburns were bright red. Bushy black eyebrows created a severe, dark line above round eyes that thick lenses made monstrously large. *The poor man must be half-blind.*

"Please," he huffed, "be seated." He pointed at a plain oak chair.

"Thank you," Laura said, "but I don't intend to take up too much of your time." Besides that, if she dared settle onto that chair, the hoops under her skirt were guaranteed to lift. Exposing an ankle was hardly the way to convince this man that she was a true lady and not some oddity of nature. And what she was about to propose would definitely tempt him to think her odd.

"As you wish." Tucking his kerchief back into his pocket, he put one hand on the back of his chair. "How may I help you?"

"I—I'd planned a pretty little speech," Laura said. "But now I wonder if you might prefer that I just get to the point." She looked around her at the piles of paper covering every flat surface in the room. "I can see that you're a busy man."

The inspector twirled the tip of his waxed mustache with a fat finger. "Proceed."

Laura nodded. "I am here to request that you administer the pilot's examination. Tomorrow."

The man's eyebrows shot up. "The examination is not given on demand. We offer it at specified times." He moved a stack of papers and fumbled with what appeared to be a calendar. "The next offering is at the end of May. Formal application must be made in advance."

"This is a special case." Laura said. "I suppose you've heard that before from people seeking special treatment. In this case, though, it really is unique." She gave a little shrug. "May I explain?"

The inspector made a show of removing his watch from his vest pocket. He looked down at it and grimaced. Then, with a deep sigh, he said, "All right."

"I need your help to save the *Laura Rose*."

"To save her from what?"

"From being taken away from me." Quickly, she outlined her predicament, beginning with Joe and Mama's tragic deaths and ending with the awful "surprise," courtesy of Wilson Danvers, Esquire. "And then there's the loan from Boatmen's," Laura said.

"I hope you aren't accusing Boatmen's of—"

"No. Of course not. It's a very highly respected institution. The thing is, Mr. Davies, all of this mess wouldn't be a mess if only folks would be patient. A second trip upriver would see everyone satisfied. More than satisfied."

"I don't see how a pilot's examination plays into the situation."

Sweat was streaming down the man's face. With a doubtful look behind her at the suspect chair, Laura moved it closer to his desk and perched on the edge. The hoops rose, but the effect was concealed by the oak panel that formed the front of the inspector's desk.

With a sigh of relief, he sat down opposite her. "I do see that you're in an unfortunate circumstance. But I do not see how my giving the pilot's examination would address any part of it."

Laura swallowed. "Everyone knows that the pilot's salary is one of the largest expenses any steamboat owner pays. I've been told that some of the best pilots command upward of seven hundred dollars a month. Over the course of a trip up the Missouri, that's a lot of money."

"And a good pilot earns every penny."

"Oh, I'm not arguing that," Laura said. "But if I could avoid paying it—can you see how it might help?" She paused. "I grew up trailing my brother. Learning what he learned from our father. I piloted the *Laura Rose* from Sioux City to Fort Rice and back without my brother. Then I brought her back to St. Louis with nary a new scratch." Again, she waited. The inspector didn't seem to be following her. Or maybe he was being willfully obtuse. "I'm asking you to give *me* the examination, Mr. Davies. Tomorrow. So that I can pilot my own steamboat upriver. Pay the debts. And keep my home."

Davies sputtered. His face grew red, then redder.

"My own mother said it, Inspector: Who better to be the first woman pilot west of the Mississippi than the daughter of Captain Jacob White? The sister of Captain Joseph White?" Laura forced what she hoped was a winning smile. "We've always been known as a steamboating family. You'd be making history, Inspector Davies."

He grunted. "I'd be making myself the laughingstock of St. Louis, that's what I'd be doing."

Laura leaned forward and placed one gloved hand on the edge of the cluttered desk. "Please. The *Laura Rose* is all I've got in the world. I'm a capable pilot. If you don't believe me, ask the crew. Any one of them will tell you."

Davies began to twirl the tips of his waxed mustache. "Now, what kind of gentleman would I be if I questioned the word of a lady? Of course I believe you. It's not as if your little accomplishment isn't the talk of the town."

Little? She'd single-handedly piloted the fully loaded *Laura Rose* past other wrecked steamers, in spite of sandbars and sawyers. She'd managed the last leg of the journey under a weight of grief and loss that had been known to crush even the brawniest of men. What about any of that was "little"?

"Please do not misunderstand," Davies intoned. "My staff and I have all the respect in the world for what you've done. Who would have thought a tiny little thing like you would prove equal to piloting a Missouri River packet—and never a pound of cargo lost? It's an admirable accomplishment."

For a moment, Laura felt hopeful. "I had a good teacher. You know that Papa and my brother were among the best pilots on the river."

"May they rest in peace."

"But don't you see? That's just it, Mr. Davies. They *can't* rest in peace if I lose the *Laura Rose*. It's my *home*. And whether you or any other man wants to admit it, I know what I'm doing at that wheel."

With a great sigh, Davies leaned back. His chair groaned. "Now, now, Miss White. No one is questioning your skill. But let's not aggrandize the accomplishment, either. The *Laura Rose* had only to reach Fort Rice. You didn't face the rapids around Cow Island. There were no Indian attacks, no groundings to speak of. In short, Miss White, the most dangerous parts of the journey were still to be faced, and it was—apart from the unfortunate personal challenges because of the illness in your family—a rather problem-free journey, at least when it comes to navigating."

Laura clenched her fists. What did he know of what she'd faced? Of the interrupted sleep and the knotted gut? She'd wept and trembled with fear. But she'd done what needed to be done, and if the self-righteous toad sitting across from her right now would only listen, she could do it again. She wanted to shout at him. Instead, she forced herself to take as deep a breath as her infernal corset would allow. "Of course I don't deny that the river helped. We had high water. But that doesn't mean it was easy."

Davies shrugged. "Life presents us all with difficulty, and you have my sympathies for yours. But if you'll permit me to say so, it's simplistic to think that my giving you the examination will solve your problems."

She did not want to appeal to him as a weak female, but reason wasn't doing any good. And so Laura let a few of the tears of frustration she'd been holding at bay escape. "Please. I've lost everyone I love. Everything but the *Laura Rose*. You have to help me."

"Even if I were to agree to that—who, pray tell, is going to entrust valuable cargo to a woman?"

Laura swiped at her tears. "There have to be other gentlemen willing to give me a chance. Men who recognize what I've already accomplished—who will see it as proof of my abilities."

"I don't deny that your recent success has been celebrated as a moment in Missouri River navigational history." The chair creaked again as Davies leaned forward and, resting his forearms atop his desk, laced his fingers together. "But it was only a moment. An exception worthy of note—and that is all."

Laura shook her head. "No, sir. It wasn't an exception. I know every inch of that river as well as any man."

Davies tilted his head, much like a professor trying to get a point across to a particularly dense student. "Why would you want to stake your future on that fickle river, when all you need do is accept the inevitable? Settle down. Enjoy St. Louis society. Don't you want a home?"

"I have a home. She's tied up at the levee."

"You have been under a terrible strain, and you have borne it all remarkably well. I for one admire the way you've persevered and triumphed. No one can deny that your story is a tale worth telling. The Good Lord wrought a miracle in seeing you through. But miracles, Miss White, don't generally get repeated."

Laura bit her lip. More tears threatened. Blinking them away, she looked down at her gloved hands and succumbed to the only thing she hadn't tried yet. If it took simpering smiles and batting eyelashes to save the *Laura Rose*, then she would dimple and simper and bat with the best of them.

She sniffed. "I j-just d-don't know what I'm going to do. It's positively—terrifying to think of living in St. Louis. I'd be all alone. And I've never lived in a house before."

"There, now, Miss White. It's for the best. In time you'll see that. We want only what's best for you."

We? Now he was using the royal *we?* Her temper flared. The more Laura thought about it, the angrier she got, and the angrier she got the easier it was to summon tears. She let them flow. Tugging her small silk bag open, she withdrew a black-trimmed handkerchief and dabbed at her moist cheeks. "Please, Mr. Davies. I'm begging. If you will only give me a chance to take the examination, I know I can prove myself worthy on paper—just as I have on board the *Laura Rose*." Her chin trembled. She mustered more tears. "If I fail, then I'll do what everyone seems to want me to do. Just—please—don't turn me out without giving me a chance."

"Perhaps you didn't hear me before when I said it, but I'll make the point again: Any inspector who did something so outlandish as to offer a pilot's examination to a *female* would be the laughingstock of the district."

He almost sneered the word. *Female.* That brought Laura up short. Was that the real reason he kept saying no? Was he afraid of what others would say? Maybe he was afraid she'd pass. Laura met his gaze, hoping she looked gentle... beseeching. "Why would anyone laugh at a kind gentleman for being uncommonly gallant? For coming to the aid of an orphaned young woman about to lose the last shred of her inheritance?"

Davies seemed to think that one over. But he remained stubborn. "No amount of gallantry will erase the facts of your unhappy situation, Miss White. I truly believe that the best thing for you to do is to accept those facts and move on."

"I'm not asking you to erase the facts," Laura murmured, even as she drew the edge of the mourning handkerchief between thumb and forefinger. "I'm just asking you to give me a chance to redeem my papa's memory." Her voice wavered. "And my dear brother's. A fair chance to give them a legacy besides bankruptcy." She looked him in the eye, pleading, "Papa's name meant something, Mr. Davies. Something honorable. I just want a chance to avoid replacing that with a story of ruin. Please. Have mercy."

Davies looked away. Clearing his throat, he reached into his vest pocket and withdrew his watch.

Again, Laura leaned forward. "If you won't give me the examination, then issue a provisional license. For one trip only."

Still, Davies shook his head. "Even if I were willing to

do that," he said, "no one is going to trust you with valuable cargo."

"What if I were to be the apprentice—the cub—working with another pilot?" When Davies couldn't seem to come up with a protest to that, she added, "You said you respected my father. You know he would want you to say yes."

Davies twisted the mustache again. And again. Finally, he took a deep breath and said, "All right. *If* you can find a licensed pilot who will work with you—and *if* you can find cargo—*if* you conclude another successful trip—then I'll consider giving you the examination." He paused. "But it has to be a real trip. Not some lightly loaded, skim-the-surface trial run."

"I understand," Laura said. "Thank you." Finally, she stood up.

Davies waddled next to her all the way to the front door and made a show of getting out his keys so he could lock up as soon as she was outside.

As she headed back to the river, desperation returned. She still had to find a licensed pilot willing to take on a female cub. All the way home she argued with herself, always circling back to the same answer. The only person who would entertain such a notion would have to be as desperate as she. And the only person she knew who might be that desperate for work on the river was a rude, bombastic, rabble-rousing rapscallion who could navigate only on crutches.

Chapter 12

Sometime in the middle of the night that would usher in Tuesday morning, Logjam sighed, uncurled himself from his place at the foot of Laura's bed, and dropped to the floor with a thud. Laura slid to the edge of the bed and peered down at him. "I'm sorry," she muttered. "I can't sleep." The dog gave a low grunt and curled up on the rag rug.

At the first light of dawn, Laura rose and, with the dog at her side, began to pace the hurricane deck. She was making the third or fourth circuit when Bird stepped out of the galley and thrust a cup of coffee into her hands. "Land sakes, child," she said. "You keep going, you'll have walked to Fort Benton and back before we ever shove off."

Laura took a sip of coffee.

Bird's voice gentled. "It's gonna work itself out," she said. "You already got good news last night, what with Mr. Meeks getting a line on freight and that young couple booking passage. Once the crew tastes our food today, they'll be begging to sign on for another trip. You'll see. It's all good news from here on, miss."

Laura sighed. "I hope you're right, because we need a lot more good news if this is going to work at all."

"Well, now," Bird said, "ain't that just the way? It don't all happen at the same time. God shines a little light and we step

into it. Then He shines a little more. We just got to keep looking at the light and ignoring the darkness all around."

Darkness all around. That part, at least, Laura understood.

Bird headed back to the galley, but she hesitated in the
doorway. "If it's any help at all to know it, Hercules and me—
Ruby, too—been prayin' for you."

Mama's prayers were one of the things Laura missed
most. Mama prayed about everything, and just hearing those
prayers had always seemed to make things better—whether
circumstances actually changed or not. A sudden rush of
longing for Mama brought a flood of tears.

"Didn't mean to make you cry," Bird said, her voice gentle.

"I wish I could hear Mama pray again."

"I know, child. I know." Bird retreated into the galley.

Laura stood at the railing, watching as the sun rose above
the tangle of trees and undergrowth on the eastern shore of
the river. Behind her in the galley, Bird began to hum as she
worked. The melody was unfamiliar. Still, the mellow sound
soothed Laura's nerves. As the sun climbed above the tree
line, she got more coffee. Then she headed back to her cabin
to dress for the day.

❋

Playacting for the likes of middle-aged, overweight Inspector Davies was one thing. Men like Finn MacKnight were
another channel of a very different river.

When he and Joe were boys, MacKnight had mostly
ignored Laura—with the exception of an occasional yank on
her braids as the two chased by on board whatever steamboat
Papa happened to be piloting at the moment. Whenever the
family was in St. Louis, Joe and Finn found each other—most
often, as Laura remembered it, for the purpose of creating
havoc.

As they grew up, the two friends took on jobs together,

first as roustabouts and then as cub pilots. Harmless fun transitioned into darker, more dangerous things. Mama prayed harder, but it didn't seem to have any effect on either of the young men. At least not until Papa stepped in and kicked Finn MacKnight out of Joe's steamboating life.

From what little Laura had seen of MacKnight since Papa's death, he was still dark and dangerous-looking, his presence unsettling in ways Laura hadn't taken time to think about. Yet, here she was at the corner of Soulard and Eighth Streets, trying—and failing—to calm her nerves, wishing she were anywhere but here. She'd rather be evading a sawyer. Navigating rapids. Land sakes, she'd rather be grounded on a sandbar. Instead, here she was, about to ask Finn MacKnight to spend the next several weeks in her wheelhouse. About to beg, if that's what it took. The idea of being under the scrutiny of those dark eyes made her grind her teeth. Or shiver. Or something.

So much about MacKnight had long since been forgotten beneath a pall of excess and trouble. Except for one thing which was, at the moment, the most important thing: Laura could remember Papa regretting that someone with so much promise as a steamboat pilot cared more about his next drink than his natural talent. Hopefully, MacKnight hadn't washed all that natural talent away. Hopefully, he would agree to help her.

At least MacKnight had never tried anything like what Jack McCoy had attempted after he sauntered aboard this past Sunday. The memory would always make her skin crawl. *But MacKnight had had a woman waiting for him that night at the hotel.* Ah, yes. And if he tried anything like that on board the *Laura Rose*, Laura would give him a piece of her mind. Or maybe try Mama's trick of sewing the sheets up while he slept and—well. She wouldn't think about that. The very idea made her face burn with embarrassment. MacKnight would have to be on his best behavior. Surely that would be understood. Wouldn't it?

Maybe this was a bad idea. *Doesn't matter. It's the only idea you have that might work. So get moving.*

Taking a deep breath, Laura headed up the street, pausing again at the low, unpainted gate that opened onto a yard framed with flower beds. The house itself was surprising in its simplicity. She'd expected more—especially in light of Joe's apparent need to impress Adele with a big house. From the profusion of blooms inside the fence, Laura assumed Fiona liked to garden. She couldn't envision Adele ever kneeling in the dirt.

Taking a deep breath, Laura pressed her palm to her waist. She looked down and smoothed her pink silk skirt. Tucked an errant curl back up into the updo she'd spent an inordinate amount of time accomplishing this morning. Then, she glanced up at the bright blue April sky. *All right, Mama. Papa. Joe. Here I go.* And so she unlatched the gate and—there was Adele, opening the front door and calling a greeting.

"I wish to speak with Mr. MacKnight, if you please," Laura said.

Adele stepped out onto the porch. "I'm afraid he isn't here. He and Fiona had a meeting. Something to do with the family finances." She came down the steps and up the path to the gate. "They never include me in those things. I'm just a child, you know." Bitterness laced the words. Adele put her hand on the gate and motioned for Laura to step into the yard. "You're welcome to wait. They should be back before too much longer. I'll make us tea." She motioned Laura forward. "They'll be pleased to find you waiting. I think they were going to speak with you later today."

Finn and Fiona would be pleased to find her here? They'd planned to talk to her? Laura followed Adele into the house and took a seat in an overstuffed chair. Adele disappeared through the doorway that led into the kitchen.

As she sat looking about her, Laura thought once again that the house did not fit what she would have expected. It wasn't unpleasant, but it wasn't really cozy, either. Three finely worked samplers hung side by side on the far wall, each one boasting a pious poem or a verse of Scripture. Undoubtedly Fiona's handiwork.

"Here we are." Adele glided into the parlor and settled a tea tray on the low table in front of the sofa. "I hope you like Earl Grey," she said. "I should have asked. And do you take cream?"

"It smells wonderful and no, no cream." The two sat in silence for what felt like a very long moment. Laura apologized. "I'm sorry. I'm not very good at small talk."

Adele shrugged. "I am. But you didn't come to see me, and you don't have to talk if you don't want to." She took a sip of tea and then set down the cup. She put her hand to the locket about her neck. Finally, she took a deep breath and said, "Finn would help you, you know. If you asked the right way. Is that why you're here? To ask him? You can tell me it isn't any of my business. I don't suppose it is, really…except…I know you love the river and so did Joseph. We've all heard the rumors about your troubles. Joseph wouldn't want you to lose the *Laura Rose*. I'm young and silly and no one really pays me any mind, but—that's what I think. You shouldn't lose the *Laura Rose*.

"Finn would be your pilot. You just have to ask. He's proud. Fiona shouldn't have spoken for him that way the other day. It was embarrassing. What man wants a woman to do something like that? They have their pride, you know. Even men like Finn, who've had most of it shattered. There's still a remnant that needs to be preserved. Fiona meant well, but by barging in the way she did...She just shouldn't have done that."

Laura looked over at the girl, wordless.

Adele laughed. "I know that look: *Why don't you just be quiet?*" She got up. "I will be quiet and get us some ginger cakes. I'm fairly useless around the house, except for a recently discovered talent for baking."

Ginger cakes. Joe had loved ginger cakes.

❋

Finn MacKnight was still wrangling his way down from the buggy when Laura hurried out of the house and down off the porch to greet him and his sister.

"How lovely you look," Fiona said.

"Thank you. I—um. I hope you'll excuse me, but I was hoping to speak with Mr. MacKnight for a few moments." She didn't say the word *alone*, but Fiona got the meaning. With a prim smile, she said something about gardening and that she would be out back if they wished for tea and light refreshment.

"Thank you," Laura said, "but Adele was kind enough to make tea while I waited."

Fiona looked surprised. With a nod, she walked up the path that led to the back of the house.

MacKnight shifted his weight on his crutches and suggested they proceed to the narrow front porch.

"If you don't mind," Laura said, mindful of Adele possibly eavesdropping from just inside the front door, "I'd rather this be a private conversation."

MacKnight shrugged and stayed put. "As you wish."

She forced herself to look up into those dark eyes. "You were upset when your sister suggested it this past Sunday afternoon, and to be quite frank, I wasn't really open to the idea myself, but things have changed and I need"—she gulped—"I need help."

"What kind of help?"

"I've convinced Inspector Davies to give me a chance to get a pilot's license."

His jaw dropped. "How on earth did you manage that?"

"I reasoned. I begged. In the end, I appealed to his sense of gallantry."

"I didn't know he had one."

"It took a while to find it," Laura said. "Even then, he had a long list of conditions. First, a provisional license for one trip only—*if* I work under a currently licensed pilot. He said he would consider giving me the examination *if* the licensed pilot recommends it, but only after the *Laura Rose* returns from a fully loaded trip to Fort Benton and back. He was very clear about that last part—no skim-the-water, lightly loaded trial, he said."

MacKnight said nothing. Just...waited.

"I'm asking if you'd be the pilot," she said. Something flashed in the dark eyes, and she looked away, hurrying to add, "Just for this one trip. That's all. And then if you'd recommend me to Inspector Davies."

"If you do a good job," he said.

She looked back up at him. What did that smile mean? Was he teasing her or smirking? She nodded. "Of course."

"I've seen a few handbills announcing the departure of the *Laura Rose* next Monday. Does that mean you've assumed I'll say yes?"

"I haven't assumed anything," Laura said. "You know things like that have to be announced in advance. People need time to book passage. Freighters need to see that we're still in business."

"I'm not criticizing you, Miss White. I'm giving you credit for bluster."

"Bluster?"

He nodded. "Yes, ma'am. Bluster. A very effective business tactic. If you're in trouble, act as though you aren't. Show everyone it's business as usual, and very often you can convince people it's true." He paused. "Is it working?"

"Tom Meeks has already gotten several small shipments committed to us," she said. "Passengers are making inquiries." Only two, but MacKnight didn't need to hear that, did he?

"And the crew," he said. "What about that?"

"It's being handled."

"Really? How?"

Why was he asking so many questions? She was offering work. Didn't he need work? "You haven't answered my question about being second pilot. Will you do it?"

"It's *second* pilot, is it?"

Yes, it was. She might only have a provisional license, but she would be first pilot of her own steamboat, and he needed to accept that or—

"Have you considered the fact that if you take me on, you're inviting an ever-present reminder of the bad luck that seems to be hovering over and around the *Laura Rose* these days? A lot of men down on that levee think my accident was just more proof of the bad luck stalking your packet. They were saying the *Laura Rose* was cursed before you left for Fort Rice, and the recent troubles have just fueled that fire."

Laura gave a soft snort. "I don't believe in luck or curses or anything like that. It's superstitious nonsense."

"What you and I believe doesn't matter, if it keeps you from getting a good crew." He paused. "Besides, from what I've heard, you have bigger problems than that facing you: bank loans and second mortgages and debt. None of *that* is superstitious nonsense."

He was flinging words at her. Did he think she wouldn't be able to pay him? Was he defending why he was going to refuse her? Why didn't he just say it? Say no and be done with it. "Stop," she said. She even took a step back. "I didn't come here so that you could lecture me on the inevitability of my failing." Why had she ever thought that someone as self-centered as Finn MacKnight would help her? He wasn't desperate. He was just as arrogant as he'd always been. She looked toward the river. "I'm sorry I bothered you. I thought—maybe—but obviously, I was wrong." She turned to go.

"Wait."

She kept walking, fighting back tears. She would not cry until she had rounded that corner up ahead. He must not see her cry.

He called louder. "Miss White. Please."

Something behind her hit the ground. MacKnight cursed, and when Laura turned back around, he'd dropped a crutch. Whatever he'd done after that, he'd hurt himself. His face was a mask of pain as he retrieved the crutch and tucked it back in place beneath his arm before hobbling after her.

Laura swiped at her tears. "Are you all right?"

"Hardly," he said beneath clenched teeth. He nodded toward the house. "Please don't run off. Walk to the porch so I can sit down." When she hesitated, he softened his voice. "Please. Just—let's talk."

Taking a deep breath, Laura retraced her steps, opened the gate, and led the way up to the porch. MacKnight sank onto the stairs with a sigh of relief. Setting the crutches aside, he lifted his bad leg to plant his foot. For the first time, Laura looked at it. The awkward angle—how did he manage to walk at all, even with crutches? She said quietly, "I'm sorry. I didn't mean...I just...I didn't think."

"Don't do that." He practically growled at her.

"Do what?"

"We were having a perfectly acceptable argument, and you decided to storm off. I tried to chase after you. And now you're trying to mother me. My leg hurts. It always hurts. It makes me...short-tempered sometimes. That's no reason to give in and run off."

"I did not give in," Laura replied. "We were at an impasse. Then, instead of saying a simple no, you felt compelled to list all the reasons I am going to fail." She glowered at him. "Don't you think I know how impossible it all seems? I can hardly sleep for thinking of all the reasons I'm going to fail." Her voice wavered. She broke off.

"I was *not* predicting failure," MacKnight said. "I wanted you to *think*."

Laura looked over at him. "Oh, I see. You weren't yelling. You were *helping* me."

He rolled his eyes. "You're a very clever girl, Miss White. Actually quite spectacular in some ways. Refusing to bow to Danvers's pressure. Facing Phineas Davies—alone—and talking him into something he undoubtedly considers outlandish. Asking Hughes to go back to the bank when you've improved your situation. Yes, I know about that. Fiona and I ran into Hughes this morning." He paused. "Now don't get angry about that. Fiona and Ambrose Hughes are old friends. He didn't give away any confidential information. The subject came up and Hughes was very complimentary when Fiona expressed concern for you." He smiled. "Actually, he showered you with lavish praise."

"He's been very kind," Laura said. "If Mr. Hughes's goodwill could solve my problems...But of course it can't."

"Exactly," MacKnight said. "So back to what I was trying to do. As I said, you're a very clever girl, but you haven't really been in the steamboat *business*. Boatmen's is going to ask some very pointed questions when you and your Mr. Hughes make another try at getting an extension. If you don't have some very good answers to those questions, they will not hesitate to say—in a gentlemanly way that fairly bleeds kindness, since you are a lovely young lady—that there is no possible way to grant you an extension."

"But why wouldn't they do it? I've proven I can do the job. If Tom continues to have success, we'll be fully loaded when it comes to freight, probably by late Thursday. The couple who booked passage yesterday were very complimentary about the cabins. They promised to recommend us to everyone they know." She told him about the noon banquet today. "Bird seemed confident that good cooking will get us a crew. So I repeat, why wouldn't they give me a chance? What do they have to lose?"

When MacKnight remained silent, the obvious answer niggled. *Twelve thousand five hundred dollars*: the full amount of the loan she wasn't going to be able to pay back because she had to pay Danvers's clients. In less than forty-eight hours. "Never mind," she said, her voice miserable. "I know the answer to the question."

"Well of course you do," MacKnight said. "The answer to that question is obvious. The thing is, you're answering the wrong question."

She frowned. Wasn't it the only question that mattered?

"The question you need to be prepared to answer when you meet with Boatmen's is this: What do they have to *gain* by extending your loan?" When Laura didn't reply, he continued, "Bankers don't deal in hope, Miss White. They deal in reality. Oh, they take risks all the time, but they're very careful to make sure that risk is minimized. If they weren't good at that, they wouldn't stay in business for long. So, if they stick to the original terms your father agreed upon—"

"They'll get their money, but I'll be forced to sell the *Laura Rose* to get it." And what if she couldn't find a buyer willing to pay the full value? She might end up still being in debt to Danvers. Could things get any worse? Her throat went dry. She clasped her hands to keep them from trembling.

MacKnight was still talking. "If they extend, they're taking on a substantial amount of new risk."

"Because of me," Laura said.

"Well, yes, but it's about a lot more than a mostly untried pilot, so don't take it as a personal affront, because it isn't meant that way. It's business, pure and simple. After all, the term 'steamboat graveyard' isn't just a colorful phrase. It's the reality of upper Missouri River trade."

Laura clenched her fists. "But I can *do* it," she insisted, then looked at him. "All right. I need your help. I need a good crew. I need freight and passengers. But there has to be some way to convince them to let me try." She rose from the steps where she'd been sitting. "There *is* a way. And I'm going to find it."

MacKnight smiled. "Good." Then he added, "Three hundred a month."

"Wh-what?"

"My salary. Three hundred a month. It's a fair number."

"It's more than fair," Laura said. "It's a bargain."

"Well, I'm not." He patted his injured leg.

"You'll get stronger."

"And likely ask for a raise."

"Fair enough," Laura said. She hesitated. "If you're so convinced that I'm likely to fail at the steamboating business, why are you willing to take the job?"

He shrugged. "First reason: Joe was my friend—sometimes my only friend. Your father was my friend, too, although I didn't always believe that." He paused. "Second reason: If I were gone and Fiona and Adele were in danger of losing everything, neither of the Captain Whites would stand by and let it happen. Not if it was in their power to help them."

"Be careful, Mr. MacKnight," Laura said. "You'll be accused of gallantry."

Something flickered in his dark eyes, and he looked away

from her, toward the river. "I'm not being gallant. I love being on that river. It's challenging and maddening and invigorating and heartbreaking, and besting it gives a man a sense of accomplishment like nothing else I've ever known. I want that life back, and quite frankly, you may be the only chance I'll ever have to reclaim it." He looked at her. "It's business, Miss White. You need a man with a license, and I'm willing to share the wheelhouse with a female if that's what it takes to get another chance at the only life I want."

Laura nodded. "Then…thank you." After a moment she added, "I need something else. Would you be willing to accompany me to Mr. Davies's office so he'll have proof that I've met his conditions? I want him to put what he agreed to in writing." She smiled at him. "It's only good business."

MacKnight laughed. "I can't wait to see the look on his face."

Chapter 13

"But Mr. Davies, less than twenty-four hours ago you sat right there in that chair and said that if I could find a licensed pilot—"

"I know what I said, Miss White." Davies cast a scowl in Finn MacKnight's direction, which MacKnight returned with equanimity. "Had I known you would enter into an agreement with—" He broke off. Looked back at Laura. "This will not do, Miss White. It simply will not do. I have the deepest respect for the memory of your father. I believe you mentioned his legacy yesterday when you were making your case for our little arrangement."

"Yes, and you and I had an agreement," Laura said.

"And we still do. If you can find a proper pilot willing to work with you." Davies took a deep breath. Again, he fiddled with the waxed tip of his mustache. "It is in the name of your father's legacy that I'm acting right now. I already had my doubts about sending an unchaperoned female upriver with a crew full of men. Now"—he glanced over at MacKnight, then back at Laura—"I do not mean to be indelicate, but really, my dear. Reputations have been permanently ruined on much less than this."

"But yesterday—"

MacKnight interrupted, "Yesterday, you weren't planning

on hiring me. Isn't that the real objection, Inspector? It's not Miss White's reputation that concerns you. It's mine. I'm not a 'proper pilot.'"

Davies harrumphed something unintelligible. Again, Laura thought of the unknown someone who'd been waiting for MacKnight in the hotel lobby that night when he carried Joe home.

MacKnight posed a question: "What if she has a chaperone? Someone so completely above reproach that no one would so much as raise one hair of one eyebrow at our working together?"

"Well...I suppose...if I knew Miss White had someone looking out for her..."

MacKnight reached for his crutches. "Then we'll get someone to look out for her. In the meantime—I believe you were going to write something out for Miss White."

With another harrumph, Davies reached for his pen.

"On the official letterhead, if you please," Laura said.

Davies opened a desk drawer. Withdrawing an official-looking piece of paper, he began to scrawl out the terms of what he'd promised. *Licensed pilot. Approved chaperone. Successful delivery of a full load of freight to destinations along the Missouri River, including Fort Benton, Montana. Pilot's examination upon return.* When he'd finished writing, he handed it to Laura. "Does that meet with your approval?"

Forcing herself to sound as sweet as she could, Laura handed it back. "Would you add an addendum that agrees to offer the examination within a week of my return, please?" MacKnight snorted. When Laura looked over at him, he was covering his mouth with his hand, feigning a cough. But she could see the amusement in his eyes.

Davies snatched the paper back, added the addendum, then signed it with a flourish.

"I'll have my clerk make a copy," he said. "When you return

with news of a chaperone, all will be ready for your signature." He scowled at her. "Unless, of course, you have another addendum you'd like added? Tea and crumpets served mid-examination, perhaps?"

"Oh, no, sir," Laura said, as she rose from her chair. "It's all very satisfactory. I've never cared for tea and crumpets, anyway." She held her dignity until they'd gone outside. As soon as she stepped onto the sidewalk, though, she let loose a string of near-epithets. "Of all the underhanded, backstabbing, holier-than-thou, self-righteous—a chaperone! What's he going to demand next?" Her frustration spent, Laura looked up at MacKnight, who seemed to be waiting to help her up to the buggy seat. "I can manage," she said and proceeded to prove it.

"Suit yourself." MacKnight made his way to the hitching post. Reins in hand, he slid the crutches under the buggy seat and powered his way into place without the use of his right leg.

He'd barely settled next to her when Laura said, "I assume you've got an idea in regards to a chaperone."

He nodded. "It just so happens I know an upstanding woman who would do just about anything to get my sorry carcass back on a steamboat."

Laura smiled. What was it Mama had said about Miss Fiona MacKnight? A fine Christian woman. Just a bit...frozen in time. Probably the perfect chaperone. "Will she do it?"

"Let's find out."

❀

"Of course I'll do it," Miss MacKnight said.

Laura had barely had time to sit down on one of the porch chairs. Finn MacKnight hadn't had time to finish making the request. "Just like that?" Laura asked. "Don't you have any questions? Conditions?"

"Well, no, Miss White, not 'just like that,'" Fiona said, with a tinge of annoyance. "I cannot simply close up the house and walk away from my life."

"Of course not. I hope it won't inconvenience you too much."

"Inconvenience? Me? Why, no. Not at all." Miss MacKnight seemed to consider for a moment before saying, "I will miss several weeks of church activities. And I won't be able to care for the garden. And then there is the little matter of my being terrified of deep water. But no. It's no inconvenience at all. I'm certain the journey to Fort Benton will prove to be a trouble-free respite from the drudgery of my boring life."

Feeling cowed by the woman, Laura glanced over at MacKnight, only to realize that he was trying—unsuccessfully—not to smile. "I—um—I don't really know what to say."

"'Thank you' would be nice to hear," Miss MacKnight said.

Laura gulped. "Thank you. Sincerely."

MacKnight brought up the subject of what to do about Adele.

"Well, she'll be coming, too, of course," Fiona said firmly. Then she scowled at Laura. "Did you have some objection to that?"

Laura shook her head. "N-no. Of course not. I—we didn't even discuss it."

Fiona's tone was scolding when she spoke to MacKnight. "Dear brother, this is no time for us to be shirking our duty in regards to Adele." She glanced behind her into the house, then leaned forward and lowered her voice. "I don't know what the matter is, but Martin Lawrence pointedly spurned her this past Sunday. In fact, something has put her on the outs with her entire circle of young friends. I just don't know—"

At that moment, Adele called for someone to hold open the door so she could bring out the tea tray she'd prepared while everyone else talked. As she settled it atop the wheeled wicker cart at the edge of the porch, she looked around. "Well, I can see that serious things have been talked about out here." She smiled at Laura. "I do apologize, Miss White, but it's ginger cakes again."

⚙

Laura sat alone in the drafty hall while, just on the other side of a massive cherrywood door, her fate was being decided. She was doing her best to heed Bird's advice and just take steps into spots of light as they appeared. Finn MacKnight said he would be second pilot, and she stepped forward. His sister agreed to chaperone and she took another step forward. The Perrins and Bird's sister, Ruby, cooked a feast that was, as Bird had predicted, the talk of the levee. Almost the entire crew from the first trip upriver had signed back on. Another step forward. And now—whatever was going on in that room could blot out all those spots of light and pull the curtain down on her life aboard the *Laura Rose* once and for all.

Shivering, Laura rose and headed down the vast hall toward a window. She stood there for what felt like half a lifetime, going over what she'd said just now to the men who held her life on the river in their hands. *Don't dodge the facts,* Finn MacKnight had said more than once when they discussed the meeting the night before. *You aren't some dim-witted, beautiful woman hoping against hope that some kind gentlemen will do you a favor. You know what you're asking them to do, and you know why they should say no. If you start with that, you have a chance of disarming them. And then, once they're disarmed, you tell them you can do it. You convince them.*

She remembered his reaching over to tap her on the forearm. "Remember when you balled up your fists and said 'I can do this'? That's what they need to see. Just flat-out, no-apologies-offered confidence. They aren't accustomed to seeing that in a woman. It's going to surprise them. That's when you might take a side step and appeal to your father's memory and wanting to preserve his legacy."

"You sound convinced that it'll work," Laura said.

MacKnight shook his head. "I have no idea if it'll work. They'll still have plenty of reasons to say no." He'd paused. "Of which I am one."

"You're also one of the reasons I have something new to tell them," Laura said.

"Well, there you have it. Finn MacKnight, liability and asset, all wrapped up in one damaged package." He held up his hand. "Don't. I know. I'll get stronger."

Laura had nodded. As Finn departed, Laura called Logjam to her side and retired. Tossed and turned her way through yet another night. And now, here she was, alone at a window, staring down at a patch of green with a knot in her midsection the size of Texas. *Help. Please help.*

The sound of the door at the far end of the hallway opening and then closing echoed. She whirled about to see Mr. Hughes headed her way...with a *smile* on his face. He was *smiling*. "Well done, Miss White, well done. Your father would be proud."

She closed her eyes. Took a deep breath. Another. Swallowed. Fished a lace-edged handkerchief out of her black silk bag and dabbed at the tears of relief. "Thank you," she said. "Oh...thank you."

"Don't thank me," Mr. Hughes said. "I was only the conduit. You're the one who convinced them." He patted her shoulder. "And now I must get you home to the *Laura Rose*. I'll bring the documents for your signature as soon as they're ready. They'll be drawing up the new loan with the *Laura Rose* as collateral. You'll be able to repay part of it as soon as the house sells. It's a good property, so it shouldn't take too long. And the bank's terms are much more manageable when it comes to the matter of interest." He paused. "Shall I contact

Mr. Danvers to meet us in the dining saloon? I hope you don't mind, but I really would like to be there when you hand him the check that satisfies his group of...ahem...investors."

"I'd love to have you there," Laura said. All the way back to the river, her mind sang with the words Mr. Hughes had just spoken. *Home* to the Laura Rose. She smiled to herself. *Home.*

❋

Laura waited at the end of the gangplank, watching as Wilson Danvers strode purposefully across the levee toward the *Laura Rose*. As he made his way up the gangplank, she made a point of pulling Papa's pocket watch out of her pocket and checking the time. "You're a bit early, Mr. Danvers."

"I believe the language on the documents was quite clear," Danvers said, staring toward the far end of the deck and the freight the crew had loaded this morning.

"Quite," Laura said. "You gave me forty-eight hours from the moment of delivery. Mr. Hughes will verify that that was at 3:50 p.m. day before yesterday." She looked once more at Papa's watch. "I still have fifteen minutes. Mr. Hughes will be joining us any minute. Shall we ascend to the dining saloon? I've a bottle of ink and two pens waiting." Laura turned and led the way up the stairs to the hurricane deck, past several cabins—and passengers. As she passed one young couple, the husband stepped up.

"Excuse me, ma'am, but the clerk said the departure's been delayed?"

"We did think it might be necessary. Now I'm not so sure. I hope you'll stick with us."

The young man nodded. "Oh, we're staying." He smiled down at his wife. "Daisy says these are the nicest cabins she's ever been booked into."

Laura smiled at the young woman, who looked hardly old

enough to be courting, let alone married. "Thank you," she said.

"Blue's my favorite color, and I never expected lace-trimmed curtains and monogrammed linens."

"My mama insisted," Laura said, then winked at the girl. "Papa put up a fuss, but Mama won."

The young wife said something about thanking Mama.

"My parents have both graduated to heaven," Laura said, "but I do appreciate your kind words." She excused herself and headed toward the prow, where Danvers was waiting at the railing with a scowl on his face.

"Now, see here, Miss White," he said. "It doesn't appear to me that you've taken that notice seriously."

"That notice," Laura retorted, "is the reason I haven't slept this week." Just then she caught a glimpse of her lawyer. "And here's Mr. Hughes."

Moments later, Laura and the two men were seated at a table in the dining saloon. Mr. Hughes went over the document threatening legal action in painstaking detail. "Now, I just want to be certain that we all understand what's happening here," he said. "This document"—he held up two sheets of paper—"represents real estate purchased by Joseph Hudson White, for which he took out a second mortgage against the steamboat *Laura Rose*, registry number 1015A, with the United Stated Department of Commerce and Labor." Hughes read the property's legal description aloud. Then he looked at Laura. "You understand that everything in regards to this transaction is in order and perfectly legal."

Laura nodded.

"Now, this document"—Hughes laid another atop the pile—"exercises Mr. Danvers's clients' right to call in that mortgage. Which they have legally done, demanding payment in full within forty-eight hours of—" Mr. Hughes hesitated. He looked for a notation at the bottom of the document. "Ah, here it is: 3:50 p.m. on Monday, April 29, in the year of our Lord 1867." Hughes peered at Laura over his spectacles. "And you agree that this was fully explained to you, my dear?"

Again, Laura nodded.

"Well then." Mr. Hughes made a show of lining the papers up and handing them to Danvers. "You, Danvers, are legally entitled to accept payment in full or the title to the *Laura Rose*. At... um..." He looked at his watch. "This very moment, I believe."

Danvers nodded. He turned to Laura. "I wouldn't be a gentleman if I didn't offer you my sympathies, Miss White. I hope you understand that it's nothing personal."

"Of course not," Laura said. "It's just business." With a sigh, she pulled a banknote out of her pocket and handed it to Danvers.

"Now," Mr. Hughes said as he produced yet another document, "if you'll just sign here, Danvers. This verifies that the debt has been settled and that all properties represented in the recent—um—*arrangement* are now in the sole possession of Miss Laura White and the Boatman's Bank of St. Louis, Missouri." He laid the document before Danvers and, with a flourish, offered a pen.

Danvers blinked. Looked down at the banknote. Compared the amount to the amount on the document.

"Yes, yes," Hughes said. "It's a tidy profit you and your cohorts have made, isn't it? I suppose there is profit to be made terrorizing orphans and widows in their time of need. Until, of course, the Almighty takes notice. As I recall, He has a special fondness for orphans and widows."

Danvers looked over at Laura. The hatred in the man's eyes sent a chill through her. She reached down to put her palm atop Logjam's head. The dog rose to his feet. A barely audible rumble sounded deep in his chest. "I believe that concludes our business, Mr. Danvers," she said. "Please do me the honor of never setting foot on my packet again."

After Danvers had marched away, Laura sank back with a low laugh. "I suppose it's sinful to admit it, but that really was tremendously satisfying." She smiled at Mr. Hughes as she held out her hand. "And you have something more for me to sign. Can I offer you a sherry by way of celebration?"

Moments later, Laura sat reading through the papers that granted her an extension on her obligation to the Boatmen's Bank.

"It's a fair interest rate," Mr. Hughes said, "although of course it would be lower if you were in a better position to bargain. You're very fortunate that they were able to arrange for the freight insurance." He paused. "I will admit to having been worried about that."

Laura had been worried about it, too. She hadn't had any answers to that problem when Finn MacKnight mentioned it yesterday afternoon. A fully loaded steamboat the size of the *Laura Rose* could be worth nearly $100,000. The very nature of the Missouri River presented a dire threat to both, and risk was minimized by a complex set of business practices that could have been the final blow that destroyed Laura's dream. But that obstacle was out of the way, now, too. As far as Laura was concerned, Mr. Hughes—with the help of the bank, of course—had worked a minor miracle.

"I do wish I'd been able to get them to extend for another month past what's on this document," Mr. Hughes said, "but they would not budge on the matter."

Laura had already taken up the pen to sign her name to the note. She looked down at the date that seemed to have Mr. Hughes worried. *July 8.* She swallowed. "But—it's easily seventy days to Fort Benton and back. Th-this only gives me sixty-some from today. And we aren't fully loaded yet. We aren't going to be able to leave until Sunday at the earliest."

"Please don't look for trouble, my dear," Mr. Hughes said. "Do your part, and trust that the good Lord will do His." Mr. Hughes glanced toward the heavens. "You have quite a group of supporters up there now, you know. And the river has been known to be kind on occasion. It isn't always disaster and mayhem."

Laura nodded. He was right. She shouldn't let worry steal the joy of this moment. "I'm sorry," she said. "After all you've done for me, I don't mean to sound ungrateful." She signed the new contract.

As he prepared to leave, Mr. Hughes reached over and took Laura's hand. "And now, my dear, please indulge an old man." Very quickly, he bussed her cheek. "Godspeed, my dear. Godspeed."

❁

Glimmers of happiness and excitement began to pierce the sadness and gloom that had been hovering over every moment of Laura's life in recent weeks. More freight arrived by the hour, and more men than they needed applied for work. The passenger cabins continued to fill. When Laura expressed surprise at that, MacKnight said it was because gossip had made the *Laura Rose* famous—or infamous, depending on one's perspective.

"It's the human condition," he said. "Everyone loves a front-row seat to a triumph, but they love the same seat at a tragedy even more. Whether you succeed or fail, the *Laura Rose* and 'the skirt in the wheelhouse' are bound to be part of steamboating history. Everyone will want to say they were there, they knew this, they saw that with their own eyes. Why, I wouldn't be surprised if you and your *Laura Rose* are the subject of a column or two in tomorrow's newspaper."

On Saturday, Hercules and Bird came to talk with Laura with a shy boy in tow. "Tyree's been having a hard time of it," Bird explained. "His mama doesn't pay him any mind at all. The older he gets, the harder it is for him." She leaned close and murmured, "She's my sister, but she's nothing like me and Ruby. She always got men comin' 'round. Tyree's a good boy. Works hard at whatever we ask him to do."

Laura looked toward the boy and Hercules, standing near the prow and talking to Elijah North. While she watched, Logjam sidled up to the gangly boy and licked the back of his hand. Tyree crouched down and threw his arms about the dog's neck. "How old is he?"

"Nine."

"Only nine?"

"Yes, ma'am. He's tall for his age. Sharp as a needle. He won't be any trouble. I already made him his own little bed-roll. He won't take up much room."

Laura held up her hand. "Stop, Bird. I'm not hesitating because I need to be convinced. Of course he's coming with us. I just can't quite decide how to keep him busy. I don't remember much about Joe when he was nine, but I do remember stories."

Bird chuckled. "Oh, yes, ma'am. A boy needs to be kept busy, or he'll find trouble. And you and I both know there is plenty of trouble to be found on this river."

"Do you think he'd be all right with cabin boy duties? Nearly all the passenger cabins have been booked. That's a lot for Minnie to handle alone. Don't tell her I said this, but she's not getting any younger." Minnie Maloney, wife to one of the engineers, had worked as a chambermaid on every steamboat Papa had piloted for as long as Laura could remember. "Of course he'll have to put up with Minnie's bad habits. Do you think he can manage?"

Bird laughed. "I'll just tell him he has to endure, ma'am."

Chapter 14

Sausage. What an abominable odor. Adele pulled the blankets up over her head, trying to mitigate the smell. Her stomach roiled. Finally, she dropped to the floor and heaved into the chamber pot until there was nothing left in her stomach. What she wouldn't give for a cup of mint tea right now.

She sat on the floor, leaning against the bed, her skin clammy, her hands trembling. Could there possibly be a worse day to be sick? Deckhands would be arriving soon to transfer Adele and Fiona's trunks to the *Laura Rose*. Finn had already moved on board. All that remained was for Adele and Fiona to lock the house—they were leaving the key on a nail out in the barn for the couple who would tend things while they were gone—and walk to the levee.

Adele could not wait to go. She'd wanted to shout with joy when she set that tea tray down on the front porch and Fiona told her the news. Had literally counted the hours until she could be free of this house. And now...now if she didn't collect herself, everything would be ruined. Why, oh why, did she have to feel sick today?

Sausage. That had to be it. Fiona's dad-blamed insistence on using up every little bit of every single thing in the larder. Heaven forbid they "let something go to waste." It wasn't as if the house was going to be empty. Jessamine Powell had found a couple who were thrilled to keep watch over things in return for free housing. They'd even agreed to Fiona's very detailed instructions regarding the garden and sharing its produce with the various families whose names Fiona left on the list tacked to the board in the kitchen. In recent days, she'd added notes about how to trim the roses and where to bury the garbage in the garden and how to forward the mail and— goodness. Fiona had practically written a book. It would be a miracle if the tenants didn't take one look at all those notes and run screaming the other way. But by the time that happened, the *Laura Rose* would be gone from St. Louis. How far away would they be by the time the tenants arrived tomorrow? *Far away*. What wonderful words. *Far away*.

There. Maybe she was going to be all right. But the minute Adele stood up, the nausea returned. She felt dizzy. Crawling back into bed, she lay quietly, taking deep breaths, trying to regain control.

"Breakfast!" Fiona rapped on the door, then opened it. "You cannot still be abed, Adele Yvette. It'll be time to go soon."

"I'm not hungry, and I'm already packed. I'll be ready when it's time to go."

"You look pale. I do hope you're not coming down with something."

"Don't worry," Adele said. "I won't ruin Finn's chance. I'll be ready. Just—leave me be for a few more minutes. And if you have time, a cup of mint tea would be so nice."

Frowning, Fiona came into the room. She looked down at the chamber pot and rolled her eyes. "You're sick. I knew it. I just knew this would happen. I told you not to go to that cotillion last night. I knew you'd take a chill in that damp night air. Who knows what ill humors you've encountered?"

Ill humors, indeed. If Fiona had any idea regarding the "ill humors" Adele had encountered last night, she wouldn't have slept a wink. "I wanted to say good-bye to my friends." Technically, that was a lie. Adele didn't have much use for the young people Fiona approved of. Loving Joseph had set her apart from them all. They seemed so childish, now that she had been in love with a real man. Why, the girls she knew had probably never even been kissed. And as for the boys, they were just that: boys—and not one set of broad shoulders in the whole lot. Not one pair of hands that—thinking of Joseph's hands caressing her neck still made Adele blush. She hunkered farther beneath the covers.

When it came right down to it, saying good-bye had been more about gloating about the new adventure than anything else. She had expected to see jealousy when she just happened to mention that she and Fiona had been given the captain's apartment on board the *Laura Rose*.

It wasn't really an *apartment*, and Adele knew that, but it was the largest cabin on board, and Adele had seen it. Had even—almost—slept there. It boasted gorgeous furniture and a rug all the way from Persia and velvet draperies and a sitting area. It was finer than anything Adele had ever been allowed to have. She was actually looking forward to seeing penurious Fiona's discomfort at all that opulence.

Of course Adele hadn't said any of that to her "friends." Just as she hadn't let Fiona know that saying good-bye wasn't really the point of going to the cotillion. Adele had learned long ago that if she expected to get things to go her way, she had better learn to speak Fiona's language.

As it turned out, the cotillion hadn't been all that enjoyable. In fact, she'd left early when it became obvious that she wasn't going to be the belle of the ball. Not one single boy asked her to dance. And then she'd heard Lucy Powell snicker something about Martin Lawrence's saying something about Adele's unusual fondness for a certain steamboat captain. Reality struck. Martin Lawrence had been wagging his tongue. The jealous cad. Of course he couldn't know the complete truth about her and Joseph, but whatever he'd said must have been sensational.

Adele's cheeks had flamed as she'd drawn her shawl about her shoulders and slipped out the door. The final indignity came when she was hurrying home by way of the garden where she and Joe had kissed—and that was all that had happened in that garden, one kiss. Whoever was dogging her, though, had the nerve to mention a "deflowering." Just loud enough that she could not pretend she hadn't heard.

Whirling about, Adele spoke into the darkness. "How dare you impugn the honor of a wonderful man? Only a coward would do such a thing under cover of darkness. And don't think I don't recognize your voice, Martin Lawrence. Shame on you."

Martin stepped into a pool of light created by one of the street lamps. "I'm not the one who should be ashamed," he said. His hands were clenched at his sides. "I guess I know why you never so much as looked at me after Joseph White came around, don't I? You could never convince me to take liberties like that."

As if she would ever want him to. "I don't know what you think you know. Whatever it is—"

Martin interrupted her, his voice wavering with fury as he spoke. "People like Miss *Fiona* MacKnight, so they won't say anything. They wouldn't want to hurt her. But you can stop putting on airs, 'cause folks know the truth about you, little Miss High-and-Mighty. It's not likely *you'll* be snagging any rich husbands in these parts. Leastways not one who likes *fresh* flowers, if you know what I mean."

"Leave me alone," Adele said. "I hope I never see you again. I hope I never hear your *name* again." Adele pushed by him. Her heart pounding, her cheeks blazing, she hurried home through the damp fog blanketing the city. She was vaguely aware of someone following her, but she didn't glance back.

Halfway home she began to shiver. It was just nerves, she told herself. Once home, she slid into bed fully clothed, buried her face in her pillow, and sobbed. What was she going to do now? People weren't jealous of her. They *hated* her. They were saying vile things. Things no one was supposed to know. But Joseph had loved her. He'd told her so. They were going to be married.

She finally stopped crying, but she felt no better. She changed into her nightgown, but she did not sleep. At some point in the still hours of early morning, in the swirl of sadness and fear and longing and aloneness, exhaustion and emotion combined to create a knot in her stomach that would not go away, no matter how deeply she breathed or how often she told herself that everything would work itself out. And now, just a few hours later, here was Fiona, leaning down to put the lid on the chamber pot, clucking like an irritated hen.

"I declare." Fiona put her hands on her hips. She heaved a deep sigh. "I suppose mint tea might help."

You would have thought Adele was asking for breakfast in bed. "Never mind," she muttered. "I'll get it myself." She slipped out of bed, but the minute she was upright the room began to spin.

"You'll do no such thing. You're as white as a ghost. Get back in bed." Fiona headed into the kitchen rattling and slamming dishes, clearly disapproving of illness interfering with her plans.

Finn called a greeting from the front door. His crutches thumped across the bare wood floor as he made his way into the kitchen. "That sausage smells wonderful," he said. "I know, I know. I didn't think I'd come back, either, but I thought of something—something I wanted to do. Had to come back this way, anyway, so I thought I'd just—what? Adele? Sick?" Thump-thump, he appeared in the doorway. "What's this I hear?"

"I'll be fine," Adele muttered.

"Yes, you will." Fiona brushed past Finn with a cup of what Adele hoped was mint tea.

"Thank you," Adele murmured and took a sip. Which her stomach sent right back up. And this time the chamber pot had the lid on. So...

Fiona ran for the mop.

"I'm so sorry," Adele said.

"Sorry won't get us on board the *Laura Rose* this morning, now will it?" Fiona looked over at Finn. "I told her not to go to that cotillion. Crowds like that, evil humors lingering everywhere, and then that blanket of fog. A damp night, and she walked home without an escort."

"Your blessed Martin Lawrence made sure I got home safe. He followed me all the way." What was one more twisting of the facts? Besides, it was true. In a way.

Fiona looked up from the mop. "Well, thank goodness for Martin," she said. "At least *he's* concerned about what people might say about a young lady who takes it upon herself to wander the streets alone."

Adele slid farther down into the bed. "I don't care what people say." It wasn't true, but she'd never admit it to Fiona, who would sit up for days and nights on end with Finn when he was injured but resented making a cup of mint tea for Adele.

"Hmph." Fiona mopped with a vengeance, then headed out of the room.

Finn came over to the bed. "I rode over here with a couple of roustabouts to load your trunks and take them down to the levee." He looked about. "One last look, as they say." He paused. And then he looked at Adele with a sad smile and said, "I miss Joe too, you know."

Adele's eyes filled with tears. He had no idea what missing Joe meant to her right now. She'd given him everything a girl could give a man. She'd thought she was going to be a steamboat captain's wife. And now she'd lost the dream and, if Martin Lawrence was right about what people were saying, all was lost. Fiona would find out. Smothering a sob, Adele let the tears flow freely.

Finn's voice was gentle as he said, "I think missing Joe is the main reason Miss White didn't want to take the captain's quarters this run." He paused, and a furrow appeared between his eyebrows as he cast a concerned look in Adele's direction. "I hadn't thought about it, but—will that be hard for you? Staying in what used to be Joe's cabin? Because if it will, I'll talk to Miss White and we'll make other arrangements. I don't think all the passenger cabins are reserved yet."

How strange to have one of her siblings actually think of her and her feelings. Adele hardly knew how to react to that. But in the matter of Joseph's cabin she shook her head. "I expect it'll be comforting. A little like still being near him." More tears flowed.

Finn reached out and patted her on the head. It was an awkward gesture. Almost as if she were a dog. Adele didn't remember his ever doing that before. It was nice not to be scolded. *Just think what he'd be saying if he knew the truth.* But maybe…maybe Finn would understand. He'd never pretended to be a paragon of virtue. Surely not everyone would react the way those simpering fools at the cotillion had behaved. She dared another sip of tea. It threatened to return but did not. With a sigh of relief, she closed her eyes. "I'll be fine. Don't worry."

"Oh, I'm not worried," Fiona said, walking briskly into the room. "You'll be ready to go if we have to strap you to a cot and carry you on board." She looked over at Finn. "It might not be a bad idea, though, if you could have those roustabouts come back in a couple of hours. In case she can't manage to walk to the levee. It's probably a minor stomach upset. She'll be good as new in a few days. Meantime, I'll just—"

"Fiona!" Tossing back the covers, Adele set the teacup on

her bedside table and forced herself to stand up beside the bed. "I am *not* some problem to be solved. I told you I'd be fine and I will. Just let me—"

"Don't be foolish," Fiona scolded, trying to wave her back into bed. "A stunt like that could make you faint. And that's just what we don't need—you falling and hitting your head and needing stitches or worse. Get back in bed. I've just rinsed the mop and I don't want to have to clear up any more messes."

Adele had had enough. Enough of being unwanted, of being treated like an inconvenience, of being sighed over and talked about as if she weren't even in the room. And now, with the rumors going about— Taking a deep breath, she almost shouted, "Get out!"

Fiona stared at her in surprise.

"You heard me. I'll take care of myself. I'll get dressed and be ready so that your precious schedule isn't ruined. If I puke I'll clean it up. Just—get out and leave me alone."

"I didn't mean—"

Finn had been standing in the doorway. He moved aside into the hall when Adele grasped Fiona by the shoulders and propelled her out of the room before she could even finish what she was saying. Next Adele slammed the door. Leaning against it, she willed herself to take deep breaths until the almost undeniable urge to vomit passed. Closing her eyes, she stood quietly, staring down at the floor, waiting.

When she'd stopped trembling, she crossed to her bed and sat on the edge to finish the mint tea. She took a deep breath. *All right, then.* She had to think. She and Joseph had done what they had done and that could not be changed. It might, however, change her future. What would Fiona do? Adele could not imagine.

She looked over at the wardrobe, and then around her at the stark little room she'd occupied since she was ten years old. How much of a loss was any of it? Truth be told, if she never again saw Martin Lawrence or Lucy Powell or their little clique of snobs—well. That wasn't frightening at all. It might even be a relief. Laura White was finding a new life, doing whatever it took to make it happen. Maybe it was time Adele MacKnight did the same thing. Maybe she should stop waiting for someone to rescue her and rescue herself.

Rising from her bed, she crossed her room and opened her wardrobe. Grabbing a pencil and a scrap of paper, she wrote a note.

> The clothing I have left in this wardrobe should be either cut into squares to be made into one of the Ladies' Aid quilts or added to the next barrel being shipped to our missionaries. I leave the final decision to my very capable half sister, Fiona.
>
> A. MacKnight
> May 4, 1867

At long last, she had thought of something that was sure to please Fiona. She would be able to contribute generously to her missions projects. Even better, she wouldn't have to put up with her half sister ever again.

Pinning the note to a sleeve so that it would be visible the moment the wardrobe was opened, Adele took a deep breath and closed the door. Next, she made her bed. The more she moved about, the better she felt. The *Laura Rose* would not only take her away from St. Louis but also toward— something. Something she would choose for herself. Surely, in over five thousand miles of river among dozens of passengers, with dozens of cities both large and small along the way…surely she could find a place to belong. On her own terms.

Part Two

[She]...enjoys the distinction of being the only steamboat captain of her sex west of the Mississippi River...The young lady mastered the details of steamboating with but little trouble and in due season received a regular license permitting her to take full charge of a steamer. She has been remarkably successful in her calling.

—E. W. Wright, 1895

Chapter 15

At least Adele had gathered herself and managed not to delay things. Fiona would never have expected the child to be the one suffering from a nervous stomach. Thank goodness the color had returned to her cheeks on the ride to the levee. By the time the buggy pulled up to where the *Laura Rose* waited at the river's edge, Adele was nearly her old self, albeit an unusually quiet version. Fiona would suggest more mint tea as soon as they were settled.

Finn seemed to be in fine form today. He'd been thoughtful to escort them to the levee himself, and when Adele had her little episode at the house, he'd been almost solicitous. Now, as Fiona looked over at her handsome brother, her heart swelled with pride. He was going to be all right. His injured leg would get stronger—as long as he was sensible about the demands he made of it. If only Miss White would give him half a chance, he would show her the fine man beneath that rugged exterior...And who knew what that might lead to?

Now there was a thought to distract a woman in a moment of fear: Finn and Miss White. She was pretty enough, although something of an enigma as far as Fiona was concerned. She could not imagine a woman wanting to take on the responsibility involved in piloting a steamboat. Oh, if Miss White were unattractive, that might explain it. Desperate women did all kinds of things. But Laura White was beautiful and feminine in every way. She could probably marry any man she set her cap for. And yet, here she was, continuing to fight for her unusual way of life on the river. Fiona would never understand that. But Finn might—actually, Finn did. And Miss White could do much worse. So could Finn, for that matter. Now wasn't that an interesting thought?

Fiona did her best to concentrate on Finn's good fortune as she descended from the buggy and approached the gangplank, where she paused to stare at the very narrow board she must ascend. Over dark water. To navigate a treacherous river.

Finn's voice sounded from right behind her. "It'll be all right. I'd take your hand if I could, but—"

"Don't be ridiculous," Fiona said. "I'm not a child. I'll be fine." Lifting her chin, she took a step. Was it her imagination, or did the board wobble? It had to be her imagination. Dozens of people traversed this plank every day. She'd done it herself just a few days ago. Deckhands did so bearing many more pounds than she weighed.

The gangplank creaked. She stopped. Boards did not last forever. Gangplanks had probably broken before, had they not? She stared down at the water and thought of that newspaper article about the man who'd managed to wrestle a one-hundred-pound catfish out of the murky depths. Ridiculous. Catfish were just that. Fish. Bottom-feeders, at that. No mythical creature was going to rise out of that tiny strip of water and drag her down.

Closing her parasol, Fiona used it like a cane and tap-tapped her way on board the *Laura Rose*. *There. That wasn't so bad.* She moved away from the edge of the deck quickly, grateful for the realization that if a person stood in the right spot, the piles of freight almost obscured one's view of the water. Good to know. Something to remember when it came time to disembark.

She wished for a railing on those steps to the hurricane deck, but at least they weren't steep. Lifting her skirt a bit, she ascended to the next deck. And then up the steep, narrow steps leading to the texas. *A ridiculous term.* She concentrated on what Finn had told her about it. Distraction was, after all, part of managing absurdity, and surely her lingering fear was just that. It had been nearly thirty years since the incident— no. *Don't think about that. Think about the texas deck. They call it the "texas" because Texas is the largest state and the texas is where the largest cabins are located. Just below the wheelhouse. Convenient for the captain.* Convenient and comfortable.

Miss White had insisted that Fiona and Adele share the largest cabin. Which was kind of her, but also probably a result of Miss White's own reluctance to be surrounded by memories of her deceased family. Odd that, for all her declarations of "love" for Joseph White, Adele had not expressed any similar reluctance to inhabit what had been his. But then who could ever understand or predict what Adele would think or do?

A few more steps, and she would have conquered the ascent. It was certainly obvious now why Miss White eschewed hoops and seemed to have no plans to don mourning silks. Dressed like a real lady, a woman would be taking her life into her hands to try and navigate these narrow stairs in a hurry, not to mention that ladder up to the wheelhouse. And silks would likely be ruined in a day.

Oh...no. She was high enough on the stairway that she could see the opposite shore now. The blue sky. Her legs felt stiff as she moved backward. She looked down at Finn, standing guard on the hurricane deck. "There's no railing at the edge of the texas."

Adele, who had hurried aboard like a homing pigeon and scurried up both flights of stairs like a child rushing toward a bowl of candy, stood looking down at her from the top of the stairs, the very picture of impatience. "For heaven's sake, Fiona. You had to know that. It's not as if you've never seen a steamboat before."

"Well, of course I knew," Fiona snapped. "I just never quite realized how high—" She gulped.

Adele rolled her eyes and bent down, extending one gloved hand. "There's several feet of decking up here, and the view is lovely. But you don't have to look if you don't want to. We'll stay near the inside edge and you can just watch the other cabin doors and the wall go by as I lead you around to our door."

Edge. Fiona did not like that word one bit. Miss White must have come to see what the delay was. Fiona heard her murmur to Finn, although she couldn't make out the words.

"I reminded her that she was afraid of the river when she offered to do this," Finn was saying. "She said, 'The Lord is faithful. I'll manage.'"

The Lord is faithful. It was exactly what Fiona needed to hear, reminding her that she had not drowned when she was seven years old and she would not drown today. Willing her knees to unlock, she took the last few steps up to the texas. But she did not let go of Adele's hand, and she did not look anywhere but at the gleaming white wall on her left. In fact, she trailed along it with the fingertips of her free hand all the way to the open door of the cabin she would share with Adele.

✸

Laura had seen women passengers go white with fear when a child got too close to the edge of a deck, but that was about the child, not the adult. On the other hand, plenty of adults had drowned or been lost as a result of a boiler explosion or a steamboat sinking. Apparently Fiona MacKnight had read one too many of such accounts. *Poor woman.* If she was this afraid—well. On the other hand, it said a great deal about her loyalty to her brother and her determination to see him reclaim his old life as a steamboat pilot.

Hurrying after the older woman, Laura made her way past her own cabin door and around to Joseph's cabin. She stopped in the open doorway and looked in. Miss MacKnight had perched at the edge of a needlepoint chair that was part of the small sitting area in one corner. Her back was to the windows. She'd taken her bonnet off and held her hands clutched in her lap. Her eyes were closed.

"Miss MacKnight," Laura said, "there's no reason for you to put yourself through this. I'll speak to the clerk and we'll arrange for you to have a cabin on the hurricane deck. I can't do anything about the water itself, but at least there's a railing on the deck below. Those cabins all open directly into the dining saloon. That should make things easier for you."

Miss MacKnight had opened her eyes the moment Laura spoke her name. She unclasped her hands and rose, taking up her bonnet and sidling toward the trunk her brother had directed the crew to place at the foot of the massive bed. "And cause you to lose the fifty dollars a passenger would pay for a cabin? I think not."

Having finally managed to negotiate his own way up the steps and around to the cabin door, MacKnight spoke up from where he was standing just behind Laura. "It's actually $150 to Fort Benton, Fiona."

Laura flashed him an angry look. "Don't let that concern you, Miss MacKnight. The only thing to be decided is if Adele would like her own cabin below as well. For such a long journey, I wouldn't think you'd want to share the smaller space, although obviously some do."

Adele turned to look out the window. "I love it up here!

The view is wonderful. It's as if I'm a princess with permission to come up onto the dais beside the king and queen." She forced a bright smile. "That being you and Finn, of course." She reached up to untie the ribbons attached to her bonnet, then removed the jeweled hat pin holding it in place and hung the bonnet on the hook beside the door. Whatever her sister decided, it was obvious that Adele MacKnight had claimed Joe's cabin as her own.

"I've just hired a new cabin boy," Laura said. "We could arrange for him to bring your meals up here."

Miss MacKnight shook her head. "I'm not ill. I'm just— discombobulated. It will pass, I'm sure." She took a step over to the window and looked out. "I already feel better. And Adele is right. The view is lovely."

"It's even better from up in the wheelhouse," Adele said. "Windows look out in every direction."

Adele's sister paled. She glanced back at her brother. "I hadn't thought— I won't be expected to climb up there, will I? I mean"—she reached down and smoothed her very full skirt—"I can't imagine the mechanics."

MacKnight chuckled. "Well, dear sister, if you insist on the hoops, you're right to be concerned. Climbing that ladder will risk giving passing steamboats quite a view. And on a windy day, you'd risk getting blown right off the ladder."

Miss MacKnight pursed her lips. "I don't know whether to blush or faint."

"Don't do either," Adele said. "If you ask me, the whole idea of a chaperone is antiquated."

"No one did ask you," Miss MacKnight snapped. "And outbursts like that invite gossip about unmarried young ladies. I, for one, hope never to see the day when propriety is considered passé."

"Well, goodness," Adele said. "I guess we all know where

you stand." She paused. "As to the wheelhouse, though, you don't need to worry. As I said, it's windows all around up there." She glanced over at Laura and her brother. "If these two decide to carry on, they won't be doing it up in the wheelhouse."

Laura felt her cheeks burn.

The older woman scolded. "Such brazen language, sister."

"I know," Adele said. "But it made you forget to be afraid, didn't it?" She gestured about them. "Just look at it, Fiona. Isn't it glorious? If you accept Miss White's offer to have the cabin boy bring your meals up, you won't even have to leave if you don't want to. On a sunny day, I'll bet these windows will give you all kinds of lovely light for your tatting and knitting and reading. Close the drapes and you won't have to *see* the river. It'll be just as if you've taken a sabbatical to a fine hotel."

"Well, I—I hardly think Inspector Davies expected me to see the journey as a personal pleasure trip."

Adele rolled her eyes. "Of course not. Heaven forbid that you actually enjoy yourself." She headed for the door, speaking to Laura as her brother moved aside to let her leave. "Would you mind very much if I played the piano in the dining saloon?"

"Not at all. I remember Mama inviting you to play the first day you visited the *Laura Rose*. I'm quite sure she would love the idea of someone competent enjoying it." Laura smiled. "I can pick out a tune, but I'm no musician. I was always more interested in navigating and engineering than piano playing."

"Just remember that word 'competent,' Adele," Miss MacKnight said. "You don't want to be annoying the passengers with missed notes."

Adele turned back around. "Thank you, Fiona. I'll do my utmost not to be the usual annoyance." She swept out of the room.

MacKnight sighed and shook his head. "Fiona, Fiona."

"Well. She doesn't often think of others, and we're here to be a help, not a hindrance. It needed to be said."

❦

On Monday morning, Finn rose while it was still dawn and stationed himself at the top of the hurricane deck stairs. Waiting. When Elijah North finally appeared, Finn nodded, then followed North up to the texas and, finally, up the ladderlike stairs where the men positioned a huge mourning wreath just below the windows at the front of the wheelhouse.

"Nice thing to do, Cap'n," North said, standing back to take a look.

"It wasn't my idea entirely," Finn said. "Fiona got me to thinking about it."

The whole truth was that Fiona had, in her own way, almost demanded it. It all started the day Fiona had agreed to come on the trip. Adele had retired, leaving her two half-siblings to discuss the details of closing up the house. Fiona wanted to know what to pack for a lengthy stay on board a steamboat. At some point, she slipped in a comment that let Finn know that she was more than a little shocked by the fact that Miss White hadn't replaced her usual wardrobe with black. She didn't give him a chance to speak before moving on to say that while Inspector Davies might have other motives for various of his requirements, he was most certainly correct about the idea that any good family—and Captain and Mrs. Margaret White would want to be remembered as heads of a "good family"—would want their daughter's reputation to remain unsoiled. A chaperone was definitely called for. Miss White might be part of the younger generation that disagreed, but not all customs should be ignored the moment someone just didn't want to be bothered.

Surprised that her critique made him want to rise to Miss

White's defense, Finn made an effort to mellow his tone as he asked, "Am I to conclude that you don't approve of Miss White?"

"Not at all. I just find her...unusual."

"Surely you don't expect her to pilot a steamboat wearing weighted silk and knee-length veils?" He paused. "Even fingerless gloves would affect her grip on the wheel."

Fiona snorted. "Of course she has to make certain concessions. That does not mean that all custom should be thrown to the winds."

"What would you have her do?"

As expected, Fiona had a ready answer. "At the very least, a mourning wreath should be hung on the *Laura Rose* before departure. I've seen them on the prows of other vessels down at the levee. It's a nice gesture. It acknowledges the memory of the recently departed. It shows respect."

"Don't you think everything she's been trying to accomplish shows respect? More than respect, in fact. It shows her deep love for her family and their way of life. Look what she's been willing to go through to preserve it."

Fiona peered at him. "All I am saying is that it's customary to display a wreath instead of virtually ignoring their recent passing." She paused. "Of course it's not my place to dictate how Miss White conducts either her business or her personal life."

Finn stifled a sigh. *Dear Fiona of the Strongly Held Opinions.* Ah well, he *had* asked. He ordered a wreath, and when North complimented the idea, he gave credit where credit was due—which was with Fiona.

North chuckled. "Always a good idea to stay a step ahead of the strong-willed ones, eh, Captain? Wise to just pretend to see things their way, long as it doesn't cause bigger troubles down the line." He grinned at Finn. "I believe you'll do all right with Miss White, Cap'n. Just fine."

Finn said nothing, just returned North's salute, then powered himself up into the wheelhouse. He sat there for a good long while, thinking about North's comment about staying a step ahead and wondering how that was going to work in the coming weeks, as he tried to navigate a dangerous river, not to mention life with not one, but three strong-willed women. What had he gotten himself into?

Chapter 16

It was still dark when movement just outside her cabin door brought Laura instantly and fully awake. Excitement, relief, joy, and a tinge of bittersweet sorrow combined as she hurried out of bed, very nearly stepping on Logjam in the process. With a quick "Sorry, boy," she opened her cabin door just far enough to let the dog out, then began to dress, thankful that the hoops and the silks had been packed away and she could once again don simple calico. After brushing her hair and stuffing it into a snood, she slid her stocking feet into the boots Mama had despised. She hesitated before opening the door to kiss the tips of her fingers and press the kiss to Mama's Bible by way of apology. With a last glance at Papa and Joe's photographs, she headed out.

Pulling her cabin door closed behind her, Laura paused to breathe in the morning air and to look off once again toward the eastern shore of the river. Next, she glanced north toward the spot where Captain James Eads, already a St. Louis legend for constructing ironclad ships during the war, would soon be overseeing the construction of the first bridge to span the Mississippi here at St. Louis. Bridges would change everything for steamboats.

Papa had once dreamed of owning his own line of mountain boats, but the railroad, Papa said, would alter everyone's way of life—and quickly. Steamboat traffic on the upper Missouri would, of course, last for at least the life of the *Laura Rose*. He thought it worth the gamble to build her. After that, though, railroads were the future, and once bridges eliminated the natural barrier presented by the rivers, shippers wouldn't use steamboats anymore.

She grimaced at the thought of losing what she was fighting to keep, but then one of Mama's gentle reminders came to mind. *Don't let worry over tomorrow steal today's joy.* There was a Bible verse about forgetting the past and pressing on to the future, too. One of Mama's favorites. Maybe she'd look for that some evening when she'd retired and handed the wheel over Finn MacKnight. This wasn't a moment to worry. It was a moment to enjoy.

She glanced up to the heavens. *I did it, Papa. Mama. Joe. Freight and a provisional license. Passengers and a second pilot. I'm going to save the* Laura Rose. How wonderful it felt to be young and healthy and about to return to the life she loved better than anything. Descending to the hurricane deck, she popped into the galley, inhaling the welcome aromas of baking bread and fresh coffee.

After greeting Bird and Ruby, who were already hard at work making breakfast for the nearly one hundred people on board, she strolled to the front of the *Laura Rose*, lingering at the railing and looking out over St. Louis. Raising her coffee mug in a toast, she bid St. Louis good-bye, then turned toward the galley to grab a bite to eat. That's when she saw the black wreath hanging just below the wheelhouse windows.

Her spirits fell. Whoever had done that meant well, but—she did not want to head upriver standing behind an ever-present reminder of the past. She would be forced to deal with it again soon enough, when she retrieved Joe's and Mama's bodies and brought them back to St. Louis for reinterment alongside Papa. The *Laura Rose* would be decked out in mourning for that somber voyage. But for this one? This trip wasn't about sadness. It was about life. Continuing on. Surviving. Whoever had put that there—

"North and I hung it."

With a start, Laura looked toward the dining saloon as Finn MacKnight made his way toward her. He paused a few feet away to look up at the wreath and then back at her. Finally, he said, "I'll take it down. I can see it wasn't a good idea."

"You don't have to," Laura said quickly. "It was a kind gesture. It's just that—"

"It makes you sad," MacKnight said.

Laura nodded. "But I do understand. It's the custom."

MacKnight nodded. "Fiona said as much." Quickly he added, "And you're right. She— We meant well. I'll handle it." He headed around the corner in the direction of the stairs leading up to the texas.

Laura followed him. "If your sister purchased it—"

"*I* bought it," MacKnight said as he hauled himself up to the texas. "North helped me hang it." Once again, he moved quickly out of sight on his way up to the wheelhouse.

By the time Laura had gathered her skirts and climbed up behind him, MacKnight had taken the wreath down. "I'm sorry," he said. "I should have asked instead of just doing it. It is, after all, your packet."

"And now I seem ungrateful, and your sister will be hurt."

"I'll explain it. If you'll tell me how. What I mean is, if you'll explain why you don't want it. Just so I can translate it for Fiona." He paused. "She's not very flexible when it comes to custom and tradition."

Laura took the wreath from his hands and looked down at it. "When my father died..." She explained his views and his insistence that the family avoid being "somber and glum." Finally, she said, "It's not that I don't appreciate the gesture."

MacKnight nodded. "Well, I think you'll appreciate this

one more." He hopped over to the edge of the narrow decking that surrounded the wheelhouse and flung the wreath into the air with such force that it sailed over the paddle wheel in a trajectory that carried it far out into the river.

The instant the wreath landed on the surface of the water, Laura heard someone down below holler, "Ho for the dog!" Logjam was in the water, swimming after the wreath. By the time his powerful strides had carried him to it, half the crew was whooping and hollering encouragement.

"I hope he's going to be all right!" Laura gasped.

"Of course he is," MacKnight chuckled. "He's probably half seal. Just look at him."

When Logjam finally caught up to the wreath, he chomped down on it and headed back for the *Laura Rose*. Laura hurried down to the freight deck with MacKnight not far behind. As the dog got near the packet, one of the crew reached for the wreath, but Logjam wouldn't let go. Everyone watched as he made for the bank and came ashore, dripping wet. He set down his prize momentarily, shook himself dry, and then took it up again and headed for the gangplank, persisting until he'd dragged it aboard. But he wasn't finished yet. He kept dragging it until finally he placed the sodden thing at Laura's feet, chuffed softly, and sat down beside it.

MacKnight called out, "He's expecting a thank-you and a treat. After all, the way he sees it, you lost part of your steamboat and he just rescued it."

At mention of the word *treat*, Logjam whipped his head about. He sprang to his feet and barked, wagging his tail.

Laura laughed as she praised the dog, ending with, "I'll get you a treat in a little while."

She bent down and lifted the wreath, then made her way to edge of the deck. Logjam followed closely. "You don't have to retrieve it anymore," she explained. "We can throw it away now."

The dog wagged his tail.

"Toss it here, ma'am," one of the crew called from the levee. "I'll get rid of it for you."

Laura tossed the wreath. The dog surged forward, clearing the space between the deck of the *Laura Rose* and the levee. Landing with a thud at the crew member's feet, he reared up on his hind legs and chomped down on the wreath, then backed away, doing his best to wrestle it free. The roustabout let go, and the dog once again dragged the wreath back on board.

"Must be part retriever," MacKnight laughed.

"I give up," Laura said. "I guess he's claimed a new toy." She looked up at him. "I don't know how I'm going to explain this to your sister. She's going to think I'm an ungrateful... something. Hopefully we can sneak it away when the dog isn't looking. I mean, what will she think if she sees him presiding over it now? It's ruined."

MacKnight smiled down at her. "Fiona is well versed in forgiveness, Miss White. If she weren't, she'd have turned me out long ago." He pointed to the steps. "Shall we away?"

❦

The sun had just cleared the treetops on the eastern shore when Cub Pilot Laura Rose White signaled departure and backed her steamboat away from the St. Louis levee, to a chorus of answering blasts from the steam-powered whistles on more than a mile-long stretch of steamboats. Once out in the channel, she gave the order for the engineers to reverse direction and at last, the *Laura Rose* was on its way.

"Bravo," Finn said. Cupping his hands about his mouth like a circus announcer, he called out, "And the *Laura Rose* is away, drawing four-and-a-half feet, loaded with over two hundred tons of freight, thirty cabin passengers, forty deck passengers, a full crew, one chaperone, one sister, half a copilot, and one downright determined mascot."

Miss White glanced over just in time to see Logjam lurch his way into the wheelhouse.

"Can you believe that?" Finn laughed. "Not only is your dog an accomplished retriever, he's learned to climb a ladder."

"He's not my dog," Miss White said, without looking back. "Joe's the one who rescued him. The crew came up with the name. He belongs to the boat more than to me."

Finn reached down to pat Logjam on the head. "It's all right, boy. She doesn't mean to hurt your feelings. She's just a bit preoccupied at the moment. It's difficult to engage in banter when you're trying not to cry."

Miss White glanced over at him, swiping at the tears on her cheeks.

Finn smiled. "You've a right to a moment. One way or the other, success or failure, you're about to make history." He paused. "And I don't blame you for wishing it was your own family standing here to witness it instead of a man with crutches and a crooked leg."

Miss White shrugged him off. "You moved well enough just a little while ago when we were chucking that mourning wreath. Am I going to have to listen to you whine about crutches and a crooked leg all the way to Fort Benton?"

Finn considered. "Maybe only part of the way. I'm determined to graduate to a cane by Omaha." He paused. "Am I going to have to call you 'Miss White' all the way to Fort Benton? Because in my humble opinion—"

"When was your opinion about anything ever humble, Mr. MacKnight?"

"Touché, my captain."

She sniffed. "You sound as if you're mocking me."

"It's better than 'cub,'" Finn teased. "And far better than some of the other names I've heard pilots call their cubs."

She glanced over at him. "'Miss White' will do for now."

"Just listen to the two of you. Barely on our way and you're already arguing." Finn and Miss White glanced back just as Adele stepped up into the wheelhouse.

"Is your sister all right?" Miss White asked.

"Define 'all right.'" Adele plopped down on the bench below the rear wall of windows. "Is she relaxed? No. But then, I'm not certain Fiona knows the meaning of the word. Is she hysterical? That word isn't even in her vocabulary."

"Actually," Miss White said, "I was thinking more about her reaction to the fact that I took the mourning wreath down."

"What mourning wreath?"

"Fiona seemed to think it would be a nice thing to do," Finn explained. "And so I told her I'd put one up."

"But now it's down," Adele said.

Finn nodded. "Miss White was raised to look to the future. 'Don't borrow tomorrow's troubles and don't wallow in the past.'"

Adele considered for a moment. "I like that. As for Fiona, I doubt she'll even notice it's not there. At the moment, she's refusing to leave the cabin." With a glance at Logjam, she made a kissing sound and patted her leg. Logjam plastered himself against her, clearly reveling in the attention.

Miss White smiled at Adele. "Have you tried out the piano yet? I thought I might have heard a note or two earlier, but with all the noise when we departed, I couldn't be sure."

"All I did was run through some scales," Adele replied, "but I enjoyed it. I even remembered the correct fingering."

Finn sat down beside her and stretched his bad leg. "I wish you'd said something about wanting a piano."

She shrugged. "I did. A long time ago. Fiona said the MacKnights had never been musical. She called it a frivolous expense."

Miss White looked back. "I have my mother's hymnal in the trunk in my cabin. In fact, now that I think about it, there might be a small book of popular tunes as well. When your brother takes a turn at the wheel, I'll pull them out for you."

"If it's not too much trouble," Adele said, "that would be nice."

"The passengers loved it when Mama played. Who knows but that we'll pick up a musician or two on the way? We could end up with a band. Some of the larger packets hire them, you know."

Finn spoke up. "Just stay away from political tunes like 'Dixie' or 'Marching Through Georgia.' We don't need any veterans trying to refight the war on board the *Laura Rose*."

"I won't make trouble," Adele said. "I promise." She stood up. "And speaking of trouble, I'd better see to Fiona before she has another hissy fit about something I haven't done. I didn't tell her I was coming up here."

Logjam watched Adele go, then curled up in a corner of the wheelhouse.

"Have your sisters always been at odds?" Miss White didn't take her eyes off the river ahead of them as she spoke.

"What do you mean, 'at odds'?"

"I don't want to cause more trouble than there already is by seeming to take Adele's side in what sounds like an old conflict over family finances and pianos." Miss White paused. "More to the point, in light of that fact that we took that wreath down, will Fiona see it as yet another personal rebuke if I get those songbooks out for Adele?"

"I'm not sure I can explain Fiona and Adele."

"I'm not asking you to," Miss White said quickly. "It's just that I don't want to encourage Adele to do things that Fiona has forbidden in the past. The last thing I want to do is to cause more animosity between those two."

Finn cleared his throat. " 'Animosity' is a strong word, although I will allow that since being hurt and spending so much time at home, I've...um...wondered if perhaps Fiona and I both have been a little hard on Adele over the years."

Miss White snorted.

"I take it you agree."

She shrugged. "The poor girl seems to be constantly on guard. Bracing for the next lecture. As if she can barely move without someone barking at her."

Finn didn't like thinking of himself that way. He looked over at Logjam and tried to make a joke of it. "I didn't realize that Logjam and I had so much in common."

Miss White shrugged her fine shoulders. Today they were accented by a wide bit of white trim that created something of a crescent moon against green calico. Another bit of white drew the eye to her waist, and it was not the first time that Finn had been distracted by Miss White's curves. When she turned to look at him, he realized she'd said something to which she was expecting a reply. Grimacing, he reached down to rub his leg, hoping she would believe that was what was really distracting him. "Forgive me," he said. "Would you repeat what you just said?"

"If you're in pain, you are more than welcome to take a rest. On a day like today, a trained squirrel could probably pilot a steamboat on this river."

"I'll be all right," he said.

She took one hand off the steamboat's wheel and brushed a coppery curl back from her forehead. Presently she said, "Adele probably understands your difficult moods. Even the most patient person in the world tends to growl when they're in pain. Besides that, girls tend to look up to their older brothers." She glanced over at him. "Even the ones who are trouble-makers. But sisters? I don't have any experience at all with how sisters work—or don't."

Good. She believed his leg was the distraction. Now that he thought about it, it did seem that he and Adele were getting along a bit better of late. If only the same could be said for Adele and Fiona. "Well, when it comes to my sisters, it's easy to judge—when you don't know the story."

Miss White studied the river. The ship's wheel was nearly as tall as she was. What a lovely profile. She nodded. "You're absolutely right. I'm not trying to pry. It's just that I don't want to unwittingly stir up anything. In a way, you and your sister hold my future in your hands. It's going to take all our combined skill to make this trip by July 8, and it'll be much easier if I'm able to navigate the waters between the four of us as successfully as I can run a river." After a moment, she said. "All I'm asking, Mr. MacKnight, is your help avoiding snags and sandbars on board—if you'll forgive the analogy." She signaled a greeting to a steamer headed downriver.

Finn stopped rubbing his bad leg and sat back. Presently he got to his feet. Watched the shoreline pass by. This was one of the reasons he'd stayed away from his two sisters for long stretches at a time. Women always had to talk about things. Even when they said things like, "You don't have to explain" and "I don't mean to pry," they didn't really mean it.

He took a deep breath. "I do agree with you that Fiona seems a bit harsh at times. But before you condemn her and champion Adele, take a minute to think how *you* would respond to a knock at your door that presented you with a spoiled ten-year-old to raise."

Miss White looked off to the leeward side of the steamboat. She seemed to be studying something on the bank. "Perhaps I shouldn't have said anything."

Wonderful. She asked him to talk about something. Now she didn't want him to talk. *Women.* He moved forward so that he was more in her line of sight. "But you did say something." He paused. "I think a great deal of Fiona, and it won't help us get along if you continue to judge a situation you don't understand."

She glanced over. "I'm not judging your—"

"Yes, you are. Just as you judged that situation in Joe's room that night at the hotel. When I wasn't drunk. Hadn't had so much as one drink, in fact."

She grimaced, and as he watched, a blush crept up from the collar of her dress and onto her cheeks. "All right. I was wrong about the drinking. That time. But—that's not the only—" The blush deepened. "As long as we are discussing the matter, it isn't 'judging' for me to have concerns about certain things." She swallowed. "You said that you had someone waiting that night. Downstairs. You said I wasn't to worry, because the hotel was discreet."

"I—you think—?"

She made a point of staring straight ahead, and all the while her lovely face glowed. "As I said, it's not 'judging.' You told me about that yourself."

He sighed. "Adele." He repeated it. "*Adele* was waiting for me in the lobby."

Miss White looked back at him.

"It's true," he said. "You can ask her. I didn't speak her name because I didn't want to have to explain. Because, to be quite honest, I didn't really know what was going on. I hadn't talked to her yet. She and a young man had left a church social—Adele said something about the boy's being jealous of Joe. Anyway, they'd been down at the levee, and on their way back to the social—if that is, indeed, where they were headed—they encountered Joe in his...um...compromising condition. Adele ran home to get me and that's all there was to it. Except for the fact that she disobeyed my order to stay at home and followed me when I went to find Joe. So I planted her on a bench in the lobby and ordered her to wait—under threat of my putting her in a convent if she disobeyed me again." He paused. "Which, now that I think of it, fairly well illustrates what it's been like raising Adele, and just why Fiona feels it necessary to be 'harsh' at times."

Quiet reigned in wheelhouse for a few moments. Finally, Miss White said, "It seems I may have misjudged a lot about both you and your family. I apologize."

"Thank you." Well, at least she seemed to believe him about some things. Best to get the rest of it out in the open as well. He took a deep breath. "I take you back to the day Fiona met Adele. Put yourself in her shoes. You've just answered a knock at the door, and you are looking down at a lovely little girl you've never seen before. The stranger accompanying that child introduces her as your half sister. She's ten years old. The thing is, you aren't even aware that your estranged father has remarried, let alone had a child. You haven't, in point of fact, heard from him since your mother died many years ago. You can't help but wonder: Did the old man really remarry without one word to his grown children? Of course the answer doesn't matter right now. You are a woman of faith, and God would never forgive your turning a child away, and so you take her in.

"Your fiancé is not amused. He demands that you make a choice: Raise your half sister or marry him and head west to California. He has no intention of taking a ten-year-old across the continent. You choose duty over love, and God rewards you in a strange way, because you never marry. You stop hoping to have children of your own. But you tell yourself that the God you serve never promised that life would be easy, and you do the best you can to mold the pretty little girl—who proves to be a spoiled, conniving brat—into something approaching a godly young woman." He glanced over at Miss White. "And lest you think I'm being a bit hard on Adele to label her that way, here's an example of what I mean. Adele has always loved high fashion. She's never been happy with Fiona's more conservative approach to things. The one time I remember getting involved in one of their spats, it was over something Fiona was making for a church bazaar. She'd spent night after night making some fancy edging—it's called tatting, isn't it?"

Miss White glanced at him. "Mama used to tat. It's actually a bunch of knotted thread, but yes, it ends up looking like lace. It's very time-consuming work. And quite difficult, to my mind." She smiled. "I never could get the hang of it, although Mama did her best to teach me."

Finn nodded. "That's it. Fiona loves the stuff. I don't know how much of it she'd managed or how long it had taken her, but the short version of what happened is that Adele snatched it and traded it for a bonnet that Fiona had refused to buy. It was too late for Fiona to make anything else, so she had nothing to contribute to a cause she'd worked very hard to support. She was mortified. Of course she protected Adele. She didn't tell anyone what had really happened. She just said she'd tried a new design and wasn't able to finish it in time." He paused. "I only know about it because it happened when I was between trips on the river—and sober, for once. But if emotions could raise a roof off a house, our little place would have been a shambles that day. And what did I do? I left by way of the back door and went off to wait for it to blow over."

He grimaced. "So that gives you an idea of what Fiona had to deal with when it came to raising Adele—and me. It gives you one more example of what Fiona had to manage alone, because her worthless brother was too self-absorbed to help."

Miss White looked at him. "You're very hard on yourself."

"Not so. I know my failings better than anyone, and believe me, in recent days I have had ample opportunity to ponder them." He paused. "There is a bright spot in all of this past drama, by the way. Our father left a decent estate. Neither Fiona nor I were privy to the details, beyond the fact that he provided for us—as long as we raised the child he left behind. But think how that must have felt for Fiona. Her own father

knew so little about his grown daughter that he thought he
had to buy her decency."

With a grimace, Finn moved to the bench and sat down.
For a few moments, the only sounds in the wheelhouse were
the usual clanging and grunting and panting of the *Laura
Rose*, churning her way up the Mississippi.

Finally, Miss White reacted. "I shouldn't have needed to
know any of that to extend grace to Fiona—or to you, for that
matter. But thank you. For trusting me with the story."

Finn grunted. "Adele can be the most charming, the most
delightful, the most entrancing young woman imaginable.
That is the Adele you know. It's most likely the only Adele
my friend Joe ever saw. But wait a few days. I don't imagine
it will take long for my younger sister's less-charming qualities to emerge." He lifted his bad leg up onto the bench and
began to rub it. "You may have used your beauty to get your
way with Inspector Davies, but trust me: You're an amateur
compared to Adele."

Miss White changed her stance at the wheel. Her shoulders stiffened, almost imperceptibly. When she turned to
look at him, her blue eyes flashed with emotion. The afternoon sun pouring in the wheelhouse windows emphasized
the amber highlights in her hair. *Heavens above.*

"And now I've made you angry."

She shook her head. "I'm not angry. I'm embarrassed.
Because you're right. I did use my…appearance…to manip-
ulate Inspector Davies."

"Desperate people do desperate things," Finn said. "And
Fiona's had a lot of opportunity to be desperate over the years.
The thing is, the very attributes that make her so difficult are
the things that have kept our odd little family together. She's
stubborn and unyielding. A thing is either right or wrong to
her. She's maddeningly straight-laced. She wasn't always. Life
seems to have beat a sense of humor right out of her. She's

all about duty." He sighed. "And fate saddled her with two siblings who are the exact opposite. We've tried her at every turn. We've disappointed her and challenged her and failed her and through it all she has continued to do her duty. The truth is, both Adele and I owe Fiona more than we can ever repay."

For the next few moments, neither Finn nor Miss White said a word. At one point, Logjam got up and came over to Finn and snuffled along his aching leg.

"You should see to that leg," Miss White finally said. "I estimate we'll be at the mouth of the Missouri around four thirty this afternoon. I'll take her into the woodlot there, and then maybe you can take over for a while?"

Finn nodded and reached for his crutches.

"I'll hand them down," Miss White said.

"And take your hand off that wheel?"

She smiled back at him. "She's in the channel and moving steady. Take the offer while I can make it. Once we're on the Big Muddy you'll be on your own."

Finn hopped down the ladder on his good leg and called, "Ready."

Miss White leaned down with the crutches. Moments later, he was stretched out on the bed in his cabin, thinking about what she'd said about him and Fiona holding her future in his hands. A woman like her...She had to hate that. A woman like her...Titian red hair glowing in the afternoon sun...flashing blue eyes...a sprinkling of freckles...and those curves... *Glory be.*

Chapter 17

Untroubled waters and smooth landings characterized the first few days on the Missouri, but neither of those things was much comfort, as Laura increasingly worried over the ever-growing debit side of Tom Meeks's ledger. One of the culprits was the steamboat's voracious appetite for fuel. Depending on the current, the *Laura Rose* could burn through four cords of hardwood in an hour.

On Friday of the first week, roustabouts hauled nearly four hundred boxes of coal on board. It was little more than an experiment, what with wood yards positioned at regular intervals on this part of the Missouri, but once they got up north where timber was less available, premium prices reigned. Up there, having a recourse—even a filthy one that didn't burn as well in the boilers—could be the difference between success or failure. It was not unusual for steamboats north of Fort Rice to be forced to rally passengers to help scavenge for wood. The *Laura Rose* had no time for that.

Laura got her first full night of sleep the night they took on the coal and decided to lay over at the coal yard. With abundant fuel on board and no need to worry over whether or not MacKnight would sense this danger or respond correctly to that one, Laura retired relatively early and slept well past four o'clock in the morning. But still, the moment the packet churned her way back out into the channel, Laura was back to worrying and watching.

She knew MacKnight was a good pilot. She should trust him more, but she couldn't seem to do it. Not yet, anyway. Not with the most important thing in her world—the only thing she'd managed to hold on to—at stake.

On Saturday of the first week, she was on her way down to the dining saloon to get a quick lunch when the sight of several felled trees on the far bank, their tops dipped into the river, their roots exposed, made her shudder. By the time the *Laura Rose* was headed back downriver, the Big Muddy might well have eaten away the sandy bank and dragged those trees into the water. Caught below the surface, any one of them could rip through the hull, and that would spell doom to cargo and crew alike. What if MacKnight hadn't seen them?

Gathering her skirts about her, Laura fairly ran the steps to the texas and then clamored up the ladder to the wheelhouse, where she paused on the top rung and called to MacKnight, "Did you see those fallen trees on the shoreline just now? Sawyers just waiting to happen."

MacKnight looked back at her. "Didn't expect to see you back up here this soon."

"I just thought—the trees."

He nodded. "Noted, ma'am. At mile 322. Have you already eaten?"

Laura shook her head. "Wanted to make sure you saw." She finished climbing the ladder and stayed at his side for more than an hour after that, calling out every fallen tree, every new sandbar, every cloud in the distance.

Finally, with lunchtime long past, MacKnight looked over at her and said quietly, "If you'd rather, Miss White, I'll just sit back there on the bench and read a book. We can have young Tyree serve your meals up here, and you won't have to leave at all. Except to use the necessary, that is. I suppose even that could be managed with a chamber pot."

Laura's face flamed with embarrassment. "I beg your pardon?"

He shrugged. "Doesn't seem you really need a second pilot, ma'am. Or is it that you don't trust the one you hired?"

"Even my father valued a second pair of eyes keeping a lookout," Miss White snapped.

"Yes, ma'am," MacKnight agreed. "I remember him telling me in no uncertain terms that if I continued down the road I was on—being arrogant and bullheaded and thinking I didn't need any help—I was destined to failure. He said that the minute I thought I'd mastered the Missouri was the minute it would master me. I remember it like it was yesterday, because he was not a man to raise his voice at a cub, but that day, he practically yelled, 'This river, young man, demands that a man learn more than any one man ought to be allowed to know. And just when he's learned it, the very next day—sometimes the very next hour—he has to learn it all over again in a different way.'"

MacKnight paused, studied something in the distance, and made a slight adjustment to the course of the packet before continuing. "The old captain went on to give me quite the lecture about the unique nature of the soil forming these riverbanks and how the fast current chews at them, constantly changing the river's course, sometimes making it seem like the devil himself is in charge of things." MacKnight looked at her. "The thing is, even knowing all that, the old captain did trust me alone at the wheel from time to time. Sometimes for nearly half a day."

Laura looked away. She just couldn't seem to trust him. Not yet, anyway.

MacKnight looked back upriver. "Last time I brought

a packet through this stretch, there was a sandbar forming around the wreck of the *Miner*."

"They call it Miner Point now," Laura said.

He nodded.

Soon thereafter, Laura made herself a sandwich in the galley, intending to take it back up to the wheelhouse and eat there. Just to provide an extra set of eyes for MacKnight. Just for a little longer. Until she could convince herself that MacKnight really was still the pilot Papa had once trusted— and not the pilot he'd fired.

As she passed by the hurricane deck stairs, she caught sight of Elijah North down on the freight deck. He was seated at the edge of the deck with Logjam stretched out at his side, both of them looking as if they didn't have a care in the world. Instead of heading back up to the wheelhouse, Laura descended to the freight deck. As she approached, Logjam rose to his feet, stretched lazily, and then plodded over to greet her.

"You just want part of this sandwich," Laura teased. The dog chuffed and wagged his tail. "All right, but just one bite." She tore off a bit of roast beef and tossed it to the dog. He caught it midair.

North started to get up, but Laura told him to stay seated as she settled atop a lone crate of something that had obviously been moved by a roustabout looking for an improvised perch.

After a moment, North said, "It's good to see you taking the old captain's advice."

"Eating lunch on the freight deck?" Laura joked.

North smiled. "The old captain always said that when you had a first-rate second pilot, it was important to let him know you trusted him to do the job. Best way to do that, according to your pa, was to leave the wheelhouse now and again. Give the man a chance to run his own show." He nodded. "Glad to see you know MacKnight's a good man for the job. Glad to see you're giving him a chance to prove it as well. The old captain would approve." North paused. "You probably don't know it, but he did that for me a long time ago, too. Fact is, your mama wasn't the only person in the family who believed in giving folks a second chance."

"But Papa *fired* MacKnight."

"Aye. And he was right to do it. Then. The young pup was still too full of himself to know the value of what he had, training under the old captain." North shrugged. "It takes some longer than others." And then he went on to talk about the river and the weather and sundry other topics that had nothing to do with Finn MacKnight. Laura lingered, stroking Logjam's broad head, feeding him the last bits of her roast beef, and telling herself that she would trust MacKnight to do the job she was paying him to do. One day at a time. Or at the very least, one part of a day.

Fiona sat up in bed, her pillow clutched to her breast, her eyes closed, listening. *Praise be to God.* She'd lived through several days on board the *Laura Rose*. Adele had long since left the cabin, humming happily as she performed her toilette. She'd even offered to bring Fiona breakfast. No, Fiona had said, she hadn't slept well and she would rather rest a little longer. Please tell the cabin boy not to disturb her.

They had worked out a system of sorts before the end of the second day on the river. A blue scarf tied about the doorknob signaled that Fiona would like the cabin boy to stop when he had time. A red scarf signaled a more immediate request. Of course seeing the scarf would require young Tyree Briggs to come up to the texas on a regular basis, but Fiona offered what she considered a generous tip if the young man would accommodate her. In an emergency, Adele teased, she could always throw a shoe at the ceiling and hope either Miss White or Finn would hear it above the din. Fiona did not find the comment in the least amusing.

If she'd known how noisy a steamboat could be...the yelling and the rumbling, the bells and the whistles, each one of them meaning something to someone and every one of them eliciting fear for Fiona...if she'd known. Well, yes. She would still be here, so she might as well get on with it. Rising from bed, she fumbled about in the half-light until she recovered the almanac she'd brought with her. At the window, she opened the drape just enough to see the calendar and count the days. They had to be back in St. Louis July 8. Today was May 14. She only had to maintain her sanity for fifty-five more days. Then it would be over.

The boat lurched. Well, not really a lurch, but enough of a quick movement that Fiona lost her balance a bit and bumped against the bed. She clutched at the woven coverlet. Nearly sixty days of this. *Dear Lord. I can't.* A verse came to mind: *Fear thou not; for I am with thee: be not dismayed; for I am thy God...* Tears pricked her eyelids. *I will strengthen thee; yea, I will help thee; yea, I will uphold thee with the right hand of my righteousness.*

She began to whisper the verse aloud, and somehow it gave her strength to get dressed. A bell clanged. Peeking through the drapes, she saw smokestacks. Another steamboat, headed the opposite way. Toward the Mississippi instead of away from it. What she wouldn't give to fling herself across the space between them and just, please God, go *home*.

Well, you aren't going home yet, and surely you don't plan on living in this dark room for the next fifty-five days. She reached up and touched the drape. One didn't have to peer at the river to take advantage of the light. Pushing the drape back, she rummaged in her trunk for her tatting supplies and the new pattern she'd tucked in at the last minute. She'd expected Adele to complain of boredom at some point and even thought that perhaps the child would be willing to learn a new skill. But Adele seemed to delight in steamboat travel. Adele knew no fear. Which, now that Fiona thought about it, was rather worrisome. What sort of passengers had engaged the *Laura Rose*? What sort of company was Adele keeping... with what sort of men?

Worry fueled the dressing of her hair and the making up of the bed. Adele had always been something of a social butterfly, and unless Fiona could conquer her own fear, Adele would be left on her own: another kind of pending disaster Fiona had not really pondered because of the cold terror that washed over her every time she contemplated the tawny, churning river.

If only Finn could be more help in regards to Adele. But, Fiona supposed, his duties as a pilot would keep him busy, even if he were inclined to help Fiona bear the burden of chaperoning Adele. Which he wasn't. He never had been. Finn would have stopped paying her and Adele any mind at all long ago, if Father's inheritance hadn't prescribed it. When it came right down to it, she was little more than a thorn in her siblings' sides. The thought would make her cry with despair if she allowed it, but she wasn't the dramatic type. Drama was Adele's purview; drama and beauty and flirtation and so many other things that Fiona had never known how to handle when they first surfaced in her fair-skinned, green-eyed half sister. Of them all, the tendency to flirt was the one thing about raising a girl that exasperated Fiona the most.

Fiona's own experience with men was so different. Flirtation had never interested her. Of course she had never been the kind of girl boys flirted with. Her nose was too large, her eyes too small. And she was tall. Tall and slender as a fence post. She'd rejected the only chance she'd ever had and never dared to open her heart again. And then Adele grew into a beautiful young woman who attracted men of all ages.

Finn had always seemed to assume that Fiona knew how to handle it when, in truth, it mystified her. The older Adele got, the less Fiona understood her, and this recent situation with Joseph White was no exception. Had it been just another flirtation or had Adele, for the first time in her young life, truly felt the first stirrings of love? The child certainly seemed to be deeply grieved by the young man's untimely death. Grieved to the point of physical illness. But of course Fiona was the last person on earth Adele would ever confide in about such things. As far as Adele was concerned, Fiona knew nothing of love. She was too old, too unattractive, too...everything.

In recent years, Adele had increasingly treated her elder sister like a jailer. Fiona gave a soft snort at the thought. If only Adele knew just how trapped Fiona felt—had felt since Papa's death orphaned them all and saddled Fiona with the chore of raising her half sister. Did Adele know how embarrassing it was to have people assume Adele was her *daughter*? To have an ever-present reminder of her spinsterhood? An ever-present reminder of everything she'd given up in order to do her duty? And now...now here she was, trapped aboard an infernal steamboat, once again trying to deny her own feelings and fears in order to do her duty. Dear Lord, but she was weary of doing her duty.

❀

Adele didn't suppose it was very nice of her to feel this way, but she rather hoped that Fiona would wait to conquer her fears for a while longer. It was a rather heady experience to be able to socialize without a frowning chaperone. Especially now that folks knew Adele had loved the recently departed Captain White and quite possibly would have been the current Captain White's sister-in-law, if only cruel fate had not dealt an untimely death blow.

It was also great fun to be the sister of "that handsome

Captain MacKnight." Adele hadn't ever been able to capitalize on that before, but female heads turned when Finn passed by. The occasion of his graduating to only one crutch had been whispered about and commented upon until it was almost as if Finn had sprouted wings.

Portly Mrs. Chadwick's daughter, Euphemia, was positively in love with him. She'd taken to listening for the thump of his crutch and she always "just happened" to be in his path nearly every time he came down to the hurricane deck. Finn seemed oblivious, even to the fact that Euphemia and her mother had exchanged dining hours so that they could be at first setting, when Finn played host instead of Miss White.

As the days went by and the *Laura Rose* moved along the river, Adele noticed that things shifted about quite a bit when it came to which passengers attended which supper hour. Miss White was joined at table by more of the single males on board, while the single ladies—and their mothers—tended to dine at the same hour as Finn.

Adele delighted in the comings and goings. It was fascinating to learn other passengers' stories, to ask them about where they lived, and to take advantage of the fact that people seemed willing to indulge the sweet, vivacious, eighteen-year-old sister of Captain Finn MacKnight. For the first time in her life, being Finn's sister was useful. Also for the first time in her life, Fiona wasn't a constant burden.

Hopefully, if Fiona ever did conquer her fears, she would realize that the rules of etiquette were relaxed on board a steamboat. Hopefully she would hover less. After all, it wasn't that people were less proper, but travelers who shared such close quarters for days or weeks at a time formed a unique bond—at least insofar as the cabin passengers were concerned.

Adele could not have known that her playing the piano would prove to be such a boon, but the music worked a miracle, enabling her to do the impossible: simultaneously please Fiona (because Adele let her know that she was learning to play some of Fiona's favorite hymns) and hold court in a way that helped her learn about all kinds of people and places.

From her fellow passengers, Adele learned that this town had a terrible reputation. That town was growing rapidly and expected to be a regional capital soon. Reverend So-and-So in this town had scandalized his congregation by leaving town with the choir director's wife. This community had an active Ladies' Aid society that was doing its best to help the refugee slaves from the war. It was all very useful information for a young lady in search of a new home, a place where no one would question the past and would, instead, empathize with the beautiful young widow whose child would never know its recently deceased father.

Chapter 18

Making her way to one of the comfortable chairs in the corner of the large cabin, Fiona sat down and picked up her tatting pattern with a sigh. She really must find a way to resume—or begin—her duties as a chaperone. To Adele, if nothing else. The child seemed too happy—and too intent on learning hymns and mentioning it to her older sister—for Fiona to think there wasn't reason for concern. On the other hand, the idea of a chaperone in regards to Finn and Miss White was probably ridiculous.

The longer Fiona pondered the notion, the more she realized that, based on Adele's unwitting revelation of the matter, Miss White seemed blind to Finn's better qualities. Adele said that Miss White and Finn had established separate dining hours, each one presiding over a table. In addition, as the days had worn on, each pilot was increasingly alone at the wheel. Adele said it was proof that Miss White trusted Finn, and wasn't that wonderful? But then Adele thought Miss White wonderful because she was an independent thinker, interested in making her way in a man's world. Adele's newfound fascination with and admiration of Miss White were worrying. For all the battles women had to fight, why choose to fight for the right to work at a man's profession? Why not take up temperance or the vote for women? At least those causes would better society.

Fiona stared down at the tatting booklet and sighed. Whether a chaperone was truly required or not, she really must venture out of this cabin. Today. For Adele's sake, if nothing else. Again, she perused the pattern. She absolutely would venture out. Just...not yet. First, she would begin making this raised cornflower. The finished doily would look lovely stitched to a claret-colored velvet pillow. Velvet was far too sumptuous a material for the MacKnight parlor, but Jessamine Powell's exquisite formal parlor was a veritable patchwork of velvets and brocades.

Fiona had been challenged to the point of sinful covetousness when she first saw the Powells' striped-silk wall covering. The Powells had the means to make a generous donation at the next Ladies' Aid bazaar fund-raiser for such an accent piece. Fiona could just see it perched on their deep green sofa. It would look like a freshly bloomed flower rising above a verdant pasture.

She set to work with her back to the window. How good the warmth of the sun felt on her back. How fulfilling to support a worthwhile cause. It wouldn't hurt to take one more day to adjust to life on a steamboat. And besides, getting a head start on making things for the fall bazaar would be good use of her time on board the *Laura Rose*. Wasn't that what the Bible said a true Christian should do—make wise use of her time?

Perching her spectacles on her nose, Fiona leaned down to read the pattern.

1st Row. Begin an oval, work 2 D (L, 2 D 8 times) draw up, but not quite close. Begin another oval, at a short distance from the last, 2 D join to the last L of 1st oval, 2 D (L, 2 D 7 times) draw up, and work 3 more similar ovals.

Simple enough. The shuttle flew through her fingers. She moved on, and as she worked, the rhythm of the work brought comfort and a sense of purpose. The problem of Adele and the fear of the river faded.

2nd Row. Turn the work down. Tie to the foundation of the last oval. Begin an oval 2 R D (L, 2 R D 6 times) draw up, not quite close. Tie to the foundation of the next oval. Begin another oval, 2 R D join to the last L of the last oval, 2 R D (L, 2 R D 5 times) draw up. Tie to the foundation of the next oval, and work 2 more similar ovals.

"Miss MacKnight." Tyree's voice accompanied a sharp rap on the cabin door. "Miss MacKnight, you got to come see this."

"I don't need anything, Tyree."

"But you got to see." He rattled the doorknob. "Please, Miss MacKnight. You'll be glad."

With a sigh, Fiona laid the bit of knotted lace aside. Removing her spectacles, she walked over to the door, opened it, and peered out through the few inches of open space. Tyree pointed toward the prow. "It's the *Mary McDonald*, and they got a grizzly bear on board! We're stopping alongside them at the coal yard. You ever see a grizzly bear? I never. Don't you want to see it? You don't even got to go down the ladder. Just come out. Stand right here by the door and I bet you'll see it just fine."

Fiona opened the door a bit wider.

"Now isn't that sunshine nice? Don't you like that? You shouldn't be all shut up in there on a fine day like this. Why, it could rain every day for a week starting tomorrow, and then there'd you'd be, missing what you didn't enjoy today. Wishing you'd come out. I could bring your chair right out here so's you could sit in the doorway. Wouldn't that be nice? Soak up some of this here sunshine."

The boy didn't even wait for Fiona to answer him as he wrapped a bit of rope about the doorknob and then tied it off to the hook mounted for that very purpose on the wall behind the door. Fiona took a step back into the safety of the cabin.

Tyree dragged a chair out of the corner and braced it in the doorway, and before Fiona could protest, he'd taken her arm and led her over to sit in the fresh air. As the *Laura Rose* eased up to some kind of primitive landing not too far distant from the other steamboat, Fiona reached over to grasp the door frame to keep the chair from tipping. Maybe it wouldn't tip, but one couldn't be too sure, and she had no intention of providing a spectacle for the men on that other steamboat.

"There now," Tyree said. "You all situated. You sure you won't come down to the hurricane deck and get a closer look?"

"I'm fine. Leave me be."

Tyree skittered off and Fiona peered over at the faded letters spelling out the packet's name. The *Mary McDonald* had seen better days. Her paint was peeling, her prow battered. *Poor old thing. I know how you feel*, Mary McDonald, *sitting here next to the bright and shining* Laura Rose. She hadn't thought about it before, but plenty of steamboats bore ladies' names. Fiona could think of three right off, because Finn had worked aboard them at one time or another: *Cora. Emilie. Fanny Barker.* And then an odd thought sprang up. Did men name steamboats for women so that they could control at least one female in their lives?

She almost laughed aloud at her own joke. And then she glanced up toward the wheelhouse. Finn might do just fine controlling the packet bearing the name *Laura Rose*. But how were things faring between him and the live version? *Something a chaperone would generally know*. She must overcome her fear. She must.

She let out a little yelp at the sound of the gangplank hitting the decking of the primitive landing. But then movement on the lower deck of the *Mary McDonald* distracted her. She squinted. And when she realized what she was seeing, she quite forgot herself. Rising from her chair, Fiona approached the edge of the texas in a vain attempt to get a better look at the gigantic creature inside a cage positioned in the center of the lightly loaded freight deck of the other steamboat.

Curiosity got the best of her. Taking a deep breath, Fiona made her way around the corner, past Finn's cabin door, and down the narrow stairs to the hurricane deck. She hurried past the line of passengers gathered there, attempting to get a better view of the thing in the cage. At the sight of Finn at the far end of the deck, she hurried toward him. Just as she was about to touch his shoulder and slip ahead of him, the most horrible sound she'd ever heard rolled across the waters from that cage.

A collective gasp went up from the people gathered along the railing. One woman screamed. *An overreaction*, Fiona thought. After all, the animal was in a cage. At quite a safe distance, too. Fiona strained on tiptoe, and for once in her life she was pleased to be tall. She would never forget her brief glimpse of that tawny beast.

The young woman who had screamed backed away from the railing. She was pale and trembling, and for a moment Fiona forgot that she, too, should be trembling with fear. Not of a caged bear—but of the uncaged river. "Here now," she said. "Let's get you into the dining saloon for a nice cup of tea."

At the sound of her voice, Finn looked back. His voice reflected disbelief. "Fiona?"

"Yes, yes, it's me," Fiona said and took the thin young woman's arm. "Is it possible to get this poor child a cup of tea?"

"Oh, Captain MacKnight!" the woman gasped. Her face colored a bit, and Fiona wondered if the scream and the near-faint might have been manufactured. That made her wonder where Adele might be. Her eyes scanned the crowd, but there was no sign of Adele.

Finn led them toward the prow. A wide deck boasted a scattering of chairs for passengers who wished to take the air. Fiona thought they looked comfortable, and just as she had the thought a rail-thin woman settled into one of them and, setting a knitting bag on the deck at her feet, went to work. Apparently she was not impressed by the chance to see a grizzly bear. Fiona wondered why not.

When Finn directed them into the dining saloon, the trembling young woman's pale face flushed. "You needn't bother with me."

Finn flashed a gracious smile. "It's no bother at all, Miss Chadwick. We want you to have good memories of the *Laura Rose*. Here now, just take my arm."

When he retreated toward the kitchen to request the tea, Fiona realized that Finn was using only one crutch. Why, that was wonderful. And she'd missed news of his progress. Adele hadn't even mentioned it. Certainly that deserved a scolding. On the other hand, she'd seen very little of Adele, who left the cabin at first light every morning and rarely returned until Fiona lay in bed praying for sleep.

Returning from the kitchen, Finn took a seat and introduced Fiona before explaining, "Miss Chadwick and her mother will be with us all the way to Fort Benton."

Just then, a portly woman nearly as wide as she was tall

bustled into the saloon. "Oh, here you are, Euphemia. When I heard you scream—Oh, Captain MacKnight, you are a dear—Thank you so much—What—Your sister? Why, yes, yes. Of course." Mrs. Chadwick spun about and greeted Fiona. "A pleasure, Miss MacKnight. We are so pleased to see that you are feeling better, aren't we, Euphemia? Now Captain MacKnight, you must not let us keep you from your duties. However, now that your dear sister is better, we'll hope to have you join us this evening."

Finn made what Fiona considered to be a rather vague reply and excused himself to go into the galley to check on the tea. The cook—Fiona remembered she had the odd name of Bird—brought it right away, and with a tip of his cap, Finn was gone.

While Mrs. Chadwick fluttered about her daughter, Fiona thought again of Adele. A thought that led to worry. "I wonder," she asked, "if you might have seen my sister this morning?"

"Why, yes, of course. She was across that gangplank as soon as the *Laura Rose* landed. She is such an adventurous thing, isn't she? And so interested in learning about new places. Very bright, too. Dr. Ross seems to delight in spending time with her. Now I know that look, Miss MacKnight, but you must not worry. His name is Dr. Malcolm Ross, and he is above reproach. I am certain you will agree once you have made his acquaintance."

Mrs. Chadwick moved with a grace that belied her bulk. Her hooped skirt of tiers of black silk ruffles—which was, Fiona noted, outdated by a good five years—rustled as she rose and poured more tea. "Drink it all, Euphemia. No, no, I don't think lemon is a good idea right now. Nor cream. Strong tea will lift your spirits, dear. I am so happy to see that you are feeling better, Miss MacKnight."

The woman dashed and darted through a conversation like a hen scurrying after a flying insect. Here and there, never pausing long enough for Fiona to say a word. Which was just as well, for Fiona's attentions were elsewhere. Finally, though, Mrs. Chadwick sat back with her own cup of tea and, gazing toward the out-of-doors, murmured, "Your handsome brother has been very concerned about you, Miss MacKnight."

Fiona frowned. "He has?"

"Why, yes. Euphemia has been so disappointed that he couldn't join us for our nightly cribbage tournament. But of course when he explained that he needed to spend time with you—Well, that's just so admirable. To find a man so devoted to his sister. To both of them equally, it seems. He fairly dotes on Adele, doesn't he? And goodness, one can see why. Such a sweet child. And so determined to excel at the piano. We have quite enjoyed her evening concerts. Now that you are feeling better, you simply must join us at the early set. Won't you?" She glanced toward the prow. "Ah, me, and now we're on our way again."

Fiona looked toward the open doors, amazed to see that the *Laura Rose* was, indeed, moving. And she hadn't even noticed.

"We'll be at Lexington this evening," Mrs. Chadwick said, clucking her tongue as she made mention of the *Saluda*. "Such a tragedy. Our pastor's brother was killed in the explosion."

Mention of the worst disaster in Missouri steamboat history coupled with an unfamiliar rumble from the freight deck below set Fiona trembling.

"I am thankful to know we are quite safe in the capable hands of Mr. MacKnight and Miss White." Mrs. Chadwick sighed.

Safe? No such thing existed when it came to steamboating, and the *Saluda* was proof. On the other hand, Fiona reminded herself, the final verdict on that horrible event laid the fault at the feet of a reckless captain, and neither Finn nor

Laura White was reckless. At least, she surely hoped not. She did her best to calm herself and sip tea with the Chadwicks, but then the sun went behind a cloud and Mrs. Chadwick said something about their going outside to view the river when they passed the wreck of another steamboat in just a mile or two. Fiona could not help it. She did not want to see a wrecked steamboat. Excusing herself, she hurried back to her cabin.

When Tyree next came around, he explained the meaning of Mrs. Chadwick's term "early set." The *Laura Rose*'s dining saloon could seat only twenty-five diners at a time, and since they had forty cabin passengers, Hercules and Bird served and cleared twice for each meal. "Early set" for supper was at 7:00 p.m. "Second set" began an hour and a half later.

"You all work very late indeed."

"Yes'm. Hercules and me are still washing dishes at midnight most nights, while Bird sets her sponge for breakfast rolls and such. I help, even though it ain't part of a cabin boy's duties. But Hercules—he's my uncle, ya know—he says a idle child is a child in trouble. I told him he don't have to worry 'bout me makin' trouble. I like it here on the *Laura Rose*. Folks are nice to me. I like that dog, too, but he's already got hisself a person."

Fiona smiled at the unique view of the fearsome-looking dog she'd seen on board. "And who would that person be?"

"Why, Captain White. Don't you know? That dog nearly kilt a man back in St. Louis, just for tryin' to kiss her. He been guardin' her ever since. You don't need to worry, though. Logjam likes Captain MacKnight, too. He won't try nothin', even if Captain was to try and kiss Captain White."

"Tyree."

"Yes'm?"

"It isn't proper for a young man to speak of such things."

"Oh, I know that, ma'am." He smiled. "Only reason I'm tellin' you is somethin' my aunt Bird used to say. She said brothers and sisters got to watch out for each other." His smile disappeared and he ducked his head. "But my mam, she don't think she needs watchin' out for. She wants to go her own way. Told Aunt Bird to mind her own business." He paused for a moment, but then the shy smile returned. "Anyway, I just wanted you to know. You don't have to worry for your brother none."

After he left, Fiona spent a good bit of time thinking over what Tyree had said about brothers and sisters and watching out for each other. The truth was that she was tired of watching out for other people. She longed for the day when she knew for certain that Finn was once and for all on the right track and Adele—*Oh, dear.* Would that girl ever get on the right track? She was so young. So immature. So capricious in the way she approached life. She never seemed to consider the long-term consequences of her actions.

Later in the afternoon, when Tyree came back to retrieve the tea tray, Fiona introduced the topic of brothers and sisters again. "I wish to thank you for reassuring me about my brother and that dog," Fiona said. "He is a fearsome-looking beast. I'm very glad to know that he gets along with Finn. However, on the topic of 'kin,' as you say, I do have a concern."

"Ma'am?"

"It seems to me that as a cabin boy, you have opportunity to know things about people that are very delicate in nature."

"Delicate?"

"Personal," Fiona said.

"Oh. You mean like this person likes to add whiskey to

their coffee and that one spends time in a cabin they didn't pay for?"

Fiona felt herself blushing at the implication. "Well...yes. And I do hope that you know to speak of those things with others would be wrong. Gossip is a sin, Tyree."

"Yes, ma'am, I know that." He swallowed and stood a little taller. "'I said, I will take heed to my ways, that I sin not with my tongue: I will keep my mouth with a bridle, while the wicked is before me. Wherefore, my beloved brethren, let every man be swift to hear, slow to speak, slow to wrath.'" He smiled. "Aunt Bird has me memberize Bible verses. Want to hear another one?" He didn't wait for Fiona to say yes. "'And whatsoever ye do, do it heartily, as to the Lord, and not unto men.'" He paused. "That means I'm really workin' for Jesus. Even when I'm washin' out the chamber pots. So I got to do my best to make Jesus proud."

Fiona suppressed a smile. "I'm very impressed that you know all those verses. I'm also grateful for your reassurance that Finn isn't in any danger from Miss White's dog." She realized she was repeating herself and cleared her throat. "It's good to know there's nothing to worry about. Do you think— I mean, would you feel the same way about my sister? Is she safe?"

"Oh, yes, ma'am. She's got all kinds of folks watching out for her. You don't need to worry a bit. Folks love hearing her play that piano. Especially the menfolks. She gets them to singing so, and sometimes it sounds just like a church choir. They have a high old time. Miss MacKnight plays and they all follow along, 'specially since Dr. Ross came on board. He has a fine voice." Tyree paused. "He knows 'most every verse of every hymn."

It was not hard to envision Adele seated at a piano surrounded by "the menfolk." Surely Finn could have realized— now, now. There was no reason to think badly of Finn. He wasn't the one burrowing into pillows trying to block out all the clattering and clanging.

Young Tyree took his leave, and Fiona went back to tatting. She ended up having to undo much of the work for most of the afternoon. And it wasn't because she was afraid of the river.

Chapter 19

Laura sensed trouble before MacKnight signaled it. Nothing she could put her finger on. Nothing she could explain to the uninitiated. Just a still, small voice whispering that all was not well with the *Laura Rose*. Instantly she was on her feet and out the door of the dining saloon where she'd been taking tea with Adele and simpering, fearful Miss Euphemia Chadwick.

She slipped Papa's watch out of her pocket on her way up the steps to the texas. Five o'clock in the evening. They had to be getting close to the Nebraska line. MacKnight was already hopping down the ladder from the wheelhouse by the time she cleared the steps.

"Sandbar," he groused. "May have to have Elijah North give the mate a lesson or two in sounding. If he'd reported it right, we would have cleared it just fine—especially after we unloaded that half ton at Kansas City."

"Think we can get off without lightering?"

MacKnight's response was gruff: "Can't know until we take a look, now, can we?" He hurried away.

Laura peered at the landscape, trying to get her bearings. She'd been at the wheel from midnight, when they left St. Joe, to mid-morning, when MacKnight took over around Nodaway Island Chute, two other packets behind them. Hav-

ing grown up hearing horror stories about what could happen when a couple of hotheaded pilots got it in their heads to
race on this river, she'd told MacKnight to let both packets by
without a challenge. "We're only racing against the calendar
this trip."

He'd seemed to agree at the time, but Laura could see
one of the other packets up ahead. The *Colonel Kidd* was just
about to pass them on the leeward side. She gazed up at the
wheelhouse just as Jack McCoy offered what she took to be a
mocking salute. She turned away with a shudder.

And what of Finn MacKnight? She'd been doing her best
to trust the man at the wheel of her packet. She had, in fact,
just gotten to where she didn't wake with every adjustment
of steam, every change in the rhythm of the *Laura Rose*'s
machinery. And now this. If he'd been racing, he was going to
be given a very big piece of her mind. As soon as they got off
this dad-blamed sandbar.

Elijah North was waiting for her at the bottom of the steps.
"Head of that chute near Squaw Point," he said, telling Laura
where they were. "No reason we should have grounded. Not
after unloading all that freight at Kansas City."

"Do you think sparring will do it, or are we going to have
to off-load some freight?"

Elijah jerked his head toward MacKnight, who was making his way toward the prow. "Cap'n MacKnight has something else he wants to try."

"What else is there?"

"Have no idea."

North waited for Laura and together they rushed to catch
up with MacKnight.

"Do you remember *Post Boy*?" he asked, the minute Laura
reached his side.

"Famous for speed," she said, bracing herself for the admission that he'd been racing.

He nodded. "The very same. McCoy and I were part of that crew when *Post Boy* went aground like this. Seeing him go past just now reminded me. We'd been racing the *De Smet* back then and had already broken a spar the day before. All we could do to get off the bar was to off-load. When that wasn't enough, we got creative."

"I don't suppose either of you entertained the idea that racing was especially stupid under those conditions?"

MacKnight motioned for one of the deckhands to break out the log chains. "Boys like to race," he said. "Cockroaches, pigs, horses. I've even heard they race ostriches somewhere. You'd have more success convincing a man to wear a lace-trimmed bonnet than to give up racing."

Finn MacKnight in a bonnet. If that wouldn't be a sight to behold. Unwilling to vent her anger within hearing of the other crew members, Laura held her peace about racing. "Elijah says you want to try something different?"

MacKnight nodded. "With your permission."

"I'm all for anything that will keep us moving without having to off-load freight."

The first thing MacKnight did after having the log chain called out was to have a different mate resound the river for depth. When the mate called out "Twenty-six inches," MacKnight flashed a dark look Laura's way. He'd claimed there'd been a mistake and it appeared he was right. Obviously, she had a mate to give a talking-to later. Or maybe she'd let MacKnight handle that. One problem with being a woman pilot was getting the right reaction to a dressing-down.

MacKnight called for crew members who could swim. Of those who stepped forward, he chose the four tallest. "You two stand on this side of that sandbar," he said and pointed to the leeward side of the *Laura Rose*. "You two over there."

Once the crew members were in position in the water, MacKnight directed each team to grasp the ends of the heavy log chain. "Now stretch it out. That's right. Drag it along the bottom, until you're just under the lip of the prow. Now heave, men. Heave! You're playing tug-of-war with the river, and you want her to win and wash the sand that you're shifting right out from under us." He turned around and hollered at the passengers up on the hurricane deck. "Move to the back! We need to lighten the prow! Move back!"

The passengers on both decks obeyed.

"If this doesn't work right away," he called to Laura, "we'll have to take some of the freight off her prow. But I think the river's running fast enough that—"

"Ho!" One of the men in the water hollered as he slipped and went under, but he reappeared and, shaking his head, went back to work, although not before enduring more than one bawdy comment about how glad everyone would be not to have to smell him tonight, now that he'd had a bath.

Laura watched in amazement as what she would have considered little more than a ridiculous trick began to work. The crew members who were now chest high in water worked the chain back and forth, and little by little, the sand began to wash away from the prow.

"Best get up to the wheelhouse," MacKnight said. "Full steam back. I think we can get her in the channel without lightering."

Laura scurried up the steps and the ladder and into the wheelhouse. She signaled for her engineers to give her more steam and to reverse the paddle wheel. With agonizing slowness, the *Laura Rose* began to move. And then she was free of the sandbar.

From his place at the prow, MacKnight bellowed something Laura couldn't make out. She guided the *Laura Rose* slowly back into the channel and ordered the reverse in the engines that would take her forward.

MacKnight waved frantically. What did he want? When

she didn't respond, he took a step forward on his bad leg and went down. His face a mask of pain, he flailed his message to a crew member. The crew member tore across the deck and up the stairs, then came to the wheelhouse and screamed, "Hold! Jim's slipped into the channel! You'll run him down! Hold 'til he swims free!"

✴

Laura clutched the wheel for all she was worth, putting every ounce of her strength into holding the *Laura Rose* steady, seeking the magic balance between keeping the steamer from losing ground to the swift current and making headway lest she— Dear Lord, she'd nearly killed one of the crew. At long last, she saw a roustabout lean over and begin to drag the log chain back on board. One by one, the men who'd been in the water— all four of them—were hoisted back on deck. Finally, Elijah North stepped to the prow and, standing next to the capstan engine, waved to get Laura's attention. When she waved back, he turned around and motioned for her to proceed upriver.

Laura blew the whistle to signal the crew—and the passengers, for that matter—that they could resume their evening, then she guided the *Laura Rose* up the channel, wondering all the while about MacKnight, who'd disappeared from view while she was watching her crew members get pulled back on board. Was he still down on the freight deck? How badly was he hurt?

At the very next wood yard at Rush Bottom, Laura pulled the steamboat up and went in search of MacKnight, hoping to discover that he'd simply decided to stay below and get cleaned up in time to host the first set. Someone would have told her if he was badly injured. On the other hand, no one would tell her if he'd decided to seek solace in a little medicinal whiskey. The idea blossomed into a combination of dread and fear that made it hard to catch a deep breath.

But MacKnight wasn't in his cabin. Laura's concern shifted when she checked in the dining saloon and saw that the chair at the head of the dining table was empty. And, she realized, Adele MacKnight was nowhere in sight. *Oh, dear.* Had MacKnight been unable to leave the freight deck? Was Adele with him now?

Before Laura could get away, Euphemia Chadwick's mother rose from the table and came to inquire after MacKnight. "Is the captain all right? Someone said he further injured his leg. Euphemia is simply beside herself with worry. She said that Miss MacKnight was headed off to do a bit of nursing."

Oh, dear. "Thank you for your concern. I'm just going to check on Captain MacKnight now, and I'll be certain to tell him that you and Miss Chadwick were asking after him."

"Oh, no, no, that's not necessary." Mrs. Chadwick glanced back toward her daughter. "We wouldn't want to appear overly—Well, you do understand, I'm sure."

Ah. So this was more than just a polite inquiry. Laura gazed at Euphemia. She didn't seem the type of woman who would attract someone like Finn MacKnight. Laura's gaze swept the table. For the first time, she realized that the ladies on board had migrated away from her "late set" table and toward the one presided over by MacKnight. Of course.

She smiled at Mrs. Chadwick. "If you'll excuse me, I'm going to track him down and scold him for dereliction of duty in regards to hosting the meal. And it is nice to know that he was missed." She leaned close. "To be quite honest, I wasn't certain my passengers would appreciate Captain MacKnight. He's not always as...um...refined as he might be."

The older woman's cheeks brightened with a blush. "I know what you mean," she said. "But then, my dear, isn't that part of his charm? There's something about a man who is so unaware of his masculine appeal that he doesn't bother with the usual primping. It really is quite powerful."

*   *   *

Laura found MacKnight sitting alone at the rear edge of the
freight deck near the paddle wheel. Logjam lay next to him,
his chin resting on his paws. When Logjam raised his head
at her approach, MacKnight looked up. His expression transformed, but not quite quickly enough for him to mask the
pain. Laura looked down at his bad leg.

"You're bleeding," she said. She knelt and reached out.

"Leave it be," he groused, pulling the leg away before she
could touch it. "It's just a scrape. I tripped over a crate."

Laura sat down. "You tried to bear all your weight on that
leg and it gave way."

He shrugged. "And when I finally managed to get back up
again, I was so angry I didn't pay attention to where I was
headed, so I tripped over a"—he barely avoided the expletive,
but he did—"crate. You were too busy trying not to drown
Jim Bevins to see the grand display." He paused. "And even
though I once forbade you to mother me, I will admit that it's
nice of you to come check on me. I'll be fine."

"Good." Laura nodded. "Then we can talk about a couple
of things."

He tilted his head and peered at her. Nodded. "No, ma'am. I
was not racing those other packets. I've been going over some of
what I said earlier, and I could see where you might have taken
some of that as an admission of guilt. But you have my word—
which, I realize, is a bit tarnished—that I wouldn't risk the
Laura Rose. I'm nowhere near that big a fool." He almost smiled.
"Even if I do have fond memories of my champion cockroach."

Laura shuddered. "Tell me that isn't true."

He grinned. "I kept him in a cigar box. Bet you can guess
his name."

"You named a cockroach?"

"Didn't you name your dolls? At least Cigar was real.
Alive, I mean."

"I didn't have dolls," Laura said.

"Not even one?"

"All right. One. She did not fare well. She was at the wheel when her steamboat crashed, and her injuries were fatal."

He grinned. "So...that wagon you rode down a hill really was meant to be a steamboat, eh? If I recall correctly, in addition to the demise of a china-headed doll, there were stitches to be endured." He pointed to the scar beneath her left eyebrow.

Laura's hand went to the spot.

"Joe told me all about it. He thought you were amazing, you know." He paused. "I'm beginning to see exactly what he meant."

She looked away. "It isn't fair of you to bring up Joe and make me cry when I came down here to speak with you about risking my steamboat in an ill-conceived effort to further impress Miss Chadwick."

"Who's Miss—oh." He took a deep breath. "Well, now, my captain. The truth of the matter is, there is only one person aboard this packet that I care to impress." His dark eyes flashed as he looked over at her. "You can trust me. I won't knowingly risk your namesake." He touched his own eyebrow. "It's rather fetching, by the way."

When Laura didn't seem to follow the point, he smiled. "The scar. Flawless beauty is tiresome. The scar adds character."

Without thinking about it, Laura reached up again.

"And that gesture. Do you realize you do that when you're feeling unsettled?"

Snatching her hand away, Laura pointed at MacKnight's leg. "Are you sure all you did was scrape your leg? The way you're babbling, I'm concerned you might have hit your head. It's too bad we only have a doctor of theology on board. Maybe we can rouse a medical doctor at Arago. If we keep running we could make it around midnight."

"If we keep running tonight, we'll end up grounded on another sandbar. Especially if we trust Gordon's soundings." As MacKnight moved, he winced.

"You're right about Gordon," Laura said. "Who do you recommend?"

MacKnight didn't hide his surprise. "Me? You want my recommendation?" When Laura nodded, he said, "Jim Bevins. He has a personal appreciation for respecting the depth of any water we encounter."

"You don't think he'll be afraid I'll run him down again?" Laura chuckled as she reached out to pet Logjam, who rolled onto his side. "I've never seen that done before," she said.

"A cripple falling?"

"Men standing in waist-high water, maneuvering a log chain that way. You and Jack McCoy figured that out?"

"It was a stupid contest of strength," Finn said. "We weren't exactly sober at the time and we were both surprised it worked. Now that I think about it, it's a miracle one of us didn't drown."

"It's a miracle Jim Bevins didn't. I could have—"

"That had nothing to do with your skills as a pilot. You're very good. None of that was your fault."

"We should work on some way to replace—mobility," Laura said. "Hand signals might work."

MacKnight only shrugged.

All right. He didn't want to talk about it anymore. She'd bring the topic of hand signals back another time. Hopefully before they grounded again. "You were missed at first set," she said.

He sighed. "I just didn't have it in me this evening."

"Mrs. Chadwick especially asked after you."

He smiled. "And Mr. Perry Firmand will do the same if you don't host the late set." After a moment, he said, "Hand signals. Good idea."

She rose to go. "We'll talk it over another time." She

pointed at his torn pants leg. "If you don't want me to play nursemaid, that's fine, but someone needs to look at that leg and get it cleaned and wrapped up."

"I'll ask Fiona to help with it."

"Shall I send her down here to fetch you?"

"Here? Next to the paddle wheel?"

Laura nodded. "Right. Bad idea. I think she might be doing better, though. I caught a glimpse of her with Adele when the passengers were moving to the back to help us get off that sandbar." She held out her hand. "Let's go. If we hurry, we can make the second setting together. There's no reason for you to go hungry." MacKnight seemed about to ignore the hand up. She waggled her fingers. "Take the hand, MacKnight." He did, and she braced herself and hauled him to his feet. "Was that so bad?" She handed him his crutch.

"I might need more help," he said. "Could I maybe put my free arm around you? You could help me to the stairs."

"You really are a rapscallion, aren't you?" Laura moved away, but she couldn't hide the smile.

The two of them were at the top of the hurricane deck stairs when Adele called, "Finally! There you are!" She held up a black metal box. "Bird sent me to find Mr. North and he gave me the supply box. I've come to tend your wounds, dear brother." And then she prattled on about Fiona's having fainted dead away at some point when Laura was up in the wheelhouse doing her best not to drown poor Jim Bevins.

"I leave you in good hands," Laura said as MacKnight prepared to follow Adele to the texas and his own cabin. "If you don't feel up to the dining experience," she said, "I'll have Tyree bring a tray to your cabin." She lingered at the bottom of the stairs, watching as MacKnight hobbled after his sister. What was it Mrs. Chadwick had said? *There's something about a man who is so unaware of his masculine appeal that he doesn't bother with the usual primping. It's very powerful.*

Mrs. Chadwick wasn't altogether right. Finn MacKnight was very well aware of his masculine appeal. Not bothering with "the usual primping" was, in fact, part of it. But yes, it was very powerful. As were those forearms of his. Those massive hands. And those shoulders. *Oh, my . . . those shoulders.*

He'd referred to her again as *my captain*. She didn't mind.

Chapter 20

With a quick intake of breath, Fiona came instantly awake. Something was different. A sound…a tremor…what was wrong?

"It's all right," Adele said. "You're safe. I talked to Finn just a little while ago. We've made some good distance since that sandbar, but the wind's coming up now. He said if it kept up, we might have to pull in and tie up for a while."

Fiona lifted her head and stared through the gloom to where Adele was sitting in a chair beside the bed. She'd lit a lamp, and in the pale light, her blonde hair shone like a golden halo. She was still fully dressed.

"H-how—?"

"Mrs. Chadwick had smelling salts with her. We were able to revive you enough so that you could manage the stairs—at least in part. Some of the men helped."

Thank goodness it was dark. Her face would be aflame with shame. She remembered how the *Laura Rose* lurched to a stop. She had looked out the window to find they were in the middle of nowhere. Taking a deep breath, she left the cabin, trailing her fingertips along the outer wall of the texas deck cabins, until she descended to the hurricane deck.

She'd found Adele at the head of the crowd, leaning hard against the railing like a child at the circus. She remembered worrying that if that railing gave way, Adele would be hurled into open space, land on some pile of freight below, and—she could be killed. But scarcely had the thought ensued when someone shouted for the passengers to move to the rear of the steamboat. Fiona sidled along the narrow aisle, past the cabins and toward the paddle wheel, and Adele came to her side. "If this doesn't work," Adele had said, "they'll probably have to lower the skiffs and start to take freight off. Maybe both freight and passengers."

Fiona had looked over at the skiff hanging on this side of the *Laura Rose*. She heard the engines below, straining against the river. She thought of the *Saluda*. The *Lucy Walker*. The *Sultana*. All those words brought horrible tragedies to mind, tragedies caused by overworked boilers in situations much like this one. Lives were lost. People drowned. The engine chugged. The paddle wheel creaked. Fiona looked back at the skiff. Then at the swiftly running river. Bile rose in her throat. She swallowed.

"Fiona," Adele said, trying to wrest herself free. "You're hurting me. Please let go."

But Fiona couldn't manage to loosen her grip. Adele had pulled free. "It's all *right*, for heaven's sake. It's not even much of a sandbar. We'll be free in just a mo—"

A louder creak and the sound of metal on metal and the very floor beneath them lurched. Fiona had let out a screech. Her heart raced. They were wrecking. The shudders were proof. There was a rip in the hull and they were going down. Fiona had slammed herself against the wall of the cabin behind them, trying in vain to find purchase. Something to hold on to. Anything. The boat was tipping. She was going to be thrown into the water.

"Somebody help!"

Adele was yelling for help, too.

Dear God. I'm going to drown. And that was the last thing Fiona remembered.

She looked away from where Adele now sat. "I thought—"
A sob interrupted Fiona's words. She turned onto her side,
clutching a pillow to her. "All I could think about was that
water. Going into that water. I felt the deck tilt and—"

"It wasn't really out of the ordinary, at least according to
Finn," Adele said. "He didn't even want to take credit for getting us off the sandbar. Then again, he wasn't in much of a
mood to talk. I was bandaging his leg."

Adele, bandaging a leg? Would wonders never cease? Fiona
lifted her head. "Finn's hurt?"

"He got caught up in the moment and took a step without
his crutch. Took a tumble. Scraped his bum leg." She paused.
"He was going to ask you to see to it, but you were...um...
indisposed. So I took care of it."

"You?"

"It's just a scrape. I washed it and put some disgusting salve
on it." She shuddered. "Honestly it felt like I was smearing
phlegm on his leg, but Bird said it's practically a magic potion.
He'll be good as new in a few days—except for the serious
blow to his pride." She forced a low laugh.

Fiona took a deep breath. "What time is it? Where are we?"

"It's probably near midnight. We're somewhere in Nebraska.
Miss White was hoping to make Brownville by dark, but the
river had other ideas. I don't imagine anyone's very happy
about this wind." Just as she said the words, a sharp gust made
the windows rattle. Again, Fiona tensed.

"Why don't you sit up and let me take your hair down?"
Adele said. "I could brush it for you, if you like. Papa used to
do that for me when I had nightmares."

Fiona reached up to check on her only attribute—her
thick, abundant, wavy hair. If she didn't see to it, she would
have a tangled mess to deal with in the morning. Helping
her would make Adele feel useful, and that would be a good
thing. Fiona sat up and, still clutching the pillow, moved so

that Adele could begin to remove hairpins, which she did with surprising gentleness.

"You do have beautiful hair," Adele said as she began to work the brush through it, first just down at the ends and then working her way slowly up, so that tangles came out without too much snarling. "One hundred strokes. Isn't that what they say?"

The brush against Fiona's scalp gave her goose bumps of pleasure. No one had done this for her since—well, there was that one time when Albert talked her into taking down her hair. He'd taken her for a drive and surprised her with a picnic. And who knew what else he'd had in mind? She'd brought an abrupt end to things. But it had felt divine to have him brush through her hair.

"I didn't know you almost drowned as a child," Adele said. "It's no wonder you've been so miserable." She seemed to sense Fiona stiffen, for she hurried to say, "Finn told me when I was tending his leg. When I told him you'd fainted. I'm so sorry, Fiona."

"It's ridiculous that it still haunts me. I can't seem to will the fear away." She blinked back unwanted tears and changed the subject. "I wasn't aware that you suffered from nightmares as a child. When did they stop?"

Adele didn't answer for a while. She just kept brushing. "It was gradual."

"But you never called out in your sleep. I would have heard you. I would have come."

Again, Adele waited before answering. "I didn't think it a good idea to call out. I...um...I slept with a pillow over my head so you wouldn't be disturbed." She segued back to the topic of hair without a pause. "Let me braid it for you and we'll be finished. The packet will likely be tied up for a while. No bumps in the night to disturb your rest."

Fiona submitted to having her hair braided, all the while

trying not to think about a terrified girl-child covering her head with a pillow because she was afraid to disturb some-one. To disturb *her*. Fresh tears pricked her eyes. A clunk overhead made her jump.

"That's nothing. Probably just Miss White up in the wheelhouse. Yes, that's it. You can hear her footsteps. She'd be going down the ladder now. And there. Hear that? On the texas. And...no cabin door sounds, so she's probably going down to the kitchen to get a late-night snack. If you don't mind, I think I'll follow suit and make certain our brother's behaving himself. I reminded him of the doctor's insistence that he keep his foot up on a cushion as much as possible when he was first recovering. Of course I have no idea whether that applies to skinned shins or not, but it can't hurt to be especially careful, now, can it?"

All the while that Adele was talking, she was moving about the cabin, putting away Fiona's hairbrush, returning the chair to its rightful place in the corner, draping her own nightdress over the footboard of the bed "so that I won't dis-turb you when I come in."

Just before she left, she paused in the doorway. "I'll bring some chamomile tea with me when I come back," she said. "If you're awake when I come in, just ask for it. If you don't ask, I'll assume you're asleep. Does that suit?"

"That will be fine," Fiona said. "Thank you."

Adele closed the door. Fiona could hear her footsteps as she hurried alongside the cabin and on toward the narrow stairs. Fearless. The child was fearless. But she hadn't always been. As Fiona turned down the lamp and slipped down beneath the coverlet, she thought back to those first days after Adele was dropped on her doorstep. How Finn had gone off with a young Joseph White, both of them deckhands on a side-wheeler bound for New Orleans. She remembered Albert LaFarge's ultimatum and her quick decision to do her duty by

Adele. She remembered how deserted she'd felt. How bereft of hope. She remembered her own heartbroken tears.

The specter of ten-year-old Adele afraid to call out, terrified and without comfort, swept over her. *God forgive me.* Curling around her pillow, Fiona wept.

※

The familiar sound of a steam engine straining to power a paddle wheel woke Laura in the middle of the night. Or it woke Logjam, who woke Laura. Either way, when she opened her cabin door to investigate, the first thing she noticed was that the wind had died down.

Dressing quickly, Laura stepped outside and looked upriver toward where the *Colonel Kidd* had been tied up at sundown. Jack McCoy had sent part of his crew upriver in a skiff, and they'd sounded the depths and set floating lights out to mark the channel for safe passage. Hurrying down to the freight deck, Laura roused the crew, leaving MacKnight to sleep or wake as he wished.

Following in the wake of the *Colonel Kidd*, the *Laura Rose* slipped between the lights set out by McCoy's crew and then, at Brownville, headed for the levee while the other packet continued on out of sight. They put off the lone passenger who wanted to disembark at Brownville, and by the time that was accomplished, the lights upriver had flickered out. Laura ordered the crew to tie up until dawn could light the way.

In the half-light of the hour just past dawn, they eased past the wreck of the *Nora*, a packet slowly being torn apart by the river as she rested on the bottom, only her wheelhouse visible above the waterline. The fresh reminder of just how quickly disaster could strike made Laura shudder. She was just coming into Nebraska City where they'd be putting off freight when MacKnight hoisted himself into the wheelhouse.

"You've already passed the *Nora*."

"Nothing to it," Laura said.

"I heard there was a quartz mill on board that packet. A thirty-thousand-dollar piece of mining machinery at the bottom of the river." He looked over at her. "Heard she was running at night, too. When a sawyer ripped her hull wide open."

"Was she running lights?"

"Don't know."

"Stupid not to do that on this stretch," Laura said, "especially on a dark night. No moon at all last night." She smiled. "We crept upriver courtesy of Jack McCoy and the *Colonel Kidd.*" Taking advantage of McCoy that way was its own kind of sweet revenge for what he'd tried with her back in St. Louis. "As soon as those lights were done, so was I. I stayed put until dawn." She looked over at him. "We're coming up on Bethlehem Bar. At Brownville they said there's only about thirty inches of water flowing over it right now."

MacKnight was quiet for a moment. Finally he said, "We may regret taking on all that wood back at Keg Island." He was quick to add, "Not that I'm second-guessing my captain. I'm just thinking aloud."

"We can't risk being stranded because we underestimated cordage and end up having to send the crew ashore to cut wood."

MacKnight nodded. "I'm not saying you did anything wrong. I realize that you're the one with the most to lose. As far as I'm concerned, you make the final decision when things come up. I'm just talking it over. That's all."

Laura looked over at him. "The sandbar up ahead formed around another wreck. It isn't going to work to put men in the water and drag a chain over it."

"I know."

"But you have an idea. I can see it cooking behind those bloodshot, sleep-deprived eyes."

MacKnight nodded. "What if we loaded the skiffs with as much wood as they'll hold and tried towing them behind us?

It might lighten the *Laura Rose* just enough to let us skim across the bar—without taking the time to put cargo ashore we then have to retrieve."

Laura motioned for him to take the wheel. "Might work. I'll get the boys started on it."

"I'll do it," MacKnight said.

"No need. Save the leg. Besides, I—"

"I said I'd do it," MacKnight groused.

With a sigh, Laura leaned forward to watch as MacKnight limped along the texas and then descended the stairs. Her stomach growled. *Ah, well.* Maybe she could have Tyree bring her something when he brought breakfast up to Fiona.

Poor Fiona. There had to be something they could do to help her feel less miserable.

❊

It was nearly noon before Finn finally dragged himself back up to the wheelhouse to face Miss White. He was tired and filthy and feeling more than a little useless. For all his grand ideas, loading the skiffs hadn't worked. They'd ended up having to put freight ashore to lighten the packet. For four hours, all he'd been able to do was sit in one of the skiffs and haul it back and forth like a ferry operator. Other crew members did the heavy lifting. Even old Elijah North with his aged but strong legs had done more than Finn.

Miss White stepped away from the wheel the minute he showed up. The look on her face said she was not happy with the time they'd wasted trying yet another of his ideas.

"I'm sorry," he said, as he took the wheel. "I know what you're thinking. In the future, unless you ask for my opinion, I'll keep my harebrained ideas to myself."

"What do you mean, 'harebrained'?" she protested. "It wasn't a bad idea. It might have worked. And you don't know what I'm thinking, so don't assume you do."

He shrugged and wiped his forehead with a grimy forearm. "I'm not angry, Finn. I'm *hungry*."

He looked over at her. "You still haven't eaten?"

She shook her head. "That's why I wanted to give the orders earlier—about off-loading the wood into the skiffs. I could have grabbed something to eat when I passed by the galley."

He barely avoided cursing himself. "I'm sorry. I thought—"

"I know." Her expression softened. "Finn, could you please stop being so dad-blamed sensitive about having a bum leg? You're the only one who thinks it's much of a factor." When he only shrugged, she flashed a smile. "And besides that, you aren't the only one in the wheelhouse with a special challenge."

"Yeah, right," he snorted.

"Tell you what," she said. "Tomorrow, you can wear the petticoats and I'll take the crutch. At the end of the day, we'll compare notes."

❄

The evening after Fiona fainted and had to be taken to her room, Adele tapped on the door and slipped into the cabin just as the *Laura Rose* landed at Council Bluffs. "Oh, good," she said. "I was hoping you'd be up." She opened the drapes. "I wanted you to see something. The two other steamboats at the levee have already lit their lamps. The reflection on the water is so beautiful."

Fiona rose and walked to the windows while Adele chattered on.

"Dr. Ross says Council Bluffs is 'the metropolis of western Iowa.'"

Fiona sniffed. "It doesn't look like much from here."

"Well, I don't suppose it is much, compared to St. Louis," Adele agreed. "We'll be at Omaha later tonight. Malcolm says it's the headquarters for the Great Plains buffalo hides business. Can you imagine such a thing? A *center* for buffalo hides. He told me the numbers that were shipped last year. I don't remember exactly, but it was astonishing. I didn't know there were that many buffalo in the world. Malcolm says Council Bluffs may rival Omaha one day. The Chicago and North Western Railway just arrived this spring. It links Council Bluffs to Chicago and the markets in the city of New York, and from there to the world. Malcolm says that is just what a city needs to achieve balanced growth."

" 'Balanced growth.' My, my. He said all that?" Fiona didn't know whether to be impressed or worried about Adele's newly acquired habit of parroting whatever Dr. Malcolm Ross said. It certainly did not bode well if she was calling him by his Christian name. Look what had happened when she'd been so—familiar—with Joseph White. *Oh, dear.*

Adele suppressed a smile. She nodded. "Yes. That means growth that includes culture. Not the kind of growth that's happening up in Montana, where gold is everything and there's very little if any true culture."

" 'Culture,' you say."

Again Adele nodded. "Malcolm has invited some of us to accompany him into town. He's supposed to meet with a pastor there. Something about founding a new seminary out here in the west."

"A seminary? But—"

"Well, yes, a seminary." Adele hesitated. "Oh, goodness, Fiona. Did you think Malcolm was a doctor of *medicine*? My, no. He's a doctor of *theology*. Why do you think I've been so certain you would like him? He suggested that I ask you to join us on our excursion. Mrs. Chadwick and Euphemia are going as well. We're going to do a little window-shopping. It feels like a lifetime since I did that." She paused. "Please come, Fiona. The walk would do you good."

"You make it sound as if I'm an invalid," Fiona scolded.

"Goodness, I'd never think that. I've assured everyone who even hints at it that you're the furthest thing from a recluse that they could ever imagine."

"Recluse! People are thinking I'm a *recluse?*"

"I'm doing my best to put an end to that nonsense. And Malcolm would never say anything like that. Why, I don't believe he has an unkind bone in his body."

"I think," Fiona said, as she reached for her shawl, "that it is high time you introduced me to this Dr. Malcolm Ross." Injured or not, it seemed that Finn could have at least given some attention to Adele's behavior. He might be ignorant in regards to what had really gone on between Adele and Joseph White, but surely he could not be unaware of this seeming attempt of Adele's to latch on to another man. *Malcolm indeed.* "Where does this Dr. Ross teach, by the way?"

Adele kept talking as they walked. "Oh, he isn't teaching right now. I told you. He's come west to investigate future locations for a new seminary. He said that the West is touted as a cure for all kinds of illnesses. Did you know that?"

"He's ill?"

"Oh, no. He seems the picture of health. He's actually quite handsome in his own way, and absolutely a favorite of all the ladies. He's so charming. He listens very well and he seems to be able to talk about any topic anyone brings up. And his voice. He has the most lovely baritone singing voice." Adele sighed. "Honestly, Fiona, he's just wonderful. You'll see. Here now, just watch your step. Here we are at the hurricane deck. Just around this way. Oh. And another thing about Malcolm. It doesn't seem to matter what hymn people request that I play, he knows it. And all the verses in most cases. I realize that's probably an exaggeration, but—"

The longer the child blathered the more alarmed Fiona became.

And then they rounded the corner.

Fiona could not remember the last time she had been struck speechless. Dr. Ross did so merely by rising from the chair where he'd been sitting on the deck of the *Laura Rose* and removing his hat as Adele led her forward.

He bowed as Adele introduced her. "Miss MacKnight," he said, in a mellifluous voice that made Fiona think that oratory must be among his duties at the seminary—if he was indeed on the faculty. "It is an honor to meet you at last."

He wore a black frock coat buttoned almost to the neck, above which the slightest bit of blue showed in the form of a silk cravat tied about a pristine white collar. A very neatly trimmed beard accented the jawline. It was shaped to a *V* beneath his mouth in such a way that it seemed to accent the cleft in his chin. His hair was cropped short, revealing a modestly receding hairline. He had finely arched eyebrows, an aristocratic nose, and pale blue eyes. His smile revealed perfect teeth. And he was old enough to be Adele's father.

Chapter 21

Back from their excursion into Council Bluffs, the MacKnight sisters retreated to their cabin. Adele hung her bonnet beside Fiona's on the rack by the door. Taking a deep breath, she turned to face her sister. "Before you say anything, I know I shouldn't be purchasing any new bonnets or anything else while we're on board the *Laura Rose*. But it was fun to see that one shop, and didn't Euphemia seem to be enjoying herself? She blushes so easily—I really must stop teasing her about Finn." Adele laced her fingers together and stood almost at attention as she said, "There. A confession and repentance and a promise not to spend money, all rolled into one little speech." She lifted her chin. "And now, I'm ready."

"Ready for what?" Fiona asked.

"The lecture. I know you have one. You were making mental notes the entire time we were in town."

Fiona had been standing before the mirror hanging on the far wall, fussing with her hair while Adele talked. Now she whirled about and said, "I am quite certain I have no idea what you are talking about. Why would I lecture you? You were a model of deportment today. Except for the fact that you insist on calling Dr. Ross by his Christian name."

"He gave me permission."

"Be that as it may, he deserves to be addressed by the title he worked so very hard to earn. Especially in light of the fact that—well, it has to be said. The man is old enough to be your father, Adele."

"Not quite. He's much younger than Papa would be if he were still living. Although I get your point. Papa was well past his prime when I came along."

"Adele!"

"Well, it's true, isn't it?" She paused. "Now that I think of it, Mama and Papa were probably just about the same distance apart in age as Malcolm and me. So why shouldn't I call him by his Christian name?"

"Private family matters aside," Fiona said, "it is unacceptable for you to be so familiar with a gentleman of Dr. Ross's standing."

Adele sighed. "I suppose you're right." When Fiona's expression changed from disapproval to shock, she burst out laughing. "You should see your face. I really must find a way to agree with you more often."

"Do you? Do you really agree with me about the matter? Because it would be a great relief to hear you say it."

Adele hesitated. "Say what? That I'll stop calling Malcolm 'Malcolm'?"

"Well, yes. Of course. But I am also hoping that you will see reason when it comes to the other matter." Fiona took a deep breath. "Surely you can see that Dr. Ross is much too old for you."

"Too old for—me?" Adele stared at her. "Glory be, Fiona—I never—" When Fiona's face began to color, either from embarrassment or anger, Adele put her hand to her mouth. Finally, she managed to speak. "I never intended any such thing. I'm no more interested in Malcolm that way than—than Finn is in Euphemia Chadwick." She sighed. "And isn't that getting very tiresome? She's willfully ignoring the obvious."

"What do you mean, 'ignoring the obvious'?"

She really couldn't help herself, could she? One mention of Finn would immediately draw Fiona away from any other topic of conversation. "That Finn was meant for Miss White, of course." Adele rolled her eyes. "I know you don't have a romantic bone in your body, Fiona, but even you can't have missed how perfect they are for one another. It's only a matter of time, and they'll see it, too."

"Really, Adele." Fiona sighed. "All the world does not turn on romance."

"Well, maybe that's what's the matter with everyone. They don't have anyone to love—or, what's worse, anyone loving them." Adele reached for the handle to open the cabin door. "*Will* you come down to the dining saloon with me? Please? I'm sure everyone—including Dr. Ross, no matter what you may think—would be very pleased."

Fiona gave her hair a last pat. "Well, of course I'll come."

Adele smiled. "Everything's going to be all right, Fiona. You'll see."

❇

Eleven days out of St. Louis, and not nearly halfway to Fort Benton, Laura stood up on the texas next to one of the tall smokestacks, looking down toward the Omaha levee, watching as a handful of new cabin passengers made their way on board. One was a veiled woman dressed in full mourning, accompanied by what Laura assumed to be a maid—at least based on the latter's rather shabby dress.

The mourning garb drew Laura's thoughts upriver toward Sioux City. Until today, she'd managed not to think about it too much, working long hours and falling asleep as soon as her head hit the pillow, day or night. But Sioux City was only a couple of days away now. The idea of facing that levee and the memory of her last view of Mama as she headed up the rise toward the place where she and Joe would both die brought bitter tears to her eyes.

She didn't want to stop in Sioux City. In fact, she wanted Finn to be the one up in the wheelhouse as they chuffed past, so that she wouldn't even have to *see* the place. That wasn't going to happen, though. They had freight on board bound for Sioux City. And even if she wanted to, Laura couldn't just leave Finn in charge and hide in her cabin until they were headed upriver again. Adele was going to want to visit Joe's grave. Neither she nor Fiona would understand Laura's not paying her respects.

If only they could wait until they were on their way back downriver. Until they'd finished fighting the river current. Until they'd managed their way over the fifteen sets of rapids between Cow Island and Fort Benton. By then, Laura would have a better idea of whether she'd won or lost her *Laura Rose*. Once they'd made it past the rapids on the return trip. Once they were headed downriver with the current. By then, she'd know if she could put flowers on graves and whisper good news, or if she'd have to admit to failing her family and losing her legacy.

With a sigh, Laura turned away from the Omaha levee and headed back toward her cabin. She didn't want to see anyone. She just wanted to curl up and take a nap. Thinking of napping made her wonder where Logjam might be. She hadn't seen him most of the morning. Just yesterday she'd realized that the dog had taken to dividing his attentions between her and Finn. She could not imagine Finn letting a dog into his bed—even if he had brought the rug from his own cabin up and tossed it in a wheelhouse corner so that Logjam could lay on something besides the rough wooden floor.

"You're spoiling him," Laura had said.

"He's earned it," Finn replied. "Retrieving wreaths, defending you from varmints, keeping the ladies at bay." And then he'd winked at her. "Miss Chadwick wrinkles her nose every time Logjam comes near. Apparently, she thinks he smells."

"He does." Laura smiled. "Just not as bad as a lot of other varmints on the river."

"You wound me, Miss White," Finn said, slapping his hand over his heart as if he'd been shot. "Guess I'd better buy some cologne at Omaha."

"I thought you were enjoying the repellant factor of a smelly dog," Laura said. "You want to counteract that?"

"Only when I'm in the wheelhouse," he said.

That had all happened just yesterday. Less than an hour ago, Finn had headed across the levee and into Omaha as soon as they'd landed—with Adele on his arm and Fiona walking alongside them—not exactly on Dr. Ross's arm, but close enough that it made Laura smile to see it.

"Goodness," she'd said, when Finn mentioned going ashore with them. "First Council Bluffs and now Omaha? Your older sister is turning into a gadabout."

"I'm as amazed as you, but she insists she wants to go along. I think the real motivation is a renewed concern about Adele." Finn paused. "Of course she hasn't actually said the words, but I think Fiona has some idea that Adele has designs on Dr. Ross."

"You can't be serious," Laura gasped. "I mean—I hardly expected her to observe an official mourning period, but... Dr. Ross? He's far too...mature, isn't he?"

"Hopefully," Finn said. "In every sense of the word. But he does seem to enjoy her company. Adele's taken to sitting with him at meals."

"I thought she was absent from my set last night because she was dining with Fiona in their cabin."

Finn shook his head, then forced a smile. "Of course the good that has come out of all of it is that Fiona is going ashore with us. To be quite honest, at the moment I don't really care what's motivating that. I've been worried about her."

Remembering the conversation, Laura felt a twinge of regret. Finn had invited her along, but she'd refused. She wasn't in the mood to take a stroll. Didn't want to leave the *Laura Rose* at all, for that matter. The farther upriver they went, the less successful she'd been at keeping the haunting specter of defeat at bay. If this was to be her last trip upriver, she wanted to spend every possible moment on board.

Back in her cabin, she lay down. But she missed Logjam. No matter how she tried, she couldn't get comfortable. When she opened her eyes, the first thing she saw was Mama's Bible. It had been in the same spot, right there atop the small trunk beside the cabin door, since St. Louis. Just sitting there, unopened. Of course Mama would want Laura to do more than just treasure it as a memento. Mama would want her to take in what it said.

With a pang of guilt, Laura picked the book up, and was surprised when it fell open to a page that, while not particularly familiar to Laura, had obviously been important to Mama. The binding was beginning to give way at Psalm 116. As she scanned the psalm, Laura remembered the first time she'd found Mama weeping quietly after Papa died. This very book had been open on Mama's lap—opened to this very place. Laura had gone to her and, sliding to her knees to look up into Mama's face, she'd said, "It isn't fair. He should be here. It isn't fair."

Mama had nodded. Then she'd patted the space beside her. When Laura moved, Mama began to read aloud, her voice wavering and, on occasion, breaking.

> I love the LORD, *because he hath heard my voice and my*
> *supplications.*
> *Because he hath inclined his ear unto me, therefore will I*
> *call upon him as long as I live.*
> *The sorrows of death compassed me, and the pains of hell*
> *gat hold upon me: I found trouble and sorrow.*

Then called I upon the name of the LORD; O LORD, I
beseech thee, deliver my soul.
Gracious is the LORD, and righteous; yea, our God is
merciful.
The LORD preserveth the simple: I was brought low, and he
helped me.
Return unto thy rest, O my soul; for the LORD hath dealt
bountifully with thee.
For thou hast delivered my soul from death, mine eyes from
tears, and my feet from falling.
I will walk before the LORD in the land of the living.
I believed, therefore have I spoken: I was greatly afflicted: I
said in my haste, All men are liars.
What shall I render unto the LORD for all his benefits
toward me?
I will take the cup of salvation, and call upon the name of
the LORD.
I will pay my vows unto the LORD now in the presence of all
his people.
Precious in the sight of the LORD is the death of his saints.
O LORD, truly I am thy servant; I am thy servant, and the
son of thine handmaid: thou hast loosed my bonds.
I will offer to thee the sacrifice of thanksgiving, and will call
upon the name of the LORD.
I will pay my vows unto the LORD now in the presence of all
his people, in the courts of the LORD's house, in the midst
of thee, O Jerusalem.
Praise ye the LORD.

Mama sat quietly for a moment after she finished reading.
Finally, though, she said, "We've been brought low, Laura.
Just like the one who wrote these words." She reached over
and took Laura's hand. "But we *can* call on the name of the
Lord, and He *will* help us." She paused. "But that's not my

favorite part of this passage—at least right now." She swiped at a tear. "Right here"—she pointed to one line—"it promises, 'I will walk before the LORD in the land of the living.'" She looked over at Laura, and even with tears streaming down her face, Mama managed a smile as she said, "That's where your papa is right now. He is walking before the Lord in the land of the living. We can't see him anymore, but he's there. I believe that with all my heart." She paused. "And someday...I'll be there with him."

On that day a little over two years ago, Laura had peered over Mama's shoulder at the open Bible and the place where Mama had underlined the words "land of the living" and "the sacrifice of thanksgiving." Now she traced the two phrases with her own finger, even as she remembered saying, "I can't thank God for taking Papa. I won't." She felt the same way today. It was too much to think that God expected her to thank Him for taking all of them—Papa and Joe and Mama. But Mama hadn't seemed to think it was expected.

"Neither can I," she'd said. "But I can thank Him for you. And for Joe. And for so many things."

Mama hadn't tried to hide her grief. She'd cried many more tears after that one day. And yet in the midst of the sorrow there'd been something else. Something beautiful. Something good. Something admirable.

Again, Laura read the psalm that had meant so much to Mama. If anyone had called upon the Lord, it was she. *Maybe you should try it.* The thought came suddenly, and just as suddenly, Laura refused it. God listened to people like Mama—good people who loved and served Him. And while she liked to think of herself as a good person, Laura didn't know God well enough to actually converse with Him in a personal way. As if He was there, listening.

You should try it. Just try.

Setting the Bible aside, she reached for the union case and

opened it, staring down at the photos of Papa and her and Joe. Opening the back of Papa's watch, she looked at a young Margaret White. *I need help, Mama. What if I lose the* Laura Rose? Fear gripped her. She looked about her with the fresh realization that everything important she owned in the world was in this tiny cabin, either tucked beneath her bed or in the trunk across the way. What a sad commentary on a life. She'd lose everything and have to start over.

"A sacrifice of thanksgiving." Again, she looked at her belongings. She supposed that, even if she lost the *Laura Rose*, there would be something left. She wouldn't be destitute. *And I'd have friends to help me.* The first name that came to mind gave her pause as she realized that, when it came right down to it, she would be thankful for Finn, even if she lost the *Laura Rose*. After all, if it weren't for him and his sisters, she wouldn't have had the chance to even try. So, yes, she supposed she would be thankful for the MacKnights, no matter what happened.

As for Finn, she no longer thought of him as dark and dangerous-looking. He was almost a friend. Sometimes, when she caught him looking at her, those dark eyes of his held something that made her tremble. But not with fear. With some new emotion that drew her to him in a way that was almost frightening.

For heaven's sake, stop thinking about him that way. He needed a job and you needed a pilot. Remember when he said that? He said it would be good business for the two of them to work together, and it is. Good business. That's . . . all.

Again, she looked down at Mama's Bible. "I will take the cup of salvation and call upon the name of the LORD." If all else failed, she supposed she could try that. But for now—for now, she would continue to fight the river and the calendar and, with Finn's help, she would win.

Back out on the texas, Laura glanced up at the sky. *And I*

will be thankful. When all is said and done, and I'm back in St. Louis with time to spare...I'll be thankful. I promise.

And then what?

Well...then she'd take the pilot's examination and pass. And then there'd be more trips for Laura as the unchallenged captain and licensed first pilot of the *Laura Rose*. Smiling with the thought of how that would feel, she walked toward the prow. She gazed at the massive piles of buffalo hides on the Omaha levee waiting to be shipped downriver and then eastward.

You can't control the river. Finn's words returned as Laura looked east. At times it seemed like she couldn't control anything: neither the river nor the ever-changing world of commerce on which Papa had built his family's life. And even if Papa's prediction was right, even if steamboating lasted for a dozen years or more until the railroad expanded into the territories, the *Laura Rose* herself wasn't going to hold up more than a few years. Like any other mountain boat, she was expected to last only five years or so; the river was that hard on the shallow-drafted vessels that plied her treacherous waters. Even if Laura beat the odds and made it back in time to keep her packet, it would be for just a little while.

Once again, the question returned. *And then...what?* Once again, Finn MacKnight's face came to mind, unbidden. *Just...stop. All you need to be thinking about right now is July 8.* July 8 would require all her skill and courage. All of it. As for the rest...Well. She'd face that on July 9.

Chapter 22

Laura was just descending to the galley to make herself a very strong cup of coffee when a lone rider approached the *Laura Rose*, dismounted, and dropped the reins of his horse—as if that was all it would take to keep the animal under control. The man strode up the gangplank and onto the freight deck with purpose. A couple of moments later, Laura nearly collided with the stranger and Elijah North, who'd escorted him to the top of the hurricane deck stairs.

The man wore a beaded and fringed buckskin coat and breeches, and his feet were clad in moccasins. When he removed his wide-brimmed hat, thick blond hair cascaded down his back in waves that curled about his shoulders. He had to be at least six feet tall, and while he was not handsome, he did "cut an impressive figure," as the saying went. At the moment, though, he seemed uncertain as he glanced about, as if looking for someone else.

"I was hoping to speak to the c-captain," he said.

Laura looked over at Elijah, whose expression said that he was enjoying himself a bit at the stranger's expense.

"Yes?"

The man frowned. "Well...can I?"

"Can you what?"

"S-Speak with the c-captain."

"You can and you are."

The stranger looked to Elijah North, as if waiting for an explanation.

Elijah nodded. "Captain Laura White, owner and first pilot of the *Laura Rose*."

"You're joshin' me." The man frowned over at her. "*Ladies* d-don't run this river."

"Is that right?" Laura snapped. "Well, thank you for your commentary on my virtue."

She glanced toward town. Finn and his sisters and Dr. Ross were just now at the far edge of the levee, headed this way. "My second pilot's on his way back on board, and I mean to be under way in less than ten minutes, so unless you want to state your business to *me*, you'd best get off my packet." She turned toward the steps leading up to the texas and from there, to the wheelhouse.

The man's tone changed and he called after her. "I d-didn't m-mean any offense, m-ma'am. I j-just never—I'm looking to earn my way upriver. W-Wait—please. I—I'm sorry, ma'am. T-Truly."

Laura turned back around. Her heart softened. Mountain man or buffalo hunter or whatever he was, he wasn't much past twenty years old, if the thinness of his beard and the smoothness of his fair skin were to be believed. His stutter worsened markedly when he was nervous. That either embarrassed him or made him angry, because his face was turning red.

"I've been away from p-proper s-society s-so—" He broke off. Bit his lower lip. "I d-didn't m-mean any offense."

Laura gentled her tone. "I have a full crew. And even if I didn't"—she looked pointedly at his outlandish garb—"it's obvious you don't have experience on this river. I can't hire anyone who needs training. At least not on this trip. You'll have to seek passage elsewhere, Mr.....?"

"L-Landon," the man said. And then, in a quick burst he said, "Nate Landon" and offered his hand.

Laura shook it, even as she looked down at the levee. "I hope your horse is gentle." She nodded to where Adele stood, stroking the animal's broad neck.

"As a kitten," he said.

Logjam loped down the gangplank and approached the horse. Laura tensed. "It won't kick him, will it?" As she watched, the horse lowered its head and snuffled Logjam.

Landon seemed equally worried. "I hope that d-dog don't bite."

Laura smiled. "From the looks of things, both critters are quite safe." She watched Fiona tuck her hand beneath Dr. Ross's arm and follow him up the gangplank. Adele was lingering by the horse while Finn waited—not so patiently, Laura thought, although she couldn't exactly say why she thought so, other than the fact that he kept looking up toward the texas.

When she raised a hand in greeting, he took his hat off, held his arms out, and turned about slowly, as if inviting her inspection. He'd cut his hair. And shaved. She'd forgotten how handsome he was when he wasn't hiding behind a tangle of dark hair and two weeks' worth of beard. *Glory be.*

"Ma'am?"

Laura turned back to Landon. "All right," she said. "I'm listening." Landon stuttered his way through explaining that he had opportunity to sell a buffalo calf or two, if he could acquire them and get them back to Omaha. From there, a dealer would see to transporting a number of "exotic" animals east. Apparently there was something of a trend among the very rich in regards to private zoos on their estates. Landon had been part of the crew that captured the grizzly bear on board the *Mary McDonald*. As he talked, he seemed to calm down. His stutter faded a bit.

"I need p-passage," he said. "You take me, I supply your t-table. Antelope, b-buffalo—as much as you want. I shoot b-better than I talk." He offered a shy smile. "Much better. I c-can guard your crew. Cut wood. Anything it takes to earn m-my way." When Laura didn't say anything, Landon coaxed, "P-please. Captain. You won't be sorry."

"Most of the time," Laura said, "when folks on board a steamboat catch sight of game, there's a lot of excitement, a lot of noise, a lot of shooting—and not much else."

Landon nodded, as if he agreed. "B-but I can track. You put my mare and me off when you stop for wood. We head overland and m-meet you at the next stop with fresh game. P-prairie chicken potpie. Roast hump of buffalo. Your p-passengers will thank you."

"Buffalo, you say." Laura folded her arms. "Even if you did bring one down, how would you transport several hundred pounds of meat back to the river?"

"P-pack mules," Landon said and motioned toward Omaha. "T-tethered at the top of that hill."

Laura looked over at Elijah. "Do we have room for Mr. Landon, his horse, and mules on the freight deck?" Before Elijah could respond, she looked back at Landon. "And feed. How will you feed them?"

"Already outfitted. The mules are l-loaded with sacks of grain. I c-can picket them to graze when we stop for wood. As for water—" He mimed dipping a bucket into the river.

"And if you dip a bucket and fall in," Laura said. "Then what?"

Landon shrugged. "Then you own a f-fine saddle horse and t-two mules." Another faint smile accompanied the words, "I can't s-swim."

Laura was still pondering the idea when Finn appeared at the top of the stairs. She introduced the two men. "Tell my second pilot what you're proposing." Landon did, and Laura asked him to wait a moment while she conferred with Finn. Together, they walked away, pausing near the door to her cabin where Laura asked, "What do you think?"

"The only real question is if he can deliver on his promise and supply the galley."

Laura nodded. "My thought exactly." She glanced back at Landon. "He says he's an excellent shot."

"If he is, it'll save you money—and time. It could add up."

Laura nodded. She called back to Landon. "How long before you can have your animals on board?"

"Minutes," Landon said. Clapping the hat back on his head, he hurried off.

Adele came skittering up the stairs, her face flushed, her eyes aglow with excitement. "Did you see him? Isn't he something? I thought mountain men were all scruffy and smelly. He's nothing of the kind." She clasped her hands together. "What a stir he's going to cause among the ladies!" She barely took a breath. "And did you see Fiona? She actually crossed over to the levee and back without fainting. That's the second time today. Thanks, of course, to Dr. Ross." She paused and looked at Finn. "Mark my words. She's going to be fine now. You'll see." And then, with another excited comment about watching "the mountain man" lead his horse on board, she was gone.

"Well," Finn laughed, "I don't know about you, but I've had entirely enough excitement for one day."

"Fiona really did seem to take that gangplank without hesitation," Laura said. "I was watching from up here and glad to see it."

Finn nodded. "I don't quite know what to make of it, but yes." He smiled at Laura. "I suppose we'll have to be more careful now, what with our chaperone on duty and all."

Laura nodded at his cane. "You do look rather dapper, Captain MacKnight. It suits you."

"The cane or the barber's work?"

"Both. Miss Chadwick is going to be all aflutter."

"Just what I was hoping for," he muttered.

"She'll approve of the cologne, too."

❦

Fiona stood at the railing next to Dr. Ross, watching a wild-looking young man lead a red horse on board, and she did not know what to think because she was rather enjoying herself. How could that be? Oh, she still started at a sudden change in the sounds of the steamboat. She still feared the current and the Indians everyone seemed so certain they would encounter in coming days. And the idea of traversing rapids made her shudder. And yet, somehow, she seemed able to live with those fears now. Why, she'd even managed her way down that dreadful gangplank not once, but twice, both at Council Bluffs and now at Omaha. And she'd enjoyed herself in those places. Not moments ago, in fact, she had very nearly wanted to purchase the sweet little bonnet Adele had tried on. What was happening to her?

"The lad says the mare is as gentle as a babe. Just look at the way she trusts him, stepping up that board as if it's nothing more than a path to the barn."

Fiona looked to her right and into Dr. Ross's fine, blue eyes. "A dumb animal only knows to follow its master," she said. "The horse isn't able to anticipate danger—except, of course, in the case of smoke, which she would smell. And then you wouldn't be praising her calm, because she'd be using all her power to run away."

"Aye," Dr. Ross said, "and in the case of smoke, likely run straightaway into the very thing she feared most. 'Tis wiser to follow her gentle lord's leading, do ya not think?"

Fiona felt the sting of rebuke. "It's always *wise* to follow the Lord," she said. "It's just not always *easy*."

"Well of course not," Dr. Ross said, his voice mellow. "We must not think that just because a thing is *simple* it will be *easy*. Those who think the words synonymous are in for a rude awakening. 'Tis a *simple* thing to board a steamboat. But for a creature who fears the noise or the water or any other thing, it can be the most difficult thing in life."

Fiona felt her cheeks warm with a combination of embarrassment and anger, the latter directed at Adele, who had obviously been talking about her behind her back. She directed her attention to the animals without further comment. The first of the mules balked halfway up the gangplank. When it planted its hooves and leaned back, a murmur of laughter rippled through the passengers gathered at the railing. Unruffled, its buckskin-clad owner took the kerchief from about his neck and wrapped it about the mule's head, covering its eyes. The creature relented and followed him on board.

"There now," Dr. Ross said. "He hears his master's voice, and all is well."

Feeling even further chastised, Fiona stepped away from the railing and remained silent until the steamboat's bell clanged and the whistle shrieked departure.

"I'd be most honored if you and your dear sister would accompany me into the dining saloon," Dr. Ross said, and he smiled at Adele with open affection. "Would you favor us with a hymn, my dear?"

Adele said that she would be delighted and headed off without a backward glance. Dr. Ross offered his arm. The poor man seemed to have no idea Fiona might be upset by the idea that he felt it necessary to remind her about the wisdom of following the Lord. *And why should she be upset? He'd only spoken the truth—and with a gentle smile, at that.* A phrase from the Bible about "speaking the truth in love" flashed through her mind. With a smile of her own, Fiona took Dr. Ross's arm. Together they made their way to the dining saloon. As soon as Adele began to play, other passengers came inside, and the *Laura Rose* turned upriver accompanied by a choir of voices singing, "Jesus, lover of my soul, let me to Thy bosom fly, While the nearer waters roll, while the tempest still is high…"

❋

The *Laura Rose* ascended to Sioux City beneath blue skies and with the added boon of untroubled waters and plentiful fuel. But Laura's mood did not reflect their good fortune, and as he guided the steamboat to the levee, Finn worried. The farther north they'd traveled, the more troubled she'd become. Finally, when they were tied up at the Sioux City levee, Laura asked him to host her set at the evening meal.

"I won't be in any mood to socialize when we get back from the cemetery."

"You shouldn't face things alone," Finn said. "Let me go with you."

"Didn't you hear what I just said? Your sisters will be there."

She'd almost snapped at him. Finn tilted his head to peer at her, even as he reached for his cane. "But you don't want to go at all."

Laura shrugged. "I just—I'd rather wait until I know if I've failed them or not before I—" She paused. "It's silly, I know. They aren't really there. Still, I can't seem to keep from envisioning myself standing at their graves, telling them either that I've saved the *Laura Rose* or—"

Finn interrupted, "Whatever happens, you haven't failed anyone. You can't control the river." The expression on her face spoke volumes, every one of them cause for concern— if he was reading her correctly. What would happen if they couldn't make it back to St. Louis by July 8? He gentled his voice. "We can't control the river, but I can control this. Let me handle it for you." He moved to the wheelhouse door. "I'll tell my sisters that we don't have the time. We need to off-load our freight in a hurry and be on our way."

Laura hesitated. "They won't understand. It seems callous. Worse even than tossing a mourning wreath into the river."

"There's nothing wrong with wanting to wait until after we make it back to St. Louis. You can come back when you don't have so much hanging over your head. I'll make them understand." He was about to head down the ladder when he turned back. "I meant what I said just now. Whether we're back in St. Louis by July 8 or not, you haven't failed anyone. As beautiful as she is, the *Laura Rose* is going to rust and warp and wreck—either on this river or because she's just plain worn out. You hold your head high, my captain. You've nothing to be ashamed of."

Her eyes filled with tears. She looked away. "You sound like my mama, preaching about things that don't last—'wood, hay, and stubble' she called it—from some verse in the Bible."

He forced a grin. "Me? Preach? You must be overtired, Miss White—although I do consider it an unexpected honor for you to think of me as having anything in common with your saintly mother."

"I can't lose everything Papa strove to create," she said. "I will *not* be a failure."

He wanted to reach out and shelter her in his arms. To somehow convince her that everything would be all right. Instead, he said, "After I speak to my sisters, I'll get after the crew. You be ready and I'll signal the all clear to shove off." He descended the ladder and limped away.

Laura called after him, "You're a good friend, Finn MacKnight."

He smiled back at her. "Don't tell anyone. I've a bad repu-tation to live up to." She smiled, but the sadness in her blue eyes sent a pang of regret through his heart. How he wished he could pay off her debt. Promise her a pilot's license. Make her dreams come true. Maybe even be a part of those dreams.

✵

"But this is my only chance," Adele wailed and sank down to perch on the chest at the foot of the bed in the cabin she shared with Fiona.

Finn sat down beside her. "It isn't. We'll come back. Fiona was disappointed, too," he said. "But she understands."

"Fiona probably doesn't even care," Adele muttered. "And even if she did, she wouldn't let it show. Not with Dr. Malcolm Ross sitting right across from her down on the hurricane deck." She sighed. "At least *that's* working out the way I want it to."

Finn frowned. "What do you mean... working out the way you want it to?"

"Dr. Ross and Fiona. At least until he leaves us at Fort Benton. I suppose it'll be up to the two of them after that."

Finn decided to ignore the implications. "We can always come back later in the year. By rail. When Laura doesn't have the added pressure of this deadline hanging over her head."

Adele's eyes glimmered with tears as she looked over at him. "It's 'Laura' now, is it?"

Finn shrugged. It had been "Laura" in his mind for longer than he cared to admit. "I'm counting on you not to give me away," he said. "She wouldn't like knowing it."

"You're wrong about that," Adele said. "She's changed in the way she feels about you." Finn snorted disbelief. "Snort all you want. It happens to be true."

"How would you know such a thing?"

"She trusts you more. With the steamboat. And... I don't know. Just something in her expression when she looks at you. It's... softer, somehow." Adele took a deep breath. "It's all right about not going to the grave," she said. "I understand. Joseph and I—" She broke off. Shook her head.

"Joseph and you…what?"

"Nothing," Adele said. And then, after a moment, she added, "He really was fond of me, you know."

"I never thought otherwise."

"And I cared for him, too. Just not—not in the way I should have."

Finn looked over at her. A tear trickled down one cheek. "What's this?"

Forcing a little laugh, Adele pulled a handkerchief out of the bag on her wrist and dabbed at the tear. "A guilty conscience." She took a deep breath. "He was so handsome. And I was desperate to get away. To get my inheritance and be quit of…everything." She began to cry. "But then he wrote such sweet letters…and…" She gulped. "Oh, Finn. I haven't always been a very nice person."

Finn barely managed to swallow nervous laughter at such a wild understatement. But then he remembered confessing to Laura White about his own regrets when it came to Adele. "Dear girl," he finally said, "in my lifetime, I've *rarely* been a nice person—at least in my heart and mind, where it counts." He put his arm back around her and gave her an awkward hug. "We've given Fiona a lot to worry about, you and I."

"I don't blame her for not liking me," Adele muttered. She looked up at him. "But she seems to like you, no matter what you do. And I've resented you because of it." She sighed.

Finn cleared his throat. "I don't understand why she's that way. It's almost embarrassing sometimes. On the other hand, it's finally made me want to be someone better. If I can."

Adele nodded. "I know what you mean. After we came on board the *Laura Rose*, and she was so afraid and so embarrassed about being afraid, but she couldn't seem to do anything about it—I began to feel sorry for her. And then you told me what happened when she was little, and I don't know—I guess it made her seem more human somehow." Finn gave a little laugh, and Adele looked over at him. "You know what I mean."

"Yes," Finn said. "I believe I do."

"She's always so prim and proper. So determined to be *perfect*."

"She demands a lot of herself."

Adele nodded. "And of everyone else, too." She sighed again. "And here we are in Joseph's beautiful cabin, and I didn't love him the way I should have. I feel so guilty about that. The longer I'm here, the worse I feel about it. About everything I've done." She began to cry again. "I don't want to feel guilty anymore. But I don't know what to do about any of it. I can't be like Fiona. I can't be all sober and serious. Even if I could I wouldn't want to settle down with someone like Martin Lawrence. I'd hate it. I want my life to be exciting. That was the main reason behind my romance with Joseph. But then I took things too far, and—" Her voice was miserable. "I've ruined everything. I can't go back to St. Louis."

Finn dropped his arm from about her and leaned back. "What on earth are you talking about?"

"You know what I'm talking about," she said.

"Stop." If she was confessing what he thought she was, Finn wasn't surprised, but he didn't want her to know that, and he most definitely didn't want to hear the details. "Don't say another word. No one needs to know."

"That's just the thing," Adele said. "Everyone back there already knows. Everyone who matters, anyway."

"And who, pray tell, is 'everyone who matters'?"

"Martin Lawrence. Lucy Powell. Their parents. Eventually, Fiona will find out. And when she does, she'll send me away."

Finn's mind raced. The church brats might be motivated

to hurt Adele, but if they gossiped, Fiona would also be hurt. Again.

"She'll hate me even more than she already does."

"Fiona doesn't hate you."

"Why wouldn't she? I ruined her life. Yours, too. Except it didn't ruin yours quite so much, because men can do what they want anyway. No one expects them to stay at home and raise children and be models of virtue." She paused. "That's one of the things I like so much about Laura."

"Do I even want to know what you mean by that?"

"Oh, goodness. As far as I know, she's as pure as the new-fallen snow. What I mean is she's brave enough to find her own way. I wish I could be like that." She sniffed. "I've been trying. Getting off at every stop, trying to imagine starting a new life. But then, when I think about packing my things and actually doing it, when I think about being all alone—" She dabbed at her tears.

"Laura's an exception to just about every rule there is," Finn said. "She's known what she wanted to do since she was a girl running away from boarding school. That's not normal—I mean, it's not common."

"All I know is what I don't want to be," Adele said.

"What's that?"

"Myself."

At that moment, the cabin door flew open and Fiona let out a little gasp. "Here you are! I was worried—thinking— Well, never mind about that. Here you are." She looked from Adele to Finn and frowned a question in his direction. He shrugged and gave a little shake of his head. *Not now.* She had a pamphlet of some kind in her hand. She held it up. "Dr. Ross gave me a copy of a lecture he gave at the seminary last year." She paused. "We've had something of a debate just now and he thought I'd want to read more on the subject. Which of course, I do." She set the pamphlet on the little table in the corner and looked to Adele. "But then Mrs. Chadwick invited us to play cribbage, and Dr. Ross is hoping that you'll play the piano for a hymn sing later this evening." She paused. "I am sorry about the cemetery, my dear. We must try to understand."

Adele tucked her handkerchief back into her beaded bag. "Finn explained," she said.

With the help of his cane, Finn stood up, then drew Adele up beside him. As he gave her another one-armed hug, he leaned close and whispered, "Don't you dare run off. I'll have to chase you down and it will hurt my bum leg."

Adele looked up at him. Her eyes filled with tears. She nodded. "All right."

"Promise me."

She nodded again. Then she looked over at Fiona and gave her a weak little smile. "Thank you for coming to get me," she said. "It's nice to be wanted."

Chapter 23

The Missouri was kind to the *Laura Rose* after she left Sioux City. Laura steered her up to the levee at Fort Randall in record time. The passenger in mourning disembarked there, apparently to keep house for a recently widowed brother who was one of the officers at the two-hundred-man garrison. Nate Landon left the *Laura Rose* as well, with a promise to meet up with them twenty miles upriver when they stopped at Whetstone Agency to put off more freight.

"If I'm not there," he said, before leaving the deck, "go on to P-Pocahontas Island. And be ready to hang some meat."

"But that's another thirty miles or so," Laura replied.

"By water, yes," Landon said. "But Red and I travel as the c-crow flies. W-we'll be there."

Two days later, Landon's return caused no small stir on board the *Laura Rose*—especially on the part of Adele, who'd invited herself up to the wheelhouse to watch Pocahantas Island come into view.

"There he is!" she said, pointing into the distance. "Oh my! He must be a very good shot indeed."

Adele descended the ladder and hurried away. Finn chuckled and nodded toward the island. "Logjam seems to think that red mare is some kind of pet," he said, just as the dog trotted down the gangplank and, lifting his fine head, touched noses with Landon's horse. When Landon handed something to the dog, Logjam danced away, then plopped down and began to devour it.

"Well, Mr. Landon knows how to win friends." Laura smiled. "Let's go see what he's brought us."

Adele had lingered at the top of the gangplank. While the crew transferred fifteen cords of wood onto the *Laura Rose*, Hercules oversaw the hanging and processing of an antelope and two deer. Bird, Tyree, and Ruby combined forces to ready two dozen prairie chickens for roasting.

Laura had expected Landon to reboard and go upriver with them, but he left his mare behind when he strode up the gangplank. "Th-there's news of b-buffalo off to the west," he said. "I n-need to s-see if there's anything to it." Glancing at Adele, he jerked his hat off his head and nodded a greeting. "Ma'am."

Adele spoke up. "How does one hear news in the middle of nowhere?"

Landon smiled. "'N-nowhere' is h-home to m-me."

Was it her imagination, Laura wondered, or was Nate Landon blushing?

Finn asked, "Should we have the men ready to defend against Indians? It's hunting season for them, too, right?"

Landon nodded. "If the report about b-buffalo is true, they'll be t-too busy hunting to worry about f-fireboats." *Fireboats*. That's what the Indians called steamboats. "T-tell you what," Landon said. "If I see trouble brewing, I'll m-meet you sooner. Warn you." He turned to go.

Adele tugged on Finn's sleeve. "He likes Bird's biscuits. We should get him some."

Laura and Finn exchanged curious glances and Adele hurried away, presumably to speak with Bird on the subject of biscuits for Nate Landon. Landon busied himself saddling his red mare, and it wasn't long before he was loping off into the distance with his pack mules trailing behind—and a dozen of Bird Perrin's biscuits tucked into a saddlebag. Laura had Tom Meeks write out an IOU and nail it to the door of the primitive lean-to where the wood hawk lived when he wasn't off somewhere cutting or hauling lumber to the river, and the *Laura Rose* backed away from shore and headed on its way.

When Laura climbed up into the wheelhouse later in the day to take a shift, she was surprised to find Elijah North standing beside Finn, scanning the hills with a spyglass. "Can't hurt to keep an extra watch," Finn said. "I thought maybe I'd have some of the crew load their weapons come sundown—if that's all right with you."

Laura agreed as she reached for the wheel. "You're in for a treat tonight," she said. "Bird has outdone herself with the potpies. Best thing we've offered passengers since leaving St. Louis."

Finn nodded. "I don't doubt it, but I'd just as soon take an extra turn up here. Elijah and I make a good team."

Elijah spoke without taking the spyglass away from his eye. "I see steam up ahead. One, maybe two other packets." He looked over at Laura. "Wouldn't hurt to try and catch up before night falls. Safety in numbers and all that."

Laura realized that Finn was worried about what Landon had said about Indians. "Are you trying to protect me?"

He glanced over at her. "And if I am?"

"If I'm too afraid of Indians to be up here in the wheelhouse, I've no business thinking I can be a pilot."

"And who said anything about your being afraid?" Finn looked over at Elijah. "Did you accuse her of being afraid?"

"Wouldn't think of it," Elijah said.

Finn nodded. "That's right. No one thinks you're afraid." He smiled. "Maybe it's me who's afraid. The truth is, I don't think I'll sleep a wink, and I might as well not sleep up here in the wheelhouse as to not sleep in my cabin. At least up here I'm accomplishing something while I'm not sleeping."

"I think I'd argue—if I could follow the train of thought in all of that."

"How about you bring Elijah and me some of that potpie? You can man the spyglass while Elijah eats and then take the wheel while I do. And then we'll fight some more about who's man enough to be in the wheelhouse when there's a threat of a possible Indian attack." He grinned. "But I'll win."

"I would like a chance at some of that potpie before it's all gone," Elijah said. He didn't even look behind him.

Laura glanced over at Logjam, who'd been curled up in the corner, but who was now sitting, ears erect, whipping his head from one person to the next as the conversation bounced back and forth. "I suppose you'd like some potpie, too," she said. Logjam gave a little chuff and bounced on his front legs like a child begging for candy.

Finn laughed and Laura gave in. She'd be a fool to be angry about someone wanting to protect her. Joe or Papa wouldn't have wanted her up in the wheelhouse either. It was the most vulnerable spot on the steamboat. If Indians did decide to protest the presence of a steamboat on the river, they'd fire at the person who was most visible, and that was the man—or woman—inside the windowed wheelhouse.

As she made her way down to the kitchen, Laura paused to gaze out at the rolling hills, dotted with the blues and whites and yellows of spring-blooming wildflowers. She thought about what Nate Landon had said about the "nowhere" being home, both to him and to the tribes living there. What was it like, Laura wondered, to feel at home in that vast sea of grass? She couldn't imagine it any more than she could imagine living in a tepee.

She'd heard that some tribes whose ancestral lands were along the Missouri farmed and lived in semipermanent earthen lodges, but her only experience with Indians was glimpsing their temporary camps from the deck of a steamboat. More often than not, places like that were gone by the time the steamboat passed that way again. Still, she'd seen the results of warriors venting their anger against a steamboat in the scars caused by arrows and splintered wood railings struck by gunfire. Papa had known the captain who was killed at the wheel of a steamboat a few years ago. That might have been a rare and singular event, but it still had the power to strike fear into the hearts of passengers and crew alike, when whispers of Indians were broadcast from steamboat to steamboat.

Thinking about that kind of danger and Finn's insistence that he would win the fight about which of them might be "man enough" to be at the wheel in the next few hours made Laura realize that she liked the idea of his wanting to protect her. It made her feel less alone. Less lonely. In the wake of that new sensation, Laura admitted something else to herself. She cared about Finn's safety, too. Very much.

✹

The *Laura Rose* did indeed manage to catch up to the steamboats that Elijah had seen in the spyglass. When Laura saw the *Silver Bow*, she smiled. Papa had been friends with George Grant, its captain. "Let's call on Captain Grant and see if he's heard anything beyond what Landon told us."

"We should talk to McCoy, too," Finn said, nodding toward the *Colonel Kidd*.

Laura snorted. "No, thank you."

"Just because he passed us by a while back?" Finn teased, "It wasn't a race, remember?"

"It isn't that. I just—I don't want to be beholden to Jack McCoy for any kind of help. Ever."

Finn glanced at Elijah, as if waiting for the older man to add to what Laura had said, but North just gave a little shrug and excused himself to have one of the skiffs lowered.

Captain Grant received Laura with a kiss on the cheek. "Your father would be so proud of you," he said. After offering his sympathy for Mama and Joe, he expressed the same concerns Laura and Finn had over Indians. When Laura mentioned Nate Landon's opinion of things, Grant's response surprised her.

"Landon, you say. Nate Landon?"

"Yes...why?"

Grant shook his head, then started to laugh. He looked up and shook a finger at the stars just now beginning to glimmer in the darkening sky. "You old goat," he said. "Looking out for your little girl, aren't ya?" And then he smiled at Laura. "Your papa clearly has the ear of the Almighty, my dear. Nate Landon grew up with the Sioux. In fact, young as he is, he's well on his way to becoming something of a legend in Dakota Territory. Not long ago I heard the Union Pacific has been trying to lure him away from the territory. They want to hire him to help feed the crews building the Transcontinental. And to help keep the peace with the Indians. So far, he's resisted all offers. But if you've got him attached to your packet, you won't have to worry about any Indian trouble. In fact, I wouldn't be surprised if he's already seen to that."

Laura explained Landon's pursuit of buffalo. "At least that's what he claimed to be doing."

Grant nodded. "No reason to doubt the young man," he said. "But that's even better for you. If he meets up with them, you can be sure he'll convince his Sioux brothers not to fire on a packet helping him satisfy his current customers."

Captain Grant invited Finn and Laura to dine with him, and later that night, as Finn rowed them back to the *Laura Rose*, Laura asked what he thought about what Captain Grant had said about Nate Landon. "Do you think it means we can let down our guard?"

Finn shook his head. "Not that I doubt what Captain

Grant said, mind you. Nor do I doubt Landon's skill. I just doubt the constancy of the Sioux—even when it comes to a 'white brother.' It only makes sense to prepare for the worst."

"And hope for the best?"

"Exactly."

Which turned out to be a good idea, because with the rising of the sun and the resumption of the trip upriver, the worst descended, not from Indians, but from the fickle Missouri River. First, the *Colonel Kidd* went hard aground mid-morning. The *Silver Bow* and the *Laura Rose* steamed past. Next, the *Silver Bow* hung up on a sandbar near yet another wreck that was in the process of creating a new island. When the *Laura Rose* took on wood a few miles upriver from the stranded packets, the wood hawk wasn't present to collect, and so another IOU was left nailed to the door of a log cabin.

The *Laura Rose* didn't run aground that day. Her challenge came after sundown, from the occupants of a skiff that came out of the night and pulled up alongside her, just as Laura was climbing down from the wheelhouse. First, there was a stir down below—angry voices and shouts. Finally, the clomping of heavy boots on the steps up to the hurricane deck. As the company of men made their way past the passenger cabins, Laura was right above them on the texas, and she could hear what they were saying. She hurried down from the texas and around to the dining saloon in their wake, following a trail of filth and grime from their boots, along with the aroma of unwashed bodies and cheap whiskey. The three men barged right into the dining saloon, demanding to see the "thieving captain."

Finn had been presiding over the second set. He rose from where he was seated at the far end of the table, and when he caught sight of Laura, he said, "She's right behind you."

The obvious leader of the trio of men wheeled about. He wore a tattered coat, and as he shouted demands, spittle showered his scraggly, tangled beard. Out of the corner of her eye, Laura saw Euphemia Chadwick slump in her chair, the victim of yet another faint. Dr. Ross, who'd been seated between Miss Chadwick and Fiona, rose from his chair. As he approached the man who was shouting, one of the men with him whirled about and raised a clenched fist. Dr. Ross's blue eyes turned to ice. The man lowered his fist. Mrs. Chadwick fanned her daughter.

The man kept shouting, but he spoke with such a thick accent—German, Laura thought it might be—all she could make of any of it was that he thought the *Laura Rose* owed him for some wood taken at one of the woodlots downriver. She let him yell until he seemed to run out steam. When he finally sputtered to a stop, she said, "We'll talk outside" and waved for him to follow her, relieved when both Dr. Ross and Finn came along.

"Vell," the man muttered. "Vat are you going to do 'bout dis?" He was looking at Finn.

"I'm not going to do a thing," Finn said, then looked over at Laura. "Captain White?"

"*Captain?* A captain in a *dress?*" The man roared with laughter, then punctuated his opinion of such a phenomenon with curses.

Finn's voice was calm but cold when he said, "You'll want to stop that kind of talk if you don't want to be thrown off this boat."

"And who vill do dis thing?" the man asked, "da cripple or da skirt?"

"He'll have help," Dr. Ross said, just at the moment that Logjam slipped up behind them all and pressed himself between Laura and Finn. Dr. Ross glanced down at the dog. "Both human and animal."

"I gather," Laura said, willing her voice not to shake as she stared at the man, "that you think we owe you some money."

The man waved a card in her face. "You took wood belonging to Charles W. Smith. I am who collects for him," he said. "Four dollars fifty cents for each cord of hardvood. Three dollars fifty cents for da rest. You pay me now." He held out a grimy paw.

"First of all, that's an outrageous price," Laura said. "There was no sign posted at the woodlot as to the charge, so I'll assume it's the same as everywhere else, which is a dollar less a cord than you just quoted. Second, when the sawyer isn't present, I settle accounts through their agents in St. Louis."

The man shook his craggy head. "Is no *gut*," he said. "Mr. Smith deals in cash only. You must pay."

"And I will," Laura said. "But not to someone who arrives like a thief in the night, dripping mud all over my dining saloon and frightening my passengers half to death."

The man took a step toward Laura. A low rumble sounded. Logjam stepped forward, planting himself between Laura and the unwanted visitor. "I heard about you," he said. "Da female vat thinks she vill be real riverboat pilot."

"I believe you know the way off my boat," Laura said and looked toward the side where the skiff was moored.

"Not until I get my money," the man said and moved as if to grab her.

Quick as a flash, Finn cracked the outstretched forearm with his cane. With a roar of pain, the man staggered back just as Logjam launched himself through the air. The man's "friends" took off.

"Logjam, no!" Laura cried out. The dog hesitated. "No." Laura's voice was calmer this time, and the dog looked back at her. "Come away. Let him go." With a great sigh, Logjam let the man go.

"Ve are not finished," he said.

"We are for now," Laura said. By then, all the diners had gathered at the saloon door. Laura was aware of Adele and

Fiona MacKnight in the center of the group. Finn and Dr. Ross followed the man to see him off the boat. Laura's knees went weak as the men disappeared from view. When she reached out to support herself with both hands on the railing, Fiona was at her side in an instant.

"Well done, my dear," she said. "Well done. And now you'll want a strong cup of tea." She took Laura's arm and guided her into the dining saloon, where the rest of the passengers greeted her with applause. Logjam followed and sprawled next to Laura's chair, and by the time Dr. Ross and Finn came back, Tyree had set a steaming mug of tea before Laura.

Finn stopped as he went by and put his hand on her shoulder. He leaned close. "Are you all right?"

She reached up and squeezed his hand. "I'm fine," she said. "Thank you." And then, to hide the fact that she was blushing, she looked across the table at Dr. Ross. "And thank you, Dr. Ross."

"A pleasure to be of service, my dear," the doctor said. His blue eyes twinkled as he said, "If you want something a bit stronger in that tea, I believe you've earned it."

Chapter 24

𝒯he *Laura Rose* made seventy-five miles the day after the woodlot incident and over a hundred the next. In the wake of nearly miraculous progress, Laura began to feel better about her chances of meeting the deadline. Together, she and Finn even managed a couple of all-night runs, thanks to the light of a half-moon that seemed to be magnified in the clear air.

When damp, disagreeable nights and gloomy, overcast days arrived, Laura determined not to complain. After all, she thought, the danger of Indian attack was less in bad weather. When they consistently avoided sandbars and passed other boats that had run aground, Finn insisted that it was thanks to Laura's uncanny ability to interpret even the slightest variation of the ripples on the surface of the water.

"Now I see what Joe was talking about when he praised the way you can read the water," he said late one evening as they tied up at a woodlot.

Laura thanked him even as she turned away, lest he notice that the compliment had made her blush.

With the arrival of the new moon and darkness so thick that it was as if the steamer had found her way inside the mouth of a dark cave, night navigating had to come to an end. With the boilers silenced, every sound seemed amplified.

Whether she lingered on the texas or up in the wheelhouse, Laura could hear voices down in the dining saloon.

Most nights, someone asked Adele to play the piano, and when the music began, Laura listened. Adele always began with a few less-familiar melodies, and for a while no one sang, but then, after a brief pause, she would switch over to the hymnal. As she played, Dr. Ross's clear baritone rang out. One night when the selection was "Nearer, My God, to Thee," tears sprang to Laura's eyes. It was one of Mama's favorites. The words of the second verse washed over Laura as if they were meant only for her. "Though like the wanderer, the sun gone down, darkness be over me, my rest a stone; yet in my dreams I'd be nearer, my God to Thee." How she longed to hear Mama's sweet voice again. To hear Joe's laughter. To feel safe in Papa's embrace. *To be nearer to God. To think of Him as "her" God.* Descending to her cabin, Laura opened Mama's Bible and, once again, began to read from the Psalms.

She read praises to God, and even though she didn't feel all that close to God herself, she still looked toward the heavens and whispered, "Thank You. For the chance to keep the *Laura Rose*. For Finn's help. For...Nate Landon." Had God perhaps sent Nate Landon her way? The idea that God might care to provision the galley was a new one to Laura, and yet she had no doubt that Mama would have seen it that way. Mama saw God in a lot of the things other people called "luck." And, Laura realized, in the things other people called "bad luck."

"He isn't a genie like the ones in the *Arabian Nights*," Mama had once said. Laura didn't remember the occasion, but she remembered Mama's gentle voice and her quiet acceptance of the course of things as being guided by God. "He does what's best in light of eternity." Mama had spoken with such calm assurance that Laura's remembering it now produced a tangible ache in her midsection. And a slight pang of regret. She wanted God to act on her behalf—but only if it meant she would be sitting aboard the *Laura Rose* on the evening of July 8, staring across the levee at St. Louis.

"I can't help it," she whispered, almost as an apology to God—and to Mama. Because if God's will didn't include her keeping the *Laura Rose*...Well, then what? Opening her door, Laura slipped outside and sat down with her back against the cabin wall, looking up at the night sky. A phrase from Mama's psalm came to mind. *I will walk before the* LORD *in the land of the living.* How she wanted to believe that about Papa and Joe and Mama. Not as just something one said to make others feel better, but as something that resonated from a place deep inside. Longing for that kind of faith grew so strong that tears slid down Laura's cheeks. She started when she heard footsteps on the texas.

Finn came around the corner. "Are you all right?" His voice was gentle.

Laura gestured up at the sky. "Just looking at the stars," she said. "Thinking."

"Want to be alone?"

She was tired of being alone. "Do you enjoy star-gazing?"

He sat down beside her. "Yes. I believe I do."

"I was reading Mama's Bible just now," she said. "That hymn Adele played was one of her favorites."

After a moment, Finn said, "I am so sorry, Laura."

"For what?"

"Everything. Your father. Your brother. Your mother." He paused. "I can't imagine it."

"I didn't cry," she said. "I knew that if the crew thought they were at the mercy of some weak female, they'd leave and I'd be stuck. So I didn't let myself cry. Not until I got her back to the levee. And then—Elijah pointed to a break in the clouds and told me they were watching. He said they were proud." She took a ragged breath. "That's when I cried."

Finn reached over and took her hand.

"I'm so afraid," she whispered.

"It's going to be all right."

"But what if the June rise isn't enough? What if we can't get past the rapids?" She swallowed. "What if I lose everything? Everything I have left that matters?"

He squeezed her hand. "Fiona would say that the things that really matter can't be lost."

"I wish I could believe that," Laura said. With a sigh, she leaned over and put her head on his shoulder. He kissed the top of her head. She closed her eyes, and for one brief moment, nothing mattered but the far-off yips of coyotes, the nearer sounds of insects, sawing away in the tall grass, and the warmth of the friend sitting next to her, holding her hand.

❈

Nate Landon made good on his promise to meet the *Laura Rose* at the Whetstone Agency, and once again he'd had success. This time, his mules were loaded down with buffalo meat. He'd ridden through a pouring rain, and Laura took one look at him and suggested he stay on board for at least a few days. "You're worn out," she said. "You need to dry out and get some rest."

"You s-sound like my s-sister," Landon said.

Remembering what Captain Grant had said about Landon's being raised among the Sioux, Laura was surprised. "You have a sister?"

"N-Not anymore. But she w-would have s-scolded m-me like you just d-did."

The young man's sad smile went straight to Laura's heart. "Cabin number nine on the leeward side is empty," she said. "You've earned it." She had Tyree deliver a bowl of hot soup to Landon's cabin after they got under way, along with the message that Landon was invited to dine in the dining saloon that evening, but only if he felt up to it.

Finn overheard her and teased, "Should I be jealous? After all, I've never been invited to dine at the captain's table."

"There's something about that boy that tears at a woman's heart."

The next time she saw him, Laura noticed Finn limping worse than usual. "What's this?" she asked.

"It's nothing."

"That's not nothing. What have you done?"

He looked over at her with a knowing smile. "It's the damp weather. Does it tear at your heart to see me so miserable?"

Laura glowered at him. "You really are a rapscallion, aren't you?"

"Through and through." And then he tilted his head and looked at her with something in his dark eyes that made her heart beat faster. "Do you like rapscallions, my captain?"

She made a show of thinking about it. "Well, I will say that having a rapscallion on my side who knows how to wield a cane seems to come in handy."

He nodded. "I'll settle for that. For now." And he limped away.

✸

It was none of her business of course, but Fiona didn't understand why Dr. Ross was still on board the *Laura Rose*. Adele had said—and Dr. Ross had confirmed—that he was seeking possible locations for a new seminary. But the *Laura Rose* was in the wilderness now. Military forts and Indian agencies were only suitable for missions. As for Fort Benton at the end of the trek, Fiona had heard more than she cared to know about that abominable place from Mrs. Chadwick, who seemed strangely excited about joining the husband who'd finally sent for her and her daughter to help him run some kind of general merchandise store at the end of the earth.

Dr. Ross didn't seem to have a missionary spirit, and yet he stuck with the *Laura Rose*. When Fiona asked about the seminary prospects, his answers seemed purposefully vague. There really was only one logical reason for the man's lingering on board the *Laura Rose*, and concerns over that replaced fear of the river as the principle reason for Fiona's inability to sleep.

"You must speak with him," she said to Finn. "It's ridiculous."

"I would, if I thought what you're thinking was even remotely true," Finn said. "But it isn't. Dr. Ross sees the same things in Adele that everyone does. She's charming, intelligent, and musically gifted. He enjoys her company. Frankly, so do I, now that she's stopped being such a self-centered brat."

Fiona pursed her lips. "She's up to something. I just know it." She sighed. "Although perhaps my concerns are misplaced. Most recently, I'd say Mr. Landon occupies far too much of her conversation. You should have seen her that evening when Miss White invited him to table. The child was fairly mesmerized by every word that came from that young man's mouth."

"And who could blame her for that?" Finn said. "Don't tell me you don't find him interesting."

Fiona sputtered an "Of course" followed by the usual sermonette in regards to Adele's general propensity for flirtation and outrageous behavior.

"I realize I haven't been around her very much on this trip," Finn said, "but I just haven't seen anything to be concerned about. Have you considered that maybe the only thing's she's 'up to' is remaking herself? And if that's it, don't you think we should let it happen?"

"She took him biscuits," Fiona said.

"Well now, that's surely cause for alarm," Finn said, his tone gently mocking. "On the other hand, it was also thoughtful. And kind."

Fiona shrugged. "What was she up to that day when she was crying on your shoulder?"

Finn sighed and shook his head. "Have faith, Fiona."

"Surely you don't believe all that nonsense about how much she loved Joseph White."

"What I believe," Finn said, "is that she sincerely wants to change. And in some way I don't quite understand, Dr. Ross seems to be helping the process."

Fiona snorted. "She's playing at religion," she said. "She monopolizes Dr. Ross's time and attention, asking all kinds of questions—until that other young man is on board. And then she seems predictably distracted—with 'being kind,' as you put it."

"I think she's sincerely hoping for better things, both for herself and for her relationship with you and me. And God, I suppose."

"If only you were right," Fiona said, her tone laced with doubt. "But I won't be able to rest until you find out for certain. I'm the last person on earth Adele would ever confide in. But she seems to trust you. Please, Finn. Will you speak with her again?"

With a sigh, Finn promised. And he really did intend to keep the promise. He would have—if the Missouri hadn't intervened with a vengeance.

⁂

"No-no-no!" As the rudder caught, Laura lost her grip on the ship's wheel. She grabbed it again only to realize she didn't have the strength to fight it—and even if she did, it was better to run aground than to break a rudder. With a shudder, the

Laura Rose was dead in the water, grounded on a sandbar that seemed to have appeared out of nowhere and, as far as Laura knew, spanned the entire channel. The firemen released steam from the boilers, the paddle wheel stopped, and by the time Laura had descended to the freight deck, the crew had lowered one of the skiffs to check on the situation.

"It had to happen," Finn said. "There's no one able to ascend this time of year without grounding a few times."

Laura knew he was right, but she wasn't finished castigating herself. She should have watched more carefully. She should have traveled more slowly. She should have done something differently. Anything. Because they had only seventeen days to cover a good three weeks' worth of Missouri River. There was no time for grounding and lightering and whatever else they were going to have to do in the next few hours. And if they didn't get off this bar quickly, they were going to run out of wood, because the coal was gone and she'd listened to Finn and passed a woodlot this morning.

She paced on the deck, her hands on her hips, only mildly aware of Logjam at her side, pacing right along with her. The skiff returned and Finn told her what she already knew but did not want to believe. "It's a hard grounding. No backing up or going around it. The only way is over."

Laura barely managed to swallow the mild curse that came to mind. "Well then." She looked over at the crewman standing next to Finn. "Man the winch. We'll be sparring our way off the bar." The crewman saluted and headed off.

The agonizingly slow process took most of the afternoon. First, each of the two poles carried on either side of the bow was placed in the sand and angled toward the front of the boat. Once each of the spars was connected to the winch by a line, the steam-powered winch drew up the lines attached to the poles, eventually lifting the entire steamboat up off the bar and dragging it forward. Every time the boat made progress, the spars had to be lifted out of the sand and replanted a short distance forward. It was late afternoon before the *Laura Rose* was over the bar. Which was grand, except that they'd used up so much fuel running the steam-powered capstan engine to power the sparring process that Laura didn't think they were going to make it to the next wood yard. And they didn't.

The crew loaded into skiffs and began combing the shore for every piece of driftwood they could find, and as soon as there was enough to stoke the boilers, the *Laura Rose* inched upriver again. When night fell, there was nothing to do but tie up and wait for daylight to reveal more wood to scavenge. Laura shut everything down and went to her cabin. She was in no mood to talk to anyone. But Finn wouldn't let it be. He came knocking.

"I was wrong," he said. "You were right. We should have saved the coal—or taken on more wood."

"And if we'd done things my way," Laura said, "we would likely have had to unload it all to lighten the boat—in addition to sparring."

"Maybe. But we wouldn't be out of fuel."

"It's not your fault," Laura said. She pressed her lips together and fought back tears of frustration.

Finn looked north. "We can't be that far from a woodlot, can we? The way this dad-blamed river changes, I'm hardpressed to know exactly where we are from moment to moment. To tell you the truth, I don't remember this bend we've just come around at all."

"It probably didn't exist the last time you were up this way," Laura said. "I remember Papa complaining about the blankety-blank river cutting a new channel that was going to add a good ten miles to the trip—ten miles of looping river just to get a quarter-mile closer to Fort Benton. He said if he didn't know better, he'd think the Indians had cast a spell on the water so it would do whatever was necessary to keep the fireboats from coming back."

"Don't give up yet."

"I'm not giving up," Laura said. "I'm facing reality. We're seventeen problem-free days from Fort Benton. It's at least two problem-free *weeks* back to St. Louis."

"That makes it exactly July 8 when you tie up at the levee."

"You and I both know there is no such thing as a problem-free trip on the Big Muddy."

Finn changed the subject. "Tyree said Bird's roasting the last of the antelope for the late meal. Come and eat."

"I'm not hungry."

"Doesn't matter. Come and eat anyway. There's no point in brooding in your cabin."

"I do not brood," Laura protested. She reached up in a vain attempt to smooth her hair back into place.

He caught her hand, and his voice changed as he said, "Do you have any idea how beautiful you look after a frustrating day of piloting this packet?"

"Wh-what?"

His dark eyes smoldered. "I mean it. Those red curls around your face..." He reached over and tugged on a longer curl. "This one trailing down your back..."

"Don't be ridiculous," she said. "I'm a wreck."

"You're breathtaking."

"I—I—"

Gently, he pulled her to him, so that they were standing so close that when she looked up at him, his lips were only inches away. "I've wanted to kiss you since the day you came looking for me, intending to yell at me for running aground while racing your steamboat. Do you remember? You were so angry." He traced her jawline. "You're particularly fetching when you're angry, my captain."

"B-but I'm not angry now."

"Yes, well... You're beautiful when you aren't angry, too. And when you're tired. And afraid. And happy. Really, just about any time of the day or night."

Laura was about to lift her lips to his when a familiar voice called her name. Finn spun her about—although he didn't quite let go. She was standing in front of him and she could feel his hands at her waist as she faced Adele and Fiona—and Nate Landon, all three of them standing at the top of the stairs that led down to the hurricane deck. At least Adele was smiling. One glance Fiona's way, and Laura felt her face begin to burn. She took the slightest step away from Finn, and he dropped his hands from her waist.

True to form, Adele spoke first, even as she reached for Landon and, taking his arm, propelled him forward. "Mr. Landon knows where we can get wood."

Landon pointed off to the east. "M-maybe two hours that way."

"But we've only got your two pack mules," Laura said. "Even if every hand on deck goes, they can't carry enough to make it worthwhile."

"The w-wagon," Landon said. "The one on b-board that's b-bound for Fort Benton. My mules will pull it." He paused. "They won't like it, but I c-can get them to d-do it. Mr. N-north said there's harness in one of the shipping crates. He j-just has to f-find it."

"It'll take most of tomorrow," Laura said.

"We don't have to wait," Landon replied. "I know the way. E-Even in the dark."

"How could you possibly?"

He took a deep breath. "Cabins," he said. "An abandoned h-homestead." He paused again. "M-my pa's."

The reality of what Landon was saying washed over her. *He was raised by the Sioux.* And he'd had a sister. What had happened to her? To his parents? Laura shuddered to think.

Landon seemed to anticipate the rest of her questions. "We might run into Indians. B-but they know me."

"I can't ask you to do that. To go back there."

"Y-you didn't. I offered."

"Are you sure?"

He nodded. He glanced over at Adele and smiled. "I want to help."

Laura looked up at Finn. He shrugged. "Might be the answer to the prayers we didn't think to pray."

"I'll call a meeting with the crew. Ask for volunteers." She motioned for Landon to follow her down to the freight deck. "How many men do you think you'll need?" She and Landon talked as they descended the stairs, and within the hour the wagon had been floated across to dry land, the mules hitched, and half a dozen armed men had headed east across the prairie. Laura was grateful—and worried. Finn had insisted that he accompany the wood crew. *Please, God. Don't let anything happen to them. To him.*

Chapter 25

Fiona stood at the railing of the hurricane deck, watching as the wagon bearing her brother disappeared into the distance. She glanced over at Miss White. There was no mistaking the meaning of that expression. Apparently, Adele had been right about Finn and Miss White. They had been about to kiss just now. And how did she feel about that? She smiled in spite of herself, because if there was anything in which her opinion would not matter it was Finn's choice of a wife. A *wife*. Would it lead to that? Would Finn finally settle down? Again, the notion made Fiona smile, for whatever happened with Finn and Miss White, the term "settling down" would probably not apply.

Surely you can see that they are perfect for each other. Adele had said that, and for once Adele was probably right. *Adele*. With a sigh, Fiona realized that with Finn distracted by romance, dealing with Adele would once again be entirely her responsibility. When the child tugged on her sleeve and mentioned Dr. Ross's conducting a prayer meeting in the dining room on behalf of the brave men headed into possible danger, Fiona said, "In a moment. First, I'd like to speak with you about something. In private."

Adele looked wary. "But—why? What have I done?"

"Just come along, please," Fiona said and led the way up the stairs. As soon as they were in their cabin, she said, "There is no reason to beat about any bushes. Once and for all, I want it settled. You are to stop this nonsense with Dr. Ross."

Adele frowned. "Wh-what?"

"Please, Adele. We know one another far too well for play-acting. Dr. Ross is a fine man. But he is a man, and as such, he is not immune to being flattered by the attentions of a beautiful young girl who appears to hang on his every word. As I said before, he *is* old enough to be your father, and well, not to speak ill of our own papa, but his behavior is hardly an example that should be followed. I realize that since the war, liaisons between young ladies and older men have become more common, but you must stop. You're not truly interested in the dear man, and he does not deserve to be trifled with."

Adele plopped down on the top of the trunk at the foot of the bed. "I am *not* flirting with Dr. Ross, and I'm not 'pretending to hang on his every word.' I'm not pretending anything." She opened her mouth to say more. Closed it. Frowned. And then allowed a little laugh. "You really still think I'm interested in Dr. Ross...as a *man*?" She covered her mouth with her palm. "Oh, my goodness, Fiona. I told you before—you can't be serious. Tell me you aren't really serious."

"I fail to see anything amusing about the situation." The child would not stop laughing. Infuriated, Fiona stomped her foot. "I demand that you stop this instant! You may have made a fool of Joseph White, but you will *not* make a fool of Dr. Ross, do you hear me?" It was all she could do to keep from shaking the girl. Happily, the mention of Joseph White stilled the laughter.

"Wh-why would you say such a thing about Joseph?" Adele said. Her cheeks grew red.

Fiona sat down. "I should not have brought that up. I spoke out of anger."

"You can't just say something like that and then refuse to talk about it. How did I make a fool of Joseph?"

"By toying with his affections. Just as you have persisted

in toying with Dr. Ross. And now—Mr. Landon, it seems. Adele, you have to stop. A woman's reputation...You only have one. A ruined reputation is nearly impossible to repair."

Adele leaned forward. "Dr. Ross doesn't have any interest in me. Not the way you mean it. Nor do I in him. He's like a kindly old grandfather to me. Or a wise pastor." She paused. Looked over at Fiona. "If anything, he's interested in *you*."

"Don't be ridiculous."

"I am not being ridiculous," Adele said. "There isn't any other woman on board who can hold her own in a theological discussion the way you do. Now that I think about it, Dr. Ross may have never met *any* woman quite so well versed in such things. Mrs. Chadwick just spouts whatever her Methodist catechism says, and Euphemia—well, I'm sure you realized this afternoon that Euphemia doesn't have any opinions of her own about much of anything."

Adele continued, "If anyone is being ridiculous, dear sister, it's you. Sparring with a man like that over whether or not free will exists and how a sovereign God would allow sin in the first place and the nature of prayer and—goodness. Whatever happened to asking a man about his favorite kind of pie or his grandchildren or—something normal?"

Fiona lifted her chin. "The things you just mentioned are very important theological issues, and I happen to find them quite fascinating."

Adele just shook her head. "And all the while you're missing the point that Dr. Ross finds *you* fascinating."

"That's ridiculous."

"Do you have any idea how often you say that? It's ridiculous how often you tell other people that what they've just said is ridiculous."

The two women sat in uncomfortable silence. Finally, Fiona spoke. "If I misunderstood your intentions in regards to either man, I apologize."

"You did." Adele paused. "Of course it's true that I've never met anyone like Mr. Landon. And I'd have to be blind not to notice how handsome he is. But really, Fiona, can't a girl just think to do something nice without everyone assuming there's some ulterior motive? I remembered Mr. Landon saying something about Bird's biscuits reminding him of home, and I just thought—I thought it would be nice. That's all. I don't expect you'll believe it, but it's the truth. As for Dr. Ross…yes. He interests me, but not for the reason you think. I've never known anyone that devout to be so kind." She winced. "I'm sorry—that didn't—"

Fiona cleared her throat. "I quite understand." Her voice wavered. "I have thought a great deal about what you said that night after I fainted. When you were brushing my hair. About how you were afraid to bother me when you were a little girl…when you had those nightmares." The quiet in the cabin pressed in. "I wept after you left. It's terrible that you felt that way. That you had no comfort."

Adele shrugged.

"And the piano. I really did think it was a frivolous request. I didn't think you meant it. But that shouldn't have mattered. Not then. You were only a frightened child." She looked out the window for a moment, trying to regain her composure.

"Why did you hate me so much? I mean, I know why you hate me now. But then—why?"

Fiona frowned. She shook her head. "I didn't—I do not—hate you." She sighed. "But I have resented you. There's a difference, although I don't suppose it matters." Something made her go on. "When you first arrived, I was engaged. We were going to head west together, but then my fiancé demanded that I make a choice between you and him."

Adele looked up. Her brow furrowed. "And so because of me, you lost your chance at love?"

"I thought so at first. Later, though, I realized that because of you, I didn't enter into a marriage I would have regretted. Only a very selfish man indeed would have done something like that. It would have been an unhappy life." She looked over at Adele with a sad smile. "Having you in my life has always reminded me of my failures. My poor choice of a man. My sour moods. My tendency to make impossible demands of myself, and then to fail to meet them—over and over again. The fact that no matter how hard I try, I always fall short."

"But—doesn't everyone? I mean, isn't that why Jesus died? Not that I'm any expert, mind you. But Dr. Ross read me a verse the other day about falling short."

Fiona nodded. "I know it well. 'For all have sinned, and come short of the glory of God.'"

"Yes. That's the one. And then another one about God giving a free gift."

"'For by grace are ye saved through faith; and that not of yourselves: it is the gift of God: Not of works, lest any man should boast.'"

"Yes. That's it. That's the one." Adele smiled. "A free gift."

Fiona looked at her with surprise. "You and Dr. Ross speak of these things?"

Adele nodded.

"But—why?"

She shrugged. "I can't tell you." And then, after a moment, she said, "Do you think it's true? That God really would forgive anything? I mean—I've always pictured Him as kind of angry all the time. You know, staring down with a scowl, tapping his foot, wondering why on earth I don't do better."

Fiona sighed. "I suppose that's my fault. That's how I've always treated you, isn't it?"

"But do you think Dr. Ross is right—that God really will forgive anything?"

"You're only eighteen years old, Adele. I can't think you've done anything that would be all that hard to forgive."

The girl's eyes filled with tears. She leaned down and covered her face with her hands. "I did. With Joseph. I'm so sorry, Fiona. I just—He was nice to me and I liked him, and I wanted to get away. I wanted Papa's money and for everything to change. And Joseph liked me, but I—"

"Hush," Fiona said. She moved to sit beside Adele and put her hand on her shoulder.

"I'm so sorry. I've ruined everything. I've ruined everything for *you*, because Martin Lawrence knows and Lucy Powell knows and I'm sure they've told their parents by now and—Well, you said it. A girl only has one reputation, and once it's ruined—" As she sobbed, Adele choked out her determination never to return to St. Louis, her plan to use this trip upriver to find a new place to live. And her fear. "I can't even do that right," she finally said, sobbing. "Because I'm too afraid to run away."

"Shh." Fiona began to rub the weeping girl's back, making slow circles, trying to help her calm down. "I won't hear of you running away. In fact, I won't allow it."

"Finn said the same thing, but you *would* allow it if you knew what I did."

"I do know about—the other matter. We'll work it out. I don't know how, but we will."

Adele looked up at her with an expression of horror. "You—know?"

Fiona nodded. "When you were sick the day we left? I thought perhaps—"

"So did I. I'm not, though. I must have been so upset that things—But I'm not." She paused. "Is that why *you* were so upset?" She answered her own question. "That's why you were so upset. You thought I was in the family way."

"I was angry, and in my anger I was cruel," Fiona said. Her voice wavered. "Please forgive me."

After a moment, Adele stopped crying. "Dr. Ross says that

God doesn't love us because we're good. He says that God loves us even if we aren't."

" 'God commendeth his love toward us,' " Fiona quoted, " 'in that, while we were yet sinners, Christ died for us.' "

"I don't understand which God is real," Adele said.

"What do you mean?"

"Yours or Dr Ross's. I mean—is God angry and demanding, or is He kind and loving?"

The question pierced Fiona's heart. "I think," she said, "that we should ask Dr. Ross that question. Together."

⚓

Laura sat up half the night waiting for Finn and the crew to return with the wagonload of firewood. Logjam gave her the first indication that they were near when he rose from where he'd been lying next to her and peered into the darkness, every inch of him tense as he lifted his great head and sniffed the wind. When Laura stood up and put her hand on the dog's head, he leaned into her, but his gaze never left the distant horizon.

"Are they coming? Do you hear them?"

Logjam chuffed and wagged his tail. He stepped toward the stairs, then hesitated.

"It's all right, boy. Go on."

The dog leaped away. In the still night, she heard him clatter down the stairs. Seconds later, she heard rather than saw him land on the riverbank as he leaped off the prow and charged toward whatever it was he'd heard. At first, Laura thought she must be imagining it, but gradually she realized that she really was hearing Logjam bark. And then the sounds of a wagon rattling across the prairie toward the steamboat.

It seemed to take hours for the crew to finally come into view—dark shadows, headed her way, led along by horse-shaped gray ghosts—Landon's two mules, plodding steadily along. *Thank God*. Laura looked up at the night sky. *Thank You*. Once at the riverbank, the men unharnessed the mules. Laura heard the word "picket" and realized Landon was going to let his mules graze until morning. She was waiting at the top of the stairs when Finn finally arrived, and it seemed the most natural thing in the world to step into his arms and hug a welcome.

"Success," he said as he held her. She sensed his looking off into the night as he murmured, "That's a sad, sad place." After a moment, he said, "We tore the cabin down. I think it gave Landon an odd kind of pleasure to do it. Maybe it helped him make peace with it. I don't know."

Laura stepped away and, taking Finn's hand, led him to the railing. "Did he mention his sister?"

Finn took a deep breath. "There's no grave, if that's what you mean." The implication hung on the air. Finally, Finn cleared his throat and said, "We should be able to leave at first light," he said.

"What about Landon?"

"He's going to head off on the hunt again."

"I wish he wouldn't. I mean—being alone again. So soon after what he's gone through."

"I think he wants to be alone," Finn said. "He said he'd meet up with us again at Cow Island." He gave a little laugh. "How was supper with Fiona? Did she deliver any sermons about the bad example we set for Adele last evening?"

"I hardly saw them. They dined at the opposite end of the table, and they were huddled in a corner of the dining saloon talking to Dr. Ross when I retired."

"But you didn't really retire, did you?"

"Logjam and I had a perfectly lovely evening lounging on the texas," she said.

"So you weren't waiting up for me? Worrying about me? Obsessing about me?"

"I might have thought about you once or twice." She looked up at him. "I'm glad you're back."

"I brought you something," he said. "Close your eyes."

She closed her eyes. When something soft brushed against her upper lip, she inhaled. *Roses.* She reached up and took what proved to be a cluster of tiny blossoms from Finn's hand.

"One little wild rosebush growing beside what used to be the front door of that homestead." When he looked down at her, his dark eyes sought her lips. But then he only smiled and reached for her hand. "Come along, my captain. I'll walk you home."

Strolling next to Finn, feeling his rough, calloused hand closed about hers, Laura thought back to his teasing her about staying up worrying about him. The thing was...she had worried. If anything had happened to him out there in the night...She gulped. If anything had happened to Finn...

"Good night, my captain."

They were here. At her cabin door. Laura looked up into Finn's dark eyes. "I did worry," she said. "About you." She ducked her head, pretending to savor once again the aroma of the roses he'd brought her.

He leaned down and kissed her cheek. Her nose. And then...her lips. *Glory be, but the man could kiss.*

✵

The wood the crew brought back to the *Laura Rose* fired the boilers well enough for them to make it to the next woodlot with fuel to spare. Over the next couple of days, the river began to rise, and as the river rose, so did Laura's spirits. If the weather held, if the rise lasted, if the Lord willed...maybe. Maybe they would make it back in time. *If the Lord willed.* There was still hope.

At least twice a day it seemed, someone caught sight of wildlife, and when they did, a general spirit of excitement rippled through the passengers. They saw antelope and deer, wolves, and, one morning right after breakfast, a tawny mountain lion loping along a distant ridge. Strangely enough, the morning before they reached Cow Island, half a dozen buffalo were sighted heading for the river. There was nothing to do but wait for them to cross. When one of the crew members managed to get off a shot, Laura whirled out of the wheelhouse and down to the freight deck to tell the men in no uncertain terms to let the beasts be. She had no intention of stopping while they tried to wrangle a half-ton carcass aboard.

The last night before the challenge of the first rapids, two other packets approached and laid to near the *Laura Rose*. The night was clear and bright, and as she gazed across the way to the other steamboats with their lights reflected on the water, Laura looked up at the night sky and smiled. She thought of what Elijah North had said about God's letting Mama and Papa and Joe look down from time to time. She realized that for the first time, pain hadn't been the first response to her thoughts of them, and she smiled. *Do you see me? Finn and I are going to do it. We're going to save the* Laura Rose.

That sense of peace and contentment didn't last long, for early the next morning, soundings proved that the river had begun to fall. They were racing the unknown again. Was the fall only temporary, or did it mean that the June rise was over? If it was the latter, then getting over the fifteen sets of rapids that stood between them and Fort Benton would take too long. With that prospect in mind, the *Laura Rose* set off upriver at three o'clock in the morning, with Finn at the wheel and Laura peering through the spyglass, worrying more and more with every mile.

"We'll make it," Finn said. "Whatever it takes, we'll make it over."

"At least we have a full moon," Laura said. "Maybe we can just keep running."

"We'll do our best," Finn said.

"But what if our best isn't—"

"Laura." Finn's voice was gentle as he called her name. "Just keep watch. Tell me what you see."

✵

They were paying fifteen dollars a cord for wood now. "That's robbery," Laura said when a wood hawk came aboard demanding cash.

"If you don't want to pay it," the man said, "you're welcome to pass me by."

Of course she couldn't, and he knew it. And so Laura opened the safe and paid the man. "I don't how you sleep at night," she said.

"Right well," he replied and smiled as he turned to go.

They met another packet coming down from Fort Benton. The report was bad. "Only thirty inches at Dauphin Rapids," someone hollered as the boat went by. The *Laura Rose* was drawing forty. They'd run aground if they didn't lighten the load and reduce the draft by at least ten inches.

"We'll have to off-load," Laura said, barely hiding the despair in her voice. And so it went. The next week was a continual process of struggling to make it over one set of rushing waters or another, off-loading, sparring, sending skiffs back to pick up freight that had been left on shore, traveling only a half mile when they needed to go at least five. Even the moonlight didn't make much of a difference.

Laura barely slept. Her sense of desperation mounted. *Help me.* It was all the praying she could do. *Help me. Please. Help me.* At last, the *Laura Rose* launched out of the last set of rapids and onto the part of the Missouri known as the "rocky river," because the channel was straight and narrow, cut through rock. Here, the water was smooth and free of any timber. There were no sandbars, no sawyers, and the way was clear to Fort Benton for the last 172 miles. But as Laura stared out at the barren, rocky banks, she felt no sense of accomplishment. It was over. Even a miracle wouldn't carry them back to St. Louis by July 8.

※

Finn was at the wheel when the *Laura Rose* landed at Fort Benton on June 28. Once the packet was tied up at the levee, Finn turned to speak to Laura. "Don't give up," he said. "We aren't beaten yet." He reached for his cane. "I'll see to the off-loading. We'll be ready to head back downriver in record time."

Laura said nothing. She was still up in the wheelhouse an hour later, sitting on the bench that ran along the back edge of windows. Logjam was at her side, his head resting on her knee. When Finn appeared, the dog looked over momentarily. But then, with a sigh, he put his head back on Laura's knee.

"The freight's unloaded," he said. "We can wait for a few hours and hope to pick up some shipments and passengers for downriver, or we can leave right way. I remember what you said about Davies insisting on freight, but you just might be able to fight him and win on that point." When she didn't so much as look up, he said, as gently as possible, "What do you want to do?"

"I don't know."

Finn sat down beside her. He took her free hand and kissed her palm. "I wish I could buy you out of debt."

She pulled her hand away, then leaned forward and covered her face with her hands. Just as Finn was about to pull her into his arms, she stood up and, taking a deep breath, crossed over to the wheel. Then she turned about. "We might as well check the lay of the land about freight or passengers. The least I can do is make the trip as profitable as possible."

Finn reached over to pat Logjam on the head. "All right," he said. "I'll see to it."

He relayed Laura's order and then went to stand near the steam capstan at the bow of the *Laura Rose*. He looked toward the distant hills and the thin clouds scudding across the sky. *I don't know what to do. I'm not asking for me. I don't deserve anything but Your anger. But, God...* He turned and looked toward the wheelhouse and the letters that spelled out the name *Laura Rose*.

Elijah North approached. "Never saw her so low," he said, nodding toward the wheelhouse. "Not even that day in Sioux City when she got the news from the doctor about Mrs. White and the Captain. She's always been able to dig down and find the strength."

"I don't know what to do," Finn said. He looked toward Fort Benton.

The crew had headed off in the direction of the long row of false-fronted buildings as soon as North told them they were free to take some time ashore. He'd warned them about getting left behind if they overindulged and didn't respond to the ship's bell when departure sounded.

Finn remembered Fort Benton. Oh, there were freighters and general merchandise stores, a livery and a blacksmith. The place had grown since the last time he was here, thanks in large part to gold fever. Mostly, though, Fort Benton, which had begun life as a fur-trading post, was little more than a long line of brothels and saloons. The former never had held any allure for him. The latter, on the other hand—He looked back up at the wheelhouse and wished with everything in him that just knowing he was with her would have helped somehow.

We aren't beaten yet. That's all he'd managed to say. He'd meant a lot more than that. But as he replayed the scene in his mind, all he remembered was Laura pulling away from him.

Again, he looked off toward the town. What could it hurt to at least take a little walk?

❇

Adele and Fiona disembarked with Mrs. Chadwick and Euphemia. Together, the ladies picked their way across the levee and toward the largest of the buildings in view, which, Mrs. Chadwick said, was to be her new home. "Just for a year or so," she said. "Until we can build something suitable." She turned to her daughter. "Come along, Euphemia. Papa will be so pleased to see us." She opened her parasol and looped her arm through her daughter's.

"B-but...Papa said it was a city. He said..." Euphemia sounded like a kitten mewling a protest as her voice faded.

"Well, it is a city," Adele said, trying to find something to say that would cheer the woebegone Euphemia Chadwick. "And just think: The Chadwicks are getting in on the ground floor. That's exciting!"

Euphemia did not look excited. She looked as if she was considering another faint. But she seemed to think better of it after looking about. Adele stifled a smile. There was nowhere to land that wasn't covered with filth. And no Finn MacKnight to lean on. Taking a deep breath, Euphemia marched on.

Chadwick's Merchandise was a false-fronted building with a raised boardwalk and two large windows displaying all kinds of things Adele assumed people needed for life on the frontier. The only thing that remotely interested her was a small display of buttons, but one glance told her they were nothing special. The interior of the store was a mishmash. Fiona looked about her with barely disguised horror.

"Well, well," Mrs. Chadwick clucked. "I can see that you and I have our work cut out for us, Euphemia."

Euphemia only nodded. But then a balding string bean of a man peered into the store from the back room, and everything changed. "My girls! My girls! Praise God from whom all blessings flow!" He glanced behind him, calling out to someone Adele couldn't see. "Here they are, Burrows, the very beauties I was just pining after!"

Mr. Chadwick was dressed in somewhat shabby clothes, and the apron he wore was smudged with dust, but none of that mattered to Mrs. Chadwick and Euphemia, for they fluttered and laughed as Mr. Chadwick hugged and kissed them and then exclaimed over Adele's beauty and Fiona's lovely bonnet until Adele decided that Mr. Chadwick was one of the most charming men on earth, and Mrs. Chadwick and Euphemia were very lucky to have him. In fact, as she saw the color come back to Euphemia's pale face, Adele decided that Fort Benton might be a wilderness, but a woman could do worse than to share a life with someone as loving as middle-aged Mr. Arnold Chadwick.

The man who trailed Mr. Chadwick out of the storeroom was another story entirely, and one glance at Fiona told Adele that her suspicions were correct. Mr. Burrows was drunk and, from the look of his rumpled clothing and equally rumpled hair, he had been imbibing for some time. But then, just when Adele had decided to categorize Mr. Burrows as a member of a lower echelon of Fort Benton society, the man reached out to steady himself and an impressive gold ring flashed.

Mrs. Chadwick introduced Adele and Fiona to her husband, and at the mention of their association with the *Laura Rose*, Mr. Chadwick turned to his drunken friend. "Here, here, Burrows. Take courage, old man. Who knows but what these fine ladies are the very answer to your predicament?" Mr. Chadwick smiled up at Fiona first, but Fiona's scowl seemed to ward him off and he turned instead to Adele. "Is it true, then, the *Laura Rose* leaves within the hour for St. Louis?"

"I believe so," Adele said.

Chadwick cupped his friend's elbow as he said, "Well now, Elmer. Come along. Nothing ventured, nothing gained, as

they say. Let's hurry down and see what we can arrange." He
nodded to his wife and daughter. "You'll watch the store now,
won't you, girls? I won't be gone long. Just have to see if we
can get Burrows on board and on his way." He glanced over at
Adele. "Elmer's had a terrible shock, you see. News of illness.
His dear wife."

Adele glanced at Mr. Burrows.

Mr. Chadwick leaned in, speaking in a stage whisper, "He's
a good man. Not at all like what it seems. He's just been at a
loss is all." He turned back to his friend. "Sober up, Elmer.
We'll get you on your way home now. Take heart." Talking
all the while, Chadwick pulled his stumbling friend along,
through the door of the mercantile, out into the daylight, and
toward the *Laura Rose*.

Adele and Fiona bid the Chadwick women a somewhat
disorganized adieu and followed Mr. Chadwick. When Fiona
said something about the situation, Adele couldn't help but
remind her that she had, after all, defended Finn through
many years of similar behavior. "Maybe he *is* a good man," she
said as they hurried along.

Fiona clamped her mouth shut.

A flash of red caught Adele's eye. She reached over and
put her hand on Fiona's arm and with an exclamation of joy
cried, "Look!" It was Nate Landon, riding toward them leading his two mules, each one bearing what looked like a carcass, until one moved and the mule skittered sideways, clearly
displeased with its burden. "He's done it. Oh, aren't they dar-
ling?" And without a thought to the mud splattering the hem
of her skirt, Adele drew Fiona along toward the *Laura Rose* to
get a better look at Nate Landon's buffalo calves.

❊

"I am so sorry." Mr. Elmer Burrows leaned against the railing of
the hurricane deck for support even as he took another sip of

the coffee Bird had brought out at Laura's request. "I'm not like this. Not really." He blinked. "I just—" A sob interrupted whatever he was going to say. He looked at Mr. Chadwick. "You tell her, Arnie. I'm no good." And with that, Burrows slumped into a nearby chair. Grasping the coffee mug with both hands, he leaned forward, his shoulders shaking as he sobbed.

"He'll be a model passenger," Mr. Chadwick said, "once he's sober." He lowered his voice. "And likely the wealthiest passenger you'll ever tow back to St. Louis. Word has it that Elmer took a good many thousands out of his claim last month alone."

Burrows stumbled up. "I'm rich," he said and looked at his friend. "You go get it. All of it. Bring it on board." He looked at Laura. "If you'll take me back to St. Louis—get me there as quickly as you can—I'll pay you. Whatever you want." He dabbed at his watery eyes with a none-too-clean kerchief. "Maggie." He practically moaned the name. Again, he looked over at Chadwick. "Nothing will matter if my Maggie—"

"Now, now, Elmer." Chadwick patted the man on the shoulder. "I'll hurry after your things." He looked at Laura. "Do we have an agreement, Miss White? Will you transport my friend here back to St. Louis as fast as your packet can go?"

Laura hesitated. Where was Finn when she needed his advice? At least she believed Mr. Chadwick to be an honest man, but this other fellow? And all this drama about a sick wife. She was about to send both men packing when Dr. Ross approached.

"Miss MacKnight thought I might be of assistance," he said.

Once again, Mr. Chadwick explained "poor Elmer's plight."

Dr. Ross drew Elmer to sit down and leaned close, listening while the drunken man blubbered his way through a tale

that Laura didn't know whether to believe or award as the
best piece of fiction she'd ever heard. Either way, it was past
time they shoved off.

"I'm going to ring the bell announcing our departure," she
said to Chadwick. "That'll signal my crew to head back to the
steamer. You'll need to hurry if you intend to bring anything
on board."

Chadwick scurried away. As Laura watched the man
clamor back up the steep rise to Fort Benton, she caught sight
of Finn. *Finally.* Relief flooded through her, but the minute
she got downwind of him, her smile faded. He'd been in a
saloon. He didn't seem inebriated, but still—

Nate Landon's arrival made it impossible to discuss anything further. He led first one and then the other mule on
board, and for the first time Laura realized that somehow
they were going to have to create a corral on the freight deck.
How was Landon going to manage to keep the calves fed?
And cleaned up after?

Landon and another crew member lowered one of the
calves to the deck. The moment the creature's hooves found
purchase, it decided to make a break for it. Landon was in the
animal's way, but not for long. The calf banged into him and
Landon hit the deck with a resounding thud. Adele shrieked
and ran to his aid. Fiona called Adele's name, and in the ensu-
ing melee Finn staggered a few steps, sat down on the deck,
and began to laugh.

Heartsick, Laura retreated. Once again, she rang out
departure. She was still up in the wheelhouse when Elijah
North signaled the all clear from the prow of the freight
deck. And she was still in the wheelhouse—alone—when
Adele appeared at the top of the ladder a few hours later, with
whom but Dr. Ross in tow. Laura spoke to the elderly gentleman first. "I thought you were getting off at Fort Benton."

The man's blue eyes spoke empathy. His voice was warm

with caring as he said, "No, I'm bound for St. Louis now, the same as you."

"But—I thought—"

He nodded. "Yes, yes. I know. I just didn't feel right about leaving the *Laura Rose*. The original plan was for me to disembark at Sioux City and then return to St. Louis and make a full report." He climbed the rest of the ladder into the wheelhouse and came to stand beside her. "Sometimes the Lord seems to whisper other possibilities. I always try to listen when He does that. And now I think perhaps I know why I was supposed to linger."

Adele cleared her throat. "I just came up here to tell you that Finn's going to be all right," she said. "He didn't want you to worry. He said he'll be back up here in no time."

Laura forced a smile. "Thank you. I was worried."

"He said you would be." She seemed about to say more, but then she thought better of it. "Really, Laura. *You don't need to worry.* He's fine."

Whatever the expression on the girl's face was meant to convey, Laura wasn't understanding it. Adele seemed to realize that, but she didn't offer any more in the way of explanation. Instead, she turned to Dr. Ross. "Don't forget about your engagement this evening."

"How could I forget the promise of such charming company?" he said.

Adele kissed the old man on the cheek and left.

Dr. Ross was quiet for a while. Finally, though, he said, "One thing a Missouri River packet provides is the opportunity for long conversations—or cribbage tournaments, depending on one's wishes." He paused. "I have so enjoyed getting to know the MacKnights." He sighed. "And poor Mr. Burrows."

Laura looked over at him. "You believe his story, then? About his wife and his gold?"

"I do," he said. "He's rather compromised at the moment, but I think the desperation is real."

"Then I'm even happier that you've decided to stay on board," Laura said. She forced a smile. "Mama would like the idea of the *Laura Rose* having its very own chaplain."

"I rather like the notion myself," Dr. Ross said. "And you, Miss White. Is there some way I might be of assistance to you?"

She grimaced. "Not unless you can stop the calendar or somehow levitate this packet and fly it back to St. Louis by July 8." *Or erase Finn's being drunk again.*

"I thought I might pray with you. *For* you, if you'd allow it? I wonder if you're perhaps tempted to think that God has forgotten you. Please don't listen to that lie. Hold on to hope."

Laura put her palm to her mouth to stifle a sob. Her eyes filled with tears.

"Do you have a Bible, my dear?"

Laura nodded. "My mother's." She swallowed. "She... um... She was partial to the Psalms."

Dr. Ross smiled. Nodded. "Some of the most profound poetry ever written," he said. He bowed his head and began to pray aloud.

Laura didn't really know what she'd expected, but Dr. Ross didn't pray like any minister she'd ever heard. Like Mama, he spoke as if the Almighty was right there in the wheelhouse with them. It made Laura feel as though she was being wrapped in love and drawn toward the Almighty.

"And, Lord, please let Miss White know that You are the Lover of her soul. That she is not alone. That You will guide her to a place of peace where she can lay her burden down and rise up with joy unspeakable. Please show her Yourself so that she can know the peace that passes understanding. I ask these things in the mighty name of the Lord Jesus Christ. Amen."

The prayer concluded, Dr. Ross stood quietly, gazing out at the landscape until finally Laura said, "Thank you, Dr. Ross. One of the things I miss most about my mother is her prayers. At times, I had a sense that she was standing in the very throne room of God." She glanced over at him. "Just now, you made me feel that same way."

"If your mother was a praying woman, I imagine she taught you the gospel from the time you were small. Am I right?"

Laura nodded.

"Then you know that you don't really need anyone else to usher you into the King's presence. That has already been made possible through the cross."

"I know you're right," Laura said. "I just—I don't suppose I've taken it to heart. In the way you mean it. In the way Mama believed it."

"Well, perhaps you'll find your way to just that in the days ahead," Dr. Ross said. "In the meantime, a person could do much worse than to read those Psalms that were so precious to your dear mother. I can't tell you how many times they've given me words when I just didn't know what to say to God."

After a few moments, Dr. Ross left Laura to pilot the *Laura Rose* southward, back toward the rapids, back toward Sioux City, and finally, back to St. Louis and the inevitable. And none of it would be impossible to bear, if only Finn MacKnight would show his face.

✹

Finn peered into the mirror above the little washstand in his cabin and grumbled at himself. "Coward. Time to confess." With a trembling hand, he splashed some cologne into one palm and then swiped his newly shaven jaw. Taking a last glance in the mirror, he reached for his cane and headed off to find Laura. She was in the dining saloon, watching Fiona and Dr. Ross play cribbage. Thankfully, she had her back to the door. Finn tightened his grip on his cane and looked over at Adele for courage. She nodded and leaned over to speak to Laura.

For a moment, Finn thought Laura might refuse to acknowledge him, but Adele said something else, and finally Laura rose and came to where he was waiting.

"I...um...We need to talk," he said. "Please." He reached out to cup her elbow. She allowed it, but her expression was guarded as he led the way out onto the hurricane deck and around to a place where they'd be alone and out of sight of the passengers in the dining saloon.

"I'm sorry," he said.

She lifted her chin and said nothing.

"Sorry for letting you spend these last few hours alone, assuming something that isn't true."

She looked up at him. Frowned.

"I went into Fort Benton, and I'll admit it. The lure was there and it was strong." He looked away from her. Raked his fingers through his hair. "Stronger than it's been in weeks." He paused. "I stood in the street looking into one of the saloons for a while, thinking about the looming heartbreak that I can't seem to keep away from you, no matter how hard I try." He swallowed. "I went in. Stepped up to the bar, even." He glanced at her. Her mouth was a thin line. Her jaw was set. Heavens above but she was beautiful. He took a deep breath. "And then—I *really* thought about you—not the *Laura Rose* and not the river or the trip or any of it. About *you*." His voice wavered. He shook his head. "And I turned my back on the past. Once and for all. I walked out of that place...knowing I'd never set foot in another one." He ducked his head, trying to get Laura to look at him. "What you saw down on the freight deck was an honest fall. I had been in a saloon, but my tripping had nothing to do with whiskey...and everything to do with you."

She gave a soft snort. "You can't possibly blame me because you tripped on the freight deck."

"There were buffalo calves and mules and Nate Landon nearly getting knocked into the water and Adele screeching and Fiona scolding and there you were...taking charge, righting things, taking it all in stride. I took one look at you and took a step and—I fell."

"I *didn't* take it all in stride." She swiped at tears. "I'm tired of being alone. Tired of fighting to keep this—*thing*. I keep thinking *And then what?* I mean, say there is a miracle and I do save the *Laura Rose*. Well...then what? Bridges are coming. The railroad's coming. The future is coming, and—"

"That's what I want to talk about," Finn said. "The 'then what.'" He took a deep breath. "What if we face it together?" For a moment, she didn't move. But then she leaned in. She wrapped her arms about his waist and rested her head against his chest. He held her close, afraid to speak for fear she'd pull away.

"I'm sorry," she said.

"For what?"

"For assuming the worst."

"You had reason. I smelled like a saloon. And then I stumbled."

"But I don't mean to be that way. To always think—" Her voice wavered. "I don't know what to think. That's the real problem. I'm just so...sad. I miss Mama and Papa and Joe. So much. And...I don't know. Maybe the *Laura Rose* isn't the most important thing. Maybe it's important because of the people it represents. But they're gone. And...I don't know." Little by little, she stopped trembling. Finally, taking a deep, ragged breath, she relaxed in his arms. "I have an idea," she murmured.

"Anything."

"Let's run the lights tonight. And every single night that

we have to. Let's keep moving and never stop. Not for one minute."

"What if we run aground? Break a rudder? Split one of the spars?"

"At least I won't have lost without a fight." She stood on tiptoe and kissed his cheek. "And we'll face the 'then what' together."

Chapter 26

As her steamboat approached the St. Louis levee on Friday, July 12, Laura stood at the railing on the open deck just outside the dining saloon, looking out over the city and wondering if she was facing the end of her dreams. A few days ago, when they'd stopped in Omaha to let Nate Landon disembark with his buffalo calves, she'd received a letter from Mr. Hughes. The house Joe had bought to impress Adele—the house that had caused so much turmoil for her—was sold. Mr. Hughes had arranged for repayment of that much of the loan. But would it matter? She still hadn't met the terms of the agreement.

She'd spent the morning preparing to face once more a group of businessmen disinclined to listen to a female. Adele helped her arrange her hair in "the latest style." When Laura discovered a rip in one of her fingerless black lace gloves, Fiona loaned hers.

"You look beautiful, my dear," Fiona said and kissed Laura on the cheek.

"Godspeed," Dr. Ross said, for he was still on board, with no plans to leave until he learned the news.

Finn met her at the bottom of the gangplank, having hurried home the moment they landed and changed into his best suit—complete with top hat. "As I've said before...breathtaking." He offered his arm.

"I'd say the same about you, but a lady isn't supposed to let on."

He covered her hand with his own, and together they headed for Hughes and Son, and the meeting that would decide at least part of the future. They paused for a moment to look back toward the *Laura Rose* and the people standing there—Fiona, Adele, Dr. Ross, Hercules, Bird, Ruby, and Tyree up on the hurricane deck and, down below, Tom Meeks and Elijah North, with Logjam standing next to Elijah.

Please don't let me fail them, Laura thought. But then she looked up at Dr. Ross and remembered everything he'd taught her in recent days. Everything she was just beginning to believe. Belief didn't mean she wasn't afraid, though, nor did it mean that she would willingly let go of the *Laura Rose*. And yet, if that happened, there would be a "then what," and it might not be so bad.

Mr. Hughes's office had always been a friendly place for Laura. Today, it was terrifying. As she and Finn walked into the boardroom together, half a dozen men rose from the leather upholstered chairs around the scarred mahogany table. Mr. Hughes was at the head of that table. He introduced each man in turn, and with each nod, Laura felt less like a competent businesswoman and more like a frightened girl.

When Finn unexpectedly said that he would wait outside, Laura held on to his arm. *Don't go.* He turned away from the other men in the room and said quietly, "You don't need me for this. Just remember to answer the right question." With a wink, he left the room.

Mr. Hughes cleared his throat. "Gentlemen. Shall we begin?"

Laura took the seat to Mr. Hughes's right, and as soon as she'd done so, the other men sat down. None of them seemed inclined to look her in the eye. She did not think that bode well. Once again, she felt weighed down with fear and the prospect of loss. But it was honest fear, not desperation.

When Mr. Hughes once again introduced her, she thought she might be ill, her stomach hurt so. Taking a deep breath, she said, "Thank you for agreeing to meet with me, instead of simply demanding that I come in and sign over my home." She forced herself to make eye contact with each man at the table. "I believe I have proven myself a worthy pilot. Captain MacKnight will vouch for me."

She looked over at Inspector Davies. "I met your demands in regards to a licensed pilot and a chaperone. The *Laura Rose* successfully delivered over two hundred tons of freight to its destination on the way upriver. While it's true we had few passengers and less freight on the way back, we kept our crew and our passengers safe, and"—she allowed a little smile—"we fed them better than most of you gentlemen eat here in St. Louis, thanks to three of the best cooks on the face of the earth.

"The only thing we didn't manage was to return by this past Monday. Any Missouri River pilot can tell you that the time allowed was within reasonable limits. I should have been able to do it. I was not, and I take the blame. At one point we ran out of wood. At another I misjudged the river and we grounded on a sandbar. I did my best, but as it turns out, on that trip, given the conditions we faced, I needed more time. Four days more, to be exact.

"Everyone in this room knows that as soon as my accounts are settled, I will be able to repay the note in full, along with the fair rate of interest to which I agreed." Her voice wavered. "From a purely business standpoint, there is no reason for you to demand that I give up my packet. From a purely business standpoint, there is no reason for you"—she looked at Inspector Davies—"to deny me the chance to take the examination that, if I pass, will make me fully licensed to operate a steamboat on the Mississippi and Missouri Rivers."

She took another deep breath. "The *Laura Rose* is my home. I'm quite certain that I don't have to belabor the point of what she means to me. You all have children to whom you hope to impart a legacy. The *Laura Rose* is my father's legacy to me. I've done everything within my power to honor it and to keep it. Now it's in God's hands."

There was a moment of silence, and then Mr. Hughes said, "Does anyone have any questions for Miss White?"

No one did. That's when Laura realized that it hadn't really mattered what she said. They'd already decided what they were going to do. She'd lost her *Laura Rose*. Laura pushed herself away from the table and rose. The men in the room leaped to their feet. "If you will excuse me," Laura said and left the room. She didn't wait for Finn to ask. She merely shook her head, as tears flowed freely. "Well. That's done." She forced a little smile.

"We won't give up," he said. "We'll find a way."

"It doesn't matter," Laura said, and her voice broke. "I mean—it does matter. It's terrible and it will hurt until the end of my days, but as much as I love that river, it's not the most important thing." Reaching up, she wrapped her arms about his neck and pulled him close for a kiss. Which was interrupted by a most pointed clearing of the throat. She looked over.

"If you would, my dear," Mr. Hughes said.

Taking a deep breath, Laura grabbed Finn's hand. "I want you with me," she said.

And it was a good thing Finn was there, because Laura would need him to verify that she had not dreamt it. That yes, she really had heard the words. Inspector Davies spoke first. He went on and on about it, but the essence of the matter was that he was willing to give her the opportunity to take the pilot's examination—

"Monday?" Laura said.

Davies scowled. "You should not take this examination without ample preparation, Miss White."

"I understand. And you agreed to give it within a week of my return. Shall we say Monday?"

He nodded. "I am at your service."

Next, a Mr. Abernathy rose. Clearing his throat, he looked around the table at the other men before saying, "You are to be congratulated, Miss White. You made your case very well. As a result, we have agreed that as long as the books your clerk presents for review show no irregularities, we will release the note. Full ownership of the *Laura Rose* will pass to the heirs of Captain Jacob Grant, as soon as your responsibility to the bank is satisfied. We expect that will happen within the next thirty days."

Laura reached for Finn's hand and hung on—speechless. Mr. Hughes beamed. "You've won, my dear." He pointed to the ceiling and winked at her. "Heaven smiles." He leaned close. "Not a man in the room could justify taking the *Laura Rose* away from such a fine pilot over a mere ninety-six hours."

As soon as Laura, Finn, and Mr. Hughes were out in the hall, Hughes said, "We have a celebratory dinner to plan."

Laura finally found her voice. "Could we postpone until I have the results of Monday's examination? We've a lot to do this evening. I'll stop in personally with a report and we can make plans then—if that's all right?" Hughes agreed and took his leave.

"I'm surprised you postponed with Mr. Hughes," Finn said as the two of them made their way back to the river. "You said we've a lot to do this evening?"

Laura nodded. "We have to make contact with all our customers and let them know we're available to haul freight. And I want to meet with that Mr. Abernathy at some point and talk investments. I've been thinking about some of the things

Papa was concerned about in regards to the railroad. What would you think of investing in land? St. Louis is bound to grow. And do you think Fiona and Adele would consider moving on board the *Laura Rose*? No, I don't suppose Fiona would, but what about Adele? She really is such a good hostess. And then there's the matter of the wedding. We'll want Dr. Ross, of course. Oh, there's so much to do. But first—I quite forgot." She pulled him over into the shade of a building and looked up into his dark eyes. "All right. I'm ready."

He arched one eyebrow. "Ready for what, Miss White?"

She glowered at him. "Really, Mr. MacKnight. Aren't you the one who's always advising that I be sure to answer the right question? How can I answer if you don't ask?" There it was. That smoldering something in those dark eyes that made her tremble. She held her breath.

Waited.

And then faltered, because Finn didn't ask. In fact, he just...stood there. She ducked her head and fiddled with the veil on her bonnet. *Didn't he want to ask?*

Finally, Finn moved. He caught her hand. "There's something—missing."

She looked up at him. Frowned. What could possibly be missing? Hadn't she done everything in her power to build a life for herself—for them?

"You've never said the words, my captain."

The words.

He stood looking down at her gloved hand as he said, "What was it you called me...a 'rapscallion'?" He gave a little shrug. "I still am, you know. I mean, are you certain you know what you'd be getting into? Are you certain you want to put up with—everything?" Finally, he looked in her eyes.

"What on earth are you talking about?"

Again, the hesitation. The doubt. He gave a little shrug. "I might not be worth the trouble."

He's afraid. The idea that Finn MacKnight might be afraid of love made Laura want to throw her arms around him and kiss him right there in public. And propriety be darned. Instead, she smiled up at him. "You *are* a great deal of trouble, Mr. MacKnight. You're a rapscallion and an entire host of other things that are maddening and infuriating and—amazing." She paused. "I love you, Finn Graham MacKnight, and I cannot imagine my life without you. Are those the words you've been waiting to hear?" She repeated them: "I love you." Perhaps it was only her imagination, but Laura thought she detected a little tremor of something pass between them. She grinned. "Did I manage to answer the right question?"

He nodded. "You did." And then he kissed the back of her hand and murmured, "I love you, too, my captain. Will you marry me?"

THE END

I love the LORD, because he hath heard my voice and my
    supplications.
Because he hath inclined his ear unto me, therefore will I
    call upon him as long as I live.
The sorrows of death compassed me, and the pains of hell
    gat hold upon me: I found trouble and sorrow.
Then called I upon the name of the LORD; O LORD, I
    beseech thee, deliver my soul.
Gracious is the LORD, and righteous; yea, our God is
    merciful.
The LORD preserveth the simple: I was brought low, and he
    helped me.
Return unto thy rest, O my soul; for the LORD hath dealt
    bountifully with thee.
For thou hast delivered my soul from death, mine eyes from
    tears, and my feet from falling.
I will walk before the LORD in the land of the living.
I believed, therefore have I spoken: I was greatly afflicted: I
    said in my haste, All men are liars.
What shall I render unto the LORD for all his benefits
    toward me?
I will take the cup of salvation, and call upon the name of
    the LORD.
I will pay my vows unto the LORD now in the presence of all
    his people.
Precious in the sight of the LORD is the death of his saints.
O LORD, truly I am thy servant; I am thy servant, and the
    son of thine handmaid: thou hast loosed my bonds.

*I will offer to thee the sacrifice of thanksgiving, and will
    call upon the name of the* LORD.
I will pay my vows unto the LORD *now in the presence of
    all his people, in the courts of the* LORD*'s house, in the
    midst of thee, O Jerusalem.*
Praise ye the LORD.

Psalm 116

Afterword

Nate Landon was present at Promontory Summit, Utah, when three spikes—one gold, one silver, and one of iron— were driven to mark the completion of the transcontinental railroad on May 10, 1869. Because of his association with William F. Cody of buffalo-hunting fame, Nate was called upon to help Cody operate his *Wild West*. After touring Europe with Cody's production, Landon retired and took up ranching in the sandhills of Nebraska.

Dr. and Mrs. Malcolm Ross lived out their days in Omaha, Nebraska, where Dr. Ross taught history and ancient languages at Brownell-Talbot School for Young Ladies. His wife, Fiona, was beloved by Dr. Ross's students, who soon learned that beneath Mrs. Dr. Ross's stern exterior there resided a tender heart with an uncanny ability to understand the less-compliant young ladies boarding at the school. Mrs. Dr. Ross called her beloved husband "Dr. Ross" to the end of their days together—even in the privacy of their home.

Adele MacKnight Darrigade lived out her life as the beloved wife of a very romantic professor of French whom she met on board the *Laura Rose*. She settled with him in Annapolis, Maryland, at the United States Naval Academy where she was the belle of many a ball. She had once told her sister, Fiona, that she wanted her life to be interesting. As God would have it, it was.

The Captains MacKnight enjoyed several more years piloting steamboats up the Missouri River. Their first two children were born on board the *Laura Rose* and spent their childhood on the *Jacob White* before the MacKnights headed west to join family in Omaha, Nebraska. As early investors in land, the railroad and, eventually, the refrigerated cars needed to move beef from the West to eastern markets, the MacKnights enjoyed both financial success and the knowledge that together, they could handle the what-ifs of life—as long as they made sure that they had answers for the right questions.

Author's Note

I hope you've enjoyed the trip aboard the imaginary *Laura Rose* with Captains Laura Rose White and Finn MacKnight. Historical fiction fans often wonder what's real and what isn't in the books they love. The short answer to that question is that I put imaginary people into places that are as historically accurate as I can make them, based on literally countless hours of research. The spark that becomes one of my books originally flickered because of something I 1) read in a diary or a history tome or an archival collection, 2) heard from a historian in a class or at a public lecture, or 3) saw at a museum or historic site.

For me, the past is exciting and teeming with people and events that amaze me. But my love of history is more than just an academic pursuit. In 1996, I experienced one of the most challenging times in my life. In that one year, my best friend died, my parents died (within six weeks of each other), my husband was diagnosed with an incurable form of cancer, and one of my children was diagnosed with a chronic, life-threatening illness. Learning about the women who survived the 1800s gave me strength and perspective. Life was hard, but I wasn't straining snakes or toads out of well water before I could make my morning coffee. I hadn't had to stand at three small graves (three of my four children would have died in a world without antibiotics). When the weather turned cold, I didn't have to rely on a pile of dried buffalo dung burned in a woodstove to keep us warm. Reading the words of women whose faith empowered them to face incredible trials "way back then" also encouraged me. In other words, women's history came to mean something to me personally.

A Captain for Laura Rose was inspired by both a place and a person. The place displayed the entire cargo from the *Bertrand*, a steamboat that sank in 1865 and was rediscovered, with its cargo intact, in 1968. Part of the display included calico fabric samples and a woman's coat. Signage mentioned two sisters en route to Fort Benton, Montana. I was hooked. Women and steamboats. Women and the wilderness. What would that have been like?

I first "met" Captain Minnie Mossman Hill, the first licensed female steamboat captain west of the Mississippi, while researching for another steamboat novel. The fact that she was petite and lovely (I found a photograph of her dressed in a stunning Victorian gown) didn't hurt when it came to fueling my imagination. After reading about Captain Hill, I created Laura Rose White to ply the waters of the Missouri River in 1867—a very different place and time from Captain Hill's Columbia River in 1886.

Of course the next challenge was to learn how to pilot a steamboat. For that part of the journey, I headed to Love Library on the campus of the University of Nebraska and checked out a small mountain of books. I visited the Steamboat Arabia Museum in Kansas City, Missouri, and I plied the Internet, concentrating mostly on academic articles in the historical reviews I could access through JSTOR, an online library and database (I was working on my master's degree in history at the time).

The most amazing thing I found in my research was an 1867 steamboat logbook detailing the journey from St. Louis,

Missouri, to Fort Benton, Montana. If you'd been in my home the evening I discovered that logbook, you'd have heard a whoop of delight. Why? Because it not only answered a mountain of detailed questions but also suggested some great scenes. I will always believe that what really happened is much more interesting than anything I could imagine on my own. Without learning real history, I would never have thought to put a woman pilot or a grizzly bear or soldiers or a Nate Landon or a Logjam on board a steamboat.

I sincerely hope that you had as much fun reading about them as I had creating them.

Discussion Questions

- For the person who chose this book for book club discussion: What made you want to read this book? What made you suggest it to the group for discussion?
- Do you think you would have enjoyed travel by steamboat back in the late 1800s? Why or why not?
- What was your favorite scene in the book? Why?
- Is there a bit of dialogue or narrative that particularly resonated with you? Why? Share it with the group.
- Which character did you most love to hate? Discuss the things that contributed to his/her character flaws. Have you ever known anyone like this person? If he or she came to you wanting help to change, how would you counsel this person?
- Which character did you most identify with and why?
- Envision yourself walking through an old cemetery. You come across Laura Rose White's grave. What does her epitaph say? What about the other characters in the book?
- If you could change one thing about this story, what would it be?
- What do you think will be your lasting impression of the book? What spiritual lesson will stay with you?
- Why do you think works of historical fiction are so popular with readers? What appeals to you the most about these types of books?

About the Author

Stephanie Grace Whitson is the bestselling author of over twenty inspirational novels and two works of nonfiction. A lifelong learner, she received a master of arts degree in history in 2012 and has a passionate interest in women's history. When she isn't writing, speaking, or trying to keep up with her five grown children and perfect grandchildren, Stephanie enjoys long-distance rides aboard her Honda Magna motorcycle named Kitty. Her church and the International Quilt Study Center and Museum in Lincoln, Nebraska, take up the rest of her free time. Visit her website at www.stephaniewhitson.com.

Look for Stephanie Grace Whitson's next historical novel

DAUGHTER OF THE REGIMENT

Maggie Malone has no interest in the war between the states. She wants to let "the Americans" settle their differences while she and her family tend their farm in the part of Missouri known as Little Dixie. But when her brothers join the Irish Brigade and bushwhackers take advantage of their absence, Maggie must set out on a journey that will launch her into the thick of battle. Along the way she forms an unexpected friendship with a Southern belle who is exactly the kind of woman Maggie has grown to hate, and a gentleman officer she can't seem to resist. Raised with her brothers to plow, hunt, and tend cattle, Maggie long ago accepted that she's not the kind of woman a man like Captain John Coulter would ever notice, much less love. But surprises await Maggie Malone as she discovers that in wartime the cords of friendship and love tie unlikely people together in bonds that can't be broken.

Available from FaithWords March 2015 wherever books are sold